To H, who helps me believe in magic.

And to A. I love you, jerk face.

HOCUS POCUS
& THE ALL-NEW SEQUEL

Written by A. W. Jantha

Based on the screenplay by Mick Garris and Neil Cuthbert

Story by David Kirschner and Mick Garris

AUTUMN
PUBLISHING

Published in 2022
First published in the UK by Autumn Publishing
An imprint of Igloo Books Ltd
Cottage Farm, NN6 0BJ, UK
Owned by Bonnier Books
Sveavägen 56, Stockholm, Sweden
www.igloobooks.com

Illustrations by Matt Griffin © Disney Enterprises, Inc.

A special thank you to Eric Geron, Lindsay Broderick,
Megan Logan and Susan Gerber

0822 001
2 4 6 8 10 9 7 5 3 1
ISBN 978-1-80368-483-3

Printed and manufactured in the UK

PART ONE

THEN

On All Hallows' Eve, when the moon is round,

    a virgin will summon us from under the ground.

We shall be back!

And the lives of all the children of Salem shall be mine!

–Winifred Sanderson

October 31, 1693

Last words, as recorded

in the journal of Samuel Parris

MAP
OF
SALEM VILLAGE
1693.
BY L.G. MUP
1866

ROYAL SIDE

BEVERLY

NORTHFIELDS

SALEM WOODS
THE SANDERSON HOUSE

ACCESS GATE
PERSHING CHAPEL
BILLY'S GRAVE
MAIN GATE
CEMETERY

NORTH RIVER

COLLINS COVE
SALEM NECK
CAT COVE
WINTER ISLAND
HALFTIDE ROCK

SALEM COMMON

SALEM HARBOUR

N
W — E
S

WILD THINGS

SALEM, 1693

The world was full of wild things then. It brimmed with oak and hemlock and dark whispering places that turned you round and round until there was no turning back.

The womenfolk said that on early mornings, near the harbour, you could hear echoes of witch song, which sounded like birdsong but more bitter. The menfolk said godliness would save them from any witches, but they honed their axes and twisted new rope just the same.

The witches said there was nothing so sweet as the shinbones of little girls. Or perhaps a well-braised scapula with sparrow spleen compote. It was all in the preparation.

They lived near town, the witches, but not so near as to be a bother, until a milk cow died or a child took sick. Then the town would start to mutter about the Sanderson girls – Mary and Sarah and especially Winnie – who had not been girls for a very long time but who did not merit the title 'ladies'.

Someone always intervened.

They're no bother, someone would say. *Just batty girls playing in the woods.*

Leave them be, someone would say. *Don't you remember how kind their mother was, and how generous?*

It all made perfect sense at the time, but once the people of Salem left the town meeting and went back to work, not a one of them could remember who that someone had been.

That is, until Emily went missing.

SALEM, 1993

"Knock-knocks," said Dani, grinning up at her sixteen-year-old brother as she trotted down the street. Leaves drifted through the air around them – thin slips of yellow and broad, shaggy orange things the size and shape of their dad's hands – and the morning was just starting to break open and turn the world gold.

Max rolled his eyes and swung his bike in a big loop to match her slow progress. "Can you please *not*?"

It was Halloween, and the houses on both sides of the little neighbourhood street were decked out with cobwebs and tombstones, giant spiders and jack-o'-lanterns – some of which were already starting to sag a little with mould.

Dani giggled as she ran through the pale tendrils of a ghost horde gathered in a tree.

"Ta-tas," she said, a little louder. Her pointed black hat sported a thin orange trim around the brim, which matched her sun-patterned jacket and striped skirt. She'd dressed as a witch, but in her own words, "a fancy one". The grin she gave Max, though, was more impish than witchy.

Max glanced behind them to make sure the street was still as deserted as when they had left for school. "Seriously, Dani. Not the place."

He should've known better than to talk about Allison Watts to Jack, because Jack still lived in Santa Monica, and Max's house had a shared phone line and a nosy eight-year-old.

"YABOS," Dani squealed.

Max blushed hard, looking over his shoulder. "I'm going to leave you," he said. "Find your own way to school." He spun another loop, catching too much speed on the turn. He stopped short before hitting the curb.

Dani stopped, too, eyes sparkling with mischief beneath the brim of her witch's hat. A few strands of tawny hair stuck to her red lipstick. "Then Mom will ground you forever," she said.

"Maybe that wouldn't be so bad," he muttered.

Dani put a sympathetic hand on his shoulder. "Oh, don't be that way," she said. "Then how will you ever see Allison's bazookas?"

Max groaned, leaning forward over his handlebars. "Please stop," he begged. "It's not even like that."

"It sounded a lot like that." She tugged on his sleeve to get them moving again.

Max relented, bike wobbling as he pedalled slowly beside his sister. "That's why you shouldn't eavesdrop on people," he said. "You lose context. One day you'll know what that means."

"Does it mean you saving up to run away to Jack's house and become the next X-Ray Glasses? Because I heard about that, too."

"The X-Ray Spex," Max muttered. "You know, I don't have to walk you to school any more if I don't want to."

It was true: one of the few perks he'd been promised about their family's move from LA to Salem was that they'd live far enough from school that Dani would qualify for bus pickup. But the previous night she'd said the bus made her lonely, and she'd begged him to bike ahead and meet her one stop early so they could walk the rest of the way together. He'd agreed against his better judgement. She was still his little sister, after all, and as long as she'd been going to school, they'd been walking together. But now he was paying the price for nostalgia.

"But you do want to," said Dani, dancing through the graveyard on someone's front lawn. "Or you would've said no." She stepped on a button and a plastic corpse with matted black hair sat up with a shout, making her shriek and race back to the pavement.

As they rounded the corner, Max saw, at the top of the hill, the skinny blond and the no-necked bonehead known as Jay and Ernie. In the two weeks since his family had moved to Salem, Max had avoided any run-ins with the town bullies, but he could already tell they were the kind of boys whose preschool teachers, searching for something nice to say during parents' evening, would've settled on *persistent*.

Jay and Ernie's lackeys seemed to appear out of nowhere as they swaggered down the middle of the road, the embellishments on their faux-leather jackets glinting dully in the morning light.

"You know," said Max, wheeling around, "I think

Mom told me they're handing out candy at the side entrance."

He felt bad about lying to Dani, but she'd get more than enough Airheads and Pixy Stix later.

"Hey!" she protested as they approached the annexe door. "There's no candy—"

But her brother was already gone, speeding off towards Jacob Bailey High.

SALEM, 1693

It was not unlike Emily Binx to stray so close to the wood.

Her mother had often scolded her for doing precisely that, though she tried not to scold too hard, for nine-year-old Emily was a serious child, and pious, paging through her prayer book without minding where her footsteps took her.

Emily was old enough to know the rumours about the Sanderson sisters, but she also knew that whenever she ran across any of them in town, they were kind to her. It was rare to see Miss Winnie or Miss Mary or Miss Sarah smile, what with their crooked backs and twisted, dusty faces, but when they noticed her, they beamed and clapped – well, Mary and Sarah, anyway – and praised her pink cheeks and pretty hands. Her mother never praised those things, for fear of encouraging vanity and sin. Even sceptical Miss Winnie would pat Emily's shoulder awkwardly and tease that she should return to her mother lest Winnie eat the little girl right up.

All this to say that Emily was not afraid of the wood as others were, and was especially less afraid than her brother, Thackery, who, like his best friend, Elijah, was seven years older than Emily and of an age when boys found anything at all to do with girls or women highly suspect.

So when the wood began to creep into her dreams, it didn't startle Emily.

In the dreams, the field between Salem and the trees smelt of warm hay and fresh flowers, and its waves of trailing sweet grass tickled her arms and legs as she walked.

In the dreams, the edge of the field ran right up to the edge of the wood and then stopped, as if perplexed about where to go next.

In the dreams, the wood was cool and welcoming, and the air tasted faintly of damp soil and crumbling bark – a taste that seemed as sweet as almond cake to young Emily, for it promised an adventure to rival her well-worn copy of *Pilgrim's Progress*.

Thackery had begun to dream of that place, too – that knife's edge between the world he knew and the world of witches – but his dreams were thick with moss-coloured smoke and the press of hands upon his skin, and the taste of sweat and bile and river muck. The dreams made him wake, night after night, more tired than the day before, but he didn't tell his parents or his sister or even Elijah, for he feared the dreams meant something dark about his mind – or worse, about his heart.

Emily didn't tell because she was afraid her mother might scold her for letting her imagination run beyond the pages of her prayer book.

And the other children didn't tell for their own reasons, each of them more personal than the next.

SALEM, 1993

Max was kneeling beside his bike, tying his shoelace, when a shadow spilled over his shoulder and onto the grass.

He tensed, expecting Ernie's hot pickle breath to hit his shoulder any minute. To buy time, he undid his laces and tied them again, carefully. The pristine white toe and accents of the otherwise black Nikes started to blur as Max considered the best way to slip away unscathed. He wasn't about to let some mouth breather spit on his new trainers just to get a rise out of him. He'd only got them as a pity gift from his parents when they'd announced their surprise move to The-Place-with-the-Witch-Trials, Massachusetts.

"You dressed up!"

Max turned to see Allison Watts smiling down at him. He glanced down at his shirt. A burst of tie-dye swirled up at him.

"I didn't, actually," he said.

Allison smirked. "Just that California lifestyle?"

Max grinned. He hated when other people made lame California jokes, but Allison earned a pass because she'd helped him find the chemistry lab on his first day – not that he expected her to remember that now. Allison was the kind of person who helped classmates with homework in the hallway before class; who always waited the appropriate amount of time before answering teachers' questions, which turned her into a classroom hero instead of a show-off; and who had an intensity about her that made Max feel like he wanted to be part of her story. He could tell she'd become someone great one day – a president or an inventor, or the CEO of a company that made flying cars. So when Allison cracked a joke about California, Max found that it made his stomach flip in a way that interfered with his ability to grimace.

He opened his mouth to introduce himself, but no sound emerged. That day, like the past three days, he thought about asking her out, but then he thought about her rejecting him and how he'd have to awkwardly extract himself from the situation, which made walking through town with his sister howling about bazookas sound like a fun weekend activity.

Allison watched his face, which must've been cycling through expressions of both hope and abject fear. When he still didn't speak, her smile softened. "Well," she said, "I'll see you around, California."

"Bye…" Max called after her, deflated. He told himself she was a human being, not some otherworldly goddess. He told himself he should just talk to her, but the thought made him feel the way the ferry ride to Catalina Island had on his ninth birthday: weak-kneed and queasy. How was it possible that he'd fallen for her so hard in just two weeks?

As Max shouldered his backpack and walked up the concrete steps, he cut past six of his classmates, all of them crowded together and gossiping about the old Sanderson house at the edge of town.

"I'm telling you, we should go there before the party," said a girl in an orange turtleneck. Over the turtleneck, she wore a slouchy blue jumper patterned with pumpkins.

"No way," whined her friend, who wore a red vest over a white jumper and looked more excited for Christmas than Halloween. She leant against the front steps' metal handrail. "I'm not going anywhere near that house. It's creepy."

Max had to agree with the second girl. He'd seen the Sanderson house the previous weekend on a ride, and its rotting walls and sagging windows seemed to peer out of the woods as he cruised past. He'd also noticed the CLOSED INDEFINITELY signs tied along the wrought-iron fence that separated the Sanderson house – and much of Salem Wood – from the actual town of Salem.

A boy who wore a brown jumper over a white shirt threw an arm around the shoulders of the girl in the red vest. "I'll just have to hold you closer, Tess," he teased, grinning.

Tess beamed up at him. "My hero," she sighed, and then snorted. As her head settled on the boy's chest, their semicircle of friends laughing along with her, Max felt the seed of a plan begin to take root…

ANOTHER GLORIOUS MORNING.
MAKES ME SICK!

SALEM, 1693

When Emily Binx woke to the dreamy light of dawn, she first believed it was due to the cockerels crowing in the garden – but for whatever reason, the birds weren't making a single sound.

Emily crept to the window and found the roosters asleep – even the chickens, who clucked softly as they dozed. It was so strange that she slipped out of the house without changing from her bedclothes, an act that would surely scandalise her mother if she caught her.

There was a soft song in the air that sounded nothing

like birds, but also not quite like the hymns the pastor's wife led at church. It sounded more like the delicate crust on sugared almonds or the sweet cream of Christmas custard. It sounded like something that could melt or sour if it wasn't used up right away.

Emily stepped into the garden and past the clustered chickens and nodding family of sheep whose coats were thickening for winter. She petted the nose of Mopsie, the black pony her father had brought back from last year's trip to Boston, and giggled when he released a happy little snort.

She passed the milliner's house, and the butcher's, but their curtains were drawn and their houses stood silent. A downy rabbit was napping in the garden of the town's best baker, as if it had settled down to sleep in the open – unafraid of hungry foxes or rowdy boys with sticks. Elizabeth, the baker herself, was awake, though. There was a smell of boiling fruit and sugar, and Emily spotted her through the shutters of her kitchen window, humming to herself.

Elizabeth lived in a small cottage on the edge of town with her husband and daughter, though they were scarcely seen since the witch trials had begun in Salem. Those who did see her when she dropped off baked goods remarked on her simple beauty. She was a tall woman in her early twenties, with dark curly hair, and she wore her pale yellow cloak in almost any weather.

A little girl around Emily's age peeped her head just above the windowsill. The girl had clear chestnut eyes and a chipper smile, and she gave Emily a friendly wave.

"Ismay, get away from the windows," came a man's voice from within the house, hushed and urgent.

The little girl ducked away.

Elizabeth stepped up to the open window and locked eyes with Emily. "What brings you outside so early this morning, Miss Emily?" Elizabeth inquired, pushing the window open to better see the girl. "And how on earth did your mother let you outside without shoes, my dear?"

Emily giggled. "The whole world seems to be asleep."

"John Barker's ale must have been strong last night," said Elizabeth. She held up the apple she was slicing. "I'll have pie later, but you won't be allowed in until you've changed."

Emily nodded sombrely. "I'm going to find the music first," she said.

Elizabeth's demeanour turned suddenly grave. "Don't follow it," she warned.

"But it's prettier than any tune I've ever heard before, miss," said Emily.

"Beautiful things have a way of obscuring danger, my dear girl. Don't—" She stopped short as the smell of burning fruit filled the air and the sound of clumsy gurgling reached her ears. She hastened to remove the delicate preserve from the stove, but when she returned to the window a moment later, Emily was already gone.

SALEM, 1993

Max wasn't sure why everyone filing into US History at the end of the day had grins on their faces. The classroom looked as it had for the past few weeks, with orange construction paper tacked to the pinboards that flanked the chalkboard at the front of the room. On one side was a silhouette of a frightened black cat, and on another a silhouette of a witch on her broom. Above the chalkboard, Miss Olin had replaced the framed portraits of her four favourite presidents with pen-and-ink drawings of four people involved in the Salem witch trials.

Miss Olin herself sat at her desk while the class filed in, scribbling notes to herself among an array of miniature pumpkins. There was a creepy little witch doll propped up at the front edge of her desk. It was dressed in a black-and-white Pilgrim's costume and a pointed hat with an orange ribbon for decoration – exactly like the one Miss Olin herself wore that day.

Max took his seat in the third row, beside the girl in the red vest and just a few desks away from Allison

Watts. After the bell rang, Miss Olin explained – for his benefit, he supposed – that Salem tradition dictated that on All Hallows' Eve, each class's history teacher recounted the town's most popular Halloween story: one that had real witches and bubbling cauldrons and unbreakable spells. The way she said it made Max realise she was trying to express what a great honour this was for her, but he found himself concentrating on not rolling his eyes.

But when Miss Olin began to tell a story about the Sanderson sisters – who had lured a girl into the woods and killed her, then turned her brother into a cat – Max knew there was someone smiling down on him.

All he had to do was provoke Allison into an argument, which would give him an excuse to apologise and invite her to check out the Sanderson house. It wouldn't be hard. This may have been only his second Friday at Jacob Bailey High, but he knew Allison couldn't stand it when people fibbed their way through a class discussion. He'd learned that the hard way when he'd tried to impress her on Tuesday by swaggering through a devil's advocate position about states' rights – something he knew next to nothing about. He found that while Allison might be willing to help people with homework before class, she didn't find it charming if she thought you were making a mockery of something she cared about. She'd taken no prisoners and he'd gone straight home to actually read the chapter about the Continental Congress.

But now he would use one of his new talents – specifically, being publicly humiliated by Allison Watts – to his advantage.

"And so," said Miss Olin, the very tip of her witch's hat bobbing as she spoke, "the Sanderson sisters were hanged by the Salem townsfolk. Now, there are those who say that on Halloween night a black cat still guards the old Sanderson house, warning off any who might make the witches come back to life!" With a loud pop, a mess of streamers shot from her hand onto the nearest girl, making the whole class jump. Max had to admit it was a nice touch.

It was also his cue.

"Gimme a break," he sighed.

Miss Olin turned an arched eyebrow on him. "Aha," she said. "We seem to have a sceptic in our midst. Mr Dennison, would you care to share your California, laid-back, tie-dyed point of view?"

The class howled with laughter and Max again had to restrain himself from rolling his eyes at his US History teacher. She wasn't the one whose feathers he needed to ruffle.

"Okay, granted that you guys in Salem are all into these black cats and witches and stuff—"

"*Stuff?*" gasped an affronted Miss Olin.

"Fine," Max pressed on. "But everyone knows that Halloween was invented by the candy companies."

The class groaned.

"It's a conspiracy," insisted Max.

"It just so happens," said Allison, like clockwork, "that Halloween is based on the ancient feast called All Hallows' Eve." Max and the rest of the class turned to watch her take him apart. She leant forward and spoke directly to him while she did it. Her expression was serious, and for a moment, Max worried he'd really put his foot in it. "It's the one night of the year where the spirits of the dead can return to earth."

The class cheered and Allison smiled and accepted a high five from the pumpkin-jumpered girl who sat behind Max. At least she wasn't actually that upset, he reasoned. Having the whole class turn against him was a little embarrassing, but ultimately Max didn't care that they were celebrating his humiliation. He was already tearing a sheet of paper from his notebook and scribbling down his name. He'd pay Dani her weight in gummy pizzas to keep her away from *this* call.

He got up from his desk. "Well," he said, crossing the narrow aisle. "In case Jimi Hendrix shows up tonight, here's my number." He handed Allison the folded sheet of paper.

The class whooped.

Allison raised her eyebrows at him but didn't answer.

Max's heart slammed against his ribcage, a rubber ball trying to escape this risk-taking madman.

The bell rang and the class swirled out, Allison with them. Max scrambled to pack up his books and catch her before he lost his courage. Maybe if she gave him a chance he'd actually make friends in Salem and then Jack wouldn't have to lend Max his spare bunk after all.

SALEM, 1693

Thackery jolted awake to the sound of Mopsie whinnying like he'd been kicked.

He sat up straight, a layer of sweat sticking his pale linen shirt to his back, and let his ears adjust to the commotion outside the window. The sun was high – he must have slept through the cockerel crow, which meant his father would be angry because he hadn't yet milked the cow. Thackery flopped back into bed, wondering whether he could plead sick. He glanced to his left, hoping he could ask Emily to cover for him, but her bed was empty and unmade. Her church dress still hung by the fire, as did her gabled cap.

Thackery hurried out of bed and looked about the small plain bedroom they shared at the back of the house. Emily's shoes were by the door, which was very unlike her.

He sniffed the air but couldn't catch the smell of woodsmoke that would mean his mother was preparing porridge in the main part of the house. Nor could he hear the good-natured sound of his father greeting neighbours as they passed on their way back from the harbour.

Something wasn't right.

He dashed into the garden, where the chickens were scrambling as if they knew it was time for supper. Mopsie had torn himself from the tree and his lead hung limp and ominous from an upper branch. A shiver crept down Thackery's spine. From the gate of the sheep's pen, Thackery spotted Elijah Morris, his best friend, who was rubbing his eyes as if he'd just risen, as well.

"Elijah!" he called, forgetting his own shoes as he crossed between their gardens.

When Thackery grabbed Elijah's forearm, his friend turned to him, blinking as if coming out of a dream. Elijah was only a hair's width taller than Thackery – at least, that's what Thackery said – and wore an identical linen shirt and long-locked hairstyle. The townsfolk called the two of them accidental twins.

"Has thee seen my sister, Emily?" asked Thackery.

"Nay," said Elijah. "But look: they conjure."

Thackery followed his friend's gaze and saw, far past the fields that surrounded town and deep within the Salem Wood, a plume of heavy smoke crawling into the clear late-morning sky. It was an unnatural shade of pink – bright and conspicuous. It made his stomach turn.

"The woods," Thackery managed, the half-dreamt ghost of witchy hands tightening around his neck. He grabbed Elijah by the shirtsleeve, and together they raced down the lane and to the field. There Thackery caught sight of his sister's slight frame slipping into the shadow of the trees.

"Wake my father," he told Elijah, keeping his eyes trained on where his sister had just been. "Summon the others. Go!"

Before Elijah could answer, Thackery was racing towards the witching wood, shouting his sister's name. He leapt over one branch and ducked beneath another, and then lost his footing and tumbled down the steep embankment until he landed in a thick bed of browned leaves. He groaned, forcing himself up onto one arm and then further up onto his hurting bare feet.

Before him stood the Sanderson house, a cottage that sat crookedly upon its haunches and sagged in its eaves despite being younger than many buildings in Salem proper. Intricate wooden shutters obscured its windows, and weeds grew in thick drifts around the house and even between some of the floorboards of the porch. A few sported bright blue flowers despite the chill of October's last day. Thackery had no doubt that these blossoms smelt and tasted like honey but would kill someone within a few minutes.

On the house's left side, a huge waterwheel caught the tiny creek and turned, groaning from the labour. Above it, the smoke hung thick and promised something as wicked as a snake in paradise.

Emily disappeared inside as Thackery watched, helpless – trapped by a memory of clambering down there with Elijah when both of them were twelve, of daring each other to throw pebbles at the door, of his heart knocking hard against his chest when the door opened and Winifred Sanderson stepped out with her wild red hair and threatened to roast them with chicken of the woods and worm snakes' tongues.

Thackery pushed aside his memories and crossed the flat stepping stones to a low window that looked into the only room of the house. Inside, the sisters were doing the Devil's work, each of them wearing a heavy cape with a pointed hood – one green as leaves before the fall, one red as clay and one a purple deeper than an elderberry's juice. Together, the women danced and rocked slowly around his poor sweet sister. They had seated Emily in a heavy-looking chair, and she looked patiently up at them as if she expected a present at the end of it all. Her eyes widened when she saw Thackery, and he hurried out of sight and shut the window.

He wasted no time clambering past the waterwheel and ducking into an alcove just as the creak of a rusted hinge pierced the air. The high haughty voice of Winifred Sanderson rang out above him.

"Oh, look," she sighed. "Another glorious morning. Makes me sick!"

The window slammed shut again, and Thackery leant into the stone of the old building.

He was relieved not to have been caught, but it didn't help the feeling that his ribs were knotted tight with rope. Emily was trapped inside with the witches, and he had no idea what to do.

SALEM, 1993

Hundreds of students pressed through the halls of the high school and spilled out onto the street. In the anonymity of the crowd, a couple of students popped off black-and-orange streamers. A boy with a dancing skeleton knitted on his beanie shouted, "What do we want?"

"Ghosts!" shouted back the rest of the school.

"When do we want 'em?"

"Now!"

Max pushed his way through the celebrants, still baffled by their unselfconscious love of something meant for little kids.

He was grateful that Allison wore a bright red coat, because it helped him keep track of her in the outgoing tide of students.

He grabbed his bike and raced after her, slowing only because he was afraid of becoming a gross sweaty mess. His heart was beating hard enough for what he was about to do. He was going to speak with Allison, just the two of them, and he was going to invite her to visit the Sanderson house with him, and she was going to say yes, because if she didn't, he really would have to hitchhike back to LA, since the embarrassment of seeing her in class every day would be too much when all his friends were three thousand miles away. Max's parents and sister kept telling him to make the most of this move, and there he was, pedalling after his moonshot.

As he biked, he decided that he'd never seen so much

Halloween decor in one place – not even in the holiday section of a department store. There were homemade ghosts and plastic zombies and giant googly eyes stuck in trees. People had even put up yellow and orange lights, and one man was testing the fog machine in his garden before the night's main event.

Max swung past a honking car and into Salem Common, the big park that sat in the middle of town. "Allison!" he barked before he could stop himself. He startled himself even, his foot slipping and causing him to skid to a halt.

She turned and eyed him for a second before saying, "Hi." She kept walking, but she slowed a little.

"Hi," he said, toeing his way after her. "Look – I'm sorry. I didn't mean to embarrass you in class."

"You didn't." She stopped then, and Max did, too.

He took a deep breath and told himself to play it cool.

"My name is Max Dennison," he said, extending a hand.

Allison softened. "Yeah, I know," she said, accepting his handshake.

Her palm was soft and warm against his, and he thought of the intricate vases he'd seen her carrying out of the arts wing – enough to stock a mansion, because, he suspected, she'd keep working at it until one came out perfect. He wondered whether asking about her ceramics class would make him seem thoughtful or creepy.

"You just moved here, huh?" she asked, saving him the embarrassment.

"Yeah, two weeks ago." He grabbed his handlebars so she wouldn't notice his shaking hands.

"Must be a big change for you."

"That's for sure."

She smiled. "You don't like it here?"

With two questions, Max felt like this conversation was really on a roll. He shrugged. "Oh, the leaves are great," he said, looking up at their fiery underbellies, "but... I dunno. Just all this Halloween stuff."

"You don't believe in it?"

"What do you mean, like the Sanderson sisters? No way."

"Not even on Halloween?"

His heart soared. He wasn't from Salem, but this was something he could work with: the universal teenage language of apathy. "*Especially* not on Halloween," he said.

Allison seemed to hesitate, and Max wondered whether he'd misread something. No one his age could actually believe in witches and flying broomsticks and newt-eye potions. Could they?

But Allison just smiled and offered him a folded piece of paper, more suave than he could ever hope to be. "Trick or treat," she said. The look she gave him made his bones melt.

She walked off then, pulling up her red hood against the October chill.

Max smiled to himself, and for a moment he wasn't even upset that he'd forgotten to ask her about visiting the Sanderson house. He'd spoken to Allison one-on-one, and she hadn't laughed at him or anything. Maybe this meant they could be friends. Maybe it even meant that one day, if he didn't mess things up, they could be something more than that.

Max unfolded the note and saw his own name and phone number, and his stomach sank. He turned over the paper, but there wasn't anything else written on any part of it.

He *had* misread her, though he wasn't sure how. And then he'd blown it.

Max sighed and looked down at the pavement. At least he still had his sweet new shoes.

LET'S BREW ANOTHER BATCH

SALEM, 1693

"My darling," crooned Winifred Sanderson, and Thackery was sure the words were meant for Emily.

But then she added, equally lovingly, "My little book. We must continue with our spell now that our little guest of honour has arrived. Wake up," she coaxed, like a mother to her child. "Wake up, darling. Yes – oh, come along. There you are."

Thackery clambered up the waterwheel, which allowed him to enter the house through a thick-paned window on the second floor. It opened to a narrow loft that looked down into the large room, which made it the perfect hiding spot. Thackery slunk in and pressed himself as close to the floorboards as he could manage, peering down at his sister and the witches below.

"Ah, there it is," Winifred was saying. Her book was open on an angled table, and a massive iron pot was bubbling over an open fire beside her. She read from the book's pages: "'Bring to a full rolling bubble; add two drops of oil of boil. Mix blood of owl with the herb that's red. Turn three times, pluck a hair from my head. Add a dash of pox and a dead man's toe'." She turned to Sarah, the narrowest sister, and perhaps the youngest, though no one in Salem seemed to remember. "Dead man's toe," Winifred ordered. "And make it a fresh one."

Sarah Sanderson brightened then and began to dance around chorusing the command, and Thackery cringed. He thought of George Flamsteed, the kind old fisherman whose boat had capsized in late September. He'd washed ashore untouched – except that he'd been missing both of his big toes. For days after, the townsfolk had whispered about the Devil's work.

Mary tossed a toe into the pot and then flung another one at Sarah for good measure.

When a wayward digit landed upon Winifred's back, she rounded on them both. "Will you two *stop* that?" she demanded. "I need to concentrate." She turned back to her book and then, satisfied, called her sisters to the pot.

The surface of the bubbling liquid was obscured by a thick sheet of white smoke.

As Thackery spied, he chewed his bottom lip, tasting blood. Emily sat quietly off to the side, and he wondered what could possibly be going through her head. He'd seen a flash of recognition from her before, but now she sat as serenely as the doll he'd believed her to be when the midwife had first wrapped her in a clean blanket.

"'One thing more and all is done'," chanted Winifred, waving her hands over the surface of the pot, "'add a bit of thine own tongue'."

At once, all three sisters stuck out their tongues and bit down with a crunch, turning Thackery's stomach. They spat into the pot and began to stir the vile liquid with a large wooden spoon.

"One drop of this," breathed Winifred, "and her life will be mine." She caught herself. "I mean, *ours*."

Thackery looked over his shoulder, but there wasn't a single sound outside. Where was Elijah? Where was his father? Surely they'd arrive at any moment.

When the sisters began to advance on Emily, Winifred carrying the huge spoon of the dark bubbling potion, Thackery jumped up. "No!" he shouted, leaping down from the loft before they could feed any of their wicked brew to his sister.

"A *boy*," growled Winifred. "Get him, you fools!"

Thackery dodged the two younger witches, dancing around the bubbling pot so they couldn't catch him. He grabbed the lip of the pot and shoved, not caring about the searing pain that shot through his hands.

Once the poison was spilled across the ground, he rushed towards his sister, but it was too late: Winifred had given her the draught of potion left in that huge wooden spoon. The decrepit witch delicately – even lovingly – wiped his sister's mouth with her own cloak before turning to face him.

"Always keep your eyes on the prize, my boy!" She cackled as she raised her free hand. The air filled with a violent green light.

All at once, Thackery's world filled up and spilled over with hurt.

His muscles betrayed him, his field of vision blurred and went dark, and his body collapsed like a bundle of sticks on the floor.

SALEM, 1993

Max decided to take the long way home to get some time to think.

He pedalled hard through Salem, avoiding anyone

who might want to talk with him – an admittedly limited group since he was so new in town – and only slowed when he reached the edge of the graveyard marked by a wrought-iron gate topped with the words OLD BURIAL HILL.

He realised it was very broody to spend time in a cemetery, but it was also a peaceful place with rolling hills and craggy rocks that, on the northern rise, overlooked Salem and the harbour. Seeing the ocean had given him a comforting feeling his very first day in Salem. It reminded him of home and of the unending expanse of the Pacific. The idea that this place was even a little like LA made his heart ache, but it also made him feel like maybe he really could make the most of it here. Maybe his life didn't have to be so different after all.

The crest of the cemetery's hill was the kind of place he'd want to take Allison one day, after they'd got to know each other enough that she didn't think he was secretly an axe murderer. They could watch the ships come in and go out, cutting through deep blue water with rolling whitecaps, and wait for the lighthouse to come on as the sun started to go down. He could tell her about California and listen while she explained why she liked Salem, and maybe he'd find a way to like it, too.

Max rounded a section of tombstones, heading for the top of the hill.

Just then, a boy shouted, "Halt!"

Max stopped, confused, and turned to see Jay Taylor, the blond portion of the duo that terrorised Salem with poorly constructed bottle rockets and the occasional roll of toilet paper. Max groaned inwardly. Just then, Ernie popped up from behind a particularly large gravestone.

Max looked from Jay, with his straight shoulder-length hair and fingerless gloves, to Ernie, whose brown windbreaker was still too large for his thick torso, and he wondered how they'd befriended each other on the playground.

Jay tossed his blond hair. "Who are you?"

Max debated pedalling away, but the front of his bike was pointed uphill and it would take too long to swing it around. Besides, this day had to come sooner or later.

"Max," he said shortly. "I just moved here."

"From where?" Jay asked.

"Los Angeles."

Jay gave him a perplexed look and Max realised that this might be the first person he'd encountered who was too stupid to provide a 'surf's up' joke. He counted his blessings.

"LA," he clarified.

"Oh!" said Jay happily. "Duuude!"

"Tubular," said Ernie.

That train was never late. Max took a steadying breath through his nose.

"I'm Jay," said Jay. "This is Ernie."

Ernie grabbed the elbow of Jay's black pleather jacket and pulled him into a crouch. "How many times I gotta tell you?" he grumbled. "My name ain't Ernie no more. It's Ice."

"This is Ice," Jay clarified, pointing.

Ernie spun around to show off the back of his head, where his nickname was shaved in block letters.

Max chuckled. He suddenly wasn't sure why he'd been worried about these two at all.

"So," said Jay, jumping down from the gravestone he'd been perched on. "Let's have a butt."

"No, thanks," said Max. "I don't smoke."

"They're very health-conscious in Los Angeles," mocked Ernie.

Jay broke into raucous laughter, and Ernie followed suit. They gave each other a double high five and a chest bump, and Max wondered how long he'd be stuck in this new-kid hazing ritual.

"You got any cash, Hollywood?" asked Jay, coming around to block Max's way. He leant forward on Max's handlebars.

Max felt his pulse hiccup. "No," he said, trying to regain control of the bike.

"Gee," said Ernie, grabbing Max's biceps.

Max turned to him, and his heart was full-on pattering. He'd waited around too long, and even if these two were dumb, they were still bigger than him and seemed to have twitchy moral compasses.

"We don't get any smokes from you. We don't get any cash. What am I supposed to do with my afternoon?" said Jay.

Max inhaled slowly. "Maybe learn to breathe through your nose," he said.

Jay guffawed and quickly pretended to find the ground very interesting. "Whoa," he said, noticing Max's shoes. "Check out the new cross-trainers."

Max tried to pull away, but Ernie was even stronger than he looked.

"Cool," Ernie said to Jay, his grip on Max's arm tightening even further. "Let me try 'em on."

Max looked from one boy to the other, hoping they were joking. The Nikes had been the only good thing about his move to Salem.

Ernie gave him a look that said *I'm waiting*, and before Max knew it, he was biking away from them shoeless, the treads of his pedals sharp and uncomfortable even through his socks.

At least they hadn't thought to take his bike, he told himself. He was angry at himself for not getting away before Jay and Ernie cornered him. He was mad at his dad for accepting the transfer to a new management position in Salem. And he was mad at Dani for making the move look so easy when it was clearly so painfully lame.

At the top of Old Burial Hill, the cemetery chapel chimed four o'clock. Max sighed and continued biking down the hill, back towards town. Both of his parents would be home by now, as would Dani.

He'd lost his Nikes, his shot with Allison and his chance at privacy – and it wasn't even dinnertime.

SALEM, 1693

Thackery's mind went blank from the pain in his body.

When he could finally blink again, he wasn't sure whether he'd lost a few seconds or a few minutes or much, much longer. He tipped his head to the side and saw that Emily was still there, as were the three hideous Sanderson sisters.

Emily sat serenely in the wooden chair, attentive but church-quiet. Her pale skin and white sleep dress looked almost iridescent in the house's low light. Thackery watched, helpless, as that iridescence turned into a warm golden glow the likes of which one might expect to see spill from the skin of an angel.

"'Tis her life force!" said Winifred. "The potion works." She stretched her arms towards her sisters. "Take my hands – we will share her."

Fingers entwined, the three witches advanced upon Emily. They leant forward and inhaled deeply. Curls of amber light drifted away from Emily and down their wretched throats.

Thackery dragged himself to a nearby ladder and managed to prop himself up, but the world sloshed around him and he couldn't think of how words were supposed to be strung together. He watched his sister, though, and felt that his heart would break.

The sisters took a final inhale and the light around Emily disappeared behind their lips. Emily's narrow chin tipped forward and her body went limp. Her face was suddenly drawn and sallow, her skin threaded with thin grey veins as if her blood, too, had been stolen from her.

Thackery lurched towards her but only managed to vomit onto the floor. He tried to look away from his sister, but he couldn't help staring at her in horror. Emily. Dead. Dead and shrunken like a frail old woman. Thackery vomited again. He hadn't eaten since supper, and the thin bile from his stomach soured his tongue.

Sarah Sanderson spun about, running fingers through her newly golden curly hair. "I am beautiful!" she squealed. "Boys will love me!"

Mary's plump face looked nearly pleasant, thanks to the colour creeping back into her cheeks. She pouted her red lips, which still twisted to one side. "We're young!" she laughed, clapping.

Winifred hurried to pick up a mirror. Her face fell, and for a moment Thackery suspected she wished she hadn't been so generous in sharing with her sisters. "Well," she said, "young*er*." Then a surge of energy seemed to ripple through her, and she raised both arms in triumph. "But it's a start!" She cackled.

The sisters promenaded together while Thackery continued to drag himself onto unsteady feet.

"Oh, Winifred," cooed Mary, "thou art a mere sprig of a girl."

"Liar!" Winifred crowed. "But I shall be a sprig of a girl forever," she said, twirling each of her sisters, "once I suck the life out of all the children in Salem!" She turned to face Thackery and beamed, then advanced on him. "Let's brew another batch," she suggested.

"You hag," he growled. "There are not enough children in the *world* to make thee young and beautiful."

That made Winifred stop short. "Hag," she repeated distastefully. "Sisters, did you hear what he called you?"

Thackery wanted to point out that he'd been speaking specifically to her, but she spoke again before he could muster the energy: "Whatever shall we do with him?"

"Barbecue and fillet him," suggested Mary.

"Hang him on a hook," said Sarah, reaching for his chest, "and let me play with him."

"No," snapped Winifred, and then, more softly, she called for her book. The heavy tome floated through the air to reach her. The book was bound in scraps of thick, tanned human skin and roughly stitched together with thread that made the seams look like scars on a dead man's face. A metal clasp on the book's cover encircled a bit of puckered leather in the shape of an eye. "Dazzle me, my darling," she crooned. The book opened of its own accord, and she paged through it until she found the perfect spell. "His punishment shall not be to die, but to live forever with his *guilt*."

"As what, Winnie?" her sisters asked, delighted.

She stepped towards Thackery, and though he tried to evade her walnut-brown eyes and the sight of her large teeth and narrow pursed lips, his ears filled with her chanting: "'Twist the bones and bend the back'," she said, and her sisters murmured a soft spell beneath her words. Thackery winced, but Winifred went on: "'Trim him of his baby fat. Give him fur as black as black. Just... like... this'."

Thackery felt his body twisting and turning in on itself, felt his bones snapping and reshaping into smaller, thinner versions of themselves. The last spell had felt like lightning beneath his skin, but this felt like a terrible bubbling in his marrow, and even as he screamed, he heard his voice come back in a shrill yowl.

The house rattled with the pounding of fists on its doors and windows, and through his pain, Thackery heard his father's voice. But it was too late.

He dragged himself to safety under a chest of drawers and let the pain sweep over his body and through his mind, spiriting his consciousness away.

SALEM, 1993

Once home, Max went straight up to his room and flopped onto the bed.

He hated the sailboat wallpaper of his room almost as much as he did the pale purple paint that trimmed the steps leading to the small loft overhead.

He'd tried to make it look more like his last room, carefully placing his drum set to take up as much space as possible. He'd even pinned up the tie-dyed blanket Jack sent him after Max told him about the California hippie jokes.

None of his attempts, though, had worked. This old nursery didn't look anything like his room, and staring at it just made him feel more alone. So he glared at the white popcorn ceiling and listened to the quiet bubbling of the fish tank beside his bed.

The bike ride home hadn't calmed his anger – if anything, the pedals cutting into his feet had stoked it. Why couldn't his parents have waited two more years before moving? Then he'd have graduated high school and gone to college and they could have moved Dani anywhere they liked. Besides, who transferred their kids to a new school in the middle of *October*?

Max squeezed his eyes shut and sighed. October made him think about Halloween, which made him think about Allison and her note. He'd really blown it, and he still didn't get how.

Did Allison like Halloween because she liked to dress up, or because of this weird, witchy town, or because she actually believed in spells that could transform people into immortal cats? Max wasn't sure which option he preferred. He rolled over. As if it mattered. As if he'd have a chance with her either way.

"Allison," he sighed, remembering her hand in his when he'd introduced himself – his smoothest move of the day. "You're so soft," he continued. "I just want to—"

His wardrobe burst open. Max sat up with a racing pulse.

"Boo!" Dani cackled, applauding herself for such

a good prank. She was still in her costume, and her patterned skirt swished as she danced. "I scared you! I scared you!"

Max blushed.

Dani clambered over him and tossed herself onto his bed. She thrashed about, crooning, "I'm Allison! Kiss me, I'm Allison!" – which only made Max blush harder.

He stood up. "Mom and Dad told you to stay out of my room!"

"Don't be such a crab," Dani said, rolling her eyes. She stood up on his mattress to make herself taller, then began to jump, the yellow-and-orange fringe of her jacket swinging wildly. The mattress springs protested each time she landed. "Guess what?" she asked. Then, before he could answer: "You're going to take me trick-or-treating."

She couldn't be serious. "Not this year, Dani."

Dani twirled and leapt off the bed. "Mom said you have to."

"Well," said Max, "she can take you."

"She and Dad are going to the Pumpkin Ball downtown," she protested, tugging on his sleeve.

"You're eight," he said, jerking away from her. "Go by yourself." He crossed the room, sat down at his drum set and tapped out a beat on the snare.

"No way," said Dani. "This is my first time! I'll get lost. Besides, it's a full moon outside. The weirdos are out."

Max ignored her, throwing in the hi-hat. If Jack had been there, he would've plugged in his guitar and they'd have been halfway through "London Calling" by now.

Dani threw her arms around his neck. "Come on, Max," she said.

He sighed and let his sticks settle across one knee.

"Can't you forget about being a cool teenager for one night?" she begged. "Please come out. We used to have so much fun together trick-or-treating. Remember? It'll be like old times."

He jerked away. "The old days are dead," he said, restarting the beat. He knew he'd end up taking her, but he wished to god she'd just give him five minutes alone. He needed to think. He needed to listen to Green Day. He needed to *not* walk around with his kid sister dressed as Winona the Whimsical Witch.

"It doesn't matter *what* you say," Dani declared. "You're taking me."

Max tossed down his sticks. "Wanna bet?" He crossed the room again, this time climbing into the small loft that was the best part of his new room. The best part of Massachusetts, as far as he was concerned, especially now that Allison thought he was an idiot and his trainers were getting stretched out by Ernie's clubfeet. He crossed his arms and leant against the wall.

Dani's eyes narrowed and she did the thing that always turned arguments in her favour.

She screamed for their mother.

THIS IS TERRIBLY UNCOMFORTABLE

SALEM, 1693

The verdict was settled before the trial began, but the Sanderson witches' case was not helped by their refusal to show remorse.

That very same night – a dark, drizzling end to All Hallows' Eve – the three sisters stood on barrels stinking of fish, three lengths of rough rope looped around three guilty necks, and they cackled and teased the crowd as their sentences were read under the light of flickering lanterns and hungry-looking torches.

"They're mad," said the tray maker to the milliner. "When did they turn so mad?"

"When they sold their souls to the Devil in a despicable tryst with yellow hellfire and wickedness," said the milliner, as if he'd been there.

"Hmmm," mused the tray maker. "It seemed to help Sarah's complexion, though."

It began to rain then — fat drops that soaked woollen tunics and ran into well-worn boots. The judge — who was also the priest of Salem and two bordering townships and, in his humble opinion, severely overworked and underappreciated — tried to speed things along.

"What say thee, witches?" he demanded.

Sarah Sanderson tittered on her barrel. "We say thou weren't so judgy when coming to us last May for a potency potion…" She cast her eyes below the man's round stomach and batted her lashes as the crowd broke into whispers and shifted from one soggy foot to the other.

"Lying jezebel!" cried the judge.

But before Sarah could retort, the father of dead Emily spoke up. "Winifred Sanderson," he said. "I will ask thee one final time: what hast thou done with my son, Thackery?"

"Thackery?" asked the eldest witch. In the dim torchlight, her face looked like chalk against the scarlet of her curls.

"Answer me!" he shouted. His arm was around the shoulders of his wife, who wept openly into his damp jacket.

"Well, I don't know!" Winifred protested, then gave her sisters a knowing, secret smile. "Cat's *got my tongue*!"

The Sanderson witches shrieked with laughter at Winifred's joke. As the sound of it died down, Sarah chafed at the rope around her neck. "This is terribly uncomfortable," she said.

Winifred cleared her throat, and before anyone in Salem could stop them, the Sanderson witches began to sing and chant in unison: *"Thrice I with mercury purify and spit upon the twelve tables."*

"Don't listen!" cried the judge. "Cover your ears!"

The gathered mass rushed to heed him as the sisters spat into the crowd.

"Don't drop the book!" someone shouted, but it was too late. Elijah Morris, the judge's apprentice and a boy who'd lost his best friend to these wicked sisters only that morning, covered his ears, too, dropping Winifred's leather-bound spell book as he did. The heavy thing sank into the mud with a satisfying squish. A moment later it flew open of its own accord, hundreds of pages shuddering and chuckling in the wind.

Mary and Sarah looked gleefully at it, the latter clapping her slender hands.

But Winifred, the eldest, let her gaze linger on the back of the crowd, her brown eyes piercing and gone almost black but her expression somehow bemused, like a cat who'd just transformed her master into a crippled mouse. Then her attention snapped back to her spell book. A laugh tumbled out of her broad chest. "Fools!" she crowed, relishing the word. "All of you! My ungodly book speaks to you: On All Hallows' Eve, when the moon is round, a virgin will summon us from under the ground." Her delight bubbled over into her sisters, who giggled and beamed alongside her. "We shall be back!" Winifred proclaimed. "And the lives of all the children of Salem shall be mine!"

White lightning cracked across the sky, and the executioner, dressed all in black, kicked down the barrels, Sarah, Winifred, and Mary dropping in quick succession. Silence fell, and at last they were still and singing no more.

As the crowd began to shuffle off, the spell book was closed and lifted. As the book rose, the eyelid on its cover blinked open and the watery green iris searched out its rescuer.

Through a film of cataracts and rain, the spell book's eye saw thick dark curls obscuring a face, and then it was tucked beneath an arm and secreted away.

SALEM, 1993

Dani and Max had only been trick-or-treating for ten minutes, but Max was already angling to go home.

Before leaving the house, Dani had begged him

to put on a costume, and he'd relented by pulling on sunglasses, a baseball cap and an oversized suede jacket that belonged to their dad. He pulled the brim low as they walked, and the grimace on his face said that there was no universe in which this night would turn out to be fun for him.

"Lighten up, Max," Dani said, leading him to the next house. He plopped onto the porch step to wait as she sidled up to the door after a pink princess and a pirate.

"What a festive little witch you are," said the woman who answered the door.

Max rolled his eyes.

When Dani came back, pleased with both her haul and the compliment, she handed Max the extra chocolate bar she'd taken for him.

"Can we go home now?" he asked, dropping the chocolate into his bag.

"No."

As they headed back down the path towards the street, Max groaned. "Dani—" he started, but it was too late. Jay and Ernie had rolled up and were holding court with their goons. Jay was in a pumpkin-smashing contest with a beanie-wearing schoolmate, and Ernie was perched on the brick-and-concrete wall of the steps that Max and Dani had to take to return to the street.

Max pivoted, deciding to cut across the lawn and

walk down the driveway of the neighbouring house. Dani did not get the memo.

"Ding, ding, ding, ding," Ernie trilled.

At that, Jay hurried over to Dani. "Stop and pay the toll, kid."

"Ten chocolate bars, no liquorice," added Ernie.

"Dump out your sack."

Dani wrinkled her brow, unimpressed. "Drop *dead*, moron."

Around them, the boys in denim jackets and ill-advised hats let out a chorus of shocked, delighted whoops and whistles.

"Yo, twerp," Ernie quickly cut in, "how'd you like to be hung off that telephone pole?"

"I'd like to see you try," said Dani. "It just so happens I've got my big brother with me." She looked over her shoulder at Max, who was staying in the background – dreaming of dodging the boys by heading down the street but not willing to abandon his sister. "Max!" Dani said.

"Hollywood!" Ernie called in recognition.

Max stuffed his hands into his pockets and looked away.

This time, the swell of sound bubbled with laughter. "Awkward," intoned a guy with the world's smallest ear gauges.

"So," said Jay, swaggering over to Max, "you're doing a little trick-or-treating." He mimicked the action with Ernie, which gained a cheap laugh from their friends.

"I'm just taking my little sister around," Max said, stepping into Jay's personal space.

Jay hummed. "That's nice," he said. He slapped down the brim of Max's baseball cap. "Wow! I love the costume." He leant in close. "But what are you supposed to be? A New Kid on the Block?" He grabbed Max's elbow to keep himself from falling over as he cracked up at his own joke.

"For your information," Dani announced, "he's a *little leaguer*."

The boys laughed hard at that, with Ernie pretending to strike a pitch from Jay with a tiny invisible bat.

Max shouldered past them.

"Wait a minute," said Ernie, grabbing Max's shoulder. "Everybody pays the toll."

"Stuff it, zit face," said Dani.

Ernie dropped Max's jacket to turn on her. "Why, you little—"

"Hey!" Max interrupted, putting himself between Dani and the bullies. "Ice, here," he said, and pressed his own paper bag of sweet into Ernie's thick chest. "Pig out." He took his sister by the arm. "Come on, Dani. Let's go."

As he stalked down the block, Dani skipping to keep

up with him, he heard Ernie send a last volley across the road: "And, Hollywood, the shoes fit great!"

Max let go of Dani's arm and shoved his hands into his coat pockets, his face burning.

He didn't say anything as they made their way down the street. He could tell Dani was disappointed in him, which only made him more annoyed with her. It was great that she thought he could take ten other guys in a fight – but seriously? Now Jay and Ernie would never forget his face. And now that he'd given them both his shoes and his sweets without fighting back, they'd never leave him alone.

He followed Dani up the front steps to another house.

"Should've punched him," Dani finally grumbled. She didn't look at Max.

Her flip suggestion made Max's irritation flare. "He would've killed me!"

"At least you would've died like a man," she replied.

"Hey!" Max imagined that Allison would have kept her cool and turned Dani's gendered stereotyping into a teaching moment, as she'd done when their geometry teacher made a joke about girls being bad at maths, but right now he was just afraid that his little sister might be right. "You just humiliated me in front of half the guys at school," he told her hotly. "So collect your candy and get out of my life."

Dani's eyes filled with tears. She brushed past him on her way back down the steps. "I wanna go home. Now."

Max sighed as she dashed through the garden and down the pavement. He hadn't really meant that – and he certainly shouldn't have said it out loud. It wasn't Dani's fault that Jay and Ernie and their gang were so awful.

There was a display of haystacks and seasonal decor in front of another house, and she tackled one of the pumpkins as if it were one of the fluffy pillows on her bed.

"Dani," Max said, walking over, "I'm sorry." He sat down heavily on the hay next to his shaking, sobbing sister. "It's just that I hate this place," he said, snatching off his baseball cap. "I miss all my friends. I wanna go home."

"*This* is your home now," Dani said over her shoulder, "so get used to it." She sniffled and wiped snot from her nose.

Max sighed. If only it were that easy. Dani had always been better at rolling with the punches. But he also knew that just because she was, that didn't mean he should take out his own dislike of change on her. He leant over. "Yeah," he admitted. Then he asked gently, "Gimme one more chance?"

"Why should I?"

"'Cause I'm your brother."

She turned to look at him, and Max gave her an exaggerated pout. She giggled, and the sound of her laugh made him smile, too.

Max looked up past the glare of the streetlights.

"Whoa," he said, "check that out."

"What?" asked Dani seriously.

The two of them stood up.

"Something just flew across the moon," Max said.

Dani wandered closer to the street, craning her neck.

Max glanced down at her, smirked, and grabbed her around the waist, shouting.

She squealed, breaking into another wave of giggles.

"Fooled ya," Max said, dusting hay off her jacket.

Dani relaxed for a moment against her big brother, and for a second it felt like they were back home in Southern California, happy. "Let's go, jerk face," she said, tugging on his sleeve.

They walked down the path to the closest house and gasped in unison.

YABOS

"Check out this house." Max ogled the building, which was at least two stories tall, though light glowed warm through a series of windows in the roof, as well, suggesting a finished attic.

The house itself was made of white clapboard, with dark shutters framing each window. Candlelit jack-o'-lanterns, poised behind thick windowpanes and lining the red-brick path, peered at them. The sounds of a party spilled down the front steps and through the iron gate to where Max and Dani stood, looking like dumbstruck street urchins.

Max felt a pang of envy, but Dani interrupted before he could truly wallow.

"Rich people," she said matter-of-factly, shrugging. "They'll probably make us drink cider and bob for apples."

Max looked down at her, wondering how a girl her age could be so good at keeping things in perspective. Despite her prediction, she dashed up the steps and pushed open the door. Max joined her, taking in the party.

The entry hall was bigger than his and Dani's new bedrooms combined, with a staircase sweeping up one side. In the adjoining room, adults his parents' age milled around sipping wine. They were all dressed in frilly, expensive-looking clothes that reminded Max of Marie Antoinette. In a far corner, a pianist and string quartet played discreetly.

"Is this for real?" Max breathed.

"Jackpot!" Dani had honed in on the cauldron of sweets on a table in the middle of the entry hall. They dashed over to it together, and Max plunged both hands in, feeling a giddiness he hadn't experienced since he was close to Dani's age. The cauldron was almost overflowing with full-size chocolate bars, plus Gobstoppers and chocolate lollipops shaped like witches and Frankenstein's monster. Dani picked up a witch wrapped in cellophane and ran a finger over the warty nose reverentially, as if she could get a sugar high just from touching it.

"Max Dennison." The girl's voice sounded like she'd

caught a toddler with his hand in the cookie jar – or in this case, a cauldron of sweets.

Max looked up to find Allison on the second-floor landing, leaning over the wooden handrail. Like the older women downstairs, she wore a long silk dress with lots of trim and complicated buttons. The cream sleeves of the dress ended at her elbows and turned into a waterfall of white lace. She wore an expensive-looking necklace, too, made of fat white pearls and one of those medallions with a Victorian woman's profile carved into it. The dress didn't seem like Allison's style, but the smile on her face – big and broad and a bit sly – was all her, and it made Max's heart do a complicated flip.

"Allison," he said, stepping away from the cauldron of sweets.

"Oh," Dani said conspiratorially. Her eyes darted from her brother to the girl at the top of the staircase. *"Allison."*

Max shot her a death look.

Allison grabbed the flouncy skirts of her dress to prevent herself from tripping down the steps. "I thought you weren't into Halloween," she said, making her way towards them.

"I'm not," said Max. "I'm just taking my sister, Dani, around."

"That's nice," said Allison, smiling.

Max's stomach turned into a warm, melty mess. He'd never made Allison smile like that before – not like she was being polite but like she was actually impressed. He grinned back and put an arm around Dani's shoulders. "I always do it," he said proudly.

"My parents made him," said Dani smartly.

Max nudged her.

Allison's smile grew bigger as she watched the two siblings tease each other. "Do you guys want some cider?"

"Sure," said Max before Dani could protest. He shot her a warning look when Allison's back was turned as she headed into the adjoining room, but Dani only smirked at him.

Allison filled two orange paper cups with warm apple juice and returned to them.

"Thanks," said Max, taking the cup she offered him. "How's the party?"

"Boring," said Allison. "It's just a bunch of my parents' friends. They do this every year." She walked back over to the cauldron and gestured. "And I get candy duty. By the way, Dani, I love your costume."

"Thank you," said Dani. "I really like yours, too. Of course, I couldn't wear anything like that, because I don't have" – she paused, turning innocently to her brother – "what do you call them, Max? Yabos?"

Max choked on his drink. The sting of cinnamon and powdered cloves went up his nose.

"Max likes your yabos," Dani said. "In fact, he loves them."

Max looked apologetically at Allison, trying to convey both abject horror and *kids will be kids*, but probably just managing to look like a stalker.

Allison laughed and picked out a few more sweets for Dani.

Max, meanwhile, wondered how he could possibly redeem himself, or at least explain himself. He also wondered whether his parents would mind if Dani mysteriously went missing and ended up living with their aunt in Seattle.

"I'm really into witches," said Allison, admiring Dani's costume.

Max was too relieved by the change in topic to be annoyed that they were again talking about witches as if they were baseball cards or Bon Jovi.

"Really? Me too." Dani unwrapped her chocolate witch and nibbled on the tip of her hat. "We just learned about those sisters in school."

"You mean the Sanderson sisters?" A look of real

excitement came over Allison's face, the way it did when Miss Olin started talking about the Bill of Rights in US History. "I know all about them," she went on. "My mom used to run the museum."

Dani grinned, equally excited. "There's a museum about them?"

"Yeah, but they shut it down because" – Allison leant in and lowered her voice to a whisper – "a lot of *spooky things* happened there."

Max felt like his plan had boomeranged and fallen in his lap, and he wasn't about to let it slip away again. "Why don't we go to the old Sanderson house?" he asked. He hoped he sounded fearless and cool, especially since his attempts to impress her up till then had come off more like playground teasing.

Allison turned to him, startled.

Dani shook her head, looking frightened, which confused Max because she'd seemed so excited just ten seconds before.

"Well, come on," he said to Allison. "Make a believer out of me."

Allison met his eyes, and he couldn't stop himself from smiling.

He was surprised when she smiled back. "Okay," she said, smoothing her skirts. "Let me get changed. They'll never miss me."

When Allison was on her way up the stairs, Dani turned on Max. "We're not going up there," she insisted. "My friends at school told me all about that place. It's weird."

"Dani." He touched her wrist, but his eyes didn't leave Allison. "This is the girl of my dreams."

"So take her to the movies like a normal person," Dani insisted.

"Dani!" Once Allison had rounded a corner at the top of the stairs, Max sighed and sank down onto one knee, facing his sister. "Look, just do this one thing for me, and I'll do anything you say. Please?" he pleaded.

Dani looked thoughtful.

Max didn't know why Allison was giving him the time of day now, after blowing him off only a few hours before, but he suspected it had something to do with Dani. He wasn't going to let this second chance, or his little sister, get away from him.

"Please?" he begged, clasping his hands. "Please?"

Dani patted his shoulder to quieten him. "Okay. Next year we go trick-or-treating as Wendy and Peter Pan." She leant in close, her nose almost touching his, "*With* tights, or it's no deal."

Max looked longingly at the empty staircase.

Dani shrugged and spun away.

"Okay, okay," he said, grabbing her around the middle

before she got too far. Like it or not, Allison seemed more relaxed when Dani was around. And like it or not, he felt more relaxed, too. Was that weird? He didn't have time to psychoanalyse. "Deal," he said. "Deal."

Dani beamed and slapped his back.

It's Just a Bunch of Hocus-Pocus

Allison led the way, though Max knew exactly where they were going, too. She cut through the graveyard, which made Max nervous they might come across Jay and Ernie again. The last thing he needed was to be forced into a fight to defend Allison's honour – or his own.

The graveyard was eerie at night. It seemed less like a place to watch Salem Harbor and more like a place to perform weird occult rituals. The tombstones resembled crooked teeth, and the linden trees towered like gaunt, broken-boned skeletons watching them in the dark.

Dani clutched Max's forearm the whole time, and though her nails were clipped too short to dig into Max's skin, he could feel the press of her fingertips through his jacket. It almost made him feel bad about the whole thing, but he reasoned that she'd go to school the next week with the best story in her class. Really, he was doing her a favour.

They exited the graveyard, and Allison led them all the way down the street to the corner with the stop sign. She took Dani's right hand in hers, and Dani still clung tight to Max's wrist, and a fluttering feeling stirred in his belly. It was almost like he was holding Allison's hand. He'd never thought about whether or not she'd get along with Dani, but he liked that she did and he liked that she tried, and he liked that she took them to the pedestrian crossing to teach Dani good road etiquette.

A stone wall bordered the pavement. It was made of big river-tumbled rocks stuck together with crumbling mortar and stitched even more securely with creeping ivy.

"Legend has it that the bones of one hundred children are buried within these walls," said Allison, running her fingers along the time-polished stones.

"Oh, great."

Allison let go of Dani's hand as they approached a wrought-iron gate. "You ready?" she asked, looking from Dani to Max.

Max nodded, pressing Dani against his hip in case she tried to run.

"Tights," she muttered, meeting his eyes.

He nodded.

Allison looked at them both like they were on something, but she pulled an old key out of her jumper and unlocked the gate.

The three of them stepped through it, and something small and dark shot across the path in front of them.

Dani jumped and, short or not, this time Max felt the bite of her nails.

"What was that?" she hissed.

Max dragged her forward, taking her torso with him as if her feet were rooted to the ground. "It's just a cat," he said, then knelt and pointed at a fallen tree to show her. Two yellow-green eyes caught the light of a distant streetlight.

"It's not just a cat," said Allison. "It's *the* cat. The one that warns you not to go in. It's been here as long as I can remember."

"How long do cats live?" Dani whispered urgently.

Max felt around in the fallen leaves and picked up a pebble. He chucked it towards the glowing eyes, prompting a yowl.

The cat disappeared.

Dani and Allison both looked at Max, disgusted.

"I didn't think I'd hit it," he said.

Dani sighed and looked at Allison. "Max failed out of baseball camp," she said, sounding resigned. They started walking up the buckling path.

"I did not *fail*," said Max.

"Fine. Max came home crying from baseball camp."

"That was a long time ago. How do you even remember?"

"My blackmail book," said Dani.

The path petered out long before they reached the house, and the three of them were forced to trample through a thick carpet of dead leaves. Max stepped down on a spindly fallen tree, applying all his weight to make it easier for the girls to pass. Allison steadied herself on his shoulder as she did, which made Max swallow hard.

The house ahead of them was smaller than Max expected, but somehow it seemed to loom above them, as if its spirit were far bigger than the collapsing wooden porch and broken eaves. Max eyed it, feeling uncertain. He knew he was the one who'd suggested this trip, but he was beginning to think the place would cave in on them – or at least give them all tetanus.

The low wooden steps creaked as Max climbed them.

"I don't think we should go in," said Dani.

Max gave her a look and she rolled her eyes.

"Sure," she said. "Whatever."

Allison produced a second key and unlocked the door. The sound of the deadbolt disengaging was loud and final.

Max looked back at Dani, who was chewing her bottom lip as if debating whether to walk home by herself. Finally, she sighed and walked up the stairs. She muttered something about "stupid crushes" as she flipped a switch on her plastic bucket of sweets and lifted the jack-o'-lantern's glowing face. She led the way into the house, closely followed by Max and Allison.

"I can't see a thing," Dani said.

"There's a light switch around here somewhere," said Allison.

Max took Dani's makeshift torch and peered around.

When Max had biked past the previous weekend, he'd thought the house seemed creepy in an old dilapidated way, but now he realised that it was sinister in a far different manner. The air inside was both stale and a little too still – the way a house feels when everyone is playing hide-and-seek. Still, yet tingling with nerves. Still, yet anxiously watching.

A ticket counter at the front of the room displayed dusty trinkets, including postcards of Salem, and stuffed bears with patterned capes and tiny brooms, and—

"Found a lighter," Max said, plucking a Zippo from

the display case. The silver lighter was engraved with a witch silhouetted against a full moon.

He struck it and hurried over to the wall to help Allison locate the light switch. It was an industrial thing that had only been installed in the past decade or so, but when they flipped the switch it didn't work.

"Try the breaker box," said Allison, pointing. Max opened the metal panel and turned every fuse off and then on again. This time, the lights throughout the room popped to life.

The main part of the house was one big room with wooden floors, wooden walls and a high wooden ceiling. There was a loft on one side of the house, which reminded Max of the small loft in his own room. A broom was mounted near the loft, with a helpful plaque identifying it as a witch's broom, in case visitors weren't sure about the house's shtick.

There were other signs of a modern influence, too. In addition to the electric lights, narrow piping ran around the perimeter of the ceiling, each branch ending with a spigot: sprinklers in case the old tinderbox went up in flames, Max realised.

Also, the layout of the room was that of a museum, not everyday living. The furniture had been moved back from the middle of the room to make way for a series of displays that had become overrun with spider's webs in the absence of regular cleaning. On one wall was a huge curio cabinet loaded with bottles and jars. Nearby, a set of cast-iron pots and pans hung from hooks in the ceiling. Everything had a small plaque with a glaringly obvious explanation.

"Here's the original cauldron," Allison said, pointing to the squat iron pot hung above an empty circle of stones. "Upstairs is where they slept," she said, gesturing to the loft. She came around to a display case featuring a large leather-bound book. It was the biggest book Max had ever seen, as long as his forearm and thicker than the width of his hand. The cover was held together with wide, angry-looking stitches, and swirls of tarnished silver helped reinforce the corners and the spine. Along the right edge of the cover was a strange pucker of leather – almost like the closed eye of a rhinoceros, or of a person who spent far too much time in a tanning booth. A loop of silver surrounded that, too, the far edge of the metal turning into a latch that would have kept the book shut if there had been a padlock.

Allison leant down to read the information card. "'It was given to her by the Devil himself. The book is bound in human skin and contains the recipes for her most powerful and evil spells'."

She sneaked a glance at Max's sister.

"I get the picture," Dani said.

Allison laughed. "According to town records, this went missing after the Sanderson sisters were hanged. They found it in another woman's house just a few days later. I guess she wanted to try it out for herself."

Dani shuddered. "How many witches does Salem have, anyway?"

"None any more," Allison said, squeezing Dani's shoulder. "Present company excluded," she added, and tugged on the tip of Dani's hat. The little girl smiled.

"What's that?" Max asked. He crossed to the far corner of the room, where an ancient-looking cast-iron stand supported a tall cream-coloured candle. Its surface was decorated with complicated etchings of trees and fire and, at the base, small humans running in fear. But they had nowhere to run since they always ran into one another.

"Oh." Allison pitched her voice low. "It's the Black Flame Candle."

Max looked at the nearby plaque. "'Black Flame Candle. Made from the fat of a hanged man. Legend says that on a full moon, it will raise the spirits of the dead if lit by a virgin on Halloween night'."

He looked around the quiet old museum. There was no one there but them, and this seemed like the perfect way to make their night more memorable. It would give Dani something else to tell her friends — and Allison, too. He liked the idea of Allison telling her friends about him, even if it was about him doing something silly.

"So let's light this sucker and meet the old broads," he said, pulling the lighter out of his pocket.

Dani, looking aghast, shook her head vehemently.

"Wanna do the honours?" Max asked Allison.

She was smiling but looked unimpressed. "No, thanks," she said, rolling her eyes.

It was the eye roll that threw him. Did that mean she *wasn't* a virgin? Did he care?

Out of nowhere, a screeching cat leapt onto the back of his neck. Its claws were sharp needles, and there were so many of them. Max fell to his knees, shouting. He wrestled it off and dropped hard onto his shoulder. The startled creature slunk under an old chest of drawers. "Stupid cat!"

"Okay, Max," said Dani. "You've had your fun. It's time to go. Come on, Allison." She took Allison by the hand, and the two of them headed for the door.

"Max, she's right," said Allison. "Let's go."

But Max had finally caught his breath. "Oh, come on," he said, not ready to head home just yet. He liked Allison, sure, but she was also the only person who'd given him the time of day in Salem, and he couldn't make it another two years there if he didn't have friends. "It's just a bunch of hocus-pocus."

That made Dani put on her mum voice: "Max, I'm not kidding this time," she said. "It's time to go."

Max shook his head at what a little kid Dani was being. Sometimes she acted so mature that he forgot, until moments like these, that she was only eight.

He opened the Zippo and held it to the candle's dusty wick.

"Max, no!" shouted Dani. The candle caught instantly, and Max grinned. But then he saw what a strange flame it was: it flickered yellow and orange around the edges but had a cool black heart.

Max's expression changed to one of concern. "Uh-oh."

BURNING RAIN OF DEATH

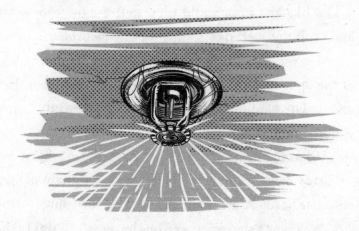

One by one, the light bulbs around the room burst in flashes of brilliant white. Each time, Dani squealed, her hands covering her eyes. Allison let out a quiet, frightened sound as the last bulb shattered and left them in the dark.

A breeze picked up, tumbling Dani's hat from her head. She uncovered her eyes and looked up, amazed. The heavy ironwork chandelier creaked loudly on its chain. Allison pulled Dani closer to her, and Max began to cross the room towards the two girls. A brilliant green light shot through the gaps in the floorboards, and the wood began to tremble and jump, threatening to rip away from the nails keeping it in place. Allison and Dani screamed, jumping towards the nearest wall. Max tried to steady himself by grabbing on to some nearby furniture, but it felt like the whole house was shaking

– and like the floor could very well decide to open up and drop them all into some unknown world.

Max was deciding whether to attempt a running leap at the door when the house became still and went dark again. The three stood quiet for a moment, as if they weren't sure whether it would start all over again.

"What happened?" Max finally asked, breathless.

Dani picked up her witch's hat and shoved it back onto her head. "A virgin lit the candle," she said.

There was a sharp *pop*, and one by one the lights in the chandelier relit – this time with real flames. Around the room, candles came alive with a soft *whoosh*. Beneath the huge cauldron, an equally large fire roared to life, and the kitchen hearth fizzed as if someone had thrown in a handful of lit sparklers. The sparks quickly caught the display tinder and burst into a warm fire.

The air cracked open with a delighted cackle, and Allison and Dani dived away from the front door just as it blew open, its knob slamming into the wall.

Max had hidden, as well, ducking under a heavy dining table near the spell book's case. When he lowered himself to the ground and looked up at the door, his eyes grew wide.

Three women were silhouetted in milky moonlight and framed by the open door: the first with long blonde hair and a narrow waist, the second with two wild swoops of hair near the crown of her head, and the third with dark wiry curls twisted into the shape of a crooked cornucopia.

The woman in the middle marched into the house. She wore a floor-length emerald dress with a high collar and a creeping black pattern that seemed determined to smother the green. A gold clasp cinched the dress at her waist, and her underskirts were a brilliant blue. As she came into the light, the unnatural red of her hair became obvious. "We're home!" she declared.

Max felt dizzy. *This can't be happening,* he thought. *They can't be real.* He glanced in Allison's direction, but she was out of his line of sight. Was it a prank? A weird Salem-centric way of getting back at him after he made fun of Halloween? But he recalled the way the Black Flame Candle burned.

Beside the woman in green, the other two women clasped hands and began to dance and jump about, giggling. One – the blonde one – wore a low-cut rosy dress with filmy sleeves that gathered at her wrists. The other wore layers and layers: an orange dress beneath a red vest and a matching wool cape. Her tartan skirts were intersecting lines of black and grey and, depending on the light, a dozen other colours.

"Oh, sweet revenge," said the redheaded witch. "You see, sisters? My curse worked perfectly."

"That's because thou art perfect, Winnie," said the brunette, touching her elder sister's shoulder. *She means Winifred*, thought Max, remembering Miss Olin's story. *Winifred Sanderson.*

The three witches laughed, and Winifred hurried across the room, her brunette sister trailing her.

The blonde witch waited until they'd gone, then popped up onto her toes and reached into the rafters over the door. She was tall and thin, and her hair flowed in gentle waves down her back and over the creamy skin of her chest. She grinned as she found the thing she'd been feeling around for. She pulled down what appeared to be a length of twine.

"My lucky rat tail!" she crowed. "Just where I left it."

"But who lit the Black Flame Candle, hmmm?" Winifred asked, crossing towards the strange flame. She paused, fingers on her lips, then noticed the case with the huge spell book. She gave a delighted gasp and hurried over to it, tapping her long nails on the glass.

"Come on, sleepy head!" she cooed. "We have work to do. I missed you – did you miss me, too?"

The brunette sister sidled up behind her. "Winnie," she whispered.

"Yes, Mary?"

"I smell children."

"Sic 'em!"

The three witches slipped into line, with Mary leading. She sniffed the air eagerly.

"It's a little girl," she declared.

Behind her, the blonde Sanderson nibbled the tip of her rat tail. Max knew that they were headed right for Dani, but he didn't know what to do. He spotted her crouched behind the old ticket-taking counter, chewing her bottom lip. He gauged the distance between himself and Mary, wondering how long he could keep the sisters occupied if he leapt out of hiding.

"Seven," Mary said, sniffing again. "Maybe eight. And a half."

"Let's play with her!" trilled the blonde.

"You'll frighten her, Sarah," said Winifred.

Sarah began to sing softly. *"Come out, little children; I'll take thee away—"*

Dani raised her eyes to the ceiling, pleading with some higher power to help her.

Winifred closed a hand over Sarah's mouth. "Come out, dear," she said. "We will not harm thee."

"We love children!" Mary agreed, slamming a hand on the counter.

Winifred gave her an ugly look, but it was quickly wiped away when Dani popped up in front of them.

"I thought thou'd never come, sisters," she said, adopting the worst British accent Max had ever heard.

"Greetings, little one," Winifred said warmly.

"'Twas I who brought you back."

"Imagine," said Winifred. "Such a pretty little" – she swallowed thickly – "child."

Sarah giggled.

"And she's so well fed, isn't she?" said Mary, going around the counter. "Plump!" she exclaimed, poking Dani in the ribs. Dani shrieked. "Plump!" Another jab, another squeal. "Plump! Shish ke-baby!"

Winifred rescued Dani just as Max was about to barrel across the room. "Tell me, dumpling," she said, placing Dani's hand on her arm as she led her deeper into the house, "what is the year?"

"Nineteen ninety-three."

Winifred pushed Dani into an ancient straight-backed dining chair.

"Sisters," she said eagerly, "we have been gone three hundred years."

"Well, Winnie, how time flies, huh?" said Mary. "When you're dead?"

The sisters all laughed, and Dani laughed, too, clearly hoping to please them. She kept going after they had finished, until her eyes landed on Mary's hungry face. Then her laughter died into a nervous chuckle. "It's been great fun," she said, getting up. "But I guess I'd better be going."

"Oh," Winifred said, pressing her back into the chair, "stay for supper."

"But I'm—I'm not hungry," said Dani.

"But we are," said Mary with a dangerous smile.

This time, when Dani tried to get up, Mary and Sarah each caught her by an arm and lifted her, kicking and screaming, towards the cauldron at the heart of the room.

"Hey!" shouted Max, springing out of his hiding place. "Let go of my little sister."

"Roast him, Winnie," Mary growled.

"No," Sarah breathed, touching Winifred's arm eagerly. "Let me – let me play with him."

Winifred heeded Mary rather than Sarah and shot a bolt of bright, branching lightning at Max's chest. He lost consciousness briefly as he hit the ground but woke to a pain snaking through his whole body. He groaned.

"Max!" screamed Dani.

Winifred threw her magic at him again, dragging him across the floor and pinning him to the wall.

"I haven't lost my touch, sisters," she said, cackling. "See?" She flung him around to face her.

Max gasped at the feeling of knives in his bloodstream. The pain was sharp and sudden and made him think that his heart would give out. He tried to cover his chest, but his hands were pressed against the wall by an invisible force.

Sarah nestled into his neck. She smelt like wet earth and orange pomanders and honey.

"Hello," Winifred said to him. "Goodbye." This time her green lightning bolts lifted him from the ground. His body skimmed the wall, moving slowly to the ceiling. He couldn't see straight – could hardly keep enough wits about him to continue to breathe. He whimpered, but the sound was drowned out by the electric crackle and hum.

Mary held Dani tightly as the little girl shrieked her brother's name over and over again.

"Mary," Allison said, and as soon as the witch turned, she struck her over the head with the broom she'd retrieved from the wall display. As the brunette witch stumbled around, Allison grabbed a frying pan from the rack and slammed it over her head, making her hair even more crooked.

"You leave my brother alone!" Dani shouted at Winifred, then struck her with her bag of sweets. She lashed out at Sarah, as well, for good measure.

Max crumpled to the ground, weak and exhausted.

When Dani crouched down to tend to him, the black cat reappeared and leapt onto Winifred's neck. It flexed its claws into the softest parts.

"Get him!" Winifred shrieked, spinning about. "Get this animal – get this beast off of me."

"Max, let's go," Dani said, pulling at his jacket. He forced himself up and stumbled after her towards the door, where Allison waited for them. He was about to join them when he realised they couldn't just leave the Sanderson sisters inside. They'd find their way to town eventually, and he didn't want that horrible lightning magic let loose on anyone else. The witches still struggled to get the cat off of Winifred, who spun wildly about.

"Get out!" he shouted at the two girls. "Go, go, go!"

The witches finally flung the cat off of Winifred.

Max stopped short before reaching the door. *How do you kill a witch?* he thought. In *The Wizard of Oz*, Dorothy did it with a bucket of water – but he didn't have a bucket.

Then he remembered the sprinklers.

When he was sure the girls were gone, he hoisted himself into the loft and rose on unsteady feet. "Hey!" he called, drawing the witches' attention up. "You have messed with the great and powerful Max and now must suffer the consequences. I summon the Burning Rain of Death."

The sisters tried to figure out what he meant, talking over one another.

"Burning what?" asked Sarah.

"Burning Rain of Death," repeated Winifred.

"What does he mean by—"

"Rain, did he say?" asked Mary.

"I don't know. Burning—"

Max drew out the lighter again and snapped it. When the flame popped up, the Sanderson sisters gasped.

"He makes fire in his hand," muttered Winifred, impressed.

Max lifted the lighter towards a spigot on the sprinkler system and waited until they all began spouting water throughout the house.

The Sanderson sisters screamed, rushing away to try to escape the falling water.

Max leapt down from the loft but slipped in a puddle, falling hard on his back.

The cat jumped onto his chest. "Nice job, Max."

Max gasped, recoiling. "You can talk."

"Yeah, no kidding," said the cat. "Now get the spell book."

Max couldn't move but wasn't sure whether that was from shock or a broken spine.

The cat batted a paw at Max's face. "Come on," he ordered, "move it!"

With that, Max shoved himself to his feet and

grabbed one of the posts that held an information card for the witches' cauldron. He used it to shatter the glass to the spell book's case and pulled it out, ignoring the shards of glass that dug into his skin.

The witches were too afraid of the water to chase him, instead cowering in an alcove near the kitchen.

"My book!" cried Winifred. "He's going for my book!"

Max dashed to the door and down the front steps, the spell book clutched to his chest. He could hear Allison calling to him, and he followed her voice down towards the street and through the property's front gate.

Inside the house, Mary and Sarah wailed.

"I'm dying," Sarah cried, her blonde hair and red dress soaked and dripping. "I'm too pretty to die."

And yet they weren't dying. Winifred drew a palmful of water to her mouth and tasted it.

"Winnie!" shrieked Mary in warning.

"Shut up!" Winifred spat back. "It is but water."

Mary tasted a few drops for herself. "Most refreshing," she quipped.

Sarah extended her tongue. "It is!" she said, then tried to swallow as much as she could.

"You idiot," Winifred said to Mary. "The boy has tricked us, and he's stolen the book. After him!"

Before they left, Winifred rescued the Black Flame Candle and stuck it in a tall kitchen cupboard, safely away from the strange metal clouds in the ceiling that spilled rain all over her mother's furniture and carpet.

Then the Sanderson sisters ran through the old wood, as they had not done in three hundred years. They arrived at the front gate, and the three of them stopped, elbow to elbow.

"'Tis a black river," said Mary.

"Perhaps it is not too deep," said Sarah.

Winifred grabbed her roughly by the arm and flung her ahead of them. Sarah shrieked, leaping, but when her heels touched the ground they didn't fall through.

"'Tis firm!" she exclaimed, gathering her skirts and doing a skipping dance on the asphalt. "'Tis firm as stone."

"Why, it's a road," said Winifred, joining her sister.

Mary took a few careful steps to join them.

"Sisters," said Winifred, drawing attention back to herself as usual. "My book."

They began to walk down the road together but were interrupted by the sound of fire engines and ambulances. Red and white lights flashed through the sky, lighting up the witches' faces.

The sisters screamed in fear and turned, desperate for the comfort of the wood.

OTHERWISE, IT'S CURTAINS!

ax, Allison and Dani took a long way through the wood that the cat seemed to know by heart. It led them weaving through trees, stitching over and under fallen branches and the leaning columns of half-rotted trunks.

In the distance, Max could hear the eerie whine of emergency vehicles, no doubt called by the sprinklers going off on what was still considered public property.

The group, still led by the cat, emerged at the edge of the road. He leapt off the curb without even looking, and Allison and Dani followed him without having to be asked.

"Whoa, whoa, whoa," Max said, pulling up short. "This is the graveyard."

"Yes, it's the graveyard," said the cat, as if Max were

one of the most annoying people he'd ever met — and perhaps he was. "Witches can't step foot here."

Max looked at the girls and waved a deflated hand at the cat. "He talks," he said.

"At least he's not trying to electrocute us," said Dani, which Max thought was a fair point.

"Is this a Halloween thing?" asked Allison. "Did the Sandersons cast a spell on you?"

The cat slipped through the gate without answering. "Follow me!" he called. "Over here." He paused, waiting for Allison to pry open the gate. She did, and they filed through and into the abandoned graveyard. Max was careful to shut the gate after them. If there had been a lock, he would've bolted the thing and taken the key with him.

"I want to show you something," explained the cat, "to give you an idea of exactly what we're dealing with."

They threaded through the quiet trees of the graveyard. The tombstones weren't arranged in careful rows, as they were in most graveyards Max had seen. Instead, they appeared in clusters or alone in unexpected places. Some parts of the graveyard even looked more like a park, with benches and fountains and the occasional mausoleum.

They walked for what seemed a long time, until they

arrived in a clearing. They stopped at a tombstone near the edge of the woods.

"'William Butcherson'?" Max read, crouching near it.

"Billy Butcherson was Winnie's lover," said the cat, "but she found him sporting with her sister Sarah. So she poisoned him and sewed his mouth shut with a dull needle so he couldn't tell her secrets, even in death. Winifred always was the jealous type."

Allison looked at the cat in wonder. "You're Thackery Binx," she said.

"Yes."

"So the legends are true," she added.

He paused, perhaps unsure how to respond. "Well, follow me," he finally said, leading them deeper into the graveyard. "I want to show you something else."

"Teenagers again," grumbled one of the men who had arrived in the noisy red vehicle. A stream of such men had rushed into the Sanderson house, and now they were filing out in a more orderly fashion.

"Every year they break into that house and do something stupid," agreed the man walking back to the street with him. Water dripped from his helmet. The captain had made him climb up and fiddle with the sprinkler system when they found the house empty.

"I hate Halloween," said the first man.

Sarah, crouched in the bearberry bushes next to her sisters, bit her bottom lip as the two men walked by. She'd never been acquainted with a man who looked quite so dashing in suspenders and oversized trousers. She stretched her neck, risking being spotted to keep the gentlemen in her line of sight a little longer.

"Who—who—who are they?" stuttered Mary, ducking further into the bushes as if she could balance out her sister's derring-do.

"Boys," said Sarah wistfully.

"Perhaps they are the keepers of Master's red vessel?" Mary asked hopefully, eyeing the vehicle at the bottom of the road. A contraption near the top threw off red-and-white sparks. "His demon drivers?"

"They are witch hunters," corrected Winifred, sounding disgusted. "Observe," she added, "they wear black robes and carry axes to chop the wood to burn us."

Mary made a frightened sound. "Hold me?" she asked, snuggling her red-haired sister.

Winifred batted her away.

Sarah, meanwhile, was snacking on a spider she'd discovered on a nearby vine.

"Sisters," hissed Winifred. "Let me make one thing

perfectly clear." The fiery vehicle had refilled with the witch hunters and tore away. "The magic that brought us back only works tonight, on All Hallows' Eve," said Winifred, getting to her feet and brushing off her skirts. "When the sun comes up, we're dust."

"Dust?" asked Mary.

"Toast."

"Toast?"

Winifred turned to her two sisters. "Pudding!" she shouted, throwing up her hands.

Mary shrieked, and Sarah shuddered then leant towards Mary and whispered, "Do we like pudding?"

"Fortunately," said Winifred, looking off into the moonlit woods, "the potion I brewed the night we were hanged would keep us alive and young forever."

Sarah beamed and hopped excitedly.

"Unfortunately," trilled Winifred, turning on her heel and pushing past her sisters towards the sagging porch, "the recipe for that potion is in my spell book, and the little wretches have stolen it. Therefore, it stands to reason – does it not, sisters dear – that we must find the book, brew the potion and suck the lives out of the children of Salem before sunrise. Otherwise, it's curtains. We evaporate! We cease to exist!" She gave each of them an accusing look. "Does thou comprehend?"

"Well, you explained it beautifully, Winnie," Mary

rushed to say. "The way you sort of started out with the adventure part, and then you sort of slowly went into the—"

"Explained what?" asked Sarah.

Winifred pursed her lips and then seemed to make up her mind. "Come!" she shouted, shoving open the door of the house. "We fly."

Eventually, Binx took Max, Allison and Dani to a small gravestone whose inscription was nearly invisible in the low light of the full moon. Max knelt to get a better look, running the tips of his fingers over letters and numerals time had sanded down. The gravestone marked the burial of a beloved daughter and sister who had died on the 31st of October, 1693. The name read: EMILY BINX.

"Because of me, my little sister's life was stolen," said Binx, studying the grave marker.

Max sat down, wrapping his arms around his knees. He could hear the wistfulness in Binx's voice. Max had never seen a cat look sad before, but Binx's expression was unmistakable, even with a muzzle and whiskers. Dani knelt down across from Max, and Allison perched on a weather-worn rock between the two of them, Winifred's spell book tucked safely in her lap.

"For years," said Binx, "I waited for my life to end so I could be reunited with my family, but Winifred's curse kept me alive. Then one day, I figured out what to do with my eternal life: I'd failed Emily, but I wouldn't fail again. When the three sisters returned, I'd be there to stop them. So for three centuries, I guarded their house on All Hallows' night, when I knew some airhead virgin might light that candle."

"Nice going, airhead," said Dani to her brother.

"Hey, look, I'm sorry, okay?" said Max, getting to his feet. He paused, then said hopefully, "We're talking about three ancient hags versus the twentieth century. How bad can it be?"

"Bad," said Binx.

Allison drew back the cover of Winifred's heavy spell book.

"Stay out of there!" shouted Binx.

Startled, Allison slammed it shut. "Why?" she asked, looking up.

"It holds Winifred's most dangerous spells," said Binx. "She must not get it."

Max grabbed the book from Allison and tossed it on the ground. "Let's torch the sucker," he said, striking the silver lighter. He held it to the pages of the book, but the flame reared back as if a force field ensconced the thing.

"It's protected by magic," said Binx.

The sound of cackling broke the air and the group turned. The three Sanderson sisters hovered above them, each perched on a wood-handled broom. Sarah, on the left, wore a rich purple robe and a tight bodice the colour of pressed wine grapes. Mary, on the right, was dressed in dowdier clothes, but they were the crimson of blood drops on snow. And Winifred, in the middle, wore forest green trimmed in faded gold.

"'It's just a bunch of hocus-pocus'!" Winifred quipped. "Sarah. Mary," she said, gesturing at her sisters. They veered off on their brooms in either direction.

Sarah went straight for Max. "Brave little virgin who lit the candle," she crooned, "I'll be thy friend."

Allison snatched up a dead branch and brandished it at the witch. "Hey!" she yelled. "Take a hike!"

The dried ends scraped at Sarah's skin and cloak and she winced and cried out, peeling away.

Winifred smiled at her book, still on the ground where Max had left it. "Book!" she called to it. The thing lifted off the ground and began to float towards her. "Come to Mummy!"

Binx leapt on top of it, and both he and the book fell back down to earth.

"'Fraid not!" he called.

"Thackery Binx, thou mangy feline," Winifred said, sounding almost impressed. "Still alive?"

"And waiting for you," said Binx.

"Ah! Thou hast waited in vain. And thou will fail to save thy friends, just as thou failed to save thy sister." She pointed the end of her broom at him and dived.

"Grab the book!" shouted Binx.

Allison nabbed it, and the group bolted away from Winifred. They ran for the protection of the trees, but Mary cut them off, grinning as she bore down on them. They dodged her and she sailed past, no doubt circling to reassess.

Max pulled Dani close to him, sheltering her with one arm. "They can't touch us here, right?" he asked Binx.

"Well," said the cat, "*they* can't."

Dani turned to him. "I don't like the way you said that."

The Sanderson sisters, still perched on their brooms, reappeared out of the woods. Sarah licked her strawberry-coloured lips. Winifred grinned widely and guided her broom closer to the three friends. Max realised that they'd returned to where they'd started – the grave of Billy Butcherson.

"Unfaithful lover long since dead," Winifred incanted,

gesturing with unnaturally long knotted fingers, "deep asleep in thy wormy bed."

Allison clutched at Max's arm.

He wrapped his other arm tighter around Dani.

Her small fingers dug into his skin through his jacket.

"Wiggle thy toes," chanted Winifred, "open thine eyes, twist thy fingers towards the sky. Life is sweet, be not shy. On thy feet, so sayeth I!"

The ground began to tremble, and the earth over the nearby grave split, soil flying up as if it were boiling water. A coffin shivered out of the cut in the ground.

"Max," Dani whimpered. "Max."

He pulled her away from the grave. His pulse pounded in his ears and his whole body went slick with sweat.

The coffin lid burst open and a corpse dragged its way out. He grunted, shaking earth from his matted hair.

That's when he spotted Max, Allison and Dani, who were watching him with horror. Billy Butcherson jumped, startled by their presence. The kids screamed and rushed away.

Billy looked around, confused, and spotted the gravestone behind him. He sighed.

"Hello, Billy," Sarah said, waving.

He smiled through the stitches keeping his lips sealed tightly shut.

"Catch those children!" shouted Winifred. "Get up! Get up! Get out of that ditch!" Billy pushed himself out of the broken bits of his final resting place. "Faster!"

Binx led his human companions through the woods, ducking under fallen branches and weaving between various tombstones and mausoleums. "In here," Binx said, stopping near what looked like a storm drain.

Allison helped Dani slip through first and then jumped in herself. Max spotted Billy Butcherson scrambling through the woods and grabbed a nearby branch, dragging it back as far as he could. When Billy was close enough, Max released the branch and it flew forward, knocking Billy's head from his shoulders.

Max whooped, but the headless body started towards him again and Max hurried into the drain.

Allison helped him to his feet at the bottom.

Dani stood nearby, coughing hard.

"You okay?" Allison asked her.

Dani grunted.

Allison handed the Sandersons' spell book to Max.

"What is this place, Binx?" Max asked, tucking the book under one arm.

"It's the old Salem crypt," Binx replied. "It connects to the sewer and up to the street."

"Charming," Allison said wryly.

"We need to find my parents," said Max. "They'll know what to do."

"Your parents?" asked Binx sceptically. "Adults always show up too late."

"Max is right," said Dani. "Mom fixes everything."

Binx seemed to take Dani's word more seriously than Max's. He thought about it for a moment, then shrugged. "We might as well try," he said. "I don't have a better idea."

"They're at Town Hall," said Max. "Can you take us there?"

The cat gave him a look as if to say, *Am I an immortal cat who's been living in the same town for three hundred years?*

Just then, Max noticed a skeleton suspended from the vault's high ceiling. "Uh, don't look up, Dani," he said.

"Don't worry," she replied. Her eyes had been steadfastly focused on the ground since they'd arrived. "I won't."

"Relax," Binx told them. "I've hunted mice down here for years."

"Mice?" groaned Dani. "Oh, god."

But they had to choose between that and an undead colonist with a mandate to capture them, so rodents it would be.

OLD SALEM CRYPT

Winifred groaned when she saw her reanimated ex scrounging in the dirt to find his own head.

"Ah, crust," she said. "He's lost his head." She launched herself and her broom into a tight, angry circle. "Damn that Thackery Binx!" she cried. "Damn him!"

Beneath her, Billy bleated through his mouth stitches.

"Which way did they go?" Winifred asked, guiding herself closer to him.

He couldn't speak, of course, but he didn't point the way, either. She realised he must have got directionally confused when his skull went spinning. She looked around the graveyard and noticed a tunnel entrance partially hidden by climbing vines. The twigs around it were broken as if they'd been repeatedly trodden on.

"Billy," she snapped, turning back to his desiccated corpse. "Listen to me." His skin and spine crackled and popped as he forced his head back onto his body. "Follow those children, you maggot museum, and get my book. Then come find us; we'll be ready for them." She drifted backwards, offended by the intensity of the dislike in his eyes. "Quit staring at me. Get moving down that hole." With that, she led her sisters back over the graveyard fence, muttering "Damn. Double damn!"

Winifred landed lightly on the walk beyond the graveyard gate. In the distance she could see the bell tower of the small graveyard chapel, its delicate lines and single bell outlined white by the pale moon.

As Winifred hurried to the fence, she felt a shock of remembrance from having walked that precise path before. She'd stood there and clutched the gate and watched a graveyard wedding take place more than three hundred years before – had watched another Sanderson say her vows in the only place where Winifred and her sisters didn't dare intervene.

"They're here," Winifred said. She could've meant the children, or she could've meant the wedding party. For a moment, even Winifred wasn't sure.

The fence was wrapped with tendrils of dead and dying English ivy, and as she pressed her fingertips to the rough bodies of the vines, she imagined her own mortality and shuddered. It brought her back to the year 1993 and to the task very much at hand. "The children," she said, her voice gaining strength. "And that flea-riddled cat. I know they're here, but where are they?" She turned her face towards her brunette sister. "Sniff them out, Mary." She ignored Sarah entirely, who had started to climb the gate – but to what end, if they could not step foot on hallowed ground?

Mary clenched her fists and breathed deeply. "They're, they're…" She pressed her face against the iron bars and gave a plaintive sigh. "Oh, I can't. They've gone too far. I've lost them."

Winifred snatched the lobe of Mary's left ear and dragged her away from the fence. "I'll have your guts for garters, girl," she said, shoving her sister away. "Confound you!" Mary clutched at her aching ear, snivelling. "Very well," said Winifred, almost to herself, "we must outwit them. When Billy the butcher gets here with my book, we shall be ready for them." She turned back to her third sister. "Sarah! Let us start collecting children."

"Why?" asked Mary softly.

"Because, you great buffoon," Winifred said, wondering why the Devil had cursed her mother with so many senseless offspring, "we want to live forever, not just until tomorrow. The more children we snatch, the longer we live."

"Right," Sarah said brightly, pointing at Mary. "Let us fly."

"Fly!" agreed Winifred.

"Wait," Mary said, causing the other two Sandersons to turn. "I have an idea." She plucked the brooms from her sisters' hands. "Since this promises to be a most dire and stressful evening, I suggest we form a calming circle."

"I am calm!" said Winifred.

"Oh, Sister," Mary said gently. "Thou art not being honest with thyself, are we? Hmmm?" She leant in, as she might to a little girl. "Come on. Give—gimme a smile."

Winifred allowed a bashful grimace and then hopped into place, starting the calming circle. Mary and Sarah followed suit, each placing a hand on Winifred's shoulders. It wasn't a real spell circle, perhaps, but it made Winifred's younger sisters happy – and on very rare occasions, that was magic enough.

Allison and Max let Binx lead the way through the dark, dripping tunnels that snaked beneath the streets of Salem. Dani did a better job of keeping up with him, perhaps because she knew he'd do a better job of catching any mice or rats than Max would.

When he decided his little sister and the sarcastic cat

were out of earshot, Max cleared his throat. "So," he said, not daring to look at Allison, "about earlier. I want to apologise."

"For lighting the candle?"

"Um. No, but I'm sorry for that, too."

"For ignoring us when we said it was time to go?"

"Uhhh." Max scratched the back of his head awkwardly. "Yeah, sorry for that, too."

"For your Rico Suave stunt with the phone number?"

"I knew you were upset about that."

"I wasn't upset about it," Allison said. "Just embarrassed. For you. You know, you don't have to be someone you're not just to ask a girl out."

There it was, sitting between the two of them: the spectre of Max asking Allison on a date. Because that's what the whole thing boiled down to, right? He'd been too chicken to catch her in the hallway, just the two of them, and tell her that he liked her and wanted to buy her ice cream, if she was okay with that idea. Instead, he'd escalated and escalated and now three undead witches had put Dani on a dinner menu.

Max knew it, but he didn't know how to answer Allison. He didn't know what to do to make things right.

"Yeah, I get that," he finally said. "But I guess I wanted to apologise for what Dani said earlier. About

– well, about you. It was embarrassing, and I'm sorry she did that."

"What did she say about me?"

"About your costume. About your, uh." He stopped talking and gestured lamely at his chest.

"You mean how she told me you've talked about my boobs?"

Max blushed. "Yeah," he said in a small voice, thinking that he'd rather be lost in those tunnels and facing death by sewer alligators than having that conversation.

"You don't have to apologise for her," said Allison. "Dani didn't do anything wrong. You might want to apologise for yourself, though."

Max cleared his throat. "Yeah," he said, for what felt like the hundredth time. "I – uh. I am sorry. I was an idiot. Like, a total idiot. But I wanted to tell my friend back in California about you, and he got bored with me talking about other stuff, so I thought—" He cleared his throat again. "But yeah, it was dumb. And it was my fault, not his or Dani's. I do get that."

"Thanks," Allison said, uncrossing her arms. Max sneaked a look at her face and determined she meant it. "I appreciate it. It's just a little weird, you know?"

Their footsteps echoed lightly off the walls as they continued following Binx's shadowy lead. Up ahead, they heard Dani telling Binx something about space travel.

"I know," Max said. "And I do know you're so much more than your—um..." He blushed, realising he was about to make the same mistake all over again.

Allison laughed aloud this time. "You really aren't quick on the uptake, are you?" She laughed again, and the sound of it bounced along with their footsteps, making Max's heart flutter.

"So what other stuff?" she asked.

"Hmmm?"

"The other stuff your friend didn't want to hear about. What was it?"

Max wet his lips. He didn't really want to tell her such personal stuff, but then again it was about *her*, so it was hard to use that defence. Besides, he had already got in a mess by saying the wrong thing.

"Like, the vase you made in sculpture class last week was sick. All those dots of blue and white in the glaze? It was awesome. And when Nancy fell asleep in chemistry and you slipped her the answer when Mrs Jackson called on her? That was really cool of you. I like that even though you're the best person in the class, you don't rub it in."

Allison smiled, eyes downturned as she carefully picked her way around a pile of mushy leaves. "Yeah, well," she said, "Nancy's parents are getting divorced; she deserves a break. Also, I am *not* better at chem than everyone else. Charles is."

"Charles is just louder," said Max.

Allison tucked a lock of hair behind her ear. "You really noticed all of that stuff?"

"Yeah," said Max. "I hope it's not creepy."

She laughed again. "It's not," she said. "I like those things about me, too."

"I just like that you work so hard. I don't know what you want to be when we, you know, grow up or whatever. But you *are* going to be it, Allison. You don't give yourself any excuses. That's – well, it's attractive."

"Thanks," Allison said again. Max could hear her smile in that single, simple word.

He waited for her to acknowledge that he admitted he liked her, but she didn't – not directly. Instead, she said, "I like the way you treat Dani. You were a total idiot back there with the candle," she added quickly. "But I can tell how much you love her. You're more *you* when she's around. More humble. I like that."

"She's got a lot of dirt on me," he joked, shrugging. "Plus, she's smarter than I am, and she's eight. It's hard not to be humble."

At that, Allison grinned. "What I meant was, I wish you acted around other people the way you act around her. It's a good look on you."

Max scrutinised Allison's face, but it was too dark to tell exactly what she was thinking. He opened his mouth to ask, but Binx's voice cut through the dark, making them both jump.

"Here we are!" called the cat. "Up and out!"

"Think soothing thoughts," said Mary in her most centred voice. The sisters grasped arms and leant into one another, revolving in a slow circle. "Rabid bats," she suggested. "Black Death. Mummy's scorpion pie."

With that, they broke apart and arranged themselves in a line, each sister lifting her face to the full moon.

"Mother," they breathed in unison.

A massive vehicle rolled up and stopped right in front of them. A set of doors near the front folded open with a mechanical gasp.

Inside, a man, perhaps in his forties, perched on a tall seat behind a set of controls. He took a look at the sisters and gave them a lecherous grin. "Bubble, bubble," he said, "I'm in trouble."

Winifred blushed. "Tell me, friend, what is this contraption?"

"I call it" – he spit a wad of gum through the window beside him – "a bus."

Winifred stroked her cheek with a two-inch fingernail. "A bus," she repeated. "And its purpose?"

He opened his arms to welcome them in. "To convey gorgeous creatures such as yourselves to your most" – he paused, drawing a fisted hand towards his chest – "forbidden desires," he finished meaningfully.

Winifred giggled. "Well," she said. "Fancy." She glanced at her sisters and back at the swaggering driver. "We desire children," she said.

He laughed loudly at that. "Hey, that may take me a couple of tries, but I don't think there'll be a problem. Hop on up."

Winifred led the way, as was the Sanderson practice. Sarah sidled onto the driver's lap.

"How does it work?" she asked, planting two hands on the wheel in front of her.

"Oh, gumdrop," the driver said, "it's already working."

The door hissed shut and the bus trembled back to life. He helped her guide it onto the road. Sarah squealed, clapping, and the bus veered into the opposite lane.

The driver sat up straighter and grabbed on to the wheel.

Sarah wrested it back for herself, and as she did, her head bobbed into his field of vision.

A black cat appeared in the middle of the road, as if out of nowhere, and Sarah gunned the accelerator.

The bus clanked, one set of wheels bucking up a

couple of inches, and then dropped back into place and kept going.

"Whoa!" said the driver, peering around her shoulder. "Speed bump."

Sarah pressed the button in the middle of the wheel, delighting in the high-pitched toot of the bus's horn.

"Binx?" called Dani, distressed. Seconds before, Max had lifted off the manhole cover overhead and started to climb out of the drainage tunnels, but he had ducked back down, shouting "Look out!"

Now the cat was nowhere to be seen.

Max hurried to push the heavy metal disc off again. He pulled himself up and then helped Dani and Allison climb out, too.

"Oh my god," Max said when he spotted Binx's flattened body in the middle of the road. He didn't react quickly enough to block Dani from seeing.

She cried out and buried her face in Allison's jumper. "No…" she sobbed.

"It's all my fault," Max said, starting to pace.

Allison took his wrist. "Max, it's not your fault," she said.

Dani grabbed on to his sleeve. "Look!" she said.

The three of them watched, amazed, as Binx's sides inflated like a balloon, as if he were taking a very deep breath. There was the sound of air filling desperate lungs and the soft snap of bones realigning.

Binx rolled over and looked up at them, shaking his head as if to clear it. "I hate it when that happens," he said.

Max, Allison and Dani exchanged looks.

"What?" said Binx, bowing into a stretch. "I told you: I can't die." He took a step towards Dani. "Are you all right?" he asked, studying her small face.

She nodded energetically. "Yeah," she said with a tear-streaked smile.

He darted over to bat at her shoelaces. When she giggled, he took a step back, seemingly satisfied. "Okay," he said, his yellow eyes peering into her pale green ones. "Then let's go find your parents."

Amok! Amok! Amok!

inifred and Mary sat across the aisle from each other at the back of the bus, ignoring their sister Sarah's shenanigans. Outside, creatures milled about, going from house to house in the strangest clothes.

Mary leapt to her feet. "Stop!" she yelled.

The bus screeched to a halt and everyone turned to her.

"I smell children," she said, grinning.

"Marvellous," said Winifred, standing, as well.

Sarah hopped off the driver's lap and hurried towards them.

"Hey, cupcake," the driver said, grabbing her arm. "Don't I get your phone number? Your area code? You want my route schedule?"

Sarah simpered. "Oh," she said, batting a hand as if suddenly shy. "Thou wouldst hate me in the morning."

"No, I wouldn'tst!" he insisted.

Winifred gathered up her satin skirts and hurried to Sarah's side. "Oh, believe me," she said to the man, "thou wouldst." She extracted Sarah's arm from his grip and gave him a warning look.

"Party pooper," he grumbled.

Winifred turned up her nose at him and led her sisters off the bus.

Ahead of them stood a small house whose garden billowed with crimson smoke. Pitchforks jutted out of the soil.

"What is this, sisters?" Winifred asked, eyeing a short figure in a plush turtle body. It waved and scuttled off. In fact, creatures wove past the sisters from all directions, ducking and dodging and giggling as they criss-crossed the road. They were unlike any of the creatures Winifred had seen during her three hundred years in Hell – but then again, her own circle of reference had been somewhat limited and rather monstrous. Simple ghouls and goblins served as waiters in Lord Satan's palace, and the Sandersons had never received an invitation. Instead, they'd whiled away their hours with the likes of chupacabras and bunyips and terror beasts, and a towering black-caped man who never showed his face.

"What are those?" asked Mary, clutching Winifred's sleeve. She jumped at the sight of a small white figure with a smooth round head and the letters NASA tattooed over its heart. "What's that?"

"Um…" said Winifred. She tried to get a better look at the faces of the quick-moving fiends. "Hobgoblins," she said decisively.

A miniature angel glided over and curtsied, gold wings bobbing. "Bless you," she said sweetly.

The sisters shrieked and shrank back as she dashed away.

"Enough," Winifred said, catching her breath.

Mary trembled as she looked around. "Oh, sisters," she fussed, "I'm very confused. I smell children, but I don't see children." She gave a plaintive cry. "I've lost my powers!"

"Enough, enough," Winifred repeated, slapping her gently on each side of her face.

"Sorry," Mary said with a sniffle.

"We are witches," Winifred insisted. "We are evil. What would Mother say if she could see us like this?"

The three witches lifted their brooms towards the eastern sky and said, in unison, "Mother."

A sharp, high laugh broke through the night.

The witches turned and saw an old man clad in red, white hair settled in wisps about his ears.

"Master!" they cried. One by one, the sisters deposited their brooms at his gate, propping the handles against the slats of a pristine white fence, and hurried over, bowing and scraping at his doorstep.

"What kind of costumes are these?" the man asked.

The witches bowed deeply, arms extended. Even in Hell, they'd only seen Lord Satan from afar, when he passed through on a black chariot to survey his domain.

"It's the Sanderson sisters, right?" he asked.

The sisters simpered and clapped.

"At your service," Winifred said.

"Haven't seen you for centuries," said Satan, which made Winifred blush because she hadn't thought he would remember their first and heretofore only meeting, when she'd pledged herself to the sisterhood of red witches and received her spell book. "Why don't you come in?" he asked, waving them through the door.

They assembled in the main room of the house, which was surprisingly homely and cluttered.

"I want you to meet the little woman," Satan told the Sandersons.

"He has a little woman?" Winifred whispered to Mary.

"Sounds tasty," she replied.

The man leant over a plush chair to speak to a woman whose face was hidden by a table lantern.

"Petunia face."

"What?" she snapped.

"We have company."

"I don't care who—" She sat up and the Sandersons gasped at the colourful twists wrapped through her curls.

"Sisters," Mary whispered, "Satan has married Medusa. See the snakes in her hair?"

The woman snarled at the sisters, who stepped back, fearful of waking her snakes.

"My three favourite witches," said Satan.

"Aren't you broads a little old to be trick-or-treating?" asked Medusa.

"We'll be younger in the morning," Winifred told her.

The woman snorted. "Yeah, sure," she said. "Me too." She left her drink on a nearby table and retreated up the staircase.

Mary walked over to experiment with the box the woman had been observing. It seemed to transport the watcher to another world, and she sat down on the comfortable chair before it to get a better look. In the box, a small dog scuttled across polished wooden floors, and Mary laughed and shouted, ducking and turning her own body to help it avoid obstacles.

Winifred wandered into another room and let out a

delighted sound when she found Satan's torture devices – wooden mallets and knives arranged along a metal strip for ease of access. There were two circles of fire, as well: one boiling a pot of water and another that seemed to be cooking sugared mud.

Winifred returned to the main part of the house just as Satan's wife came back down the stairs. They both laid eyes on Sarah, who was dancing slowly with the Devil.

"Master," she said softly.

With that, the woman of the house made the lights brighter and stormed down the stairs. "Okay, that's it," she snapped. "Party's over."

Sarah broke away from her dance, and Mary sat up quickly.

"Get out of my house," said the woman.

"Pudding face," her husband pleaded, approaching her.

"Shove it, Satan," she snapped.

"Oh," said Sarah seriously. "Thou should not speak to Master in such a manner."

"They call me Master," the man said, pleased.

"Wait till you see what I'm gonna call you," said his wife. She threw some brightly coloured bags at the sisters. "Take your Clark Bars and get outta my house."

Winifred stalked forward, putting herself between

her sisters and the pale, tired-looking woman. "Make us," she said.

"Honeybunch," said the old man.

"Ralph," the woman said sharply, "sic 'em." A small furry demon leapt up and chased the sisters from the house.

The demon stopped at the doorstep and trotted back inside. The sisters ran the rest of the way to the road, where they paused to catch their breaths.

"My broom!" Sarah cried, realising it had gone missing.

"My broom!" echoed Mary.

"My broom," Winifred huffed. "Purloined. Curses."

They started down the road on foot. "Sisters, look," said Mary, holding up a chocolate bar she'd taken from the house. "'Tis the chocolate-covered finger of a man named Clark." She bit into it. "Mmmm—ew—" She spat it out. "It's candy," she said, aghast. "Why would the master give us candy?"

"Because he is not our master," said Winifred sharply.

"He isn't?"

"And these are not hobgoblins," Winifred added. She tore the mask from a passing creature, revealing the startled face of a small blond boy. "See?" she said, gesturing.

"Cool it, man!" cried the boy.

Mary touched his arm. "A child," she said hungrily.

The boy hit her with a bulging fabric sack. "Weirdos!" he shouted as he ran away.

"Weirdos?" repeated Sarah.

"Sisters," said Winifred, "All Hallows' Eve has become a night of frolic. Where children wear costumes and run amok."

"Amok," chorused Sarah. "Amok, amok, amok, amok, a—"

Winifred elbowed her in the stomach and Sarah doubled over, clutching her abdomen.

"Oh, Winnie," pleaded Mary. "Just one child."

"We haven't the time, Sister," said Winifred. "We must find my book. Then thou may have as many children as thou desires."

Mary hummed. "Boiled and toasted and sautéed and roasted and—"

"Yes, yes," Winifred interrupted, knitting her fingers together eagerly. "But first, the book."

I Put a Spell on You

At last, Max and the girls homed in on Salem's Town Hall, a two-storey red-brick building with the sound of a live band spilling out and down the street. The windows of the second floor were washed with purple light from the party happening inside, and a banner above the double doors read SALEM'S 16TH ANNUAL TOWN HALL PUMPKIN BALL.

"Oh, great," Max said, leading the group across the street. "How are we ever gonna find Mom and Dad in this place?"

"I'll wait outside," said Binx, jumping into the low branches of a nearby tree. "If anything happens, shout for me."

Max eyed the noisy building. "How will you hear us?" he asked.

"I won't," said Binx. "But it might help you feel better."

Dani held out her arms and Binx relented, leaping into them. Max jogged up the steps to open the door for Allison and Dani.

"I should be eating Peanut M&Ms right now," Dani muttered as she stalked past.

"Actually," said Max, "you should be in bed."

She rolled her eyes. "I'm going to find Mom," she called to Max before disappearing between a policewoman and a jellyfish.

Town Hall's second floor was a huge ballroom, and it was packed with half the adults in Salem. On the raised stage, a skeleton in a top hat sang Sinatra's "Witchcraft". The band members were dressed as skeletons, too, and they really blasted the brass. Max wondered, fleetingly, whether their drummer would give him lessons.

The whole audience was dressed up, and they seemed to have gone all out. Max spotted a sequinned Viking, a knight in a full suit of silver armour and a timely Bill Clinton.

"Are you sure your parents can fix this?" Allison shouted over the music. "What if they don't believe us?"

"What choice do we have?" said Max.

Two strong hands grabbed Max by the shoulders, and he shouted, spinning around. "Oh," he said, relieved, "Dad."

"It's not Dad," said his father in a forced Romanian accent. "It's *Dad*ula."

Max winced at the terrible joke.

"Oh, my goodness," his dad said, taking Allison by the hand, "who must this charming young blood donor be?"

"Dad!" Max snapped. "Something terrible happened."

"Dani?" his dad asked immediately, letting go of Allison. "What's wrong? What—"

"No," said Max, "Dani's fine."

His dad's face grew stern. "Good," he said, then turned to Allison and excused himself. He put his arm around Max's shoulders and pulled him off to the side. "What is it?"

"It's—it's complicated, okay? Promise you'll believe me."

"You know I can't do that in advance. Shoot, Max. Look, whatever it is, just tell me."

Onstage, the skeleton did a complicated dance turn and leant into his microphone: "'*Cause it's witchcraft, that crazy witchcraft.*"

Across the room, Dani sidestepped a costume that made the wearer look like Aladdin seated on a flying carpet. She peered into the mouth of an alligator. "Mom?" she asked hopefully. The reptile shook its head and waddled off.

She turned and nearly crashed into a blonde woman in a red bustier, the cups of which were built out into two spiralled cones.

"Mom?" Dani asked, aghast. She nearly dropped Binx. "What are you supposed to be?"

Her mother looked flustered. "Madonna," she said, and gestured to her costume. "Well, you know," she continued, suddenly self-conscious. "Obviously. Don't you think?"

Dani sighed. "Come here," she said, holding Binx out towards her mother in hopes that he would speak.

"What?" asked her mum, crouching to hear her daughter better.

Dani pointed to Binx's head with one hand. "This cat, okay?" she said. "He can talk. My brother's a virgin. He lit the Black Flame Candle. The witches are back from the dead, and they're after us." She took a breath. "We need help."

Her mum paused and then placed a worried hand on Dani's cheek. "How much candy have you had, honey?"

The words came tumbling out of Dani as she realised that her parents might actually not believe her: "Mom, I haven't OD'd. I haven't even had a piece. They're real witches, they can fly and they're gonna eat all the kids in Salem. They're real."

"All right," her mother said warily. "Let's... just... find your father."

The jazzy skeleton wrapped up his crooning. "Thank you, ghouls and ghoul-ettes!" he said to the crowd, grinning as the applause swelled and died down again. The band immediately began an up-tempo cover of Jay Hawkins's "I Put a Spell on You".

The Dennison family convened, with Allison looking on from the sidelines.

"Guys," Mr Dennison said impatiently, "I love you, but enough is enough. Just calm down."

Max fumed. "But they're gonna come—"

"Don't you see how crazy this sounds?" insisted his dad.

Dani caught sight of something across the room. "Max!" she shouted. "Max! They're here!"

Max turned away from his dad. His eyes rippled over the crowd. When he spotted the three witches – Winifred apparently telling off Mary and Sarah sucking face with a mummy – Max took off. He ignored his parents' pleas for him to come back and instead scrambled onto the stage. He wrestled the microphone from the skeleton.

"Cut the music!" he shouted.

"Hey, man, I'm in the middle of a song," complained the singer.

"It's an emergency," Max told him, still speaking into the mic. "Only for a minute." He turned to face the crowd. "Will everybody listen up, please? Your kids are in danger."

The crowd gasped, and startled adults pressed closer to the stage.

"Three hundred years ago," said Max, "the Sanderson sisters bewitched people, and now they've returned from their grave."

The roomful of people laughed.

"Hey, I'm serious," Max insisted. "It's not a joke. I know this sounds dumb, but they're here tonight. They're right over there," he added, pointing to where the sisters stood, each of them looking nervous.

A spotlight scanned the crowd and stopped on the three Sandersons, and everyone gasped again, stepping away from them.

Winifred recovered the fastest. "Thank you, Max," she said, tapping her long fingernails against her chin, "for that marvellous introduction."

The crowd laughed, and this time a smattering of applause also washed through the room.

"I put a spell on you," she said dramatically, throwing her hands in the air. The keyboardist took this as a cue and began to play a fizzy, sparkling tune. "And now you're mine," said Winifred with a mischievous smile.

Max heard Dani shout above the appreciative murmurs: "Don't listen to them!" She was right, he knew. What if the witches decided to *actually* put a spell on everyone? He leapt off the stage to help his sister as their parents dragged her towards the exit. Allison trailed helplessly behind them, trying to reason with Max's mum without being disrespectful.

"You can't stop the things I do," said Winifred, then broke into a trill: "I ain't lyin'." She pirouetted to scattered giggling. "It's been three hundred years, right down to the day. Now the witch is back, and there's hell to pay. I put a spell on you," she repeated, working the crowd and making her way to the stage, then breaking into full-throated song: *"And now... you're miiiine!"*

The snare drum rolled and the brass flared. "Hello, Salem!" she called, smirking at the children's attempt to warn the parents. "My name's Winifred! What's yours?" She sashayed to the edge of the stage. *"I put a spell on you, and now you're gone!"*

"Gone, gone, gone!" sang her sisters, taking over the two mics reserved for backup singers. *"So long!"*

"My whammy fell on you," crooned Winifred, *"and it was strong."*

"So strong," sang Sarah and Mary, *"so strong, so strong!"*

"Your wretched little lives have all been cursed," sang Winifred, grinning when the audience cheered. *"'Cause of all the witches working, I'm the worst! I put a spell on you... and now you're mine."*

Max and Dani's parents deposited the kids near the front door.

"Take your sister home," said Max's dad. "It's too late for pranks." He took his wife by the hand and led her back into the crowd.

Max, Allison and Dani didn't head downstairs right away. Instead, they watched in horror as the whole ballroom danced to the witches' song.

Someone bumped into Max and he turned, ducking when he saw Billy Butcherson stumbling towards them through the delighted crowd. Dani screamed and grabbed Allison, dragging her in the other direction.

"If you don't believe, you better get superstitious," sang Winifred, having the time of her life. *"Ask my sisters—"*

"Oooh, she's vicious!" they chorused.

"I put a spell on you!" belted Winifred. *"I put a spell on you!"*

Mary and Sarah joined her, and the three of them began to dance towards the crowd. *"Ah say ento pi alpha mabi upendi,"* they chanted.

"Ah say ento pi alpha mabi upendi!" repeated the crowd.

Max suddenly felt lightheaded, and the air seemed to fill with the smells of fresh-baked cookies and brownies.

"It's a spell!" Max shouted, pressing his palms to his ears. "Don't listen!"

Dani and Allison followed his example, but the adults within earshot ignored him.

"In comma coriyama—" sang the witches onstage.

"In comma coriyama!" the adults crowed back.

"Hey—"

"Hey!"

"Hi—"

"Hi!"

"Say bye-byyyyyye!" Winifred belted out, waving dramatically at the crowd, then added, with a smirk: "Bye-bye!"

The crowd roared and whistled as the lights cut to a crimson wash.

As the band struck up the next song, Winifred could be heard cackling as she sealed the curse: "Dance, dance, dance until you die!" Sarah pranced off the stage after her, swinging her skirts.

"Good work, Winnie," said Mary, catching up to them.

"Of course it was," said Winifred. From behind the velvet stage curtains, she watched the result of her dirty work. "Now these silly parents will be occupied without a thought for their darling children at home in their darling beds. We will have a feast tonight, sisters! But first, we must find my book."

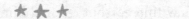

The kids ran down the block and into an alleyway behind Allegra's, one of Salem's most popular restaurants. The alley was filled with stinking rubbish bins and discarded kitchen equipment – including an industrial oven and some broken blenders – waiting to be hauled away.

Max kicked the oven, cursing. He only managed to hurt his foot, so he limped back and leant against the closest brick wall. "This is really bad!" he shouted.

"Max, come on," said Allison, startled. "Calm down."

"Look," he snapped, "I want you to take Dani back to your house and don't let her out of your sight."

"Max, I'm not leaving you," said Dani.

The restaurant door crashed open, and Max, Dani and Allison ducked behind the piles of rubbish. A chef stepped out to pick a lobster out of the fish tank. Just as the door swung shut behind him again, Binx's eyes widened. "Uh-oh," he said, and jumped down to share the kids' hiding place.

The three witches strolled up, following Mary, who sniffed loudly as she walked.

"I smell…" she muttered, tasting the air. "Winnie, I smell… I smell…" She paused. "Scrod." She withered under Winifred's hateful look. "It's a bottom dweller," she explained. "You know, you can eat it sometimes with lovely bread crumbs, a little bit of margarine. Oooh – or olive oil is good." She began to stutter and devolve from nerves.

Winifred gave a disgusted sniff in her direction and abandoned the alley, but Sarah stepped towards the rubbish bins, her blue eyes wide as she searched for the source of some feeling she couldn't quite put her finger on.

"Sarah," Winifred said shrilly, though she didn't bother to wait for her. "Sarah!"

As Allison tried to inch past the oven, its door fell open and blocked her way. She reached for the handle to close it, then paused and turned to Max with a conniving smile. "I have an idea," she said.

Mary and Sarah followed Winifred through town, towards a slender ironwork gate. Behind the gate was the largest building the witches had ever seen, its dark windows peering out of red-brick walls. They'd come because of the smell, which was strong enough that even Winifred, whose sense of smell was poor, had caught it as the wind switched.

"What is this place?" breathed Sarah.

"It reeks of children," Mary said, almost humming in delight.

"It is a prison for children," explained Winifred. She opened the creaking front gate and let in her sisters, then cast a spell to unlock the prison's heavy front door. Above the door, tall white letters spelled the words JACOB BAILEY HIGH SCHOOL.

The hallway was wide and quiet when the sisters crept in – wider than the river that once ran through town, and quieter than the nights when they went down to it to fish out dead fish and fishermen.

As they shut the door behind them, the place filled with an unholy howl. "Welcome to high school hell," said a dark and warbling voice. "I'm your host, Boris Karloff Jr." This announcement was punctuated by a thunderous crash and a crescendo of evil laughter. The sisters wove from one side of the hall to the other, trying to determine where the sound was coming from and how to avoid its owner.

"It's time to meet our three contestants," the disembodied voice continued. "Sarah, Mary and Winifred Sanderson. Read any good spell books lately?"

The sleek, dark body of Thackery Binx flickered through an open door. He hissed at the sisters and scampered off.

Winifred began to lead her sisters towards him when a pleasant female voice said, "Hello, welcome to the library. *Bonjour, bienvenue a la bibliothéque.*"

The sisters looked at one another and then shuffled into the dark room and down a narrow hall. They found themselves in a distant wing, where strange carvings sat on narrow white pedestals.

"I would like a book," the woman said. *"Je voudrais un livre."* Her voice came from within a small room lined with metal. The sisters slipped past the iconography and into the room, which smelt strongly of burnt clay and children. The sisters grinned at one another, then looked for the source of the voice and the smell. A black box with a red blinking light sat on one shelf. The woman repeated her last request, but her voice filtered through the mesh panelling of the box.

"I think she's trapped inside," said Mary, sounding sorry for her.

Winifred's eyes fell to the floor, where mounds of clothes – socks and sleeveless tops and shorts in coordinating colours – lay scattered.

"It's a trap," she said, but before she could turn, the heavy metal door swung shut. Even before she saw the girl's face through the window, she knew that she and her sisters were toast.

Winifred reached for Sarah's arm. She was more afraid than she had been three hundred years before, on the night she'd got them caught by the townspeople. Then as now, it was because of things she hadn't bothered to do. Her mother would have been so angry at her, were she there. She'd have criticised her and told her she should be more thorough, more thoughtful. More like—

There was a click, and the room grew warm enough to make Winifred sweat.

She muttered spells beneath her breath – every spell she could remember, in fact – spells of protection and revenge, spells for clearing storms and finding a lost pair of spectacles.

The three children – and even that damned cat, who looked awfully pleased with himself – peered through the narrow window of the box.

Winifred's hair began to smoke and then alighted, and so, too, did the lace hem of her dress, and then she yelled "Wretches!" and she and her sisters burst into flames.

DEAD MAN'S TOES!

Allison wanted to check the kiln for debris, but Max worried that seeking the witches' smoking bodies would scar Dani for life. Instead, the two of them decided to put the kiln on a longer second cycle, hoping that the Sandersons would have mostly turned to ash by morning. They'd sneak back in the next day or Sunday to clean it out, and by Monday morning no one would have any idea what had happened in the arts wing.

Max turned to Dani, then, who had moved away from the kiln door when the witches started to burn. She held Binx close to her, petting him and kissing the top of his head.

"It's done," Max said to her, and when the words sank in, Dani beamed up at him.

"Really?"

He ran over and scooped her up, spinning her around and nearly knocking over an unfired ceramic skull that someone had made.

"Really," he said softly against the side of his little sister's head. His own body relaxed, then, as all the adrenaline seemed to pour out of it.

Allison walked over and put one hand on each of his shoulders, which sent butterflies careening through his digestive system.

"Let's get home," she said. She was looking at Dani, but it sent a happy shiver down Max's spine.

Allison took Max's hand when he set Dani down, and they all slipped out of the school, breaking into a run as they neared the ironwork gates. Dani whooped, and the sound of her celebrating made it all feel real to Max, too.

"Farewell, Winifred Sanderson!" shouted Binx, leaping from Dani's arms to the rain-slicked street and racing about not unlike a dog after its own tail.

Max grabbed Allison around the waist, spinning her, and then set her down and gave Dani a big kiss on the cheek. Dani squealed but didn't push him away. Instead she grabbed his face and kissed his forehead, grinning.

Binx dashed away, leading the jubilant kids down the block. Leaves fell around them like confetti in oranges and browns and golds. They crossed into a park, and Allison took off after Dani, towards a grassy field where Dani could show off her handstands and cartwheels.

Max relaxed against the park fence and looked up at Binx, who had settled onto the nearby branch of an oak tree. "We did it, Binx," he said, grinning. "We stopped them."

"I've wanted to do that for three hundred years," Binx said thoughtfully. He paused and then added, "Ever since they took Emily."

Max's smile faded into a serious look. He turned to face Binx, who was silhouetted against the opalescent moon. "You really miss her, don't you?" he asked.

Binx looked away without answering, but Max could see the pain and self-loathing knitted across his small furry face.

"Man, you can't keep blaming yourself for that," Max said. "That happened so long ago."

Binx's narrow shoulders shifted up in a small shrug. "Take good care of Dani, Max," he said. "You'll never know how precious she is until you lose her." He leapt out of the tree and headed across the park, slipping into the shadows.

"Hey, Binx!" called Max, straightening. The cat turned and looked at him. His eyes seemed to glow yellow in the low light. "Where do you think you're going?" Max asked, walking towards him. "You're a Dennison now, buddy. One of us."

"Come on, Binx!" Dani called from the clearing. "Let's go home."

"Home," Binx repeated wistfully. He glanced from Max to Dani and then scurried after her as she linked one arm through Allison's and headed back to the pavement.

As Max watched them saunter ahead of him, he thought about how he'd hated Salem as soon as his parents had announced their move – even before he knew anything about the town or their house or Allison Watts. "Home," he said. The word sounded weird to him, but it also sounded right.

In the cool October night, wisps of vapour the colour of moss-green algae or fresh growth on old branches filtered across the moon's full face. The vapour slipped through low-hanging clouds but didn't become part of them, and after a few minutes the vapour began to fall back to earth, as if weighed down by the condensation that had begun to bead on grass blades and window glass.

It funnelled down the chimney of Jacob Bailey High

School's kiln, and when every last breath of it was inside the school, it whirled and churned and knocked down the reinforced metal door. Winifred strode out of the kiln, hacking and batting at the smoke still hanging in the air.

"Hello," she muttered testily, "I want my book. *Bonjour, je veux mon livre.*"

Her hair was even wilder and wirier than before – and the grin plastered on her face was murderous – but she otherwise looked just the same as when those bratty kids first trapped her. Her sisters followed her out of the broken kiln in similar condition, Sarah trying desperately to wipe black ash from her sleeves and skirts.

"Find them," Winifred ordered, turning on Mary.

"W-what?"

"The boy and that blasted girl," she said. "And that child with the wretched cat. They have my book and that book is our last chance to stay in this world. Find them."

"I—I don't know," stuttered Mary.

"You don't know?" said Winifred scornfully.

"Well, Winifred, everything smells like smoke now."

"What are you good for, then?" demanded Winifred.

"I—well—I don't know. I—I'm still your sister, Winnie." She quailed under the look Winifred gave her then. "Never mind!" she yelped. "I didn't mean it!"

Spinning away, Winifred swung angrily at the nearest sculpture, grabbing a cobalt blue vase and throwing it onto the concrete floor. The vase shattered into a dozen pieces. Winifred groaned. "Just find them," she said over her ash-dusted shoulder.

Max caught up with the others and led the way home. He could tell that Dani was getting sleepy because she kept repeating herself, and because her eyes stayed closed a little too long when she blinked.

He took her hand as they passed by Town Hall, where the Pumpkin Ball was still going strong. The lead singer's vocals poured through the open door: *"Jump, magic, jump; dance, magic, dance..."*

"Getting back into the kiln tomorrow's going to be easy," Allison said wryly. "All the adults are going to be asleep till lunchtime."

Max yawned into the crook of his arm. "That doesn't sound so bad," he said.

Allison smiled at him and shook her head.

When they reached the Dennison house, the lights inside were still out. Max unlocked the door as Dani checked the bowl of sweets they'd left on the porch.

"Aw, man," she grumbled. "Only Almond Joys are left."

Allison patted her back reassuringly. "Don't worry; you can have whatever's left over at my house."

"Promise?"

"Only if your brother brings you over tomorrow," Allison said, smiling at Max.

Dani rolled her eyes. "There'd better be Twix bars if I'm covering for you two."

"Mom?" Max asked, leading the girls inside. "Dad?" He flipped on the light. His parents' coats were nowhere to be found. Nor were his mum's keys, which she always had trouble tracking down despite dropping them on the entry table each time she came home. His dad had left behind his Swiss Army knife, though, and Max plucked it up and pocketed it just in case. He had a feeling that after their night, he'd be paranoid of witches for the rest of his life.

"We got a new cat!" Dani said, pushing past him. "Mom?"

Max looked at Allison. "Well, I guess they're still partying," he said, stepping out of her way. "Come on in."

They went to Max's room, because Dani always liked to sleep there when she was anxious. She said that even monsters were afraid of the stink of teenage boys. Dani gave Binx a bowl of milk before slipping under Max's covers. "You're my kitty now," she said, petting

Binx's head. "You'll have milk and tuna fish every day, and you'll only hunt mice for fun."

"You're going to turn me into one of those fat, useless contented house cats," Binx said.

Dani giggled. "You betcha."

Allison chuckled, watching them. She and Max were sitting on a pile of pillows near the staircase that led into the bedroom's loft. Allison grabbed a nearby blanket and wrapped it over her shoulders, then leant into Max. He was sure the sudden acceleration of his heartbeat would startle her, but her breathing was soft and steady. He wrapped one arm around her gingerly, afraid to disturb her, and she pressed her cheek more firmly against his chest. He wanted to touch her hair but was afraid that might be too forward. Instead, he tucked his fingers around her elbow and thought about how he might ask her on their first proper date. Part of him still wanted to take her to the hill in the graveyard that overlooked the harbour, where he went to think, but after all they'd been through, it seemed a bit creepy. Maybe he'd take her to a movie, like Dani had suggested.

"You know, Binx," Dani said sleepily as the cat finished his milk and leapt up to snuggle into her arms, "I'll always take care of you. My children will take care of you, too. And their children after that, and theirs after that. Forever and ever…" She trailed off, and when Max looked over, he saw that she was fast asleep.

The night had gone quiet. It was so late that all the children of Salem were tucked into bed. So late, in fact, that their babysitters had fallen asleep, as well, drifting off as they waited for their employers to come back from the Town Hall Pumpkin Ball.

As a result, the town felt deserted and eerie beneath the harsh light of its own streetlights.

Jay and Ernie didn't seem to notice, however.

Long-haired Jay perched on the hood of an old black car, while stocky Ernie leant against the front bumper, unwrapping fun-size chocolate bar after fun-size chocolate bar and stuffing himself silly. Toilet paper cascaded around them from the branches of a sycamore tree that had mostly shed its leaves for winter. The boys knew the local police would unfairly presume them guilty if a stranger's house – or worse, a classmate's – ended up decked out this way, so instead they'd TP'd Jay's house. In the morning, his parents would just look disappointed and point them towards the stepladder.

"You wanna smash some pumpkins?" Jay asked, toying with a half-empty roll of toilet paper.

"No," said Ernie around a mouthful of chocolate.

"Well, then you wanna look in windows and watch babes undress?"

"It's three o'clock," Ernie said. "They're undressed already."

Jay flung the paper away. "Well then, you think of something."

"I don't feel so good."

"That's 'cause you're eating too much candy, you oinker," Jay said, smacking the latest bar from Ernie's hand. He hated when Ernie got this way – so fixated on one thing, and usually a thing that was totally boring and didn't involve Jay at all.

The witches saw the boys before the boys saw the witches.

Mary, who had been desperately sniffing the air for what felt like two hours but was probably merely minutes, was the most excited to spot them.

"The boy, Winnie!" she hissed, tugging on her redheaded sister's sleeve.

"Are you sure that's the right one?" Winifred asked.

Mary was not, but she knew that Winifred did not like insecurity.

"I am," she said. "It must be."

"It *must be*," said Winifred, "or it *is*?"

"It is!" Mary said with more conviction than she felt.

"Good," said Winifred. Her voice grew darker and more vindictive then: "The girl who trapped us in that fire box is mine. I'll teach her to try and burn a witch."

Jay and Ernie were, to an outside observer, old enough to be more men than boys, but the night was heading towards dawn and the Sanderson sisters were not eager to discriminate.

The witches crept up behind them. As they did, Sarah danced through the soft, waving curls of white paper, spinning and smiling.

Mary homed in on the strongest scent in the street: without a second thought, she pressed her nose against the larger boy's left foot.

"Yo, witch," Ernie said, smacking her with Max Dennison's nearly empty bag of sweets. "Get your face off my shoe."

Mary scuttled backwards, fixing her hair. "Oh," she said, frightened more of Winifred than of this boy with the strange hair and the useless weapon. "Wrong boy. Oh, sorry, Winnie."

Sarah plucked up a scrap of toilet paper and swung it about, watching the thin material make exquisite shapes as it caught the air.

Winifred threw her hands up. "Why, why, why was I cursed with such idiot sisters?" she demanded.

Sarah did a little twirl. "Just lucky, I guess."

Mary snorted before she could stop herself, and Winifred let out a tearless sob.

The three sisters turned away to try to find their original targets.

"Oh, man," said Jay. "How come it's always the ugly chicks that stay out late?"

One by one, the Sandersons turned. Sarah in particular looked prepared to turn someone into a box turtle or slug. Something slow on the road and sweet on the tongue.

"Chicks?" prompted Winifred.

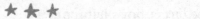

Winifred managed to bring the boys to their knees thanks to a particularly well-delivered lightning bolt. She gave them over to her sisters to drag back up the road to their house in the woods. Once there, she summoned two of her favourite cages from the wardrobe. They'd once housed Winifred's prized phoenix twins – the ones Mary set free out of pity at the age of twelve.

Winifred was happy to have them empty now, for she shoved one boy into each cage and sealed the doors with iron locks. The cages crackled with electricity as she used her magic to rehang the huge iron things on their ceiling hooks. The impertinent boys wept and pleaded for pity without pause.

Winifred ignored them. Their suffering would teach them not to disrespect their elders – even if they wouldn't have much time to live out that lesson. "We haven't much time left," she said. "We shall have to make the potion from memory."

"Let us outta here," whimpered the blond boy, who had told Sarah that his name was Jay.

"Yeah," said the other boy, who called himself Ernie. "We're really sorry."

"We think you're really cute," Jay added with effort, hoping to win them over.

"Hush!" snapped Winifred. She began to pace. "I can't think," she muttered to herself.

"Remember, remember," her two sisters chanted in low voices, trailing her across the room. She hated when they did that, but both were stupidly convinced that it worked. "Remember, Winnie, remember."

"Now I remember!" Winifred cried, whirling around.

Mary and Sarah gasped and jumped back.

"I was here," Winifred said, ignoring them. She pointed to where the podium stood. "The book was there. You, Mary – you were here."

Mary beamed at being remembered.

"Sarah, you were in the back," Winifred added,

fluttering her hand dismissively. "Dancing, idiotically. And the book said—"

Mary leant in. "Yes?"

"I remember it like it was yesterday," Winifred said, grinning.

"Yes?" said Mary.

"Oil of boil," Winifred recited, the long nail of her pointer finger dancing through the air as if reading a spell, "and a dead man's nose."

Jay and Ernie exchanged a suffering look. *Nose?* Ernie mouthed. Jay cringed. Is this why the old ladies had kidnapped them? To turn them into potion ingredients?

"Dead man's toes!" Sarah crowed.

"She's trying to concentrate," snapped Mary, shooing her away.

Sarah shrugged and wandered off, nibbling her lucky rat tail.

"No, his thumb," said Winifred softly.

"Thumb?" asked Mary.

Ernie chewed anxiously on his left thumbnail.

"Or was it his gums?" asked Winifred. "A dead man's buns…?"

"Buns," said Mary. "Buns. Sounds like—"

"Mums?" asked Winifred hopefully.

"Mums. Funs… funs…"

"Chungs," said Winifred.

"Chungs?" Jay asked, turning to give Ernie a startled, anxious look.

Ernie drew a finger across his neck to make Jay shut up. "Dead man's chungs," he said breathlessly.

"No," said Mary. "There's no such thing as chungs."

Winifred made a helpless sound. "You're right."

"I am?" asked Mary. Then, with more certainty: "I'm right."

"It's no use," said Winifred. "I don't remember the ingredients. I—I—I've got to have my book!"

Behind her, Sarah grabbed the base of Jay's cage and spun it around, making him whimper and clutch at the hammered iron bars. She giggled.

Winifred went to the kitchen and retrieved the Black Flame Candle, which had been merrily flickering the whole night.

"Behold, sisters," she lamented. "The candle burns to a stub. Soon our time will be spent, and we will have wasted our last chance."

"Curtains," Mary whispered, finally putting together Winifred's earlier rant.

"My dress is made of curtains," Sarah said, before trading Jay's cage for Ernie's and twirling in the other direction.

Winifred stalked past both of her sisters and threw open the nearest window. She leant out and released a high-pitched keen: "Booo-ooook!" Her shoulders sagged. "Come home," she pleaded. "Or make thyself known."

Mary petted her back as Winifred dissolved into a fit of sobs.

COME! WE FLY!

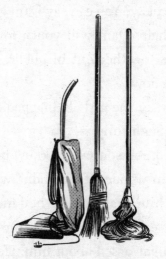

Allison began to stir, which woke Max from one of the deepest sleeps of his life.

"Hi," he said to her, unable to hide a smile.

She smiled back. "Hi," she said sheepishly. She picked up the clock near her hip. "Oh my god," she said. "It's five o'clock. My parents are gonna kill me. I should go." She leapt up and grabbed her jumper.

Max stretched. "I wish you could stay," he said.

Allison looked at him. At first a worried look passed over her face. She was unsure of what he meant and where he wanted this to go. But his dopey grin made her relax.

"Hey," Max said, straightening as he woke more fully and realised she was worried not only about being out so late but about being out late with a boy. "We'll figure it out together, okay? You can say Dani got sick on sugar and I needed help. Dani will vouch for you. Plus, my parents saw us together out in public. They know we weren't – you know…"

"Maybe I'll say the girls kidnapped me as a prank," Allison said thoughtfully.

Max nodded. Allison would know best, he realised, but it made him wonder if she didn't want her parents to know about him at all. Maybe he'd misread her again and she didn't really like him back. Or maybe she did, but she was embarrassed about him. He got to his feet and stuffed his hands into his pockets.

"I'll walk you back," he offered.

Allison glanced at Dani, who was still asleep. The dark curving line of a black cat was pressed against her cheek.

"Poor Binx," Allison said.

Max looked at him then, too. "Yeah, poor Binx," he said, thinking of their conversation at the park. He couldn't imagine being separated from his family for so long. Dani had meant well when she said a dozen generations of Dennisons would look after him, but Max knew that her promise wasn't much comfort to Thackery Binx.

"We owe him a lot," Max added.

Allison nodded.

"Look," he said. "Can we find some kind of way to help him?"

Allison thought about this proposal. "The book," she said. "The witches used it to put the spell on him. Maybe there's a way in here to take it off."

She dropped her jumper on Max's cluttered desk and walked back to the loft's staircase, where she plopped down on the bottom step.

"I don't know," said Max. "Binx told us not to open it."

Allison picked up the spell book. Every time she picked it up, it seemed to get heavier. "But the witches are dead," she said. "What harm could they do?"

Max nodded, thinking that over. "Well, just be careful."

"I will," Allison said, smirking. She undid the clasp that strapped the cover closed, then reached for Max's arm. "Hold my hand," she said.

He did, happily.

Allison took a breath and lifted the cover. She skimmed the first page, which included a list of names she assumed belonged to former owners of the book: Gunnilda Arden, Odelina Arden, Isolde Fitzrou, Mathilda Picardy, Eve and Amice and Frances Harvey, and then Cecily Sanderisson, Emma Sanderisone, Druscilla Sanderson, Winifred Sanderson, and last, Elizabeth Sanderson.

"That's odd," Allison said, examining the final name on the list. She ran a finger over it.

"What is?" Max asked.

"The last name on the list isn't Winifred's," she said. Shaking her head, she turned to the first page of spells. Max leant forward to rest his chin on her shoulder. "Nothing here so far," she said, flipping to the next page.

Winifred Sanderson left the window of her childhood home and dragged her tired body to a fainting couch in the corner. This was the same chaise upon which her mother had birthed her and each of her sisters – quietly and all alone, as was a witch's way.

Mary and Sarah and even the two imprisoned boys watched as Winifred settled herself onto the fainting couch and began to weep into her hands and ash-streaked skirts. The sun would rise soon, and she'd expire in this small house alongside her hopeless sisters. And then what? The thought made Winifred sob even harder. She was afraid to go back to the place filled with fire and brimstone and catty witches – or worse, to go to no place at all. The idea of death chilled her to her marrow.

"Oh, Winnie," said Mary gently. "Do you want to hit

me?" She knelt and placed a hand on her sister's wrist. "Would that cheer you up?"

Winifred batted her hand away, and Mary sighed, straightening. She helped Winifred put her feet up. "There you go," she said, plucking up a fan and opening it to wash some fresh air over Winifred's face.

"This is the end," said Winifred. "I feel it."

"No," Mary said reassuringly, pumping the fan with more gusto.

But Winifred didn't believe her. No, Winifred knew that she would draw her last breath in the same house wherein she'd drawn her first.

"We are doomed," Winifred insisted. "I feel the icy breath of death upon my neck." The thought made her sick. She'd always been destined for more than these four walls. She'd been destined for greatness. Her tea leaves had always said so, which meant something, Winifred thought, even if she'd nudged the leaves around once or twice to properly decode them.

"Mary?" She looked around blearily, as if she couldn't see her sister right next to her. "Take me to the window. I wish to say goodbye." She struggled to rise, and Mary hurried to help her. "Goodbye. Goodbye, cruel world. Goodbye to life." Winifred reached the open window and leant heavily on the windowsill.

Mary worried that not even the house's sturdy foundation could keep her sister on her feet.

"Goodbye to all that," Winifred said sadly.

As she did, she noticed something in the distance and straightened.

"Sister!" she said, reaching for Mary's arm. "Observe!"

Over the dark tree tops, near a full, heavy moon, shone a thin beam of reddish light.

"They opened it!" crowed Winifred, energy pumping back into her body. "Ha-ha! Just when our time was running out. Come! We fly!"

She dragged Mary to the wardrobe. Sarah trailed behind them. Their own brooms were gone, leaving only a few objects meant for cleaning left by the humans who had turned their beloved house into a shop. Winifred, who was the first to look inside, snatched up the only broom. Sarah took the mop, holding her nose at the smell, and Mary fussed over the upright vacuum cleaner.

"What about us?" Ernie called after the witches' retreating backs.

Jay hushed him, but not before Sarah turned to them with a sultry, conniving smile.

"Oh, we'll have plenty of time for you," she said. She blew them a kiss as she followed her sisters through the front door.

Allison, who was becoming impatient with the number of spells in the huge book, turned to a new page.

"Oh, listen to this," she said, happy to have found anything useful at all. "'Only a circle of salt can protect thy victims from thy power.'"

There was a yowl, and Binx leapt onto Max's lap and shoved the book shut. He climbed on top of it to keep Allison from reopening it, then hissed at Max and Allison in turn.

"We were just trying to help you," said Allison.

Binx batted at her shoulder. "Well, don't!" he said. "Nothing good can come from this book." He turned to swat at Max's face. "You got it?"

With that, he leapt down and padded back over to where Dani was sleeping.

Max looked apologetically at Allison. "Maybe we should go now," he said.

She hesitated before nodding. "Okay," she agreed, sounding disappointed. She set the book back on the loft's staircase and followed Max out of his room.

"Come on," he said. "I'll walk you home."

Come, Little Children, I'll Take Thee Away

Max peered into one of the other rooms accessible from the upstairs landing. "Mom?" he called. "Dad?" He turned back to Allison, shrugging. "They're still not home," he said. "That's weird. Must be having a great time."

"I dunno," Allison said, leading the way downstairs. "Something's not right. I'd feel a lot safer walking home if we had some salt."

Max led her into the narrow kitchen. The only window was set over a steel sink, and the cherry-patterned curtains were drawn back to let in a little moonlight. The space was clean but not yet unpacked: boxes were stacked, unopened, against one wall, and Max suspected they would be for a while.

"My mom's not much of a cook," he said apologetically,

swinging open a set of white-painted cabinet doors and climbing onto one of the tiled counters to inspect the highest shelves.

"Sounds like my kind of lady," Allison joked. "When I'm an adult, the only thing I want to make are chocolate chip cookies."

"Milk or dark?" Max asked.

"Dark," said Allison, as if the answer were obvious.

"Oh, no way," said Max. "They're cookies. You gotta go milk."

Max found a spare container of salt behind a bunch of sugar packets and spices that the previous homeowners had forgotten. He made a triumphant sound and tossed the paper cylinder to Allison. Then he dropped down to sit on the same counter she was leaning against.

Allison turned the container over in her hands, then paused and smirked.

"What's it say?" Max asked, leaning in. He noticed that Allison smelt like green apples and cinnamon.

Allison glanced at him, then back to the canister. "It says, 'Form a circle of salt to protect against zombies, witches and old boyfriends'."

"Yeah?" Max asked. "And what about new boyfriends?"

As she studied his face, Allison's lashes fluttered against the tops of her cheeks. Max noticed the hint of a smile around the corners of her mouth, so he leant forward. He skimmed the dip of her lip right below her nose, and he felt his pulse kick up to a dangerous RPM.

A crash thundered down the stairs, and both Allison and Max pulled away and looked at the ceiling.

"Dani," Max breathed.

He jumped down from the counter just as Allison pushed off towards the stairs. On his way up, he checked his jeans for the reassuring weight of his dad's pocket knife.

"Dani!" Max called as they rounded the upstairs landing and barrelled back into his bedroom.

Dani had pulled the covers over her head, her hair just poking out of the top.

Max exhaled with relief and tossed his coat on the floor.

"Max," Allison said. "The book is gone."

He walked towards the narrow staircase that led to the loft. Sure enough, the book had disappeared. Allison snatched his wrist. "I'm telling you," she said, "something's weird."

Max hurried over to his sleeping sister and yanked back the covers. "Dani, wake up," he said.

But it was not Dani in his bed.

Sarah Sanderson sat bolt upright, beaming. "Trick or treat!"

Allison shrieked and leapt away. Max backed towards the wardrobe, but its plantation doors accordioned open.

Mary and Winifred Sanderson strode out, both grinning. Winifred clutched the spell book, its patchwork front cover facing him. Mary had one hand around Dani's mouth and another around a large knitted sack.

"Looking for this?" Winifred demanded, waving her book.

"Or this?" Mary asked, tightening her fingers around Dani's face.

Max looked from Dani to the book and realised Binx was right: the spell book was dangerous, and it must've somehow betrayed them. Even as he thought this, the strange pucker of skin on its cover shivered a little and then opened, blinking blearily. It *was* an eye, and by the looks of it, the thing had been cut from a person's face.

Max shouted with disgust, stumbling away. Winifred raised her free hand and hit him with a bolt of white lightning. Max flew into the air and crashed into his drum set. Cymbals and drums went everywhere as he collapsed.

Allison popped the salt open and began to shake it wildly around the room.

"Salt!" said Winifred. "Ha! What a clever little white witch."

Allison brandished the container at her.

"But it will not save thy friends," Winifred continued. "No. Come, sisters." She plucked up her skirts and started up the stairs to the loft. "The candle's magic is almost spent. Dawn approaches."

Mary followed her, still clutching a struggling Dani. Sarah trailed after them both, looking from Max's prone body to Allison. She gave the girl a dark look, then stuck out her tongue and hurried after her sisters.

Dani bit down hard on Mary's finger. "Let me go!" she shouted when the witch had freed her mouth. "Put me down!"

Winifred launched lightning at the loft's small window, and the wall exploded in a shower of sparks and smoke that turned from pink to green to grey. The blast knocked Allison off her feet and sent a cascade of wooden boards down the stairs.

Allison pushed herself back up and dashed for the stairs to the loft. "Dani!" she called between coughs. But the witches had flown away, and they'd taken both the spell book and Max's little sister with them.

Allison turned back to Max and shoved the snare drum off his chest. "Max, are you okay?" She helped him sit up.

He blinked groggily. "Where's Dani?"

★ ★ ★

Winifred gave a joyful shout as she led her sisters across the night sky, the three of them soaring high above Salem. The world below was full of so much more light than when she'd last been alive, including a slender lighthouse north of town that emitted a steady revolving beam. And yet it felt familiar and wonderful to have wind whipping through her curls and over her ankles and to have the smell of salt and frightened children in her lungs.

"Use thy voice, Sarah," Winifred called over her shoulder. "Fill the sky. Bring the little brats to die!"

Sarah peeled off then, veering down so her words would carry to prepubescent ears. Even from her height, though, Winifred could hear the sweet strains of Sarah's voice:

> *Come, little children,*
> *I'll take thee away*
> *into a land of enchantment.*
> *Come, little children;*
> *the time's come to play*
> *here in my garden of magic.*

The song filled Winifred's mouth with the taste of her mother's maggot-apple pie. It was the treat she had always asked for on her birthday, both because she loved the sweet fruit and the flaky crust and because she loved to watch her mother's hands powdered with flour as she crimped the edges and wove the top crust together with quick, practised fingers, pressing the wormy creatures back into the sugary goo before they could wriggle their way out.

Winifred clutched Dani's small body tighter. "My mother could not live forever," she whispered into the girl's ear. "But I'll make sure her rightful daughters do."

Dani squirmed and whined like a maggot herself, but Winifred's heart was full and warm and her teeth were ready for the crunch of crystallised sugar on a buttery crust, or for the roasted knucklebones of a towheaded girl – whichever Mary wanted to prepare first.

Max and Allison picked their way into the loft and looked out over Salem's dark streets. It was nearly six in the morning, but kids were out in hordes, some of them holding candles and others carrying torches and some empty-handed. A few of them were still in costumes, though the majority wore pyjamas and nightdresses. All of them walked as if transfixed. They headed south in a silent, shuffling crowd.

"They're going to the Sanderson house," Allison said, watching the scattered throng snake up the road and out of sight.

"Hey!" Max shouted down to the sleepwalking children.

Allison grabbed his arm. "It won't work," she said.

"Hey!" he yelled again, ignoring her. "Don't listen to them!" But just as with the adults at the Pumpkin Ball, nothing seemed to get their attention.

Allison shook him. "Max," she said. "Max, I figured it out. Winifred said 'The candle's magic will soon be spent, and dawn approaches'. The Black Flame Candle only brought them back for this one Halloween night – and unless they can steal the lives of children, when the sun comes up, they're dust."

"Yeah," Max said, turning to her, "but how can we make the sun come up? And they've got Dani. We need a miracle."

Allison gave him a helpless look. She looked back at the road and the flickering warmth of candles and torches dotting the eerie scene.

"I have an idea," she said. "Can you drive?"

The candles in the Sanderson house flickered low, and their yellowed wax softened and dripped down iron holders and wooden furniture in slow, slick rivulets.

"Can you pick the lock?" Jay asked Ernie.

"My kit's at home, man," said Ernie. He looked across the room at his friend. "Jay," he said, "I'm scared."

Jay was scared, too, but he knew he couldn't admit it. He was two months older than Ernie, and he was supposed to look out for him. So he said, "I won't let those hags eat you, Ern." *They might eat me, though,* he thought. But if they didn't, he'd be a better person. No more creeping on girls, no more breaking things that didn't belong to him and no more stealing crisps from the petrol station. That last bit had always made him feel bad, anyway. His parents ran a small business, too – the groundskeeping service for the historical lighthouse on Winter Island – and he knew how tough it could be to get by.

The boys groaned in unison when Winifred and Mary Sanderson returned, this time with Max Dennison's mouthy little sister in tow.

Mary spent several minutes tying Dani to a chair before turning to the caged boys with a conniving grin.

Winifred, meanwhile, opened her massive spell book and got to work. With a spark from her fingers, the fire beneath the cauldron leapt back to life.

Jay and Ernie protested as Mary pressed chocolate bars and gummy worms between the bars of their cages.

"No more candy," said Jay weakly.

"But we've got to fatten you up," said Mary.

"We should first eat the girl," said Winifred, almost absently, as she leant closer to the simmering potion she'd been preparing for half an hour. "Otherwise, she'll start to spoil."

She and Mary and Dani looked up when the weathered front door creaked open. Jay and Ernie looked, too, though both boys moved sluggishly, as if they'd long before given up hope of getting free.

Sarah entered, her purple cloak billowing dramatically around her narrow body. "The children," she said, beaming, "are coming."

Winifred clapped. "Well done, Sister Sarah!"

Dani tugged harder on her rope bindings, but it only seemed to tighten them.

Behind her, she heard Binx wriggling in the woollen sack that Mary had strung from the mantle. He yowled, and his claws scratched at the thick fabric. "Let me out of here," he demanded.

"If I did, thou wouldst drop into the fire," chided Mary.

"She's doing you a favour," Sarah agreed, pausing near the sack to give it a light pat where she thought Binx's head might be. He struck out at her hand, but it only prompted a giggle from her currant-coloured lips. The burlap caught Binx's claws and trapped them. As he struggled to rescue his paw, Sarah leant in closer. "Sweet kitty," she cooed. Her nose nearly touched the burlap. "You'll make a good roast." She giggled again and turned away.

Winifred finished tending the bubbling cauldron and moved instead to her book, which she'd returned to its ornate wooden stand.

"Soon the lives of all thy little friends will be mine," she told Dani, "and I shall be young and beautiful again forever."

"It doesn't matter how young or old you are!" Dani spat back. "You sold your soul. You're the ugliest thing that's ever lived, and you know it."

Winifred gave her a long, cold look. "You'll die first," she said crisply. She stalked back to the cauldron and bit off a chunk of her own tongue, spitting it into the potion while eyeing Dani. The liquid's surface erupted with huge, hungry bubbles. Behind her, Ernie and Jay groaned.

Dani's ears pricked at the crunch of tyres on gravel. It was their parents' big car: she recognised the deep purr of the motor from many weekends spent lying awake waiting for her parents to come back from friends' dinner parties. The thought made her remember those Saturday evenings with Max, when he'd order a pizza and help her with homework before starting his own. Sometimes he'd even give in when she begged him to watch *Rescue Rangers* or *DuckTales* with her instead of practising his drums.

Dani glanced at the Sanderson witches, but none of them seemed to hear the sound. Max was there to save her, she knew, and after he did, she'd never make him watch cartoons with her again unless she thought he secretly wanted to.

Winifred gave a delighted yelp, snapping Dani's attention back to the horrors at hand. "'Tis ready," the eldest witch said, giving the potion a final stir. "Pry open her mouth."

"Dani, don't drink it!" Binx called from his cloth prison.

"Shut up, you," said Winifred. She scooped up some of the bubbling liquid in her huge spoon.

Sarah hurried over to Dani and pinched her jaw. Her fingers were surprisingly strong, but Dani kept her teeth tightly clenched.

"Dani!" Binx shouted, unable to see what was happening. "Don't drink it, Dani!"

Mary went over to help her sisters. She forced a thumb between Dani's lips, then sprang back. "Ow!" she shouted. "She bit me!"

Dani brought her foot down hard on Sarah's toes.

Though both of her sisters were incapacitated, Winifred still advanced with her spoon.

The door flew open, crashing into the wall. "Prepare to die!" shouted Max. "Again."

"Hollywood," Jay said, jutting his chin at his cage's padlock.

Winifred turned to Max. "You," she said, splashing some of her potion in the process. It sizzled against the floorboards. "You have no powers here, you fool." She refocused her attention on Dani.

Meanwhile, Sarah had regained her footing and tried once more to force open Dani's mouth. Dani shook her head hard and squirmed, trying to protect her face from the witch's sharp nails. Winifred pressed the spoon against her mouth, putting it as close to the girl's nose as she could in the hopes that the putrid smell would force her to gasp or breathe through her mouth, swallowing the potent liquid in the process.

"Maybe not," Max said to Winifred. "But there's a

power greater than your magic, and that's knowledge. And there's one thing I know that you don't."

Winifred, frustrated, pulled the spoon away from Dani and whirled on Max. "And what is that, *dude*?"

Her sisters chortled like ravens.

"Daylight savings time," he said.

Mary parroted the strange phrase, mocking his accent. Sarah snorted.

The orange light of sunrise pierced the eastern windows of the house, shining warm and rosy and sure through the glass.

The witches shrank back.

"Max, get me out of here," Dani said desperately.

At once, the Sanderson sisters collapsed onto the floor, writhing in pain.

"It hurts!" Sarah shrieked.

Max ran over and cut Dani's ties with his dad's pocket knife. Once freed, Dani jumped up and ran to the fireplace to save Binx.

"Hey!" cried Jay. "Let me out of here! Help!"

Max unhooked the bag containing Binx and handed it to Dani. "Get outside," he said with a push to her shoulder.

The witches continued to whimper underfoot. Winifred pulled her cloak over her face and hands to protect her skin.

"Hey, Hollywood!" said Ernie.

Max strode over and examined the bully, whose legs were dangling out of the cage.

"Help us out here?" Ernie asked.

Max pulled his stolen shoes from Ernie's feet. "Tubular," he said, holding the Nikes up in salute. On his way to the door, he pushed over the cauldron, spilling the soul-sucking potion over the floor. It bubbled and smoked and spilled through the spaces between the floorboards as Winifred wailed.

"Let me outta here, man," Jay pleaded.

"Come on, Dani," Max said, taking Binx from her since she was struggling with the sack. "Let's go."

As they stepped out of the house, Dani stopped. "Max, I want to see her turn to dust," she said.

Just then, she spotted her mum's grey SUV. Allison was standing next to it, gesturing desperately at the headlights, which were covered in a coloured film that turned their light orange.

"Pump it!" Dani yelled, running for the car.

Max followed her, ripping the cellophane from the headlights as he passed them.

He jumped into the driver's seat, pushed Binx into Allison's arms, and revved the engine.

The dawn thinned and vanished with a roar and a rumble.

MAGGOTY MALFEASANCE

S arah rolled onto her back and stared at the high ceiling of the house she'd been born in. Firelight flickered over the sturdy roof beams, highlighting swathes of cobwebs and colonies of spiders. She went through a mental checklist from the roots of her hair to the nails of her toes. Her hip hurt a little, but then again she had fallen on it in her hurry to avoid the burning glint of sunrise. Everything else felt fine.

"I'm alive," she said, smiling.

"Damn that boy!" said Winifred, who'd collapsed first and now lay beneath both Sarah and Mary. "He's tricked us again." She got clumsily to her feet. Her face was as red as her hair.

"Oh, you're right," said Mary, shifting uncomfortably

beneath Sarah's weight. "You're always right. I don't know how you do that."

"It's my curse," said Winifred to Mary. "That, and you two. Get off me, you thundering oafs!"

Sarah sprang up, dusted off her skirts, and pulled her lucky rat tail from her sleeve. Chewing it always made her feel better, especially when Winifred was out of sorts.

Mary and Winifred scrambled up after her.

"Look," said Winifred. She crossed to the kitchen, where the Black Flame Candle waited on a cluttered counter, its mysterious flame diminished to a weak flicker. The scene on the outside of the candle had all but melted away, and the taper was reduced to a runny stub. "The candle is almost out," she said, then gained the courage to turn and examine the fallen cauldron and the puddled floorboards. "And my potion. My beautiful potion." She knelt by the cauldron, not caring that the cooling liquid soaked her clothes. "Look," she said. She knelt down even lower and peered into the depths of the pot. "There's just enough left for one child."

The room seemed to grow very quiet, and the silence made Jay and Ernie even more conspicuous. They were biting their lips and staring at each other, each wordlessly threatening mortal harm if the other made a sound.

Winifred turned to Mary. "Get the vial," she said.

Sarah took her a glass bottle whose base was wide and round and whose neck was long and thin. Carefully, Winifred ladled the last of the potion into the bottle. She pressed the cork back into its mouth and clutched the treasure to her chest.

"What luck," she said, smiling. She turned to the door through which Max and Dani had escaped only minutes before, and her voice grew sharp: "This is perfect for that little towheaded brat."

"We have a child," said Sarah, gesturing at the two hanging cages.

Jay and Ernie each pointed at the other, shouting "Him!"

Mary, for her part, leant against the front window and watched the garden with dreamy interest. "And look, Winnie: more children are arriving." She beckoned to the sleepwalkers. "Come on in," she cooed.

"Winnie," Sarah said, touching her sister's forearm, "we'll make more potion because we have the book." She pointed to the spell book, which still lay open on the pedestal.

"We haven't the time," said Winifred. "Besides, I want to get that little rat-faced kid that called me—"

"Oh," Mary said, rushing over, "don't say it."

"Ugly?" asked Sarah.

Winifred and Mary both cringed.

"She really hurt my feelings," whimpered Winifred. "She doesn't even know me." She took Sarah's outstretched hand and dried her eyes on it. "You know," she said, composing herself, "I always wanted a child, and now I think I'll have one. On toast!"

Dani sat in the back of her parents' car, clutching Binx in her lap. Max was driving, which made her even more scared because his last practice session had ended in a long argument with their dad about what constituted a rolling stop.

"There are too many kids," Max said, careering past another group of transfixed children. He recognised a few of them from Dani's class and felt a pang of worry. He leant out his window. "Go home!" he shouted, but of course they didn't listen to him. They didn't even seem to hear him. Max groaned and pounded the steering wheel. "We need to wait in the cemetery until sunrise," he said. "But these zombie kids are going to trap us on the road."

"Try that side road." Allison pointed off to the left, back into the woods. "It'll reconnect to the main road in town, and you can circle around to the front of the cemetery."

Max nodded. He knew it was a risk since it would take longer, but he also knew that it would put them closer to the clearing Binx had shown them before. From there, it would be easier to see the witches coming – and to go back into the sewers if needed.

Before any other kids blocked their way, Max veered to the left as Allison suggested and headed deeper into the trees. He clenched his sweaty fists tighter around the steering wheel as visions of careering off the road swam through his head. The engine growled as he goaded the accelerator.

The sprinklers, the kiln, the fake sunrise – how many times could they trick the witches before their tricks didn't work any longer? Max realised their time was running out – but so was the Sanderson sisters'. If Allison was right, they just had to keep them at bay until sunrise.

If Allison was right.

Max glanced at her. "Are they following us?" he asked.

Allison turned around in her seat. "No," she said.

Max smiled. "Good."

Just then, Winifred Sanderson appeared at the driver's side window, her body angled forward against the handle of her broom.

Max swerved away but kept going; Allison reached

over to steady the steering wheel and help ease them back towards the middle of the road before they skidded off of it.

"Pull over," Winifred demanded. "Let me see your driver's licence."

Max considered sticking his arm out the window to push her away, but that seemed like a terrible idea on several fronts. Instead, he gripped the wheel even tighter and banked the car to the left, knocking her and her broom out of the way. He grinned again, but this time he wiped his palms – one and then the other – on his jeans.

"We're gonna be okay," Allison told him. He nodded tightly and pressed on, taking a sharp turn onto the street that held the graveyard entrance facing downtown Salem.

He slammed on the breaks in the middle of the street and hopped out, not bothering to take the keys with him. Allison helped Dani and Binx out of the back seat before grabbing a packed duffel bag from the floor. The group hurried through the gate, breathing more easily once they were safe on hallowed ground – that is, until Max slammed into Billy Butcherson.

Dani shrieked and Allison hurried back to help him, but Max shouted at them to go. Then he pulled out his dad's pocket knife.

The girls were gone when Winifred arrived a second later, still clutching her broom. She floated near the top of the gate and shouted down at Billy, who was fighting Max for the knife.

"Catch the children!" she said.

Max winced as Billy overpowered him, forcing the knife closer and closer to Max's throat. Then Billy surprised him by levering Max's hand higher, above his head. Billy sliced through the threads that sewed his mouth shut. He released Max then and gave a dry, guttural cough. Small brown moths flew from his lips and fluttered away.

"Come now," Winifred ordered. "Kill him. Do it now!"

"Wench," Billy snapped at Winifred. "Trollop!" Max found this a bit rich since Billy had been the one running around with his girlfriend's younger sister. "You bucktoothed, mop-riding firefly from Hell."

Winifred let out a scandalised screech.

"I've waited centuries to say that," Billy told Max.

"Say what you want," Max said, shrinking away. "Just don't breathe on me."

"Billy," said Winifred. "I killed you once, I shall kill you again, you maggoty malfeasance."

Billy grabbed Max around the waist and tugged, pulling both of them into the woods.

"Hang on to your heads!" Winifred called after them.

Her taunt followed them, but she didn't bother flying over the graveyard gate, which worried Max. The witches had to be plotting something.

It didn't take long for Max and Billy to find Allison and Dani in the clearing that housed Billy's open grave – which meant, Max feared, that it wouldn't take long for the witches to find them, either.

Allison and Dani scrambled up, each holding a sturdy branch.

"Max, run!" shouted Dani.

"Max, move out of the way," said Allison, charging.

Max threw himself between her and Billy. "Wait!" he said. "No. No, no. He's a good zombie."

Allison gave the dead man a searching look.

"You're sure?" she asked Max. "How do I know you're not just saying that because you've been bitten?"

Max gave her a look, and Allison relented. "Okay, fine."

Billy followed the pair down the low hill, towards both Dani and his own open grave.

"Hi, Billy!" Dani said, waving.

Max looked at her face: her fear was gone, and she seemed to think the idea of befriending a zombie was totally reasonable. Was she so adaptable because she was still a kid? He couldn't remember ever being like that. Maybe she really did have a thing or two to teach him. He hoped they'd all survive the night so she could.

Billy helped Dani into his grave. "You'll be safe in here," he said.

Max dug through their duffel bag of supplies. He handed Allison a fresh carton of salt and pulled out a baseball bat for himself.

"You okay, Dani?" he asked his sister.

"Yeah," she said in a small voice. "I'm fine."

Adaptable or not, she was still his sister, and they both knew she was still in danger. He adjusted his grip on the bat and practised swinging a few times.

Allison opened the salt container and drew a circle of it around the grave.

"Here they come," said Binx, who was perched on a headstone. "Billy, guard Dani. Max, Allison: spread out."

They'd just taken their places when Winifred descended from the dark sky. Her dress and robes fluttered around her, caught by a light autumn wind.

"For the last time," she said, "prepare to meet thy doom."

She swooped low, heading for Dani. Max took a swing at her with the baseball bat.

Winifred veered to the side, cackling, and then course-corrected. This time, she bore down on Max. "You little pest," she said to him. "I've had enough of you."

He swung at her again, but Winifred grabbed the bat from his hands and flung it away, chortling.

Max made to run then, but Winifred was a step ahead. She opened her palm, and a branch of electricity rippled out of her skin and made contact with the nearest tree, right at the joint between its trunk and heaviest branch. Dani screamed as the branch toppled down, blocking Max's path and separating him from his friends.

Billy, who stood between Dani and the witch, glowered at Winifred. "Go to Hell!" he said.

The eldest Sanderson smiled tightly. "Oh, I've already been there, thank you," she said. "I found it quite lovely."

HALLOWED GROUND

arah and Mary – the first on a ratty mop and the second on an upright vacuum cleaner – dived towards Max and Allison. Max fled to the right and Allison to the left, splitting up the two witches as they scrambled into the woods and tried to seek shelter among the trees.

Winifred cackled, pleased that her sisters had followed her instructions for once. Billy took a step closer to her. He looked as if he was going to say something else spiteful, but Winifred gave another sharp laugh before diving straight towards him. Dani, hidden in the open grave, gave a frightened warning shout. Billy lifted his arms to grab for Winifred's broom handle, but he missed. Winifred pulled up at the last moment and thrust her legs forward, kicking him in the jaw. His head flew off for the second time that night and bounced and rolled to a stop several feet away.

In the woods, Allison slipped behind a huge pine tree as Sarah turned a corner, and waited there until she was sure she was safe. After a few heart-stopping seconds of ducking and weaving, Max dived under a half-collapsed tree and waited in the leaves until Mary swept past, calling out "Sister Sarah! I lost our dinner!"

From her safe spot in Billy's grave, Dani peeked out from between her fingers. When Winifred left to track down her sisters, who were weaving through the woods calling for Allison and Max, Dani dragged herself out of the grave and hurried over to rescue Billy's head.

Max and Allison stumbled out of the woods at the same time and spotted each other from across the clearing. Max lifted his chin in recognition, then headed straight for Billy Butcherson's grave. He froze so suddenly Allison almost crashed into him from behind. Dani had disappeared.

Allison spotted Dani first and tugged on Max's sleeve. The youngest Dennison was several yards away. She'd gingerly picked up Billy's head and was offering it to his body, which was desperately shuffling through leaves and sticks. "I think you dropped this," she said.

As Billy reattached his head, everyone heard a familiar shout. Winifred re-emerged from the woods, her sisters at her heels. She aimed her broom handle towards Dani and Billy, and before Max could run or shout or even blink, Winifred had his little sister around the middle and was lifting her into the sky.

Billy, Max and Allison took off after them, while Binx watched helplessly from where he stood before a gravestone.

"Bye-bye, big brother," called Winifred over her shoulder. She pulled from her robes a glass bulb filled with green liquid. Then she looked at Dani and gritted her teeth. "All right, you little trollimog."

Sarah and Mary waited some distance away, celebrating their sister's success by spinning in wide circles on their mop and vacuum, fingers barely touching.

"Hold on, Dani!" called Binx, dashing over rocks and gravestones in her direction.

Winifred bit down on the bottle's cork and yanked it from the neck of the bottle. She spat it onto the ground. "This will teach you to call people ugly," she said. "Open your mouth."

Binx ran up the sturdy branch Winifred had torn down only minutes before. He leapt from its highest point and knocked the vial from her hand. As Winifred reached for it, he clawed at her face and arms until she flung him away. Binx gave a yowl as he hit the ground, but he was on his feet in a moment and scrambling to shelter in the underbrush.

The potion bottle tumbled end over end as it fell, but somehow not a drop of liquid spilt. Max caught the bottle. White smoke bubbled out of the top, smelling of saltwater toffee and pond scum.

"Give me that vial," said Winifred.

Max held it over his head. "Put her down, or I'll smash it."

"Smash it," said Winifred, "and she dies."

Allison called his name and tried to run over to him, but Billy pulled her back.

"He's got a plan," Billy whispered to her. "I think."

Max glared at Winifred. She said she would kill his sister if he broke the bottle, but he knew that if he handed it over she'd just kill her anyway, slowly sucking out Dani's life force in front of him, just like Binx had told him they had done to his poor sister Emily. He couldn't be the one to sentence his own sister to that.

But he could do it to himself.

He lifted the bottle to his lips and took a long swig, swallowing the whole thing. It bubbled and burned as it went down his throat.

"Max, no!" shouted Dani.

But it was too late.

Sarah and Mary froze, shocked by the turn of events. They waited for Winifred's reaction.

Winifred gasped, recoiling as if she'd been burned.

Max smashed the empty bottle against a nearby tombstone and glared up at the eldest Sanderson. "Now you have no choice," he said. "You have to take me."

Winifred descended slowly. "What a fool you are, to give up thy life for thy sister's."

When Mary and Sarah heard Winifred's words, the two of them exchanged a look.

As she neared the ground, Winifred released Dani and grabbed Max's collar instead.

Dani collapsed, sobbing, and Billy and Allison hurried to help her up.

Winifred, who was surprisingly strong, lifted Max by only his shirt. His body had begun to glow, letting off a golden, pearlescent sheen that moved when he moved, but at a more leisurely rate.

Winifred brought Max's face close to hers and opened her mouth. A narrow stream of light peeled off from the rest of him and coursed past her lips and down her throat. Max's eyes grew wide, for he could feel the draining sensation somewhere in his chest. He felt, also, like he was growing older, as if each second were a lost year. The world suddenly wasn't so funny any more.

Distantly, he could hear Allison and Dani screaming,

but he didn't know what to do about it. For some reason, all he could think of was the red plastic car he'd got for his fourth or fifth birthday. He'd raced around in it, pedalling the thing with his feet like a Flintstone and shouting that he'd be a race car driver one day. Then he thought of the day Dani had been born, and how his father had put the small squirming pink thing in his arms and told him that now he had responsibilities, and he'd looked at his baby sister and felt a warm, comfortable weight settle around his shoulders. He thought of meeting Jack, and of hearing the Ramones for the first time, and of screaming at his parents when they sat him down and explained that his dad had taken a job on the East Coast, in Salem, Massachusetts. And then he thought of Allison and her vases and her laugh and their conversation in the sewers, when she'd told him she liked him better when he was around Dani, and how he'd realised that maybe he liked himself better then, too.

Max reached up and pushed Winifred's face away. She swatted his hand at first, but he tried again, with as much force as he could muster. As she turned her face away and had to close her mouth, the remainder of Max's life force coalesced back around his body. Having it closer to his skin made him feel more solid – and more aware of his surroundings. This gave Max an idea, and he heaved his whole body towards Winifred, scrabbling for her throat and digging his thumbs into the hollow of it. The witch gagged and pushed back at him, finally shoving him hard enough that he almost fell. He was left clinging to the handle of her broom by only his fingers.

Max pulled down hard, flipping the broom, and suddenly Winifred was unseated and hanging by only her fingers, too, scrambling to get a better hold on the prickly bristles. "Hallowed ground!" she said desperately, looking down. "Hallowed ground! Sisters!"

"Winnie!" called Mary. "I'm coming!"

The brunette witch sailed over the other children, not realising that her vacuum cleaner's cord was dangling within their reach. Dani grabbed it by the plug and dug her heels into the soft earth. Allison and Billy anchored themselves to the cord, too. Mary only made it a few more feet before the cord stopped her from going any further. She looked over her shoulder and let out a strangled cry when she realised what had gone wrong. That only made Allison, Billy and Dani pull harder on the line.

"I'm going to teach you a lesson you'll never forget," Winifred said to Max as they both struggled to pull themselves back onto the broom. They spun and spun like a top as, in the east, a sliver of orange light broke the horizon. Winifred pulled herself back onto the broom, but the promise of sunrise gave Max a second burst of energy. He just had to wait for it to reach his tingling fingers.

"Sarah!" Mary pleaded, still struggling against the spiteful humans trying to drag her onto the graveyard soil. Beneath her, the vacuum cleaner revved and whined.

Sarah flew down and grasped her sister's hand, tugging, but Billy, Allison and Dani had better leverage. With each tug, they pulled Mary a little closer to the ground.

"Let go – now!" shouted Allison. They all did at once, and the released tension sent Mary and Sarah spinning through the air.

Winifred watched her sisters arc over the treetops, trying desperately to right themselves, so she didn't notice when Max swung his body around and put all his weight into knocking her from her place on the broom.

She hit the ground with a heavy thud. Max dropped down a few feet away, panting. Winifred roared as she turned over and began to crawl towards him. Her movements were stiff and laboured, though, as if each additional pull of muscle and twist of tendon was more and more difficult to control. Her long nails, as sharp and hooked as claws, dug into the earth each time she planted her hands, and each time she pulled them back, earth and grass flew up and muddied her palms and wrists.

Max pushed himself away from her, but he was so, so tired. Gold light shimmered before his eyes.

At last, Winifred grabbed him by the front of his

jumper and lifted him up, struggling with her own aching hips as she stood. She opened her mouth to suck the life from him, but when Max looked down he saw that the curled toes of her boots had begun to smoke and harden into granite.

The stone crackled over her skin from the soles of her feet to her calves and knees and stomach and shoulders and head, until Max found himself dangling from the grasping fingers of a furious statue.

He wiggled about, ripping himself free. He grunted when he hit the ground, but the gold halo surrounding his body faded as the sun fully broke over Salem Harbor. A scrap of his shirt hung from Winifred's stone talons, fluttering meekly like a flag of surrender.

Above the graveyard, Sarah gave a squeak before bursting into a cloud of purple glitter. Mary's jaw dropped open just as she exploded in a firework of red smoke. Their mop and vacuum cleaner hit the ground with two distinct thuds.

Winifred's statue began to quiver and then crack, and with a burst it blew apart, lighting up the world, briefly, with a lime-green glow.

Max sucked in a disbelieving breath and collapsed onto his back. For a moment, his entire world consisted of his pattering heart, the sweet relief swimming through his head, and morning's grey light.

LOVE YOU, JERK FACE

ax, from his place on the ground, buried his face in both arms.

"Max?" called a tentative voice, but he was still dazed and didn't know how to answer. Instead, he heaved himself into a sitting position and looked around at the clearing, where nothing had changed and everything had changed. The witches were gone, but there had been witches. He was alive, but he'd nearly had his essence drained out through his pores. And Dani—

"Dani!" he said, turning to try to find his sister.

She was dashing down the low hill towards him.

"Max," she said, kneeling beside him. He thought he'd never heard her sound quite so gentle. "Are you okay?"

"Yeah," he croaked. "I think so."

"You saved my life," she said.

He looked at her small surprised face. "Well, I had to. I'm your big brother."

She beamed. "I love you, jerk face," she said.

"I love you, too."

She threw her arms around his neck, and he wrapped one of his own around her back.

"Come on," Dani said after a few seconds. She helped him to his feet and led him to Billy's grave. Winifred's ex was already climbing back into his broken coffin.

Allison walked over and slipped an arm around Max's shoulders. She felt solid and stable and *real* in a way that still seemed to escape the rest of the graveyard – and even Dani, who was helping Billy get settled in his coffin.

Max wound his free arm around Allison's waist.

"It all really happened, didn't it?" he asked her.

She squeezed his arm. "Yeah," she said.

The Black Flame Candle, the Sanderson sisters, his almost kiss with Allison in his parents' still packed kitchen. Binx and Billy and Dani's kidnap and rescue, and Max's own life drifting into a witch's angry mouth before his eyes. All of it was real.

Despite how unbelievable the night had been, Allison made him feel grounded just by standing near him. In fact, having Allison so close made Max think that he could take on the world, at least if he was with her. He looked back at the broken remains of Winifred's statue and realised that maybe they already had. And maybe they would have to again, but it wouldn't be so scary the second time around.

"Bye, Billy," Dani said as he reached for his coffin's lid. "Have a nice sleep."

"Hey, Billy," called Max.

Billy Butcherson paused and gave Max an expectant look.

"Thanks," Max said.

Allison waved goodbye with a small smile on her face.

Billy waved in return, then stretched his whole body with a big yawn and dropped back into the remains of his bed.

Dani looked around. "Binx," she said. "Where's Binx?"

She broke away from Max to track down the cat, but what she found brought her to her knees.

"No…" she said, gasping. Binx's body lay still and lifeless at the foot of a leafless tree.

"He's gone, Dani," Allison said softly.

"But he can't die, remember?" Dani touched his narrow shoulder. "Binx," she said. "Binx, wake up. Like last time."

When he didn't move, she broke into a fresh wave of sobbing.

"Come on," said Binx's voice, though it wasn't coming from the cat. "Please don't be sad for me."

Allison, Max and Dani all looked around.

A few feet away stood a young man – likely Max's age – wearing a billowing white tunic that was open at the collar. The warm light of daybreak filtered through his skin and clothes as if he wasn't entirely there.

"Binx, is that you?" Dani asked.

"Yeah," said the ghost. His dark blond hair was pulled back and tied in a short tail, and he was smiling. "The witches are dead. My soul's finally free."

Dani took a step towards him.

"You freed me, Dani," Binx said. "Thank you." He looked from her to her brother. "Hey, Max," he added. "Thanks for lighting the candle."

Max snorted. "Any time."

"Thackery?" The asker was a semitranslucent little girl in a white dress and white cap. She peered around the trunk of a tall tree. "Thackery Binx?" she called.

"It's Emily," said Binx, looking back at his new friends and smiling. He leant down and gave Dani a kiss on the cheek. "I shall always be with you," he whispered.

Dani nodded, and with that Binx took off and joined his little sister, hugging her and then taking her hand.

"Thackery Binx, what took you so long?" she asked, gazing up at him.

"I'm sorry, Emily," he said. The pair walked off towards the sunrise in the direction of the large iron gates to the cemetery. "I had to wait three hundred years for a virgin to light a candle."

As Max, Allison and Dani watched them go, Max placed a hand on Dani's shoulder and pulled her a little closer to him. He'd never forget Binx's caution to look after her.

The figures of Thackery and Emily dissolved into light and shadow and a trick of the sun through autumn leaves, and Max crouched to give Dani a hug.

She giggled before pushing him away.

"So," said Allison, bumping Max with her hip. "Did I make a believer out of you?"

They both laughed. "Yeah," said Max. "I guess so."

It was hard to tell who started the kiss or how long it lasted, but as soon as they came up for air they dived back in, Max cupping Allison's face in both of his hands and Allison pulling him closer by the hem of his jumper.

Dani gave them a few seconds of privacy before clearing her throat loudly. "Can we go home?" she asked. "I'm tired, and I haven't gotten a single piece of candy tonight."

Max laughed and pushed her ahead of him as they all headed back to the family car.

"Sure thing, kid," he said.

"I'm glad you saved me, Max," said Dani, as if she'd actually been debating the pros and cons. "Now I get to bug you for years and years."

Allison laughed hard at that, which made Dani laugh, too.

Max knitted his fingers through Allison's as they followed Dani to the graveyard gate. "Can't wait," he said.

And he meant it.

Jay and Ernie swung in their cages, waiting for someone to come save them.

They sang in rounds to pass the time and moved listlessly. Waiting was a painful process, but they held out hope that someone would come for them.

Meanwhile, on its podium Winifred's spell book slowly opened its eye and looked around, feeling the loss of its master. But then it rose into the air. Jay and Ernie screamed and shook the bars of their cages at the strange sight. The book soared out of the window and into the early morning light. It floated above the cemetery and through the town square, passing the crowd of adults who filed, stumbling, out of Town Hall after a night of endless dancing.

It continued flying, higher and higher, seeking its master...

It wouldn't stop until it found her.

PART TWO
NOW

I accept my fate, though you know not why.

You, all of you, despise me for things you believe me
to have done —

and yet I know that the greatest mark upon my soul
was doing nothing at all.

> —Elizabeth Sanderson
> November 5, 1693
> Last words, as recorded
> in the journal of Samuel Parris

BEVERLY

SALEM
WOODS

THE
SANDERSON
HOUSE

PERSHING
CEMETERY

SALEM
OLD TOWN
HALL

TRAVIS'S
HOUSE

ISABELLA'S
HOUSE

NORTH RIVER

COLLINS COVE

SALEM
NECK

LIGHTHOUSE

WINTER
ISLAND

CAT
COVE

ALLEGRA'S
ITALIAN PIE
SHOPPE

JACOB
BAILEY
HIGH

KATIE'S
HOUSE

HALFTIDE
ROCK

CENTRAL STREET

SALEM
COMMON

ALLISON'S
CHILDHOOD HOME
(POPPY'S HOUSE)

THE
DUSTY
ATTIC

CELLULAR
CELLAR

SALEM
HARBOR

MAX'S
CHILDHOOD
HOME

DOT'S
MUSIC
STORE

THE
ORACLE
STONE

WITCH, PLEASE

TWENTY-FIVE YEARS LATER...
SALEM, 2018

I've never been so excited for a lecture about the Articles of Confederation.

"Swap?" Travis asks as we walk into AP US History.

We always switch seats in history during the class period closest to Halloween.

But not today.

Today I have nothing to fear.

I beam at him. "Nope!" I say, a little too enthusiastically. "I'm good."

When he raises an eyebrow, it disappears behind the thick green frame of his glasses. His brown eyes sparkle mischievously. He's wearing dark skinny jeans and a red T-shirt with a demon-filled periodic table on it and the words PERIODIC TABLE OF *HELL*-EMENTS. It's a very Travis T-shirt, and I'm very glad he's not in costume, though he's been wanting for weeks to dress up in his finest suit and come in claiming to be the second black president.

I continue grinning like an idiot, so finally he shrugs, scratches at his dark hair, cut into a low fade, and heads to the third row. All around us, our classmates gossip, complain about the homework from last period, and check their Instagram and Twitter feeds. I slide my backpack off my shoulders and settle into my seat at the front of the class, taking out my textbook and class notes.

I like sitting up front because it helps me focus. Travis prefers the back because it helps him sketch comics on his tablet undetected. But Travis is a generous soul, and every year since seventh grade he's sacrificed his art for exactly one class: the history class that falls on or nearest to Halloween, when Salem tradition dictates that all history teachers drag out the tale of the Sanderson sisters, dust it off and set it on fire in front of me like a convicted witch.

But not this year.

It feels like my academic career has been building up to this day, late in the first quarter of my junior year

– a day when the teacher will finally walk in and say absolutely nothing about the Sandersons, because that teacher is my dad, and my dad does not talk about the Sandersons in public. Ever. It's supremely weird to be related to any high school teacher, but this single period of talking about the Constitutional Congress instead of witches will make it all worth it. October 31, 2018, will be the day I won't have to sit at the back of class watching thirty of my classmates make fun of a story my parents and aunt truly believe. I won't have to spend forty-five minutes dreading the tradition and then another ten avoiding eye contact with my teacher because I can't bring myself to look enthused about *their* version of the story. I think *any* version is ridiculous.

I look around the room, relishing all that I see. The laminated poster of the United States is just where it always is, as are the timelines that chronicle everything from the Revolutionary War to the civil rights movement. And just like last week and the week before, there is not a single Halloween decoration to be seen. The victory may seem small, but it is sweet.

Dad walks in from the hallway and nods at me, but he doesn't say anything as he crosses to his desk. That's our rule. It's important to have ground rules when one of your parents grades your essays *and* goes bowling with your guidance counsellor. He's wearing a tie-dyed bow tie, which is about as festive as he gets for Halloween. It's some kind of inside joke with my mum, I think, because she always gives him a dopey grin when he wears it.

He sits at his desk to fiddle with something on his computer, and music comes on. It's Dad's ritual to play one rock song during passing period, to give students some privacy in their conversations. It's the kind of thing that earns him cool points from my peers, which makes me extra grateful that he's also not the kind of teacher known for unnecessary detentions, busywork or puns. Today he's chosen "Sympathy for the Devil", which is a bit on the nose, but I'll give him a pass for the holiday. He taps out the beat with a pencil while he waits for the bell, and some strands of dark straight hair fall in his eyes.

A few stragglers scuttle in, including Dracula and a bumblebee in dress code–violating shorts. Then in comes Isabella (not scuttling, because Isabella Richards does *not* scuttle) in a flowing white top with draped sleeves and a pair of white skinny jeans. Her belt looks like it's made of gold coins or medallions, and her black corkscrew curls spiral out from beneath a golden laurel circlet. The bell whines, and Isabella slides into the seat to my right, her messenger bag thudding as she tucks it under her desk. She shoves a round shield under her desk, too. On its front, angry snakes frame Medusa's screaming face. It looks like Isabella's made the thing from foam and tinfoil, which is a very Isabella thing to do.

"Athena, goddess of wisdom and war," she says when I give her a quizzical look.

Of course she is. "I thought you weren't going to dress up," I whisper. I lean towards her, and my plastic chair creaks. I doubt that Jacob Bailey High has seen a renovation since my parents were students here in the nineties, and the furniture is constantly reminding us that it won't last forever.

"Drama extra credit," Isabella tells me, adjusting the shield so it doesn't roll away.

I glance back at Isabella and she gives me an *I know it's dumb* grin, but I find the whole thing kind of attractive. Isabella is both the last person who would ever need extra credit and the first person who will volunteer for it. She's also the kind of girl who helps freshmen find their classes on the first day of school, volunteers weekly at the nursing home in Marblehead and still gets invited to more bonfire parties in a single summer than I have in my entire life. It's not the fact that she does everything that makes her so impressive but the fact that she genuinely seems to love everything she does. When she shows up, she's all in, whether she's crafting a Greek shield for extra credit or asking me about my day.

I glance at Travis. I don't dress up for Halloween on principle – today, I'm wearing black jeans and a plain black jumper. Travis isn't dressed up, either. For solidarity. But I know he's been planning his own costume for weeks and can't wait to break it out for my mum's Halloween party tonight – my family's first-ever Halloween party, which is going to be a *real* treat. *Not.*

Travis is too busy sketching to have noticed me talking to Isabella.

The song ends, and my dad shuts his laptop and stands up. "Happy Halloween, everyone," he says. "Do you know what happened in October seventeen seventy-seven?"

Isabella raises her hand. When she gets a nod from my dad, she says, "What about in October sixteen ninety-three?"

There's a long pause as the class waits to see what my dad is going to say to this unexpected development.

I'm staring at Isabella like she just murdered a puppy.

It's an unspoken rule that there is no Sanderson-sister talk in Mr Dennison's classroom. Students think it's because he finds the whole thing ridiculous. What they don't know is that it's because the Sandersons, at least as my dad tells me, came back from the dead and tried to kill my aunt Dani twenty-five years ago. Unsurprisingly, that took the sheen off the Sandersons' story for him, though he's never talked about it outside of my family.

I look from Isabella to my dad, waiting to see how he will react.

"I didn't think you'd want to waste your time with that, Miss Richards," he says slowly.

It's enough of a window that more hands shoot up. My classmates are clearly not as excited as I am to hear about some dude-bro landowners who determined the fate of a fledgling nation.

"Mr Dennison, doesn't this relate to the evolution of criminal justice and the autocratic state?" asks Cruella De Vil, stroking a stuffed Dalmatian in her lap.

"Mr Dennison, what do the Sanderson sisters say about misogyny and unmarried women in colonial America?" asks a pirate.

"Mr Dennison—"

"Mr Dennison—"

I fold my arms over my desk and rest my forehead against them, wishing I could sink through the speckled linoleum floor.

So much for my one-year respite from Sanderson talk.

"What about Elizabeth Sanderson?" Isabella asks, her voice cutting clear and confident through the chatter.

I turn my face towards her, forehead wrinkling. *Who's Elizabeth Sanderson?*

"Elizabeth Sanderson..." My dad's voice trails off, but not in a question. He's no longer weighing whether to answer but how. "You've done your research, Miss Richards. As usual."

Isabella watches him hopefully.

I look past her to Travis, who is the only person I've shared my family's Sanderson story with since I got made fun of as a little kid. Everyone else has forgotten about Poppy Dennison's short-lived belief in witches, but not him. He has an eyebrow raised to ask if I'm okay. I shrug and look back at my dad, who's carefully rolling up his sleeves.

"Elizabeth Sanderson is an... interesting case," Dad says. "She wasn't—" He catches himself. "People say that she wasn't a bad witch or that, if she was, she never brought any harm to Salem. Still, the trials came for her and her family the way they came for so many innocent lives. It was because of Elizabeth's selflessness that her husband and daughter escaped with their lives, but she wasn't so lucky. It was a classic case of mob mentality, and she was far from the only victim."

"Do you think Elizabeth actually *was* a witch like her sisters?" Isabella asks. There's an arch tone in her voice. It's not like her to talk to teachers this way.

"Seriously? Do *you*?" The question comes from Katie Taylor, a slim, pale girl with long blonde hair who sits in the very back of every class and watches for any sign of weakness – in students or in teachers – so she can pounce. "Witch, please."

The class titters at Katie's joke, but nervously, since she's taking a swipe at Isabella, whom everyone likes.

As upset as I am at Isabella, some part of me still has the urge to turn around and snap at Katie.

"That's enough, Miss Taylor," says my dad calmly, still looking at Isabella. "It doesn't matter what I think," he tells her. "People were hunted down and killed for superstition – that much we do know. That's a terrible thing and a terrible waste of life. But were all of them actually evil witches?" He shrugs. "Sometimes the world isn't as simple as we'd like it to be."

"But you know what is simple?" I blurt, trying to save both him and Isabella. "The Articles of Confederation."

Dad gives me a surprised look, as if he forgot I was here. We have rules, and one of those rules is that I'm not supposed to be snarky in class. But I'm sending him a lifeline, and we both know it.

"Right," Dad says, straightening. He strides to the whiteboard and picks up a marker. "The last meeting of the Continental Congress happened in October seventeen seventy-seven."

A groan ripples through the room, but I'm willing to take the hit to my reputation.

Katie Taylor is the daughter of Jay Taylor, the school principal and the same guy who bullied my dad decades ago. Katie didn't get the nickname Tattletale Taylor for nothing. I'm sure my dad would be mortified if the whole school found out that he believes in ghosts and witches. Plus, my mum, who will be up for partner at her law firm soon, wouldn't be able to live it down, either.

And then there's me. I still have to get through two more years at Jacob Bailey High, and I'd really rather not do it while being called Ghost Girl or Witch Killer. I've got less than two years to work on my portfolio and my SAT scores, and the Sanderson sisters and local lore are *not* going to hold me back. Before I know it, I'll be at SCAD or RISD or NYU or another arts school where I can focus on my photography and not spend my brain cells worrying about keeping the family secret safe.

I sit up straighter, lifting my chin a little as I do.

I can feel Isabella studying me, but I ignore it.

Dad's familiar handwriting staggers across the board, and I take calming breaths, counting to five each time and willing my heartbeat to slow. I can't tell whether it's still pounding thanks to my dad's close call or because I suspect that Isabella is mad at me for derailing her question – a question that replays in my head now.

Isabella dressed as the goddess of wisdom and war, and she brought both into my dad's classroom on the worst possible day.

Brick Coven

Travis almost trips Captain America in his rush to catch me.

At the lunch bell, I'd leapt up, thrown all my stuff into my backpack and ran out of my dad's classroom like Usain Bolt. In the crowded hall, I cram my backpack into my locker, shut it and twist the lock just as Travis rests a hand on my arm. I can't look him in the eyes. I'm embarrassed by my dad and myself, and sometimes I wonder why Travis hangs out with me at all.

"Pops! You okay?" he asks, pushing his glasses up the bridge of his nose.

"Yeah," I say sullenly, meeting his eyes. "Lunch?"

Travis shakes his head. "Maybe Isabella's letting her goddess getup go to her head a bit," he says.

"It's not her fault," I tell him. Travis has known how I feel about the Sanderson sisters for so long, he sometimes forgets that he's the only person outside my family who even knows the story.

"Poppy!" calls Isabella, jogging to catch up to us. She squeezes through a group of jocks, smiling and waving at them as she does, and affectionately pinches the shoulder of her biology lab partner as she passes her. Even in damage control mode, Isabella can't help fulfilling the peppy, friendly image everyone has of her.

I groan, shutting my eyes for one brief moment and wishing I were anywhere but here.

I never dreamt I'd be trying to avoid Isabella Richards.

She finally reaches us, and notices my arms are crossed and my mouth is set in a hard line. She studies my face. "Did I do something wrong?" she asks me, reaching out to touch my arm. I recoil automatically and then kick myself for the hurt look that passes over her face. I didn't mean to, but I also can't deny that I *am* a little mad at her. Why did she go after my dad like that anyway? Wasn't it obvious that he didn't want to talk about the Sandersons? I guess not.

"Poppy?" she prompts, worried.

"I..." I shake my head. "It's a long story. Don't worry about it."

Isabella chews her lip, then nods. "Well, can I buy you pizza to make up for it?"

Pizza? My one weakness. "Travis and I brought," I say.

"No, I didn't," says Travis, shrugging and giving me a put-on pout.

I narrow my eyes at him. *Traitor.*

He shrugs as if to say I cannot possibly compare to pepperoni, but I catch the sneaky look in his eye as he glances between me and Isabella. He's been trying to get us to spend more time together so I'll make a move — but *seriously? Now?*

Travis and I have an entire conversation with our eyes, but I'm having a separate one internally. Isabella's been hanging out with us every day since the school year started, and I have no idea why. She has friends from half a dozen clubs and teams, and can bounce from cafeteria table to cafeteria table with ease. Our friendship so far has been light and fun and cruising along evenly, but if I take her up on lunch today, I know I'll have to tell her about my biggest secret. Bigger, even, than having a crush on her.

Travis leans over. "She's our friend," he whispers. "It's time."

"No," I say tightly. "I don't want to."

"Free mozzarella, Pops," he whispers. "Can't say no."

I glare at him, then turn back to Isabella, who is looking at us both like we've lost it.

"Sure," I tell her. "But I have opinions about mushrooms."

We're allowed to go off campus for lunch as long as we stay within a five-street radius of school. Most people skip Allegra's because it's on the edge of said radius, but that's exactly why Isabella likes it. It gives her a chance to get away from everyone else, she says, when she just wants to read a book or not think about Homecoming Committee or her zillion other commitments.

None of us owns a car, so it's not like we could have an off-campus lunch much further away. As we push through the school doors and into the last October afternoon, we find a clear, sunny sky with crisp air that gives my lungs just the slightest icy tingle. It's a day for apple picking or pumpkin carving or mulling apple juice with whole spices. It's so pretty, in fact, that confessing my family's deepest, darkest secret shouldn't even be on the table.

We make it a few blocks from school before any of us says anything – though Travis keeps giving me meaningful looks that I keep wilfully ignoring.

Finally, he clears his throat. "So, I found this summer course at Stanford for physics."

"Oh?" says Isabella, no doubt eager to fill the silence.

That's all the encouragement Travis needs, and he's off and running, telling her all about the kinds of experiments they do and the qualifications of the teachers. And then Isabella tells us how much she loved Stanford when she took a campus tour there last summer.

Finally, I step between them and decide to make a peace offering. "I went to San Francisco a few years ago," I say, "with my family."

"Yeah?" Isabella looks really interested to hear more, but she also looks apologetic. She's still trying to make up for making class noticeably awkward for me.

"Yeah," I say. "We drove up to Muir Woods. The redwoods were amazing. I bet I shot fifteen rolls of film on that trip."

"You're in photo class?" Isabella asks, slowing her pace ever so slightly to stare at me.

I hesitate, but then I continue walking, and she keeps up. I'd kind of hoped she'd noticed my pictures in *The Chusetts*, our monthly student paper, but the photo credits are smaller than the bylines. Anyway, part of the draw to visual art was the chance to be *behind* the lens.

"Yeah," I tell her. "I love it."

"What do you take pictures of?"

I shrug and take a second to think. *Football games. Science fairs.* But those things are to show schools that

I'm versatile, not to feed some deep artistic need. "I like to find small details that are really beautiful, but that most people would walk right past and not even notice," I finally say. When she looks confused, I add, "Like, peeling paint? That's my jam. Or the way shadows slant off driftwood. Or the veins in leaves when sunlight passes through them. My teacher says I need more range, though, so art schools will look at me. Portraits and self-portraits and landscapes and stuff. I'm working on it."

"And you develop them yourself, in a real darkroom?" she asks.

We hang a right at the corner and walk under a row of nearly naked trees.

I nod. "I'll show you how sometime. Watching the developer work on the paper – knowing it's this thin layer of silver that's making the image appear – it's like magic."

I meet Isabella's gaze, and something in her expression makes me blush.

"I'd like that," she says. She's watching me – studying me – like there's something about my face she's never noticed before.

I realise Travis has purposely fallen back. *Sly devil.*

We arrive at Allegra's. The tiny restaurant with its roof of curved sheet metal looks like it's seen better days.

The last time the place was renovated was just after my parents graduated. I've only ever been here a handful of times, but it's usually not this busy. I hold open the flimsy door and let Isabella and Travis file through and into the warm space covered with cobwebs and fuzzy fake spiders. At the counter, people dig into pizza pies and loudly chatter. Lucky for us, there's an empty booth in the back that we quickly occupy.

As Isabella slides onto the worn red leather next to me, her expression shifts and she seems to come out of her thoughts. "So, when are you finally going to get on Insta?"

I shake my head. "It's not really my thing," I say. "When you use film, you only get a few chances to get the image right, you know? You have to work for it. Being able to take a thousand shots of the same thing and use filters without really understanding how contrast or composition works – it seems like cheating." Isabella's smirking a little, and I realise that she's probably on Instagram herself, because why else would she ask? My stomach sinks. "But not *actually* cheating, obviously," I add. "I mean, it's cool. It's just… different."

I glance at Travis, but he's too busy sketching a thumbnail of Iron Man on his tablet to rescue me.

When I look back at Isabella, she's tapping a finger

against her bottom lip absently. Her lipstick is lilac matte and somehow hasn't smudged.

"Isabella! It's so good to see you!" cries someone with a thick Italian accent. Allegra herself hurries up to give Isabella a hug and a kiss on each cheek. She's a slight elderly woman with wispy white hair and a stained red apron. Isabella really *is* friends with everyone. Allegra waves to Travis and me, wishes us a happy Halloween, and calls a waitress over to take our order.

Then, before I know it, my mouth is full of tomato sauce and toppings – extra mushrooms. Travis practically inhales a slice of pepperoni pizza.

"So, I'm sorry about today in class," Isabella says, finally redirecting the conversation to the sensitive topic at hand. I knew she wouldn't let me off that easily.

"Oh… yeah…" I sigh. "Well, it's just – my family has a lot of history with the Sandersons. It's complicated."

"I'm sorry. I didn't know. I'm just *genuinely* interested in the Sanderson sisters. And I just thought, your dad being a history teacher and all, he might know more about them. But I guess it was kind of… touchy?"

"The city owns the house," I say, "but my nana used to be the museum manager, back when there was still a budget for running the place. After the museum closed down, she held on to the keys."

"Your grandma used to work at the Sanderson house?" Isabella lights up. "No way! Poppy, why didn't you ever mention this before?" She examines my face for a second. "But I'm guessing that's not the complicated part."

I look to Travis for courage, and he nods.

It's time Isabella goes from new friend to ride-or-die friend.

Before I know it, I'm spilling my family's secret to my school's class president, homecoming queen and debate team captain. Isabella listens, nodding and looking sympathetic, as I start to tell her about my aunt and parents and their weird story about a Halloween night twenty-five years ago. I also can't help looking over my shoulder in paranoia as I share their tale.

"So, I guess my dad wants to impress my mom – they weren't dating yet, remember – and he lights the candle."

Isabella gasps. "No!"

"Yeah." I hesitate and check to make sure Allegra and her staff are otherwise occupied. I drop my voice to a whisper: "And the Sanderson sisters reappeared."

"Which ones?" Isabella asks.

I think it's an odd question, because everyone knows the three Sanderson sisters, but then I remember her asking about Elizabeth. As with everything, it seems like Isabella really has done her homework.

"Winifred and Sarah and Mary," I say.

"And apparently Sarah's *real* thirsty," says Travis, still sketching.

It's weird to talk about the Sanderson witches as if they're distant relations. I study Isabella, wondering whether she thinks I'm making all of this up – or worse, if she thinks my family is insane and is going to go back and tell her mum to oppose my mum's promotion.

Isabella looks sincerely interested. "So then what happened?" she asks.

"My parents and my aunt tried to get my grandparents to help, but they didn't believe them, so instead my dad lured the witches into the arts annex and trapped them in the kiln."

Isabella puts a hand to her mouth. "No!"

"Yeah, and my mom turned it on." I roll my eyes.

"Because she's a badass," chimes in Travis.

Isabella laughs.

I can't help smiling. I admit that even if I don't believe the story myself, that part about my mum always makes me a little proud. I glance around the restaurant again, just to quadruple-check no one heard one bit of my family's story. A mum and her two small boys are seated on the other side of the room, arguing about who'll be getting the last slice of pizza. Others seated around us are too engrossed with each other to notice us. I ease up and turn my attention back to my friends.

"Anyway, the witches survived," I say in a low voice, "and they busted down the door. Then they kidnapped my aunt Dani and made a potion so they could steal her youth or something, but my dad drank it instead and rescued her. And then the sun came up and the witches went up in smoke and dust. I think they turned to stone before or something. But that's the story. My dad promised me that he wouldn't talk about it in front of other people, for my own sake. And that's why in class when you brought it up, I was quick to shut it down. Sorry."

There's a long pause and I inwardly cringe. Isabella has been patiently listening the whole time, but how could she possibly look at me the same way after a story like this?

"It's ridiculous, right?" I ask, trying to make it clear as possible that I don't share my family's delusions.

"Three of your family members would disagree," says Travis, still not looking up from his tablet.

Isabella just stares at me. "So *that's* why the kiln is broken?" she finally asks.

I relax. She hasn't blatantly made fun of me yet, which I appreciate. She's even giving me the chance to change the subject and calm my nerves for a little while.

"That's what my parents and aunt say," I reply. "I guess the school used to offer classes for ceramics and sculpture and stuff. You can blame the Dennisons for the lack of pottery in your life."

Isabella smirks. "I'll let my dad know." She doesn't usually talk about her dad, the first black mayor of Salem, because he's the only thing plenty of people want to talk to her about. She takes another bite of pizza and another sip of her drink, then says, "Well, thank you for sharing that with me, Poppy." The air seems to crackle between us. I don't realise how close she leant in until she scoots back in the booth. "So. Do you believe them? Your parents and your aunt?"

"I mean, they're my family." I sigh. "I feel like I have to believe them, but also… like, *really*?"

Isabella laughs. "Yeah. I know how that feels. I like that you try to see everything from all sides." She looks like she's going to say something else, but then she turns to Travis. "You've been awfully quiet, Trav. What do *you* think?"

He adjusts his glasses and keeps his eyes on his tablet. "There's no scientific basis for any of it," he says. "Maybe they made up the story and told it so many times, they started to believe it was real." He glances up at me. "No offence, Pops."

I wave it off. "None taken." I turn to Isabella. "Anyway, you coming tonight?"

"How is your mom okay with inviting our entire

class to your house for a Halloween party this year?" Travis cuts in. "I thought, you know, she's spooked by the holiday."

I turn to him. "She insists she's just happy it's been a whole twenty-five years since the 'Sanderson incident'," I say, putting the phrase in air quotes. What I don't tell him is that I know there's something else up my mum's sleeve. I can just feel it.

"Well, I wouldn't miss it." Isabella gives me a smile that makes my stomach flip a little. "There's no way I'd leave you hanging."

"It's not fair that you're so nice." I take another slice of pizza. "People aren't supposed to be smart, popular *and* nice. What's your weakness, Isabella Richards?"

Her smile flags a little, and for a second she looks mystified – but then it's gone. "Halloween candy," she says matter-of-factly, then grins and takes another sip of her drink.

"Dudes, hate to break it to you, but we need to wrap it up," says Travis, "or we are going to be late for class."

I look for the waitress, craning my head this way and that, as Travis and Isabella quickly finish off what's left of the pizza and their drinks. If I recall correctly, I think we can just pay at the till. Isabella digs in her pocket for her wallet, and I remember she's treating us.

"It's all good," I say, reaching for my own wallet.

"No! I insist," she says, laughing. "It's the least I could do."

That's when Katie Taylor's perky face emerges from the top of the neighbouring booth. She's recently dyed the bottom layer of her long blonde hair with streaks of blue and turquoise, and when she ties it up – as she has today in a fishtail braid – she looks like a mermaid. The kind that lures people out to sea and viciously drowns them. "I'm coming to your mom's Halloween house party tonight, too, Poppy," she says. The smile she flashes me is toothache sweet, and I feel like all the air in the restaurant has evacuated the premises. *"Wouldn't miss it,"* she adds.

Katie steps out of the booth, along with Jenny Liu, her best friend and football team co-captain. "Aw, how cute," Katie sneers, looking at Isabella. "It's good to see the loser inner circle widening." She regards me for a second. "One more witch, and it's a coven!"

She and Jenny turn on their heels and go to the till to pay, whispering and giggling the whole time. Jenny tosses her silky ombré hair as she follows Katie through the front door of the restaurant, where five other members of the football team, all in the same fur-lined shoes and oversize cashmere jumpers, have just arrived with steaming coffees. I'd wager pumpkin spice lattes. Neither Katie nor Jenny bother to look back at us, which somehow feels worse than if they had.

I think of my family and how hard I've worked to

hide this different piece of their lives. And now I've gone and told Katie 'Tattletale' Taylor. It's never long before Katie finds new ways to make someone's life a complete nightmare. *What have I done?*

"Poppy?" Isabella watches me, worried. "Who cares what Katie thinks? She couldn't hold a candle to you on her best day."

"A Black Flame Candle!" Travis chimes in.

We both shoot him a look.

I glance over again at Katie and her minions as they pile into Katie's car. "Do you think they heard us?"

"Well, this is a dumpster fire," says Travis.

I groan and drop my forehead to the table.

"I'm not going," I tell the table.

Travis touches my shoulder. "Pops, you can't miss your own party."

"You mean my *mom's* party," I correct him. "This whole thing was *her* idea, which I totally don't get, since she never even *talks* about Halloween except to warn me about waking dead witches. And now our whole class has been invited, and my dad invited all the teachers and school staff, and Katie is going to be there with my family secret up her sleeve, ready to perform a terrible magic trick in front of everyone I know!"

"Pops, breathe," says Travis.

"I mean, if she really doesn't want to go, maybe we can do something else," suggests Isabella.

"Nah," says Travis. "She'll come around."

I sigh and pick myself up. "You're right. I'm going to pull it together, and I'm going to this party, and I'm going to ignore Katie for the rest of my life," I say.

"'Witch, please' is right," says Travis, smiling and nodding. "That's my girl."

Isabella gives me a concerned look, then picks something off the pizza tray and offers it to me. "Mushroom?" she asks hopefully.

I snort at the idea that a soggy mushroom can fix this situation. "I'm stuffed," I tell her, sitting back up. "But thanks."

"I guess you could say your stomach doesn't have *mushroom*," quips Travis.

Isabella and I both turn to him. We start laughing at the same time.

"Poppy, you're a saint for putting up with this," Isabella says.

"I'll take that as a compliment," I say.

"Hey," says Travis, flashing a smug smile. "If you got it, *haunt* it."

SERIOUS SHADE

y the time American Lit rolls around, I finally
find someone who looks more over Halloween
than I do. Too bad it's a painted pumpkin sitting
on Miss Chen's desk.

At this point, I can *feel* Halloween night approaching.
Half the class is anxious to get home and primp before
a night of parties, and the other half is still licking sugar
off their fingers from the caramel apples Spanish Club
sold at lunch. As for me? I'm just plain old anxious. The
classroom is split in two sections that face each other,
which is fine for discussion classes, but now means that
every time I glance up, I see Katie and Jenny texting
under their desks. I try not to look, which of course
means I just look even more. I'm glad Isabella's next to
me. Her presence is calming, somehow.

Miss Chen, Halloween or no Halloween, wears a black T-shirt and comfortable jeans, as always. She spends ten minutes trying to encourage a class discussion that doesn't dissolve into giggles or blank stares. After her last attempt ends with dead air, she catches the eyes of everyone in class, one by one, the look on her face announcing her utter disappointment.

"Well, I can see all of you are eager to get on with your nights," she announces after silently shaming each of us. "Including, perhaps, going to the Dennisons' Halloween party. So why don't we spend the rest of the hour catching up on the reading you *clearly* haven't done?"

My classmates exchange looks like they've just won the lottery and can't quite believe it, but I feel a wave of guilt because she's only trying to do her job. Blame my empathy towards her on being a teacher's kid.

Miss Chen sits back down and picks up a wooden wand. "And the next person who talks gets detention for three days," she adds, rapping it on the edge of her desk. With a flourish, she flips the wand into the air and catches it, the tip pointing in Katie's direction like an accusation.

When Katie gives her innocent eyes, Miss Chen sets the wand back on her desk with a snap and picks up a copy of the local newspaper. She's a big fan of reading the police reports.

Katie looks over at me, and I feel the full force of her wicked smile. She mouths, *boo*.

I open my copy of *The Scarlet Letter* and flip through my notes and highlights to see whether I'll have anything intelligent to say in the end-of-unit essay. It's a welcome distraction.

Katie snorts, covering her mouth, and hides her phone under her book. She's Snapchatting, no doubt. Or in a group text with her squad about what a loser I am. *Whatever.*

Miss Chen clears her throat loudly and gives Katie a look that would melt lesser students.

"Sorry," says Katie. "Hester Prynne is just so funny." Her eyes dip back to her book and then swing up to meet mine. Her smirk grows more pronounced.

I drag my teeth over my bottom lip and stare at my book until the words come back into sharp focus. I will not let Katie Taylor get to me.

But if I were a Sanderson sister, oh, the curses I would cast.

I wish Travis were here right now instead of in Honors Chem. He'd do something to make me laugh, or at least make me feel less like a loser.

Isabella touches my forearm and then jerks back from the jolt of static that passes between us. "Whoa," she whispers, "you *must* be mad." She laughs nervously at her own joke.

I glance up at Miss Chen, who is still tucked behind her newspaper. Isabella is not one to risk detention – especially given all the extracurriculars she has to run and attend after school – so I know she must be *really* worried about me.

"You okay?" she asks, feigning reading from her book.

"I'm fine," I say tightly. I really want to tell her that I'm *not* fine, but I don't think Isabella knows what it feels like to be made fun of. She's basically gifted at everything she touches. Maybe that's what I should tell Travis: I'll never ask Isabella out, even if she's smart, beautiful *and* nice, because it's too much pressure to be with someone who is so good at life. I love my photography and I want to go to a good school and find a way to make money with my art, but that's not the same as what Isabella Richards likely wants. She's probably looking for someone perfect. Like her.

My phone lights up: it's a text from Isabella. DON'T WORRY. KATIE WON'T TALK, it says. SHE'D RATHER HOLD THE SECRET OVER YOU AND MAKE YOU SQUIRM. I chew my lip. That makes sense. I hope she's right. I look over to Isabella and see her slide her mobile phone under her book.

I glance up and see Katie giggling to herself again, but this time she's being more discreet. She looks over, catches me staring, and winks.

My phone lights up again and I look down to see that

Katie has posted on the Facebook event for my mum's party. I click it open, ignoring the sinking feeling in the pit of my stomach. She's posted to the page with the cryptic words: *Can't wait to see all you guys and ghouls! #RealWitches*

She *did* hear me at Allegra's. I'm *so* dead.

I stew in my thoughts until the bell rings.

Miss Chen's sigh of relief is actually audible. "Everyone out," she says, tossing her thick grey braid over her back. "Happy Halloween. Don't drink the blood of babies."

I stuff everything back into my bag and hurry to the door, but Katie manages to intercept me. "See you tonight," she says sweetly. "Can't wait."

"Katie, get over yourself," Isabella says over my shoulder.

Katie swivels on one heel. "*Excuse* me?"

"Don't mind if we do." Isabella takes my forearm to steer me through the door.

Thankfully, we don't zap each other this time. Her hand is warm and firm and I pray to god she doesn't notice the goose bumps rippling over my skin.

"I've got to get to debate," she says to me while still looking straight ahead once we're a good distance down the hall, "but seriously, don't let her get to you. She's not worth it. Trust me." She squeezes my arm and dips back into the crowd. She's tall enough that I can see the glint of her gold circlet over the heads of the other students.

While it's blindingly obvious that Katie isn't worth stressing out about, something about Isabella saying it makes me feel warm and tingly. *You don't need external affirmation*, Mum would say – but one could argue that you don't need cheese fries, either. Both are pretty damn satisfying indulgences.

Isabella disappears down the stairs and I lean against a wall of lockers, chiding myself for being such an idiot. I'd like to blame it on the emotional turmoil that comes with being a Dennison on Halloween, but unfortunately, this isn't that unusual for me. Acting like a grade A weirdo around the girl you have a giant, extraordinarily inconvenient – and almost certainly ill-fated crush on is a *very* Poppy Dennison move.

I've never heard anyone talk about Isabella's love life – she's too busy getting ready to run the world to expend energy on dating, presumably. But then, I doubt anyone talks about *my* love life, except maybe to speculate about whether Travis and I are secretly a thing. Which is so far from true. What *is* true is that the chance that Isabella likes me back is so remote, I'm far more likely to get struck by lightning. Twice.

"Pops."

I look up and see Travis coming down the hall with

a Jacob Bailey High baseball duffel bag slung over his shoulder. It's a relic from his one and only season on the team, before he gave up any lingering MLB dreams. My gaze slides from the duffel to his T-shirt, the top half of which is sopping wet.

"What happened to you?" I ask.

He shakes his head. "Donnie Thompson got carried away during the chem experiment," he explains. "He said saline conductivity was too boring, so he started flinging salt water everywhere. Dude needs some anger management lessons pronto." He arches an eyebrow. "But what happened to *you*?"

"Nothing," I say, suddenly self-conscious.

Travis jerks his chin at my head. I reach for my hair, thinking I've had a leaf stuck in it all period. But I realise that long strands of my hair are floating above my head like tentacles.

I gasp. "Oh, crap." I grab my head with both hands.

"That's some serious static," says Travis.

"Being the town freak must be a hair-raising experience, huh, Dennison? That's some *serious* volume," Katie quips as she breezes past with her football squad. Then she turns and calls out to me, walking backwards, "You're not a long-lost Sanderson, are you?" She feigns alarm, really hamming it up for her friends, who look on with a kind of wicked glee. *"Please, spare me your* hexes! *Think of the International Witch Tribunal! Surely they'd have your head for misuse of magic.*" She grins at her own joke and spins on her heel, flanked by her mean-girl posse, and hurries off, the cleats tied to their backpacks bobbing in unison.

Katie knows everything about my family's Sanderson secret: confirmed.

I try to shake off how upset I feel. "What's going on with my hair?" I ask Travis.

"You must be *coming into your powers,*" he teases, but he leads me to the bathroom and pushes me through the swinging door.

I run in, place my backpack down and splash water onto my hair. Desperately, I smooth down the wayward dirty-blonde strands, adding more and more water until they hang as limp and still as they're meant to.

Alone, I stare at myself in the mirror, looking like a golden retriever just out of the bath. My throat feels tight, but I try not to panic. After talking about the Sanderson sisters at lunch, some of my family's superstition seems to have wiggled its way into my brain, and I remind myself that magic isn't real and there's no way I've somehow wished myself into magical abilities just to spite my personal nemesis. I zapped Isabella with static earlier: that must be the answer. Static from my jumper or from a change in the atmosphere or something. Static and paranoia, because it's Halloween night and I'm nervous about my entire class meeting my parents.

I take a deep breath and grip the edge of the sink, willing my thoughts to stop spinning. I look at my own face, sad and pale, in the mirror once again and try to see it objectively, as if I were looking at a tree or an old house, searching to find the perfect shot. Mascara streaks down my cheekbones in little spikes, stark against my skin. My wet hair clings to me, too, snaking across my cheeks and chin and down my neck, curling around my collarbone and jawline.

My photo teacher, Ms Ahmed, said I needed to work on my range and stretch myself, and capturing this moment on film isn't something I'd normally ever do. I look scared and vulnerable and raw – and not social media ready, that's for sure. *If Katie Taylor could see me now.* But in the rawness is something sharp, like a fire beneath my skin that feels *just* out of my control.

My eyes fall to my backpack on the floor, and I lean down and root around for the smooth, solid body of my camera. I frame the shot in the mirror. Half-open bathroom stalls stand in formation behind me as I hide behind my camera, my face obscured in my reflection in the smudgy bathroom mirror. All I can see is my hair trailing water onto my jumper, and a streak of mascara that's found its way to my chin. I adjust the f-stop and shutter speed to suit the incandescent bathroom lights. I take a deep breath, hold it, and take the photo, the crisp snap of the shutter satisfying in the tiled room. I'll call this shot *Portrait of the Artist as a Drowned Rat*.

When I reemerge from the bathroom, Travis points from my hair to his shirt. "Look!" he says. "We match!"

I know he's trying to make me feel better, so I give him a weak smile.

Principal Taylor comes around the corner, probably on patrol to clear the halls. He's wearing a plaid button-down shirt like always, the collar fastened all the way to the top and a few locks of his blond comb-over falling out of place. Jay Taylor grew up with my dad, and they have a long-standing tiff because decades ago, Jay was one of the biggest bullies at Jacob Bailey High. It's not surprising, I guess, that his daughter turned out the same way – though with her own special brand of petty meanness. He looks from my dripping head to Travis's damp shirt.

"Would you care to explain why you're both soaked, Mr Reese?" Principal Taylor asks, narrowing his eyes and pursing his lips into a sharp point. He directs his question to Travis, as if he suspects it's all my fault and my friend would rat me out if asked the right question. He always does that with Dennisons, except for my aunt Dani, who could get along with even the angriest crowd of pitchfork-wielding townspeople.

"Science experiment gone wrong," says Travis, rescuing me, "but it's just water."

Principal Taylor nods slowly, his eyes flitting from Travis to me as if he's trying to look right through us.

This guy needs to ease up. It's Halloween, and for all he knows this wet look could be our extremely sad and lame attempt at costumes.

He clears his throat and continues down the hall.

"Let's go," I whisper to Travis, "before Principal Taylor accuses us of being whatever the water equivalent of a pyromaniac is." I stay rooted in place as I watch Principal Taylor come across a group of girls giggling around one of their lockers.

"Get on home," he says to them. "We're locking up the building." He looks back over at Travis and me. "You never know what wild things kids will do on Halloween night."

His words make my stomach turn: *has Katie already told him about my family's Sanderson secret?*

Travis doesn't seem to notice, or at least ignores Principal Taylor so he won't think we care. Instead, Travis slings an arm around my shoulders and pulls me towards the stairs. "Don't trip," he says. "So, I did some Googling while you were in the bathroom, to explain the static. It might storm tomorrow. It's probably a pressure thing. Or humidity. Or maybe there are extra ions in the atmosphere."

I roll my eyes. "Sure," I say.

Travis ruffles my wet hair. "Let's get you home. We got a party to crash."

BROOM SERVICE

My house doesn't exactly scream 'Halloween party'.

I mean, our house isn't usually decorated for Halloween, but we're throwing a fairly large Halloween shindig in a few short hours, so I'm slightly concerned. It's also the only house on the street without a single pumpkin or decorative gourd on its porch – and you'd better believe there aren't any fake gravestones, which my mum finds tasteless since she has a soft spot for a zombie named Billy she apparently met twenty-five years ago. That, and she generally doesn't think it's very funny to make jokes about the (living) dead. But tonight, we should probably have some kitschy knick-knacks out on the lawn, or at the very least a pumpkin. *Sigh*. What is my life?

Travis looks from the hedges of the festive house next door, which are probably 90 percent fake cobwebs, to its bales of hay stacked high and its large, painted pumpkins wearing witches' hats, to our pristine garden decorated only by a few stray yellow and orange leaves.

"So, remind me again why your parents are throwing a party to celebrate a holiday they absolutely abhor?" he asks.

"I'll let you know when I figure it out," I mutter, walking down the lantern-lit brick path. My big white house with its dark shutters and two storeys can certainly hold a good number of people, that's for sure. As I open the front door, I see there isn't even so much as an autumn wreath on it.

Inside, Dad kneels in front of the fireplace with a pile of sticks and cut logs. He's wearing a green jumper and brown corduroys, and when he turns to wave hello, I see that he has a headband on with HOLLYWOOD in white block letters.

"Hollywood sign," says Travis with a nod. "Classic."

"Thanks." My dad clicks his silver lighter and holds it to the firewood.

"Can I help?" Travis asks, even though he already knows the answer.

"I've got it," says Dad, on cue, "but Allison might need help in the kitchen."

When Nana and Grampa retired to Palm Springs a few years ago – because they'd heard so many wonderful things about California from my dad – he was sceptical about moving into his in-laws' old house. He's since become very particular and territorial about certain things – including the way fireplace wood is stacked. Maybe it's a result of getting older: Mum says Dad used to be much more laid-back. Apparently, kids even nicknamed him Hollywood for a long time after he moved here from California. But I know he got more serious after their 'face-off' with the Sanderson sisters, and even more so after my parents got married and I made my debut.

When Mum was pregnant, Dad bought a safe to lock up the stub of the Black Flame Candle. He even tried to get the Sanderson house condemned and bulldozed, but the city pushed back since it's a historic landmark. My parents are de facto caretakers, with possibly the only set of keys, even though they never go there. I'm surprised no one's made the Sanderson house into an escape room by now.

Travis and I drop our bags by the front door and head into the kitchen, where we find Mum poring over case files – which is to say, we find Mum being Mum. Her white blazer is draped over the back of her chair, but she's wearing one of her favourite blouses – crimson with cascading ruffles at the front – rolled up at the elbows, which means it was a court day, and a long one at that. Her honey-coloured hair is pulled back in a sleek bun, and her cherry-red lipstick has started to fade because she chews her lips when she's thinking. Beside her, there's a platter of dark chocolate chip cookies, and half of them are iced to look like pumpkins. *So there will be treats at the party. That's a relief.* There are two tubes of icing near Mum – one orange and one green – but she's so engrossed in her case that she seems to have forgotten them.

Mum notices us even though her eyes are still on her files. "The ones by the toaster are finished," she says, not realising Travis has already homed in on the cookies and popped one in his mouth.

"Just testing them out," he says through a mouthful. "They're *not* poisonous."

I ignore him. "Can we help with decorations?" I ask Mum. Then I turn to Travis and mumble, "If we're having this party, we might as well try to make it good."

"I would love that," she says, circling something in her file. "Give me two seconds."

Travis pours himself a glass of milk and hands me a cookie without waiting to see whether I actually want it. They're soft and still a little warm. It's my mum's special recipe. Travis stacks three on top of each other and eats them together like a cookie sandwich – in the most literal sense of the term.

Mum caps her pen and looks up. Her face falls. "Oh, Poppy, you're soaked."

I pull my still-wet hair to one side. "Yeah..." I clear my throat. My day's been so weird that if I tell her about any part of it, she'll immediately think it has something to do with witches. *The* witches. I look desperately at Travis.

"Saline conductivity!" he says, choking on cookie crumbs. He takes a gulp of milk to wash it down. "We were doing experiments to show that the more salt you have in water, the more easily it conducts electricity. But then my lab partner got bored and threw the experimental fluid on everyone."

"That seems... dramatic?" says Mum.

Travis shrugs. "High school."

Mum laughs. "Fair." She pushes back from the kitchen table and stands up. "That reminds me, it's a blood moon tonight, *so...* I want you two to be more careful than usual, okay?"

"*That's* what Travis's chem experiment reminds you of? The blood moon tonight?" I say before I can stop myself. Even though I told Travis my family's story years and years ago, it still sounds nuts every time Mum or Dad brings it up.

"What?" Mum says flatly. "The blood moon could amplify magic and—"

I cut in. "Mom." I glance at Travis, who is occupying himself with more cookies and milk, trying to stay out of it. I feel myself blushing. *Why can't my family just be normal?* Why do my parents have to believe something so out there that we get in fights over it, and in front of poor Travis? And then I cringe, remembering that I've already accidentally spilled my family's Sanderson secret to someone else – Katie Taylor. The worst possible person.

Mum shrugs and selects a finished cookie. "All I'm saying is that it's nights like these that make me wish we knew where Winifred Sanderson's spell book had gotten to."

"Mom."

"I know, I know," she says, arranging the cookies on a tray. "Some kids probably picked it up, but what if they still have it tucked in a trunk somewhere? What if someone finds it or reads from it? It's not safe to have that thing roaming around."

"Mom, it's not *roaming around*," I say. "It's a *book*." I pause a second, my mind racing, and then everything clicks into place: "*That*'s why you're throwing this party."

"*What?*" Mum spins around, takes a bite of her cookie, and leans back against the kitchen counter. She watches me thoughtfully as she chews.

Travis has also paused to watch me.

"This whole party," I insist. "Isn't it enough that you tried to get the Sanderson house condemned and locked up the Black Flame Candle in a safe? Do you have to humiliate me *and* play Big Brother, too? You're throwing this party to keep me and my friends from getting beamed up into the blood moon, or whatever it is that you think could happen tonight."

Travis's eyebrows rise in surprise.

Silence fills the kitchen.

"Okay, I didn't deserve that," Mum says. "But you have a point. Yes, I'm trying to make sure as many teenagers as possible are otherwise occupied, including you and your friends, but I promise I never intended to humiliate you. I just want to throw a party and give all your classmates toothaches while keeping anything bad from happening to you. Is that so terrible?"

I grunt.

"I promise they won't realise that your mother is a little superstitious, or that your father and I and your aunt Dani believe in witches and zombies, okay?"

Sure, watch over me and my friends. But this still doesn't solve the problem that is Katie Taylor spilling to all the party guests that my family believes in ghost stories, if she hasn't done so already.

"Or have I already embarrassed you?" Mum's voice

is deliberately calm and even, but I can tell she's hurt by the way I insist on distancing myself from this part of my family's history. She hasn't finished eating her cookie. She holds it by her side listlessly.

I think about what I'd do if I introduced Isabella to Mum and Mum started going on about the blood moon and werewolves or whatever, and the thought of that makes me even queasier. I resolve to keep Mum as far away from Isabella as humanly (or non-humanly?) possible.

I shrug. "No, you don't embarrass me," I tell her. "Besides, it's just Travis."

"Hey!" Travis says through another mouthful of cookie.

I ignore him. "But…"

"But you're afraid I'm going to say something weird tonight in front of all your classmates."

I don't say anything, but she knows she's right.

Mum comes over and tucks a strand of damp hair behind my ear. "I get it, Poppy, I do. I promise I won't say anything I wouldn't have wanted my mom to say to me as a teenager."

I bite my bottom lip. I know that despite their own hang-ups, my parents go out of their way to try to make sure my life is happy and relatively well-adjusted. "Thank you," I say with reluctance.

Mum breaks off half of her cookie and hands it to me. "Now get some more sugar in you. I need volunteers for pumpkin duty. You didn't think the house was going to be this decoration-less for the party, did you?" Then she looks at Travis. "And maybe save some cookies for our guests?"

Mum specialises in last-minute party decor, like Martha Stewart hooked to an egg timer.

Travis and I help by doing a clean sweep of the house, and by wrapping pumpkins in black tulle and patterned ribbons and arranging them in the entry hall and dining room under Mum's watchful eye. In the entry hall, we set up a Pinterest-worthy treat buffet table and dump eight kilograms of sweets into a cauldron that, as far as I can tell, Nana and Grampa stored in the garage to pull out once a year expressly for this purpose. *Well, I guess late is better than never.*

After the halls are made merry with fright, Travis and I scramble up the long staircase to my room, where we're supposed to wrap a hundred lollipops with tissue paper and ribbon to make tiny ghost party favours. I draw eyes and a gaping mouth on the tissue paper with a felt pen, then look up to see Travis lounging in the beanbag chair in the corner. We're both too big for it by now, but I wouldn't let Mum give it away – it's my BFF's favourite place to study and sketch stuff.

On either side of him are framed photos I've taken and developed: on the left, chipped paint on the steps of the cemetery chapel with the pale curl of a spring vine climbing through the cracks; on the right, a pile of smooth, round stones with grains of sand sticking to their sides and a small crab standing on top, brandishing its claws like it's supreme ruler of the world. Above it, there's a photo of the rusted balcony of the lighthouse with its grimy windows glinting in the sun, and another showing a close-up of the sinewy bark of the redwoods in Muir Woods.

Travis has a look of extreme concentration as he draws on his tissue paper. I like the way the light of the setting sun slants through the curtains and over his face. The shadows spilling down one side are striking, and I fish out my camera again and snap a photo before he can move.

He glances up. "Is that for my fan club website?"

"The Chusetts." I set my camera down on the bed. "Hey, I'm sorry about my mom."

He shrugs. "Family," he says. "Happens to the best of us."

But we both know he's just being nice. His parents

are deeply normal, and he's the oldest of four, including a five-year-old sister whom he adores. They don't have any skeletons in their family closet, as far as I know. *The skeletons in our family closet can dance and sing, apparently.*

I finish another ghost pop and pick up my laptop to find reference images for spooky ghost expressions. When I pull up the browser, I find it's on Isabella's Instagram. It's a good thing Travis is better at maths than he is at subtlety. There are a couple of selfies, a variety of bonfire shots from the summer, and pictures from various school clubs and service activities. She actually has a pretty good eye. And her reposts of baby sloths, fluffy wide-eyed puppies, delicious-looking pizza and tacos, and Jyn Erso score big points.

I come across a selfie that I'd forgotten she took. In it, she's sitting next to Travis and me on a bench, a cool September breeze tossing my hair together with her dark curls. Travis is trying to push in front of me and I'm laughing and shoving him back. Isabella is laughing, too. She captioned it *#NoFilter #NoNewFriends*, which is ironic because we only started hanging out a week before that photo was taken, a sudden friendship that came out of the blue and that Travis and I accepted fairly quickly, despite my wondering why she chose us, of all people.

"You should just set it as your home page," Travis jokes.

"Ha, ha. Very funny." Then I ask, "Hey, why do you think Isabella's been hanging out with us this school year?"

Travis holds out his latest ghost pop to me. His comic book skills are in full effect and I feel bad for the people who will be getting my ghosts instead of his. "*Boo*-yoncé," he clarifies, in case I couldn't tell from his very accurate drawing. He adds it to his pile on a silver serving tray. "I think she's been hanging out with us because we're both interesting people, and she's an interesting person, and I think maybe the two of you would be even more interesting together if you ever get the guts to ask her out already."

I sigh and roll my eyes. "I'm being serious," I say.

"I am, too," he says. "I saw you both making eyes at each other over lunch, even if you think I'm too blind to notice."

I gape at him. "Isabella Richards was *not* making eyes at me."

"Sure, whatever," he says, dashing off another celebrity face and moving on to his next ghost. "But you and I *both* know that Isabella Richards doesn't do anything that isn't on purpose."

"What do you mean?"

"She's been shooting for the Ivy League since she was teething," he says. "That girl has *drive*. She knows what she wants, and she knows there's a lot standing in her way. She doesn't waste time on stuff if she can help it." He gives me a pointed look. "Which means she isn't wasting time on you."

"Or maybe she's not wasting time on *you*," I swipe back.

Now it's time for him to roll his eyes. "Not you, too," he says. He's referring to the fact that when he moved here six years ago, half the school assumed the two of them would end up dating because they're both black.

But what if he's right and Isabella *was* flirting with me?

"You okay, Pops?" Travis asks.

I glance up and see that he looks concerned.

"Yeah," I say, looking at the damage I've done to my ghost, which is spotted all over with uneven circles. "Polka ghost," I explain, as if it's totally on purpose.

"More like measles ghost," he says, and I stick out my tongue at him.

"What I was trying to say," Travis clarifies, "is that I've had a lot of crushes, so I know what one looks like. And to me, it looks like Isabella wants to be more than friends with you."

"Speaking of which, I haven't heard much about your love life lately," I say.

"Don't try to change the subject," Travis says, raising an eyebrow. "That might work on Ms Ahmed, but I know you way too well. We're talking about you – and Isabella – right now."

"Okay, okay," I say. I won't admit it, but secretly I'm glad he's not letting me sidetrack him. Getting his angle on the whole Isabella sitch is the best thing that's happened to me all day.

"Listen, I don't want to pressure you," he continues, "but just know I'm here for you, if you end up asking her out and for some ridiculous reason she says no."

"Thanks," I say. And I mean it.

"You cool?" he asks. It's been a weird day for me, and he's worried.

"Super cool," I say. I'm thankful I have a friend like Travis. He gets me.

The doorbell rings and I startle. "I really don't want to go to this party," I tell him, as if he hasn't heard me whine about it for the past three weeks.

"It'll be good for you." He unfolds himself from the beanbag chair. "It's time."

"We can't go down now!" I protest. "We'll be the sad people who got there too early."

He laughs. "Poppy, it's your house. You can't show up late to your own party. What'll you tell people? Traffic on the stairs?" He grabs his duffel bag and unzips it.

"I know you're not big on costumes," he says, pulling out a black blob. "But you'll be the only one down there without one." He hands me the piece of fabric and it blooms into a slightly crumpled witch's hat with a dramatic curl at the tip. The edge of the brim is a bright red. Next he hands me a small black mask with gold and ruby crystals. "My mom made it for you," he says. "You're an undercover witch. One of her top sellers."

I run my thumb over the intricate pattern of swirls curling out from the eyes of the mask. His mum runs an Etsy shop in her free time, and I know she's super busy around the holidays, so the gesture means even more. "I love it," I say. "It's gorgeous. But my mom will kill me if I wear this. I mean, a *witch*?"

"Live a little," says Travis. "She's throwing a party to celebrate twenty-five years without witches. Show her you're celebrating, too." He takes the hat from me and stuffs it onto my head. "It's *boo*-tiful."

"Ha. Thanks."

"Look, we both know you had words with your mom earlier because you're feeling guilty about Katie overhearing you. But guess what? It happened, and unfortunately time travel hasn't been discovered yet, so you're going to have to live with it. Own it." He hands me a stick that looks whittled by hand. "Keep calm and carry a wand," he says, smirking. "Or, you know, try using it to turn Katie into a frog if things get really desperate. And don't worry. I got your back." He checks his phone, then picks up his duffel bag and goes to change into his secret costume.

I give an exaggerated sigh as he leaves the room, but when I turn to the mirror over my dressing table, I'm smiling. "Thank you!" I call out. "You're the best, Trav!"

I straighten the witch's hat on my head and narrow my eyes. "Let's do this."

BASIC WITCH

I descend the stairs from my room to find the entry hall is already pretty full of guests.

Huey, Dewey and Louie chat with Mary Poppins in one corner while a handful of adults dressed as different presidents are circled up in the adjoining room — I recognise two of the men from my mum's office, so I pin all of them as lawyers. I wouldn't put it past them to be discussing a case, but Mum will put an end to that if she sees it. Parties are for partying, she says. Everything else, I guess, is for work. I even spot Dad talking to Miss Chen. For her costume, she's traded her staple black T-shirt for a white one, which is actually kind of hilarious.

At the bottom of the stairs, I adjust the strap of my camera around my neck. I debated whether to bring it down with me, but it's kind of the best party accessory, because when conversations peter out, you can point at it apologetically and excuse yourself to take pictures in a less awkward location. Or even fake taking pictures until you come up with an escape plan.

Adena Jones and Patsy Roth, two girls from my year, are standing at the treat table near Juan Jimenez, one of Travis's friends. Juan is dressed as a hot young vampire, and the girls are a good and evil ballerina, respectively – one wearing heavy black eye makeup and a black tutu with red accents, and the other wearing a sparkling tiara and white tutu with silver accents.

I walk over. "Hey," I say. "Thanks for coming." I feel a wave of gratitude towards them and the universe that they're the first kids from school at our party. It would be hard to pick an easier crowd.

"Cool mask, Poppy!" says Adena.

"I love your hat!" adds Patsy. "Classic!"

"Thanks!" I say.

"These cookies are awesome," Juan says around a bite.

I laugh. "Yeah, dark chocolate chip cookies are, like, the only things my mom bakes."

Travis comes up behind me with an extra drink, which I accept as I study his secret costume for the first time. A bloody unicorn horn spirals through one shoulder, and his lab coat is carefully scorched along the bottom hem. His coat is also dirtied by splotches of green and purple and yellow, and a very realistic vampire bite drips fake blood down his throat. He's draped a stethoscope around his neck, as well, probably borrowed from his father, who's a Physician Associate.

"Mad scientist?" I ask.

"Mythical creature researcher!" he says proudly. He rips open his coat and all of us cower as if he's about to flash us. Instead, he reveals a black T-shirt with the middle ripped out and a horrible worm monster climbing out of his stomach.

Adena actually screams when she sees it, then laughs nervously at herself.

"I need to feed!" Juan shouts, grabbing Travis by the shoulders and going for the unmarked side of his neck with his mouth. The two of them exaggerate their wrestling, moving into a slow-motion fight that Travis eventually loses. The girls and I exchange smiles.

Out of the corner of my eye, I see Principal Taylor let himself in without ringing the bell, which makes me tense since it means Katie can't be far behind. He shuts the door behind him, though, so maybe she's showing up later with Jenny and the rest of their squad. Principal Taylor is wearing a ship captain's flat cap – a nod, I guess, to the historic lighthouse on Winter Island. My dad says

Principal Taylor spends most of his weekends up at the lighthouse, where he serves as a volunteer mechanic and begrudgingly gives tours. When Principal Taylor spots Miss Chen and my dad, he seems to hesitate for a split second, but then he puts on a tight, forced smile and saunters over to join their conversation. I'm surprised Principal Taylor is here, even if Mum made Dad invite all his colleagues.

"I'm shocked he's not at the lighthouse," I whisper.

"He can't turn down an invite from your mom," says Travis, and I guess he's right. She does a lot for the PTA, including convincing her firm to sponsor school fund-raisers and events. Principal Taylor would've known that an invite from my dad was really an invite from my mum.

"So, who else is coming tonight?" Juan snags a pockmarked ghost lollipop. One of mine. *Oops*. He quickly unwraps it and pops it into his mouth.

"I'm not totally sure," I say, looking away from Principal Taylor. "Hopefully not Katie."

But I know it's just a matter of time before she's here.

"Yeah," says Juan. "I saw her messing with you in English today. What'd you do to draw her ire?"

I'm trying to come up with an excuse that doesn't involve resurrected witches when my mum saves me by sweeping down the stairs. She's wearing a chic black hat over a platinum blonde wig with a long fringe and has a metallic blue lightning bolt painted across one side of her face. Her black dress is short and structured, and her hands are covered by studded fingerless motorcycle gloves.

"Mom?" I ask, shocked. She's not normally a costume person, either, but she's sure one-upped me. "Who are you supposed to be?"

"Gaga, ooh la-la!" she says, striking a pose. When I just stare at her, she hesitates. "Right?"

"You look gaga in the best of ways, Mrs Dennison," says Travis.

"Thank you, Travis," she says warmly. "Have another cookie." She points to the adjoining room, where a few more of my classmates have trickled in without my noticing. Luckily, none of them is Katie. "Poppy, why don't you start a game of charades?" she asks me. "The cards are on the coffee table."

"I dunno," I say, "that sounds—"

"Great!" Juan cuts in, noticing my mum's sharpening look before I do.

I see what Travis means about people not being able to say no to her. Usually it just rolls right off me.

"I thought it'd be fun," she tells me as the others head over to the sofa. "But if it's not *all that*, you don't have to play…"

"I'm sure it'll be a blast, Mom," I tell her.

"Oh! Your aunt Dani called. She's running late."

"As usual," I say with a wry smile.

Mum gives me one right back.

We're both passionate about being punctual, unlike my dad and his sister.

Mum takes my hand. "You look beautiful, by the way," she says.

I'd been so impressed with her costume that I'd forgotten to be self-conscious about my own.

"Yeah?" I say, cringing. "Travis got it for me. You don't think it's too... witchy?"

"It's perfect." Mum gives me a big kiss on the forehead. "Now, go have fun."

I head over to join the rest of my friends, surprised by my mum's reaction. Seeing both her and my dad in costume and unfazed by my witchy appearance, I wonder if maybe they don't dislike Halloween as much as I've always thought.

Travis goes first in charades, crouching into a ball and then climbing out of it, stretching his arms and legs as far as they can go.

"Creepy baby!" shouts Adena.

"Poison ivy!" says Patsy.

"Baby chicken!" says Cory Brody, a tall, heavyset kid who moved here a year ago and now takes chemistry with me. Tonight, he's dressed as a top-hatted magician.

Travis turns and leers at us, waving his hands to encourage more guesses.

"Demon baby under an accelerated growth spell!" yells Patsy.

He breaks character to stare at her. "*Really*, Patsy?"

"No talking," chastises Juan. The timer beeps and Travis plops down on the sofa beside me, frustrated. "Pumpkin!" he says, shaking his head.

"How was that a *pumpkin*?" asks Juan.

"I think the real question is, how *wasn't* that a pumpkin?" says Travis.

The door opens and Katie and Jenny and the rest of their football friends come in as one big swarm. All six girls are dressed as zombie football players, which isn't terribly creative.

A knot forms in my stomach. I tell Travis I'm going to get another drink, even though my cup is still full.

He gives me a worried look, but I put on my best smile and slip past the long staircase and into the kitchen.

I'm surprised to find Isabella here. *When did she arrive?* She's still in her Athena costume, the shield now strapped to her messenger bag. I'm even more surprised to find my mum here – and I'm mortified when I hear what she's saying:

"I don't know about the spirit board. I know it's a board game and all, but it's a blood moon tonight, which could amplify magic and psychic connections. Maybe just play charades instead?" She sounds very concerned and disappointed and mum-like.

"Duly noted, Mrs Dennison. I just thought it'd be a festive game we could all play."

My eyes land on a flimsy black-and-white cardboard box sitting on the counter between them, with the words SUMMON SPIRITS FROM BEYOND THE GRAVE emblazoned across the front in a dripping purple slime font. It's a cheesy spirit board. Isabella must've brought it as a fun Halloween-themed gag for the party, but Mum doesn't find the idea very fun at all, judging by the sceptical look she's giving it.

"I'm not your mother," she tells Isabella, "and I won't tell you what to do, but I just want you to know that it could be very dangerous to tempt the spirits, even if it's through a cheap board game. Especially tonight."

I feel a wave of nausea so strong and sudden that I have to summon every bit of restraint I have not to unleash at least a few Halloweens' worth of pent-up irritation on my mum. For believing such wild things. For dragging me into it – for dragging my friends into it. Of all the Halloween parties in all of Salem, Sanderson-sister superstition walks into mine and does one hell of a number on my already abysmal chances with the most interesting girl in school.

"Isabella," I say loudly, snapping my mouth into a smile. "I'm glad you could come."

They both turn to me.

Isabella recovers quickly, grinning and coming over to give me a hug hello as I try not to spill my drink on either of us.

A warm, happy feeling pools in my stomach.

"You look *amazing*, Poppy," she says, stepping back. "I love your costume."

Over her shoulder, I give Mum my best *We talked about scaring people off* face.

She shakes her head, displeased, picks up her drink, and heads back into the party.

"Sorry about that," I tell Isabella. "She's superstitious. You know. Her story."

"No, *I'm* sorry," she says. "I didn't mean to upset her with my spirit board. Honestly, I thought it'd just be a fun group game, but she caught me at the door and pulled me in here. I totally should have been more sensitive. I wasn't thinking." Isabella hesitates for a moment, worrying her bottom lip between her teeth. "Sorry, I really messed that up," she laments. "Not exactly the first impression I wanted to make on your mom. She totally hates me now."

"She doesn't hate you. And it's okay. She's just extra jumpy tonight because it's a—"

"Blood moon?" asks Isabella, an amused and understanding lilt in her voice. She smiles. "Yeah. I got that."

"But if we were ever to test the merits of a dollar-store spirit board, tonight's the night, right?" I say. I realise just how badly I must want to get out of this party if I'm playing into the Sanderson legend. "But we can't open that box here. Field trip? Sanderson house?"

She looks at me with wide eyes. "Really?"

"Yeah!" I exclaim. I can't believe I'm saying this – because my parents have always been so strict about the Sanderson house being forbidden – but Isabella looks so excited that in this moment, I really don't care. She's clearly interested in the Sandersons, and I've never been to the Sanderson house. Why not tonight?

I glance back through the open kitchen door into the main part of my own house and spot Katie breezing around the room as if *she's* the hostess of the party. She gives one startled classmate a hug, then takes another by the arm and whispers something in his ear. As she finishes, she looks over at me and smirks. His eyes follow hers. She does this again and again, and each time I feel my willpower draining through my pores and puddling around my boots. "Beats staying here and hanging out with Katie Taylor," I add.

I look back at Isabella, who looks from me to the weathered spirit board box. We've hung out plenty, but rarely when Travis isn't around. Now, alone here with her, the energy feels next-level. It's like there's something crackling between us.

"Ditching *is* pretty much at the top of the list of things I'd like to do right now," she confesses. "Plus, Sanderson house on Halloween? Poppy, you're a genius!"

"Great! Let me go get a jacket." I put a hand on the light, delicate fabric of her Greek-goddess sleeve.

"I'll come, too," Isabella says. "Just in case you need backup."

"Thanks," I say.

I feel like the worst is over. At least I hope it is.

But as we walk back into the party room, I bump straight into Katie, nearly spilling my drink all over her.

She steps back from the open kitchen door and smirks at me.

Did Katie just hear everything we said about going to the Sanderson house?

I'm kicking myself for not being more careful, but

I tell myself I'm just getting paranoid and push the concern away.

As we pass Travis and his friends, he looks from me to Katie, who's moved to the centre of the room with her zombie football squad. She keeps laughing just loud enough and glancing my way so that I know she's trying to draw my attention.

"Ugh. Why is she so awful?" I ask Travis.

"You've been *Taylored*," he says in a low voice. "She always picks out one person to make miserable."

"Have *you* ever been Taylored?" I glance from him to Isabella and back.

"I haven't," he says, "but Juan was last spring because he rejected one of her defensive midfielders, poor guy."

"Maybe her dad told her it was time to continue the family legacy of bullying," I joke.

"Yeah," Travis muses. "We *are* creeping up on graduation."

The thought of graduating soon both excites and terrifies me.

"Poppy, you ready to go?" Isabella asks me. "I feel like we've reached peak Taylor."

"Where are we going?" asks Travis.

Well. So much for being alone with her.

"The Sanderson house," says Isabella matter-of-factly.

"I have the spirit board." She winks at me, and my insides flutter.

"Your mom will be *so* pissed," Travis whispers to me with a smile.

Katie lets out a high-pitched shriek of laughter, then glances in my direction and away.

My drink spills over my wrist and I look down, shocked to find that I've crushed my cup without realising it.

"Okay, point taken. Let's go," says Travis, extracting the paper cup from my hand as I scramble for napkins to dry the floor.

Juan gallantly mops the last of my drink from my arm with the edge of his cloak.

We all look up when Katie walks towards us, her squad gathered around her in a defensive formation. *Is that a football thing?* I ignore her and tell myself she's going to breeze past – but then she actually stops short of me. Out of the corner of my eye, I see Juan take a step back, like he's afraid of being Taylored a second time.

"I see you're a basic *witch*," Katie tells me. "Cute." But her tone of voice suggests she's actually over it.

I eye her football kit. "And you're… offensive?" I ask.

"Nice one, Pops!" I hear Travis whisper.

"I'm a fullback from the dead," Katie says, deadpan.

Behind me, Isabella actually cracks up.

Katie shoots her a disdainful look, then turns back to me. "I'm surprised you're not hiding from the Sanderson sisters. I hear they're back, and they're hungry for Dennison blood."

Her friends giggle at her joke.

"What are you talking about, Katie?" Juan asks. He's trying to protect me by calling her bluff, not realising that this opening is exactly what she's been waiting for.

"Oh, Poppy hasn't told you? Her family believes in witches and zombies – like, they legit think they brought the Sanderson sisters back from the dead twenty-five years ago."

Her friends erupt into hyena laughter.

Jenny gives Katie a high five. "Score."

I feel my face go scarlet. "Stop," I say, but it comes out in a hoarse whisper. I look around to make sure my mum and dad are nowhere in earshot. Luckily, they're off in the corner by the crackling fireplace, hand in hand and giving each other their classic love eyes and a kiss.

Still no sign of Aunt Dani.

"If you think her family's so nuts, why are you here?" Travis asks Katie.

"To live-stream the freak show, of course," says Katie, waving her phone. "My fans love it. Standards for entertainment in Salem are low."

"Hey—" starts Isabella, stepping between Katie and me.

"Is something the matter here?" The clipped voice belongs to none other than Principal Taylor, whom I'm surprised to see standing behind me. He looks me in the eyes, and I see some expression flicker over his face when he no doubt notices the intense expression etched on mine, but I can't figure out what he's thinking. He tells Katie to get herself a drink.

"No, thanks," she says. The venom hasn't left her voice. "Besides, I was just catching up with Bella." She fakes a nicey-nice smile.

"*Isa*bella," she corrects, shaking her head. Her eyes are sharp and clouded, like there's a storm raging behind them. It's a look I haven't seen from Isabella before – like a warning siren in glare form. "And we're not tight, Katie."

For a second, I actually think I see Katie wince. She stares back at Isabella like she wants to say something to set the record straight.

My gaze flickers between the two of them. *Bella*, Katie called her. That's… new.

Katie rolls her eyes. "Sure," she replies to her dad. "Whatever you say." She turns, and her squad parts behind her to let her lead them to the other side of the living room.

Principal Taylor stays put. He studies my face for another second – a long dark stare that's full of what I can only guess is hate. *Seriously, what's his deal? What have I ever done to him?* He turns suddenly on his heel and practically glides out of my house. Those standing closest to the door look over but quickly turn back to their conversations.

"Let's get out of here," I whisper to my friends.

"Yes, let's," seconds Travis.

I look over at Juan and my other classmates, who are watching me with concern. But are they worried because of the way Katie treated me or because of what she said? Do they all think I'm some loser now, and that I think witches are real, too, like my family?

Isabella leads us back to the kitchen, then holds up her spirit board box. "Sanderson house?"

Travis adjusts his stethoscope uncomfortably. I can tell he wants to get me out of here before I start screaming at Katie, but I also know my parents have his parents on speed dial, and their combined wrath will not be pretty if we're caught sneaking out of a seemingly innocent party to trespass on private property.

I glance through the open kitchen door at Katie, who's whispering to Jenny.

Jeez. Give it a break.

"Sure," I reply to Isabella. "The keys are in my mom's room. Give me a minute."

I climb the stairs and slip into my parents' room, using just my phone's torch to avoid tripping on the rug at the foot of their bed. My mum keeps the two keys – one for the Sanderson gate and one for the Sanderson house – in the bottom drawer of her jewellery box, which sits on the polished top of the dressing table alongside some framed pictures.

There's a photo of their wedding, which took place a few years after they both graduated from college and moved back to Salem. There's one of me as a baby, draped in a lopsided baby blanket that my aunt Dani made out of red and yellow yarn. It was the first and last thing she ever crocheted. There's also a framed photo of my mum and dad and Aunt Dani at Halloween, back when my parents were about my age.

I pull out the jewellery box drawer and fish for the old silver keys, which are clipped to a leather key ring. They're next to my mum's favourite necklace, which she wore the night she and my dad had their first kiss. The night they woke the Sanderson sisters and sent them back to the grave. *Allegedly.* My fingers slip over the big pearls of the necklace and the Victorian-style cameo pendant. She wore it on their wedding day, too. How can they dislike the Sandersons and Halloween so much if it brought them together? How can my mum be so afraid of all those things if she doesn't mind keeping this necklace around to remind herself of them? They didn't seem to dislike Halloween or costumes or the idea of magic in this photo. In fact, they look so happy to be alive and together on this holiday. Maybe it's just me. Maybe *I'm* the only reason they've held back on the pumpkins and cauldrons and dancing skeletons all these years.

I know I should head back downstairs before I get caught, but instead I pick up the photo and hold my phone's torch a little closer to the glass. Dani was eight or nine then, and in the photo she's wearing a blue empire line dress with cap sleeves. My dad is in full Peter Pan attire, complete with green tights and feathered felt cap. My mum, who has her hair in a ballerina bun, is wearing a short green dress with fairy wings. In the picture, my dad's on one knee with Dani balanced on his propped-up leg, and my mum's crouching down to get in the frame. Her left arm is draped over my dad's shoulders, and her right crosses his chest, holding him tight. She's beaming at the camera, but he's only got eyes for her.

I believe in fairy tales about as much as I believe in witches, but I've always wanted someone who would look at me the way my dad looks at my mum in that picture. The way he still looks at her, when they think

I'm ignoring them. I think about Travis teasing me about Isabella making eyes at me today at lunch. Sometimes I don't know if I'll ever find someone who makes me as happy as my parents make each other, and the idea of that makes me so sad, like feeling a loss without knowing exactly what I'm missing.

I put the photo back on my mum's dressing table, just where I found it, make sure I've shut her jewellery box without disturbing anything, and slip back into the dark hallway and down the stairs, but not before grabbing Mum's bright red vintage coat off a hanger.

So what if we're going to the Sanderson house during a blood moon? Magic isn't real. And besides, we'll be back before anyone even knows we're gone. Not a lot could go wrong, but a lot could go right. And then, who knows what'll happen?

I kind of can't wait to find out.

CALLING ALL SPIRITS

I shrug on Mum's coat against the chill of the October air and step outside and away from the party, the hum of conversation following me onto the back porch.

Travis and Isabella are waiting for me there, where the kitchen light reflects on the white-painted railing, making the posts look like ribs surrounding my parents' colonial-style house.

"Let me get this right. You want to talk to spirits?" Travis is saying to Isabella.

"Ten bucks says they're friendlier than Katie," she replies with a laugh.

Travis, who made a grab bag of cookies, popcorn and chocolates, is snacking and leaning against my dad's grill, his white lab coat protected from soot by the grill's cover. Isabella has pulled on a white peacoat and her messenger bag over her Athena costume (minus the shield), and Travis has tied a striped scarf around his neck, obscuring his outfit's stethoscope. The bloody plastic unicorn horn seemingly stuck through his shoulder makes me smile. He may have gone as a magical creature researcher for Halloween, but in real life, Travis prefers his science with more physics and less of a pulse.

Isabella's standing a few feet away from him, down in the garden, neck craned as she stares at the moon – the blood moon – which hangs in the sky above the trees as full and heavy as a ripening peach. The light reflects off the gold circlet of her costume and washes over her upturned face. Something about her expression is eager and hopeful, like she isn't Isabella Richards, with the weight of constant pressure sitting heavily on her shoulders, but just a girl staring wide-eyed into the face of a grand adventure.

Travis turns to me. "Pops, we thought you'd never come," he says through a mouthful of sweets.

"I was gone for literally a minute." I pull my pointed witch's hat back on, though I've left the mask and wand Travis gave me inside my house along with Isabella's shield. I know I was supposed to be an undercover witch, but I guess I'll have to be an out-and-proud witch for this expedition. I loop the strap of my heavy camera back around my neck. It's a clear night for photographs, so if I get busted, at least I'll have some good photos of this blood moon. I walk down the wooden steps to join my friends, and Isabella turns to me as I spin the leather key ring around one finger.

"I got the keys," I say.

"I *can't* believe we're doing this," says Isabella, as if she's never broken a rule in her life.

Travis shrugs. "Believe it."

Isabella grins and tucks her spirit board box under her right arm. There's a giddiness in the way she carries herself. Her eyes are bright and glinting. She seems excited to check out the Sanderson house, and honestly, so am I, even if I know my parents might kill me.

Fighting my instinct to stay put, I say, "Let's go then!"

We circle my house, slip out through the garden gate, and hurry down the street, the sounds of laughter and music from Mum's party growing more distant.

Trick-or-treaters swarm Salem with sugar-crazed faces and bags full of loot. A princess waves at us. Her dad, who's dressed like a pea, throws in a good-natured nod. Buzz Lightyear and Woody aren't far behind them, their Green Army Men buckets heavy enough that they each have to use both hands to hold them. They catch up to their dad, showing off their bounty of sweets. Two kids – a boy and a girl dressed as peanut butter and jelly – shove past us rolling a red wheelbarrow full of sweets.

I pull my phone from my coat pocket. "Isn't it almost ten?" I ask my friends.

Travis nods to an adorable gaggle of kids dressed as Snow White's Seven Dwarfs. "Kids in Salem go *hard*," he jokes.

"Will you two hurry up?" Isabella calls playfully over her shoulder.

We quicken our pace. "Travis, why am I suddenly freaking out?" I whisper to him.

"Because you're doing the one thing your parents don't want you doing," he points out.

"Right. Thanks," I hiss. "Now I feel *much* better!"

We near Old Burial Hill, where the streetlights are further and further apart and the gardens are large and overgrown.

"You don't think we're going to actually *find* anything there, do you?" Travis asks me.

"Definitely not," I say. "But if getting into that rotting building twenty-five years ago catalysed the world's most bizarre love story for my parents, maybe there's something to a healthy dose of Halloween hijinks," I add in a whisper.

Ten paces ahead, Isabella stops and points at the graveyard in front of us. "Creepy, right?"

"Are we even going the right way?" Travis asks, looking around.

"The Sanderson house is just on the other side of the graveyard. Let's cut through it," I suggest. "Unless you're both too chicken?"

Isabella turns around and smiles at me. "Gumption. I like it."

"Oh, gum? I'd like a piece, please!" says Travis.

Isabella and I shake our heads, and we all stride forward arm in arm.

At the top of the hill, tucked into the woods, there's a dusty little chapel that no one ever uses. There's not much to it – just four stone walls, a handful of pews and some miraculously intact windows – but I've found myself going there more and more as graduation looms closer. There's a profound sense of calm that comes with sitting among the rows of dusty candles, the sun slanting through cobwebbed windows. Gloomy though it may be, there are few places in Salem better for being left alone than the cemetery, and with the solitude beyond that aging wrought-iron gate with OLD BURIAL HILL emblazoned atop it comes a certain amount of peace and security, even now.

"So 'Bella', huh?" Travis puts words to a question that's been nagging at me, too.

We leave the graveyard gate behind and start up the hill. There isn't a path, so we have to unlink our arms and pick our way around the headstones, which run the gamut from barely visible to morbidly ostentatious.

"Katie Taylor isn't as good at anything as she is at pushing buttons," Isabella grumbles, annoyed.

I glance at Travis, but he shrugs.

We both know Isabella's ignoring the actual question. Did the sweetest and most popular girl at Jacob Bailey High used to be friends with its most vicious bully? I think I'd remember something like that, but maybe it was supposed to be a secret.

If it's true, maybe it's too hard for Isabella to admit. She saw how awful Katie was to me today. Maybe Isabella doesn't want me to think less of her for their one-time secret friendship.

"I can't believe I let Katie get to me." I pass a towering tombstone engraved with willow branches, and for a moment, it blocks out the moon.

"*I* can," says Travis. "You care *way* too much about what other people think."

"I know," I tell him. It's a critique I've heard before – including from him. "But it's not like I can just… turn it off."

"It's a curse," Isabella chimes in. "But that's also a

good thing, in a way. It means you're a person who cares about things."

I look gratefully at her, the spirit board box still clenched under her right arm. She manoeuvres expertly around gravestones and overgrown swells of grass as if she's done it a hundred times before. She even evades an unmarked stubby headstone that I trip over a moment later.

"It's not a curse," says Travis. "It's a choice. As my mom would say, you *decide* not to pay any mind."

"Yeah, well." Isabella breathes heavily from the incline. "My mom would say you need to take them to court."

Travis laughs but shakes his head.

The chapel appears on the rise ahead of us. Its small bell tower peeks above the tree line.

"You know" – Travis pops a handful of sweets into his mouth – "when my family first moved here, I read that the bells in the chapel toll on their own each Halloween night."

Isabella glances at me, her eyebrows raised. "Poppy?"

"What, now I'm the resident expert in everything supernatural?" I slowly narrow my eyes and my mouth sets into a long straight line.

"Pretty much," says Travis.

"Well, I've never heard it ring," I say.

"It's supposed to *wake the spirits*," Travis adds, "and let them *regain their bodies*."

An owl hoots loudly nearby, and all three of us jump.

I clutch the silver keys more tightly in my hand, and then Travis and I laugh nervously.

Isabella turns her head around so wildly looking for the source of the noise that I fear it will do a complete three-sixty spin. "This was a bad idea," she says. "We should turn back."

But I press onward. "Come on, we're almost there!"

From the trees comes a series of sharp snapping noises, like bone-dry branches being broken for firewood.

I grab Travis's arm. "What was *that*?" I point with the key ring to the trees.

"A rabbit?" he says. "Or maybe a fox? Pedestrian by magical-creature-expert standards." He straightens his lab coat, showing off its brightly coloured mystery stains in the thin light of the moon.

I take a deep breath, then smile reassuringly at a frozen Isabella. "Come on, guys!" I say, hurrying forward into a grassy clearing while they follow right behind me. "No rest for the wicked." I'm thankful we left the claustrophobia and bad vibe of the house party, despite whatever we're about to do. "Once we get to the

Sanderson house," I say, "we can use the spirit board to—"

Before I can finish, something grabs my ankle.

I shriek, tumbling forward, and crash into Travis, whose body softens my fall.

"Sorry!" I'm careful to protect my camera as I roll off him.

He grunts and sits up, rubbing the shoulder that has the bloody plastic unicorn horn in it.

"Are you guys okay?" Isabella asks us.

"Yeah," Travis manages, though he sounds as if the horn actually stabbed him.

"Poppy, what about you?" asks Isabella.

I check my lens. Luckily, it's undamaged. I feel stupid for bringing it. "I'm okay."

"How'd you even trip?" asks Travis, standing.

Someone grabbed me, I think.

But I know that's impossible – there's no one around but us.

"On a tree root," I say as Isabella helps me up. I notice there *are* no tree roots nearby. My confidence wavers. "Er… a rock?" But I don't see any of those, either. It's quiet again.

I realise my hands are empty. "Crap! I dropped the keys." I pull out my phone, which is fortunately also not broken, and turn on the torch app, sweeping the beam over the grass. I take a few steps back and look in the other direction, in case the keys bounced when they hit the ground. "They're not here," I say, running my hands through thick tufts of grass.

Travis cleans his glasses on his lab coat before slipping them back on. The bold green frames seem to glow a little in the moonlight. "That's impossible. They can't have gone far," he says, turning on the torch on his phone, too.

"Well, I guess this means we should go back," Isabella says, her phone's torch app also turning up nothing. "The party's going to wrap up soon, and your mom and dad are going to realise you're missing. And if they call *your* parents, Travis, you'll be grounded until Cyber Monday."

"We're almost there, though!" I say, shining my phone into the darkness ahead. The chapel is off to our left, shrouded in crooked trees, which means the cemetery's back fence and rear access gate are just a few feet away.

"But no keys," Isabella says, seeming glad to have a solid excuse to turn back.

"My family's story aside, the house is a Salem landmark. Everyone's tried to get inside at one point," I say, feeling the desperation rising in my voice. I refuse to give up on this plan. "Anyway, the place is over three hundred years old. I'm sure we can get in without the keys."

"Isn't that breaking and entering?" Isabella asks, concerned.

"Luckily, both my mom and your mom are pretty good lawyers," I say. "Plus, my parents practically own the property. Well, my nana used to run it, anyway."

Isabella and Travis size me up.

"I'm pretty sure *my* parents broke in!" I point out. "Well, maybe they used my mom's keys. But it's pretty much the same thing. So if they find out, they can't possibly be mad at me."

"Touché," says Travis.

Isabella sighs and shrugs. "Fine."

We let ourselves out of the cemetery and hurry across the deserted, cracked black asphalt overgrown with weeds. No one ever really drives this part of Cemetery Loop. The graves here are so old and their inhabitants so long dead that no one's alive to remember them, much less go to the trouble to visit or leave flowers. The streetlights seem to reflect that, too: they're low and dim and barely give enough light to illuminate the street, let alone anything beyond it. Ahead of us is the tall wrought-iron fence that runs along the pavement between the street and the decrepit Sanderson property. The black iron spikes rise out of a low, crumbling rock wall, which seems to shrink back from the streetlights as if it's trying not to be seen.

I run my fingertips along the stone. "They say the sisters' victims were buried in these walls, *brick by brick*."

"Delightful," Isabella mutters. "You know, I kind of like this Halloween historian side of you."

"So, they were witches *and* bricklayers? Triple threats!" says Travis. "Well, sort of."

Isabella turns to him. "It's not as cute when you do it."

We reach the gate, which is fairly plain – just a big arch with wrought-iron double doors. It's locked, as expected.

"Come on." I take Isabella's boxed-up spirit board from her and slide it through the bars, then hoist myself onto the stone wall. "We can climb over."

"*Is* that something we can do?" Isabella asks.

I land with a huff and an ungraceful thud on the Sanderson side of the fence, then pick up the spirit board box. Travis joins me. Isabella hops the low stone wall and lands beside us, delighted.

Somehow, it's far darker on this side. The only sound is the rustle of dried leaves, and I get this heavy, oppressive sense that we're being watched. Probably by security cameras put up around the premises. Not by ghosts or supernatural things. No, sir, no way.

Because that's just a bunch of hocus-pocus.

I've never set foot in the Sanderson house before; I'm

not allowed. I've only heard about it from Mum, Dad and Aunt Dani, the building described through the lenses of their memories. Seeing it in person, and so close, sends a chill down my spine, but I tell myself that my goose bumps are linked to the thought of getting caught at the house. It's a squat old cottage with a sagging roof and broken, grimy latticed windows, and there's an ivy-covered waterwheel on the side that looks like it'll never spin again. The front door of the house is framed by windows that look out onto a porch with a few rotten wooden steps.

"Oh, look. Gallows in the front garden. How quaint," Travis jokes.

We make it to the front porch without further complications, but Travis's attempt to break in with one of his fake scalpels ends with the plastic blade breaking clean off in the lock.

Travis turns to us with his hands out. "No such *lock*."

"Ha, ha," I say flatly.

"Hold up." Isabella vanishes around the side of the house.

I turn to Travis. "This'll be fun. Beats my mom's party."

"You're just thrilled to be breaking rules with Isabella Richards," he whispers.

"So?" I retort, elbowing him. "Shut it."

"She can be your Isa-*bae*-lla," he sings softly with a wink. I know Travis is trying his hand at matchmaker, but he's been insufferable ever since I told him about my crush on Isabella, and I could *so* throttle him right now.

The moon, mostly obscured by leaves from the canopy of trees, peers down at us curiously.

There's a loud thump from inside the house, and both Travis and I go dead silent.

"What was that?" I whisper.

Then the deadbolt thuds and the door creaks open.

I can hear my pulse thundering in my ears.

The door opens wide enough to let moonlight in, revealing Isabella, who's grinning at us like she's just discovered Atlantis all on her own.

"I climbed the waterwheel," she explains matter-of-factly before ushering us inside the musty-smelling house.

"Now we're going *Raiders of the Lost Ark* up in here," murmurs Travis. "Nice."

I follow him into the house. It's smaller than I expected. The walls seem to press in on one another, and the sheer quantity of furniture inside doesn't help.

I shine my phone's torch around at the various tables, chairs and cabinets. "I think the Sandersons were hoarders," I whisper.

"Light switch over here," Isabella says, flicking it up

and down a couple of times. Nothing happens. "Buuut it doesn't work."

Together, our three phones' sweeping torches give the house's only room an eerie glow. The postcards and gift-shop items have been dumped into boxes behind the counter – silver lighters and small stuffed black cats with witches' hats. There's another big cardboard box by a curio cabinet that's taller than Travis. I peer in and see a mess of broken glass and weird objects – feathers and desiccated herbs and spindly bones and a handful of things that I hope aren't body parts. Everything is covered in dust.

I hold my phone overhead. In the narrow loft over the living space, I can just make out a few straw pallets wrapped in rough sheets. I point to it. "My mom said the Sanderson sisters used to sleep up there," I say.

Isabella stares up at the loft. "I can't believe I'm here," she breathes. She wanders over to a wrought-iron candlestick as tall as her chest. She touches the curved top of it. "This is where the Black Flame Candle was," she says. She looks around again. "The Sandersons lived here," she adds, as if she truly can't believe it. And I can't blame her; I can't quite believe it all, either.

"Being here definitely makes my family's story feel a little more... plausible," I say.

I see the cabinet that Aunt Dani probably crouched

behind before the witches first discovered her. There's also an overturned wooden chair that looks like the one Mum described: Emily Binx was killed here, and Aunt Dani was tied up and almost force-fed the witches' evil life force potion. Wow, it feels ridiculous to even think it. I lean over and run my palm down the chair's smooth wooden side. Oddly, the whole house gives me a profound sense of déjà vu.

Nearby, there's a big display case with cracked glass and caution tape to prevent anyone from getting cut. I sense my mum's involvement here. The placard beside the case reads THIS IS THE SPELL BOOK OF WINIFRED SANDERSON, but the slanted platform inside the case is empty.

"You know, my parents are still upset about that spell book going missing," I say.

"Oh, about that—" starts Isabella.

Travis cuts in. "Maybe Principal Taylor found it and can't figure out how to make it work. I hear there's a good spell in there for making people less grumpy. Poor Principal Taylor."

I laugh. "Or Katie's got it locked away, ready for the day she finally decides to bewitch everyone into retweeting her clapbacks." I pass the big cast-iron cauldron in the centre of the room and a pair of skeleton cages dangling from the ceiling, large enough to hold two people each, and wander over to the stand where the Black Flame

Candle used to be, but of course the candle itself is locked in a safe in our attic. My mum checks on it twice a year, just to make sure no one has got their hands on it. I've heard plenty about this particular house of horrors, but confronting it IRL is bone-chilling.

"You guys," says Isabella. She pulls an enormous book out of her messenger bag. "I know I should have told you sooner, but… I have Winifred's spell book."

I freeze. "What? How?"

"I don't know. It showed up in my room on my bed earlier today. I don't know what to do about it. It's legit the spell book. Creepy closed eyeball and all."

Travis takes it from her hand. "Whoa! It weighs a ton!"

How does Isabella have the spell book? This thing's been missing for twenty-five years.

"Let me see that," I breathe.

Travis hands it to me, and I hand him the spirit board box in return.

I inspect the leather cover, with its clumsy stitches that look like scars and silver serpent embellishments. I open it and flip through dusty pages with black and red ink in archaic font, showing spells for all sorts of dark, creepy things. I slam the book shut. It's much easier to doubt my family's story when I'm not staring right at the closed, wrinkled eyelid of the accursed artifact. "Well, *this* changes things," I say.

"So, who wants to cast a spell?" says Isabella jokingly. "Tonight's the night. It's a blood moon. And someone wanted me to have this spell book. So which spell do we choose?"

"Hey, let's ask the witches!" Travis shouts, opening the spirit board box.

"Travis, that was a joke," I say. "Right?" I'm starting to feel uneasy.

Travis takes the book from me and kneels by the cauldron, laying the mass-market spirit board out in front of him with the book open to a random page next to it. The board itself is matte black, with delicate lines curling from the sides in shining gold and silver. Letters and numbers in bold white type dominate the centre of the board. Isabella plops down beside him.

"Pops, do you believe your family's story, or don't you?" Travis sticks out his tongue.

"You know I don't," I say.

"Good. Me neither. Now lighten up. Let's have some fun," says Travis.

I force my eyes down to the spirit board and take a closer look at it, not quite sure how it works. In the middle of the board, the alphabet is printed in two arching lines. The numbers zero through nine are printed in a row below that, and along the bottom of the board are the words GHOUL, BYE. Similarly, HELL YEAH occupies the top left corner of the board and HELL NO takes up the top right corner. Centred between them is HEY, GHOUL, HEY. Not exactly traditional.

"But I still have kind of a bad feeling about—" I start.

Travis clears his throat and places his hands on the planchette. "Hello? Calling all spirits?"

The three of us sit in silence. Isabella glances at me and mouths, *Are you okay?*

I smile and nod. *Totally*, I mouth back.

"Hey," Travis whispers to us. "How are spirits with college applications? Think they can help me get into Stanford?" He looks around the room, as if expecting a spirit to volunteer.

Grinning, Isabella jabs his arm with her elbow. "Knock it off."

"If they can, I call dibs," I say.

Isabella jabs me, too, but I just laugh, and suddenly I'm not so nervous any more.

"That's *genies* for long shots and wish fulfilment, and we're short a lamp," says Isabella, also placing her hands on the planchette.

"Seriously, though," I add, resting my own hand there, too. But as the words leave my mouth, the book's pages flutter in a sudden inexplicable breeze, and the planchette slides to the top of the board and comes to a stop.

HEY, GHOUL, HEY.

THE WITCH IS BACK

No *way* is a ghost actually here in the Sanderson house communicating with us through this five-dollar toy store spirit board.

I snatch my hand away from the cheap plastic planchette, jump up, and pace around the Sanderson house, crossing from the cracked, dusty cauldron to the wrought-iron stand where the Black Flame Candle used to sit before my parents locked away the remaining stub. I don't believe in ghosts and witches like my parents do, but if I did, I'd know that this is exactly how one could get free. I take a deep breath.

Stop freaking out.

"Poppy, you okay?" Isabella sounds genuinely worried for me.

"You're moving it," I say to Travis. "Good one." I take off my basic witch hat and run a hand through my long dirty-blonde hair before putting it back on.

"I'm not," Travis says where he sits. "Cross my heart and hope to..." He isn't even looking at the board when the planchette slides on its own down to GHOUL, BYE.

Isabella and Travis glance down to where it settled. Isabella inhales sharply and takes her hand slowly off the board. Travis's eyes go wide, and he yanks his hand away from the board, too, and peers around the empty house.

"It's not us," Isabella says to me.

"So, what do we do now?" I ask, my gaze flitting between Travis and Isabella.

Isabella bolts up. "Leave. Obviously. What else would we do?"

I bite my lip and wonder, fleetingly, what it would mean if there *were* a spirit here. What if my parents and Aunt Dani have been telling the truth this whole time? I've spent so many nights staring up at my ceiling, wondering whether my relationship with my family would be less complicated if I knew what actually happened. It's All Hallows' Eve with a blood moon, so if my mum is right – if the blood moon actually *is* amplifying magic tonight – this might be my only chance to find out for sure. What if all my denying and

Halloween-hating has not only kept my parents' story under wraps but also kept me from the truth?

"No," I hear myself say.

Isabella meets my gaze. Her eyes are mesmerising – wide dark pools with long lashes.

"It's just a cheap board game," I say with more confidence than I feel.

Isabella hesitates, trying to read me. "I'm high-key over this ghost stuff," she says, "but if you want to stay, I'll stay."

"Me too," says Travis.

"Cool. We stay," I say. "Let's see what the spirits want." I kneel between my friends on the rough wood floorboards. I'm the first to reach for the planchette, and Travis and Isabella rest their fingers on it, too.

"I'm sorry about that," I say to the board, feeling a little silly talking to thin air. But at least the three of us are in this together. Well, the three of us *plus* the disembodied spirit.

The planchette slides back to HEY, GHOUL, HEY.

I glance at Travis and then at Isabella.

"Who are you?" I ask the board, my gaze locked with Isabella's.

The planchette skims along the board, and I tear my eyes from her to watch it. It points to the letter *M* and then to the letter *E*.

I laugh. "Helpful," I say.

"Great," says Travis. "The ghost is sassy."

Isabella shushes him. "Let Poppy do her thing. You go, Poppy."

"So, how long have you been dead?" I ask casually.

Isabella leans into me and whispers, "Master of ghost small talk. I dig."

I chuckle, but then my fingers seem to chase the planchette, it's moving so fast: three, two, five.

"Three hundred and twenty-five years," Isabella says, tone reverent – like she can't believe this is *actually* happening.

"Or Texas," Travis adds.

I raise an eyebrow at him in question.

"Three-two-five. It's a Texas area code."

Travis is my best friend, which means that I'm afforded the truly priceless gift of never having to laugh at his jokes. "You're right. A Texas area code makes *so* much more sense."

"That means it'd be the year..." Isabella's voice trails off.

"Sixteen ninety-three." Travis can do mental arithmetic faster than anyone I've ever known.

I meet his eyes, then Isabella's. She bites her lip and looks back at the board, studying it like it's a textbook and exams are tomorrow.

"Are you... a Sanderson?" I ask.

The planchette speeds up to the right corner: HELL
NO.

"What's your name?" I ask.

The planchette zips towards the bottom of the board
and back to the top, nudging at the corners. I glance at
Isabella, who's frowning at the board, eyebrows knit in
concentration.

I take a deep breath and repeat my question, louder:
"What's your name?"

I read the letters out as they're selected.

T-E-L-L.

Then the planchette dips out of the alphabet for a
second before diving back in.

Y-O-U.

"'Tell you'?" I repeat. "You want to... tell me
something?"

The planchette shoots to the top left corner: HELL
YEAH.

I swallow hard. "Okay. Go on. I'm listening."

The planchette skitters around the board, stopping
on letters just long enough for me to catch which ones
they are. My heart is racing. Without permission from
my brain, my mouth starts reading the words aloud
faster than I could ever hope to comprehend them.

"'Some inside and some without'," I hear myself say.

"'One believes and one holds doubt. On All Hallows' Eve ere twelve is struck, trade three souls'—"

"Um, Pops," says Isabella, "I think—"

"—'until sunup'," I finish.

"—we should quit while we're ahead," Isabella continues.

There's a pause, and the planchette makes its way to the bottom of the board.

GHOUL, BYE.

I pull my hands back, clasping them in my lap to hide the fact that I can feel them shaking.

Travis and Isabella let go of the planchette, too.

Isabella looks around the Sanderson house as if she's afraid something is about to happen.

"What the *heck* was that?" I ask.

The spell book snaps shut of its own accord, and we all scream. Then the planchette shoots off the spirit board and skitters across the room and under a cabinet. Cobwebs run thick between the bottom of the cabinet and the floor, and the open shelving reveals ancient jars of pickled things – some of which look like children's ears. We stare at the book for a long, tense moment.

"Good thing nothing weird happened," says Travis, a slight tremor in his voice undermining his deadpan tone.

The next thing I hear is Isabella shouting, and then

everything around us flies into the air. Winifred's spell book hovers, opening and glowing green around the edges. I take cover as a chaise longue and the Black Flame Candle holder rocket into the air. The display case for Winifred Sanderson's spell book flies up, as well as a wooden dining table and boxes of crap from the ticket counter. A strong wind whips through the house, swirling the spirit board, witch-hatted black cat plushies and my own witch hat, Sanderson sister postcards, and other debris.

Drawers and cabinets snap open and shut like loud, hungry mouths. An animal lunges at me, and I scream before realising it's a stuffed and mounted squirrel, jaws frozen open in an angry hiss. It bounces off my arm and flies away, back into the whirlwind. Travis and Isabella shout and raise their arms to protect their faces from flying taxidermy. It feels like the room is spinning. The wind tugs at my hair, winding it around and around, the air twisting it in a vortex. My camera flies off from around my neck. I grab the strap, preventing it from soaring away completely. The floorboards jump, making me shriek, and an unnatural lime-green light shines from beneath them, as if someone's run neon bulbs under the house.

"What did we do?" I yell over clattering and crashing.

"I'm going to go with the obvious answer and say we

angered the big dumb evil spirits, Pops!" shouts Travis.

There's a crack of thunder and bright burst of yellow lightning that seems to be coming from *inside* the house. A crash nearby – not from thunder, this time – makes me jump. I peek up to find that the dining table has landed miraculously on its feet beside me. I reach for Isabella and wince from the shock of electricity that passes between our hands. I drag her under the table with me.

"Travis!" I call. "Get over here!"

He scrambles over and joins us. "Don't have to ask *me* twice!"

Then the air goes perfectly still and all is silent for a moment before the airborne debris showers down around us at once. It thumps and patters against the tabletop overhead, including the two skeleton cages, which roll onto the ground where they rock and teeter. The three of us cluster closer together, trying to avoid the falling fragments. The spell book slams shut and lands at our feet, and Isabella quickly snatches it up and hugs it as if to prevent it from opening again.

And then the whole house goes silent once more.

I can hear us all breathing heavily.

"What *was* that?" whimpers Travis, his eyes darting around wildly. He looks at Isabella. "And where the hell did you get that spirit board? Grim Grinning Ghosts and Sons?"

"Hello? Did you not see when the spell book was floating in the air and glowing?" she retorts, waving the book.

"What spell did we just read?" I ask.

Isabella cautiously opens the book and riffles through its pages, then stops. "An *exchange* spell?" she says.

"What's *that*?" Travis asks.

"So let me get this straight – we read a spell from the book? How did the spell from the book…?" I say. My heart is still pounding, partly from the adrenaline and partly because I know this is all my fault. The blood moon. The spell book. The stupid spirit board. I never should've offered to take my friends here and perform a spirit summoning. Ever since I can remember, even when I was just a little girl, I've done everything in my power to make sure no one else heard the story my family told me – the story they swore was true. And now…

Isabella opens her mouth to speak. But she freezes when we hear the wooden slats of the front porch creaking under slow, deliberate footsteps. Isabella shuts the book and presses into my right side, and Travis clings to my left arm. We're all shaking like leaves. I pray it doesn't give us away to whoever, or *what*ever, is about to enter the house. I hear the doorknob rattle and give, and I realise we didn't lock it behind us when we came in. The front door to the Sanderson house creaks open. I take a deep breath, bracing myself. The door continues to swing back on its hinges, eventually bumping into the wall. The figure in the doorframe is towering and backlit, with a bushy crown of fire-red curls haloed by the toasted moonlight. *It can't be. Can it?*

"Try to get into the loft and down the waterwheel," I whisper to my friends.

"I'm not about to die for you," Travis whispers back.

"Shhh!" Isabella hisses. She's gone from terrified to observant.

The figure steps into the house, floorboards thudding beneath heavy shoes. It pauses, looking slowly around as if trying to remember exactly where it left something precious.

Two more sets of feet thunder up the steps, and I scrabble towards Travis, gesturing for him to move.

But it's too late.

Lights spring on.

Travis shrieks, Isabella winces, and I flip over the table to create a barricade.

Dust goes everywhere, including up my nose.

"Poppy, what are you doing?"

I stand up, hacking and spitting. My parents are in the open doorway, Aunt Dani in front of them dressed as the Queen of Hearts with high, drawn-on eyebrows, dramatic blue eyeshadow, a huge red wig and an extravagant dress. Mum's platinum blonde wig looks more frazzled than at the party, but the blue lightning bolt across her right eye and cheek is in perfect glittery condition, and her short, structured black dress didn't rumple at all on the car ride over. Dad, his Hollywood sign headband still snapped over his dark hair, is standing by an open circuit breaker box, which explains why the lights wouldn't work earlier. There must have been a power surge.

I can't believe I thought…

"Oh, thank god," I say, breathing hard and letting out a little laugh. I feel so stupid for thinking my friends and I actually brought back witches from beyond the grave. Then again, I have no idea how to explain what just happened, or how Isabella got the spell book.

Isabella also gets to her feet and hides the spell book behind her back.

Mum crosses her arms over her chest, and when I see the look on her face, I consider ducking back behind the overturned table.

Instead, I clear my throat and turn towards my aunt. "Aunt Dani, this is my friend Isabella. And Travis is hiding behind the table."

Travis and Aunt Dani often riff for hours over

family dinners, but now he sheepishly lifts an arm and gives my aunt a microscopic wave.

I kick Travis.

He only shakes his head. "I told you," he says through clenched teeth, "I'm not about to die for you."

Aunt Dani glances over her shoulder at my parents. Then she reaches up and drags off her Queen of Hearts wig, revealing her fair, honey-coloured hair tied back in a bun. She pulls it down, shaking out the shoulder-length waves. "That thing was giving me a migraine, anyway." She crosses the room to shake Isabella's hand. Isabella's other hand is awkwardly behind her back, hiding the heavy spell book. It occurs to me that this is the weirdest meet-the-family scenario ever.

After Aunt Dani greets Isabella, she leans towards me. I stare into her calm green eyes outlined in smoky makeup, and catch a whiff of vanilla, which tells me she's been frosting cupcakes. That explains why she was so late to my mum's party. She glances at my parents, and in a stage whisper, she says, "They're angrier than they look."

I stare at my aunt, whose brick-red lips are turned up in a secretive smile.

"Is that supposed to make me feel better?" I hiss.

Mum clears her throat and puts her hand on her hip. She looks around the house, then back at me, and shakes her head. "You came here tonight, of all nights…" she begins.

"We—we can explain," I say.

Mum cuts in. "You don't need to explain. I overheard Katie Taylor telling her friends how lame it is that you went to get spooked at the Sanderson house." She pauses. "Not that I think you're lame, but I *am* still upset with you. And just what have you done to this house?"

I look back at my parents, searching for the right words. I really don't know how to explain what happened, but I'm sure there must be some non-supernatural explanation. I'm not about to go down the same paranoid rabbit hole as my family. "There was a windstorm," I say. "But you're here now, and everything seems… fine?" Even I hear my voice go up an octave at the end.

"A *windstorm*? In the Sanderson house?" asks Mum. "On the night of the *blood moon*?"

Travis stands up then, quickly surveying the debris strewn around the room. "Mrs Dennison," he says, "Mr Dennison. I am so sorry – there was a cat and… we were afraid it was lost, and we chased it through the gate without even realising where we were, and…"

It's super obvious he's cobbling his lie together one piece at a time.

"Do you know how surprised we were to end up

in here?" he continues. "I've never personally been so surprised."

Mum looks shaken by the talk of a cat, and she takes Dad's hand. "Poppy, what exactly did you do?" she asks me, studying the wreckage.

I almost wish the green glow beneath the floorboards would return to swallow me whole. "We *may* have found the spell book and tried to summon the dead, but it didn't work," I say. "I'm sure it's just… draughty in here. Or something."

"The spell book!" Mum gasps. "Where is it?"

Isabella pulls it out from behind her back. "Trick or treat?"

"Where did you find it?" Mum whispers, shocked.

Isabella carefully stoops and places it on the floor, then slowly backs away from it, but doesn't offer an answer.

Dad puts his hands on his head. "What were you *thinking*?" he asks me. His voice has that shaky, frustrated tone that tells me Aunt Dani is right: he really is angrier than he looks.

"I guess we weren't?" says Isabella, looking to me for backup.

What do I say? That we came here on Halloween night to prove that their story about the Sanderson sisters and a talking cat isn't remotely true – and, by the way, jury's still out?

"Poppy, haven't we taught you *anything*?" Mum says. "This is the only thing we've ever asked you not to do – and you go behind our backs?" She's angry, but there's also an edge of hurt to her voice. "You put your friends in danger, too. Do you realise that?" She eyes the book and turns to Dad. "Oh, Max, I have a very bad feeling about all of this."

To my right, Isabella shifts uncomfortably, and hot blood rushes to my face.

"Okay, okay," Aunt Dani says, hands on hips. "Max. We didn't exactly heed the warnings about coming up here to flip through books and let virgins light candles. I seem to remember that I was the one overruled twenty-five years ago about coming to this creepy house." She glances at me and says out of the corner of her mouth, "You didn't let anyone light a candle, did you?"

I shake my head ever so slightly, and Aunt Dani lets out a small sigh of relief.

"That's not the point," says Dad.

"That's *exactly* the point, Max," says Aunt Dani, rounding on him. "Tell him, Allison."

Mum cups my cheek in one of her hands, searching my face, and I feel a horrible sinking feeling settle in my stomach.

"I'm sorry," I tell her. "I know we shouldn't have come."

"Oh, Poppy," she says gently. "We're just glad you're all okay. We love you so much and couldn't bear—"

And then Mum's expression turns to one of shock, and she's gone.

And then Aunt Dani is gone.

And Dad, striding across the room, disappears mid-step.

"What—" I start, reaching into the empty air, but my voice catches in my throat.

A pair of disembodied hands with freakishly long nails appears in front of us, gnarled fingers clawing at the air like they're prying open lift doors. The hands struggle to widen the fissure in the invisible veil, and the air seems to part further, a green glow flickering around its edges.

I see an emerald dress with white laces criss-crossing up the front, revealing a narrow length of royal blue silk. I hear an indignant huff, and then the tear opens wider still and a woman squeezes her way through, nearly tripping as she extracts one leg and then the other, her long green skirts getting caught in the narrow opening between worlds. When the woman turns to us, I see that her face is flushed and her mouth is smudged scarlet across her bottom lip and Cupid's bow. Her eyes are crazed and triumphant, and her red hair is a violent cloud above her scalp. The glowing green rip seals shut behind her.

Beside her, from a new vibrant slit, the manicured hands of a second woman grab on to the edges of the air before the tear can seal itself shut. A tall black boot emerges, followed by flowing red-and-purple skirts. Their wearer – a beautiful woman with loose blonde curls – steps out and claps with excitement, jumping from one foot to the other as the shimmering doorway closes.

A third, plumper woman forces her torso through the last flickering green opening. She grins at us with a crooked mouth, then waves at the blonde woman to help drag her fully into our world. Her dark hair is sculpted like a witch's hat over her head, and she's dressed in a rust-coloured bodice with heavy plaid skirts. The brunette clutches at the blonde as she slides through the parted air, and then the space behind her seals with a pop, leaving no hint that it ever existed.

The women look around, grinning. They are wildly impossible and yet somehow perfectly placed, as if they never left this ramshackle house.

My heart stops beating for a moment, and a lump rises in my throat.

This can't be happening. But a larger, more terrified

part of me can't quieten the chorus running through my head. *They're real. They're real, they're real, they're real.*

"What the hell?" I breathe.

But neither Travis nor Isabella has an answer for me. Travis quickly grabs the spell book and hides it behind his back. Luckily, only I seem to have noticed him do so.

My family's story was true.

And now Mum and Dad *and* Aunt Dani are gone.

The redhead takes in Isabella, then me, then Travis, and she moves down the line, her grin growing wider and wider and pushing against the edges of her face.

"We're ba-aaack," Winifred Sanderson sings.

With a swell of sinister delight, the house fills with the sound of the Sanderson sisters' cackling.

The witch is back.

WHIFFLE-WHAFFLE

Winifred, Sarah and Mary Sanderson stand before me, the first beaming, the second preening, and the third licking her lips like she's ready for an early Thanksgiving feast.

Aunt Dani has always been especially descriptive in her retellings of their harrowing Halloween night, and the sisters look exactly as she described – especially Winifred, who seems to tower above the room, wielding her confidence and authority like a weapon. Her cheeks are flushed, maybe from the October cold, and her wild eyes can't seem to settle on a colour as they comb over the three of us. "What have we here?" Winifred croons. "Something… tasty?"

Travis grabs my wrist and tugs, but I can't seem to move. I'm scared out of my mind, but I'm also angry that my family is gone and that these witches are here grinning like they've just won the resurrected witch lottery. Which I guess they kind of have. As my blood pressure builds, I feel a crackle in the air. The hair on the back of my neck prickles. Somehow, the feeling brings me courage. *You must be coming into your powers*, Travis had joked. And yet… *No.*

I don't take my eyes off Winifred. From my parents' stories, I know that she's bound to be the mastermind of it all. "What did you do to my family?" I demand.

"Do?" Winifred repeats in a needling voice. "Why, I've been in Hell, sweet girl – where your family is now."

Hell.

"It's not all it's cracked up to be," Winifred continues. "There's not much to *do* there."

"No doing at all," Sarah says sadly. She prances over to prod Travis's biceps.

He snatches his arm away from her, eyeing the blonde witch suspiciously.

Images of demons with tridents and torches flash through my mind.

What have I *done*? I never thought I was putting my family in danger. I thought that the spirit board and coming here tonight was all just a fun joke, and now… and now my family's in… Hell?

"If there was any *doing*," Winifred continues, "it was you, my dear. We heard your siren call from the other side."

"It was a lovely invitation," agrees Mary with a goofy smile, clasping her hands over her heart. "Sweet girl," she adds, parroting Winifred with a lick of her lips.

Winifred raises both hands and strikes a pose. "So, here we are!" she announces. As her arms drop back to her sides, her words gain a sharp edge: "Now, where's dinner?" She eyes me, and I know it's meant to intimidate, but it barely registers. I'm still stuck on the fact that my reading that stupid spirit board is what catapulted everyone into this hot mess in the first place.

"I didn't mean to bring you b-back. I didn't even know you were real! And now, my family. Are they…?" I pause to take a deep breath. "I didn't mean to read that spell," I say in a voice that I hope makes me sound confident and a bit dangerous. "You *tricked* me!"

"Not *I*," says Winifred. "No. It was my book. Boo-oook! Where are you, my darling?"

"Your book?" I quickly cover. "What book?"

Winifred looks around the house, squinting. "I know my dear sweet book is here. It called upon us with its spell and tricked you into reading it. You've got it, don't you?" She eyes Isabella, then me, and last Travis. "Ah, yes." She grins. "Time I show you *my* favourite trick."

"A trick! A trick! A trick!" says Sarah, clapping gleefully.

"You horrible—"

I don't get to finish my insult before lightning crackles through the whole house, the green-tinged forks of it striking everything in their path. I'm lucky Travis has better reflexes than I do, because the lightning leaves a smouldering black spot on the floor where his feet were seconds ago. I quickly realise my red vintage coat has caught fire and hastily shrug it off.

There's a tremble in the air and all the light bulbs burst at once in small showers of sparks. The few bulbs on a candelabra erupt into eerie flames, leaving us in a murky half-light.

"Here's a trick for you!" I shout, and press the shutter release on my camera.

The flash blazes in Winifred's face, and the witches wince and shield their eyes. Winifred strikes out without seeing, and I use my camera to protect myself.

It goes flying from my hands and lands with a gut-wrenching crash as I push Travis ahead of me, towards the front door, with Isabella racing just steps behind us. I feel awful leaving my family… wherever they are, but we'll have to figure that out when there aren't three evil witches about to fry the hair off our heads.

We're down the path and on the dark deserted street

before I stop to catch my breath. My parents must have had a spare set of Sanderson keys, because the gate is unlocked.

"You okay?" Travis rests a hand on my shoulder. He has the spell book under his arm.

I look at him and freeze. "Isabella!" I shout, surveying the empty street. "Where is she?"

Travis looks around. "She was right here a second ago… Wasn't she?"

I turn back towards the Sanderson house.

The windows crackle with a green-white light.

Then everything goes still.

This is all very, *very* bad.

"She's still inside. We have to go back for her!" I insist.

Travis grabs me by both arms before I can dash back onto the Sanderson property. "If we both get electrocuted, we can't help anyone, including and *especially* your family," he tells me.

Your family.

His words slam into me. Hell, Winifred said. My parents are in Hell. "But Isabella," I say. "We have to help—"

There's a distant cackle and the sound of hurried footsteps.

I pull Travis closer to me, ducking into the bushes at the side of the road.

The sisters spill down the walk and look up and down the road.

"I remember this *wretched* town," Winifred says, stepping into the middle of the street. "Back on earth for a third time," she crows. "What Mother would say if she could see us now."

At that, the three witches step forward together, lifting their faces to the moon. "Mother," they sigh.

"Perhaps she can return, if things go according to plan. But first, we have things to find, sisters."

"The spell book!" shouts Mary.

"The blood moonstone!" chimes in Sarah.

Mary takes another sharp sniff. "I smell children, Winnie," she says, grabbing the arm of the red-haired witch.

"Hush, Mary," says Winifred, brushing her off. "The whole world smells like children. It is Halloween night, and we're in for a treat."

She turns towards town and hurries down the asphalt road. "Keep up, you whiffle-whaffles! We haven't time to waste!"

"Whiffle-whaffle! Whiffle-whaffle!" Sarah crows, hopping back and forth as she bobs her head, clapping her hands gleefully. She stops to beam at Mary. A second later, they both take off after Winifred, gone.

"Come on," I say, tugging Travis back through the

gate. I'm desperate to see if Isabella's okay, and I pray she either stayed hidden or escaped another way.

The creepy candelabra lights are still on inside the house, which makes it look less frightening as we jog up the steps, but once we're through the door, I take a deep breath. I'd known the place would be trashed after that whirlwind, but coming in cold it really doesn't look like anyone could've survived this. Furniture is overturned and broken glass is everywhere. Dried herbs and pickled unknowns are scattered across the floor. Even with all the evidence strewn in front of me, I can't believe that the story is true. It's always been true.

"Isabella?" I call in a low voice, afraid that even though the witches are gone, they'll somehow hear us. I can hear my own heartbeat, loud in my ears. *This can't be happening,* I tell myself. And yet, clearly it is.

"Neon, neptunium, nickel," Travis mutters to himself as he picks over the fallen debris. He was an anxious kid, and his dad taught him to recite the periodic table of elements to deal with stress. "Niobium, nitrogen… Oh, hell no!"

I find he's discovered a shattered jar oozing a green liquid and what looks like tongues.

Across the room there's a whimper and the sound of something scrabbling against wood.

I point to where a tall cabinet is tipped against the wall, its two front legs angled over the floor.

"Are you for real?" Travis hisses. "This is the part of the movie where you peek under a cabinet and a *zombie wolverine jumps out and eats your face off.*"

I ignore him. My ankle boots thud louder on the floor than I'd like, but I try to tread as softly as possible. I lean down to peer beneath the cabinet.

Something barrels out from beneath it, careening towards my face. I shriek and fall over in my rush to back away.

"Zombie wolverine!" Travis shouts. "Zombie wolverine!"

He jumps onto the collapsed chaise longue and we both stare at the escaped animal.

It's a Boston terrier with two pointed black ears and a white streak of fur down the middle of its forehead that runs over its chin and chest. It looks up at him expectantly.

Travis gives me a sheepish smile.

"It's wolverine-*like*," I say charitably.

He exhales loudly and steps back down, then kneels to scoop up the small dog. "Hey, guy," he says, scratching its neck. "What are you doing in here?"

The dog nips his finger, and Travis cries out and drops it, falling back on one hip.

The terrier runs around in a tight circle.

"Oh my gosh, oh my gosh, oh my gosh," says Isabella's voice.

I look around, then back at the dog, confused. Realisation quickly dawns. "No…"

"Unfortunately, yes!" comes Isabella's voice again through the Boston terrier's muzzle. "When I was running out after you, they zapped me! Will I stay this way forever? I mean, I've always joked about how nice it'd be to trade lives with a dog, sleeping all day and living in complete bliss, but it kind of feels like I'm a prisoner in a dog-shaped flesh prison!"

Travis looks at me with wide eyes.

By this point, nothing surprises me.

"Isabella, relax! Oh. Sorry, I didn't mean for that to sound so much like a command," I say.

"You try relaxing after interspecies transformation! I'm a *dog*!" She starts swatting at Travis's leg repeatedly with her paw.

"That's really annoying," he says. "But I guess it could've been worse. Everyone likes dogs, right?"

We both look at Travis.

"Seriously?" I ask. I turn to Isabella. "It'll be okay. We'll get you back to being yourself."

"Please tell me you've got the spell book," Isabella says. Her face is so expressive, even as a dog, that I can almost see the real Isabella staring back at me, chewing on her lip with worry.

"Seriously? Yes, I have the spell book," Travis says, waving it.

She wiggles her stubby tail without answering and whimpers.

"So, um, I think we should get to the graveyard before the Sanderson sisters come back for us," says Travis. "Didn't you say that's hallowed ground, Poppy?"

"What? Yeah. Yes," I say, in a daze.

"Come on, come on, let's go," Isabella says.

"What about my parents?" I ask, but Isabella is bounding through the door.

"Poppy, we're smart. We're capable. We can get them back. Together. Trust me. But first we need to come up with a game plan. Now, come on!" she calls over her shoulder. "Travis is right, we'll be safer in the graveyard."

This night keeps getting weirder and weirder.

Travis and I hurry to keep up.

"Oh, I get it. A Boston terrier. Because we're in Massachusetts. Do you get it?" Travis says to me.

I give him a withering look. "Seriously, not the time."

When we pass through the gate, I spot my parents' dark saloon parked on the street outside the Sanderson house, partially hidden by some overgrown bushes.

Travis is already there, racing around and testing the

handles on each door of the car. "Locked," he says. "They must've had the keys with them when they…" His voice trails off in a way that makes my heart ache even more.

We push on to the graveyard. It's still and silent, just like before, but the tombstones take on a more ominous air with my family missing. When I shut the gate behind us, I realise that my hands are trembling. The full weight of the situation hits me all at once.

"Oh, god," I mutter, running a hand through my hair. "Oh my god, you guys, what am I going to do?" The image of my parents and Aunt Dani, their faces frozen in a moment of shock, dances in front of my eyes, just out of reach. I stop to catch my breath and end up crouching with my head against my bent knees and my hands on the top of my scalp. "Oh my god, what have we done?"

"Poppy, we had no way of knowing that any of this was even real," says Isabella. "It's not your fault. We'll get them back."

I shake my head. "I wanted to come down here and I read that stupid spell that Winifred's spell book fed to us. I should've listened to my parents! They were right! I'm an idiot." I feel a rush of hot blood to my face.

Travis gives me a worried look. "We can still be spotted from the road."

I bite my bottom lip and shake my head, barely

believing any of this. He walks over and helps me back to my feet, and together we follow Isabella deeper into the damp, dark cemetery.

"Why did this happen?" I ask Isabella. "Why did the spell book find you? Why did it work? Do you know something we don't?"

"Last week," she explains, "my parents gave me a DNA test. They thought it would be cool for me to learn more about our ancestors and stuff – our family history as Richardses, that sort of thing. This week, the results came in, and I learned a ton – like, there's a whole line of us in Louisiana who I never knew about. And you can trace my DNA back to both Ghana and Nigeria." She hesitates. "I was surprised to learn that my eighth great-grandmother was born in Salem, but she moved south more than three hundred years ago. And her mom was… Elizabeth Sanderson."

"That's why you asked about her in class," I say, realisation dawning. "That's why the book found you."

Isabella nods. "I think you may be right."

"But why now?" I ask. "You've lived in Salem for years."

Isabella frowns, considering. "No idea," she says. "Your guess is as good as mine."

"So what, you're a witch?" asks Travis.

Isabella plops down and gives her neck a scratch with

her hind leg. "Sorry. Having four legs is exhausting," she says. "Who knows *what* I am? Right now, I'm a dog. But I thought being related to the Sandersons was this cool, kind of interesting thing, you know? Some fun fact I could use as an icebreaker. And I was going to tell you, but I kind of wanted to know more about Elizabeth first, you know, if she was actually a good witch, unlike her sisters."

"Okay, so you're a Sanderson and a witch, maybe. And the Sanderson sisters are back, but I didn't see Elizabeth. And my mum and dad and aunt are in Hell. What was the spell we read exactly?" I say.

Travis crouches low and opens the spell book, and Isabella sticks a paw on the page.

"Here," she says.

"'Swap souls'? What does that even mean?" he says before reading the rest of the page. "It says that, basically, souls of the living are swapped for souls in the beyond."

"This isn't happening," I say, as if saying it can somehow make it true. I turn away from both Travis and Isabella and find my legs carrying me further up the hill. I can see the cemetery chapel from here. It looks even smaller in the dark. The bell is barely visible, the curve of its top throwing off a sliver of moonlight.

"We have to get to higher ground," I call numbly back to Travis and Isabella. "And out of the trees. If the witches find brooms, we can see them coming." That's another lesson I learned from my family: Aunt Dani only got snatched up by Winifred because she wasn't paying attention and didn't see the witch swoop down out of the trees.

I sink onto the chapel's low-slung porch and drop my face into my hands. "What are we going to do?" I feel the fear creeping over me, gaining leverage, crushing the breath from my chest. I inhale deeply and release the air slowly, trying to formulate a plan. But what do you do when your family is in Hell and evil witches are on the loose, hunting you down?

Travis sits down next to me and puts one hand on my knee and his other arm around my shoulders. "It's gonna be okay," he says.

That's when the tears start coming, spilling hot and salty down my face. When I open my mouth to breathe, I taste them on my dry lips.

"My parents," I say. "Aunt Dani."

"I know," he whispers, holding me tighter.

My whole body shakes.

Isabella comes over and places her paws on the toe of my boot. "We're in this together. Poppy, you're one of the smartest and bravest people I know. We got this."

Above us, the church bell begins to clang of its own accord.

I feel Travis and Isabella tense, and I take a deep breath.

Pull it together, Dennison, I think.

The three of us wait for the bell to quieten. At this point, I can't even bring myself to be afraid of it. I replay dropping my camera in the Sanderson house. *That's the least of my worries.*

As the last toll dies, Isabella sits up straighter. "Poppy, it's okay," she says.

"It's *not* okay!" I wipe tears from my face, angry at myself for crying, and angry that I didn't listen to my mum and did something stupid. "My family is in *Hell*. You're a *dog*!"

Travis opens the spell book again and studies the page as Isabella sits down beside him.

"Wait," Isabella says. "There. In the book. It says the spell breaks at sunrise."

I blink at them through stinging eyes. "What?"

"The spell says, 'On All Hallows' Eve ere twelve is struck, trade three souls until sunup.' Once the sun comes up, everything will go back to normal."

I sit up straighter, the lightness of hope rising in my chest at the thought of this nightmare ending at dawn. I never really believed my parents' stories about that weird Halloween night when they saved Salem and fell in love, but I always thought that if it *were* real, I wouldn't have been nearly brave or creative enough to do the things they did, like embarrassing themselves in front of everyone at the Town Hall party or torching the witches in the arts wing. If I have to accept that all this is real, the fact that the spell will break at dawn seems too good to be true. But I say, "Well, that's reassuring."

"And you heard the witches. Not a lot happens in Hell, apparently. Your parents should be safe and sound in the meantime," says Isabella. "Hopefully," she adds in a tentative voice.

"Yeah," says Travis, closing the spell book, "but I don't think those three witches are here for a one-night joyride. Last time they tried to eat kids, Poppy."

"No matter what, we can't let them get the spell book back," I say. "As long as we have the spell book, we have all the Sandersons' spells. And if this spell breaks at sunrise, we only have to keep them distracted for a few more hours before they get sent back to Hell and my family comes back to us." I look at Isabella. "And you're sure about this?"

"I'm sure," says Isabella. "But if you could help me figure out how to not be a dog any more, that'd be cool."

"Of course," I tell her, drying my face.

But another voice – a voice I don't recognise – interrupts our conversation: "It's all not *quite* that simple, I'm afraid."

The three of us turn to our left.

Two figures – a small girl and a much taller boy – are striding around the side of the chapel. They're both pearlescent, their flowy clothes and pale skin emanating warm amber light.

I've never seen them before, but from Mum and Dad's descriptions, I feel like I know them.

"Binx?" I ask, shocked.

Travis stands up next to me, wide-eyed and sputtering, not quite managing to form complete words.

The boy inclines his head. "Hello, Poppy," he says. "I'm guessing your dad's no longer a virgin."

"Gross," I say.

He tosses two keys on a key ring – the keys to the Sanderson gate and house – on the ground.

"We tried to warn you to turn back," he says, "but looks like the hint didn't really *materialise* for you."

SQUAD GHOULS

Thackery Binx's ghost appraises us, some of his floppy hair falling in his eyes, the rest pulled back in a small ponytail.

Emily stands beside him, smiling serenely. "Hello, friends," she says. Nothing's creepier than a child ghost except for two child ghosts, though Thackery, a.k.a. Binx, looks a good five years older than her, at least. Emily's blonde hair is covered by a white cap, and her matching nightdress stops just above her toes. I can see the woods through both of their filmy bodies.

The Sandersons' appearance made it clear that my family's story is true, but meeting Binx and Emily is another thing entirely. I've heard so much about them – especially Binx – that it's like meeting my parents' childhood friends for the first time.

"Ghosts," Travis hisses urgently to me. "Pops, there are *ghosts*."

"You knew there were ghosts," I hiss back. "I've told you the story."

"Yeah, but I didn't believe it!"

"Well, neither did I!" I shake my head, stand up, and take a step closer to Binx and his sister. "How do you know my name?"

"You're a Dennison. You're practically famous in ghost circles. Anyway, when we saw you approaching the house this evening, with the spell book in her bag" – he looks at Isabella – "we had a feeling you took after your dad. Speaking of which, Max, Allison and Dani arrived in Hell not long ago and asked me to keep a close eye on you three. We are able to speak with spirits on either side of the veil, after all."

"My family! Are they okay?" I ask desperately.

Binx nods. "But not for long," he says. "I'm afraid the spell book's logic isn't as straightforward as you say. The spell does not *expire* when the sun rises. It becomes *permanent*."

"*Permanent?*" asks Isabella, surprise and fear in her voice.

"Permanent dogs," Travis says. "Permanent ghosts… It sounds like we're friggin' permanently screwed!"

"Well," says Binx, crouching to get a better look at

Isabella, "aren't you a funny little thing? I guess the Sanderson witches didn't want a wily black cat around any more, so they made you a cute, simple puppy instead."

"I am not simple!" Isabella protests.

"Don't worry," says Binx, patting her on the head. "I was only a cat for three hundred years. It worked itself out. Eventually."

She stares at him, appalled.

"I don't understand," I break in. "*Permanent?* Meaning, my family will never come back?"

"It *will* be permanent," says Binx, "unless you can find the blood moonstone and destroy it in time."

Travis's face lights up. "Blood moonstone! We overheard the witches talking about that!" he says to me. "They said they were going to look for the blood moonstone and their spell book."

"What's a blood moonstone?" I ask.

"It's a magical item hidden in Salem," says Emily serenely. "But no one knows where."

"Great. And we have no clue where the blood moonstone is," says Isabella. "Now we *definitely* can't let them get back their spell book."

I look at Binx and Emily, unable to process what to do next. "Why are you still in the graveyard? My parents said you'd... crossed over that night."

"The veil is a bit permeable," says Binx with a smile, "at least for those of us who are needed."

I crouch and pick up the keys that unlock the Sanderson gate and house, then stand back up. The metal is still cool from Binx's hand, as if the keys have been sitting in the refrigerator. I pocket them. "Are you *sure* my family's okay?" My voice sticks in my throat.

Emily walks over – though her feet never seem to touch the ground – and Travis and Isabella step aside as she kneels in front of me. Her face is small and angelic, the linen cap keeping her hair out of the way. "Wouldst thou like to speak with them?" she asks sweetly.

While I trust Binx and Emily, I'd still like to see my family with my own eyes. Besides, the three of them defeated the Sanderson sisters before. They'll know what to do now. As I realise this, a swell of hope washes over me, warm and comforting. "Yes," I say, leaning towards the ghost girl. "Please."

Emily holds out both her hands, palms up. "Here," she says with a nod.

Travis and Isabella watch me, and Travis nods encouragingly.

I place my hands on Emily's. Her skin feels real and yet not. If I hold still, her hands seem cool and solid, as if carved from wood. But when I move, my own hands seem to slip through hers just slightly, with little resistance. I shiver.

"Do not be afraid," she says with a childish lilt in her voice.

Binx comes and places a hand on her shoulder. At first I think he's going to ask her to get up and leave me alone, but his dark eyes meet mine. "Close your eyes, Poppy Dennison," he says gently.

When I close my eyes, the glow of Emily's face seems to follow me into the dark.

"Clear your mind," Binx murmurs. His voice is serious and soothing.

Yeah, I'll get right on that. I only have to clear a million spinning thoughts.

"Breathe when I breathe, Poppy Dennison," whispers Emily.

I shut my eyes and take a deep breath, trying to follow the movement of Emily based on the rise and fall of her fingers, which seem to press into and through my own.

"Forlorn girl with a family lost," someone says, "seeking them at any cost."

My heartbeat quickens. It doesn't sound like Emily, and I can't tell whether it's coming from the graveyard around me or from inside my own head. I have to fight not to open my eyes and try to find the source of the voice.

"Look for them beyond the veil, past candle dark and shadows pale. Bring them here with spirits bright, then fold them back into the night." Emily squeezes my hands, and somehow I know to open my eyes.

But it isn't Emily kneeling in front of me any longer – it's Aunt Dani.

She's just as colourless and translucent as Emily was, though her hair drifts around her as if there's a soft breeze. She's scrubbed her face, but she's still wearing the costume dress. Washed-out hearts parade down her skirts.

"Hey, kiddo," she says gently.

My eyes well with tears as soon as I hear her voice.

"Aunt Dani," I say quietly.

"I knew you'd find us," she tells me.

An unexpected panic hits me as I realise how closely she resembles Emily and Binx. "You're not *dead*, are you?"

She chuckles. "Please. Those old birds can't get rid of me *that* easily."

"Poppy," comes another voice.

I look up to Binx, but he's been replaced by my dad, who looks just as pale and translucent as Aunt Dani. He's still wearing the Hollywood headband, which makes me laugh, even now.

"No," I breathe, the reality of the situation fully

sinking in. My body feels waterlogged and my mind slow. I can hear my own heart pounding in my ears. "Dad, I'm so sorry. I can't—Oh god, I'm sorry." I take a deep shaking breath, the way my mum taught me to do when I feel stressed. It got her through LSATs and the bar exam, she's always said. The thought of her makes me cry harder. "Where's Mom? Are you sure you're all okay? We're going to get you out of there."

"Your mother went to speak to the manager of this lovely wing of Hell," says Aunt Dani.

"She thinks there should be better ventilation," says Dad.

"She might organise a class-action lawsuit against Satan," says Aunt Dani. "It's unclear."

I laugh again, drying my face with one sleeve.

"How do I bring you home?" I ask.

"By undoing the spell," he says.

"*Thanks*, Dad. Real helpful."

"You and your friends need to send those witches back here before sunrise, okay?" Dani says, nodding. I meet her eyes, which are a ghostly blue. "You've got hours left."

"*Hours?* Great, no pressure," I say with a sigh.

"You're going to be *fine*," adds Aunt Dani.

"But—but what if we can't do it?" I choke out. I can't imagine a life without Aunt Dani dragging me to Home

Depot – or without Dad making popcorn with extra butter just to bribe me into watching some lame old-fashioned music documentary with him, usually one with lots of drumming and saccharine lyrics. "If we can't help you, will you… die?"

"You *can* help us," Aunt Dani says firmly. "And you *will*."

I notice she hasn't answered my question.

"You will," Dad says. "Dani's right."

Aunt Dani throws him a satisfied smirk.

"It took us landing in Hell for you to say that, jerk face?" she asks, grinning.

Dad ignores her and faces me. "You're better equipped for this than I ever was."

"But be careful," Aunt Dani says with a wink. "Blood moon magic and all."

Suddenly, Dad and Aunt Dani look towards the woods.

There's a thin glowing figure coming towards us through the trees. I would recognise that stride, straight and sure, anywhere.

Mum opens her arms as she comes near me, and I spring up and run towards her.

"Mom, I'm so sorry," I tell her.

"I know," she says. "But you don't have to be." Her arms wrap around me, warm and firm. "Though once we get back, you're on dish duty every night for the rest of your life."

I laugh, tucking my face into her hair.

The warmth of her body fades into something cool and permeable.

But when I pull away, I see another woman's face.

I break away and stumble back, frightened.

The strange ghostly woman is Mum's height, but probably twenty years younger. Her hair is black and curly around a narrow face. Her wide brown eyes are framed with long lashes. Her skin glows dark silver, as if the moonlight has worked itself into her pores, and she wears a pale yellow cloak and dress that flow to her bare feet.

"I'm sorry," she says. "You're not supposed to touch us when we're channelling through the veil."

"Who are you?" I ask, panicked. My whole body feels cold, and I can barely remember the way my mum's arms felt around me just a second ago.

"My name is Elizabeth," she says. "I woke up when Emily and Thackery did, but I didn't want to frighten you. I'd like to help you, Poppy Dennison. My sisters can be quite brutal."

"Sisters?" I ask, suddenly afraid. "Wait, you're the ghost of Elizabeth *Sanderson*?"

The youngest Sanderson sister, hanged for being a

witch after bravely ushering her husband and daughter to safety. I take another step back. She might be a ghost, but what if she still has witchy powers, like Winifred's lightning magic? And what if she *is* actually evil?

"Why are you a ghost if your sisters aren't?" cuts in Travis.

I'm suddenly aware of the cemetery, of Travis, Isabella, and Binx and Emily, who have transformed back into themselves, as well.

"When one's purpose is incomplete, work left undone has a way of keeping the dead around to return to serve the living," Elizabeth replies. She looks longingly into the distance. "Perhaps *you're* my purpose."

"Another ghost. A witch ghost," Travis says faintly, for anyone who might be keeping count. "Four Sanderson sisters."

Isabella watches Elizabeth silently.

"Sanderson was my mother's name," Elizabeth says. "And my sisters'. And yes, mine. I kept it as long as I was alive because I wanted to show that a name doesn't define who you are."

My eyes drop to her throat, which is ringed with a dark, angry bruise.

"No," she agrees, "it didn't quite work out."

"Sisters!" Winifred calls in a haughty, piercing voice that's eerie and out of place in the land of the living. "How wonderful it is to be alive again. Once we find the blood moonstone, we'll be alive forever, and we'll bring back Mother and Master and all the greats of the beyond!"

The trio have stolen a push broom, a rake, and of all things, a barely operational leaf blower from a shed at the local park and are now soaring over Salem proper. Or perhaps more accurate, two of them are soaring while Mary sputters along, trying to coax the leaf blower into staying aloft, with limited success. Below them, the town lies dark and quiet, with just a few dotted lights pricking the ground like stars.

"And look at that moon," Winifred adds. "Red as blood and wide as a bowl of kitten-paw soup. Never in my years have I seen something so beautiful. How doth a moon come to look that way, I wonder?"

"Well, actually," says Mary, hanging on for dear life as the leaf blower dips and climbs erratically, "a blood moon occurs when the sun passes behind the moon in an eclipse, and the light of the sun is filtered through—"

"Shut up, you frowzy fopdoodle!" snaps Winifred. "I don't have time for thy dithering." She pulls a hand-size rectangle from her pocket. "I want to know what this box is," she says, sitting up a little straighter to run both of her hands over the smooth surface. The thing suddenly glows with a brilliant white light and Winifred drops it, startled.

Sarah snatches the object from the air and cradles it. "Look!" she says. "It has an apple on the back, with a bite out of it." She nibbles on the corner. "It doesn't taste very good." The face lights up again, and Sarah studies the numbers written there. "It says eleven twenty-four on October thirty-first," she said. "Oooh! It is an almanac, Winnie. Or a clock without hands." She tosses it over her shoulder. "Why carry around something so boring?"

Mary shoots down to catch the thing just before it hits the ground. When she looks up, she sees Winifred charting a straight course over Salem while Sarah loops overhead in a wide corkscrew. Sarah's delighted squeals can be heard from a thousand feet below, where Mary steps lightly off of the leaf blower. She examines the box carefully and, when it lights up again, slides a finger over its screen, per its illuminated instructions.

Mary jumps when the image changes to that of a beach at sunset, the painting mostly obscured by a grid of circles and squares.

"W-Winnie," she calls, rocketing back up towards her sisters. She skims alongside Winifred. "I think it's a memory box. Or—or a spell book. For thy pocket."

Winifred shakes her head. "A spell book for *thy pocket*? Why would one ever want a thing like that?"

"But look!" says Mary, pushing on an image at random.

A new grid appears, this time with a series of images: a slice of bread with something green – cream of moss? – slathered on it and an egg spilling down its side; some young women in short dresses with smiling faces; calm water and a sandy beach with patches of tall dune grass. Each is rendered in precise detail and brilliant colours, and each is unlike anything Mary has ever seen.

She hands the box back to Winifred. "See?" she says. "Didst thou see?"

"A memory box," Winifred repeats thoughtfully, without precisely agreeing. "I wonder, Sister: would it have a memory of where the blood moonstone is?" She presses the painting Mary showed her, and the image expands as if she's leant in to look closer.

Winifred makes an exasperated noise. Frustrated, she begins tapping everywhere until the box chimes.

"How can I help?" asks a woman's voice.

Winifred quirks an intrigued eyebrow at it.

"I'm sorry, I didn't catch that," says the box.

Winifred clears her throat. "Where is the blood moonstone?" she asks slowly and carefully.

The box pauses, then replies, "The Oracle Stone is

located at The Oracle Stone, fourteen-sixteen Central Street, Salem, Massachusetts, zero one nine four four."

"Sisters," Winifred says. She guides her push broom in front of Sarah and Mary and gives each of them a light smack across the face.

Their giddy smiles turn to determined expressions to match hers.

Winifred purses her lips and then grins. "We have someplace to be."

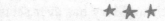

Elizabeth looks down as Emily comes over to tug on the sleeve of her dress.

The witch lifts the girl up and perches her on her hip, even though Emily looks far too big to be held. "Are you okay, my little flitter-mouse?" Elizabeth asks, checking Emily's forehead with the back of her hand. "You were very brave to channel for dear Miss Poppy just now."

Travis clears his throat. "Yeah," he says, "we're in a bit of a rush to figure out a way to send the Sanderson sisters back, so if you could…" He spins his fingers in a wrap-it-up motion.

I elbow him roughly. I assume that manners aren't unique to our spectral plane.

"Yes," Elizabeth says apologetically. "Quite right." She

sets Emily down. "I've come to help you. I only wish we'd found each other sooner tonight. I would have told you that the first rule of witching is not to trust Winifred's spell book." She gives us a commiserating look. "I *also* learned that the hard way. Once my sisters were hanged, I took up the book to try to bring Emily back from the grave, but it only led a hateful mob right to my doorstep."

Emily rests a tiny hand on her arm. "There was nothing you could have done."

Travis hugs the spell book close to him. "Well, don't worry. I'll watch it like a hawk."

"I mean, *I* would, but... dog arms and all," says Isabella. "Thanks, Travis."

"Elizabeth, we have to stop your sisters from doing any more harm, and we have to help Isabella turn back into a human and rescue my family," I tell her.

"I know," Elizabeth says. "There is much to do, and not much time left."

In the pause that follows, every fear I've ever had seems to flash through my mind. Fears of my parents dying, of disappointing them, of never being able to shake that sorrow and guilt.

And the witches doing horrible things to the world, to the town, to me and my friends...

"My sisters are conniving — or at least Winifred is. She'll have already created a plan to complicate matters."

Isabella lets out a high-pitched sigh. "Oh, great. What are we supposed to do now?"

When my eyes land on her, I see that she's lain down and placed her two front paws over her face. No one deserves to be trapped in a dog's body, especially not her.

"Yeah, what if they find the blood moonstone?" Travis asks.

"You must find it first, and I may be able to help you," says Elizabeth. "For you see, my mother gave it to me when I married: a moonstone the size of a chicken egg that had been passed through the Sanderson line for centuries. It was always given by a mother to the daughter she believed would use it most responsibly, for that moonstone has two abilities: first, if boiled in a pot of river water and herbs, it makes a broth that will grant eternal life. Second, if the stone is broken, so too is every spell cast by a Sanderson."

I glance over at Travis and his expression says, *Yeah, that's pertinent information to know.*

Then I turn to Isabella.

She's perked up – even her ears seem taller. "*Every* spell?" she asks Elizabeth.

"Any of them still in force," says Elizabeth. "You would go back to two legs." She looks at me. "And your parents and aunt would return from the world beyond the veil."

"But *I* cast the spell, not Isabella," I say.

"You *read* the spell," Elizabeth agrees, "but the three of you cast it together."

"Do you remember where the moonstone is?" Isabella asks. "We have to find it and destroy it before Winifred gets her hands on it."

"How do we destroy a blood moonstone?" I ask. "Nuke it in the microwave?!"

"*Microwave*?" Elizabeth asks.

"Forget it," I say.

Elizabeth shakes her head. "I feared my sisters would find it, so I gave it to my husband to look after, and I asked him to never tell another living soul where he hid it. And then, the day after my sisters were hanged, I knew the town would come for me and my family next, so I prepared everything for a hasty exit. We nearly made it, too. But as my husband, Jacob, and I made to leave, they came for us with pitchforks and torches. I only just bought Jacob and our daughter, Ismay, enough time to escape to the woods. I never saw them or the moonstone again." She looks at Isabella. "That stone is tied to the Sanderson family, and the Sanderson family is in your blood. You can cast a spell to find it."

"Am I the only one who thinks this sounds like – I don't know – the *worst* possible idea we could think of?" asks Travis. "Magic got us into this mess in the first place."

Elizabeth rests a hand on his shoulder. "And only magic can get you out."

Cell-Binding

The Sanderson sisters land in the middle of the deserted street, heels clicking on pavement as they cross to a squat unlit building with plate-glass windows and a hand-lettered sign reading THE ORACLE STONE. Beneath it, a second, smaller sign reads: CRYSTALS, INCENSE, TALISMANS & TEXTS.

While Winifred stalks up to the shop to let herself in, Mary finds her attention drawn by the shop next door. A banner hangs in the front window with a series of pictures of women and men laughing as they press different versions of the strange memory box to their cheeks. The text along the bottom of the banner reads YOUR CONTACTS. OUR NETWORK. CONNECT MORE.

Mary looks at the object in her hands doubtfully and presses the buttons again until she finds an outline of a head and torso. Beneath the image is the word CONTACTS. She presses it, and a long list of names appears. Chewing her lip, Mary follows Winifred to the front of The Oracle Stone.

A group of three men in costumes comes staggering down the street, laughing loudly. One has his arms draped around the shoulders of the other two. He looks, Winifred thinks, as if he's been too long in the brewer's cold cellar.

"Excuse me, good sir." Sarah puts a hand on the arm of the man in the middle. He has high cheekbones and a perfect smile. She squeezes his forearm with barely masked excitement. "Could you help a lady in need?"

The group swivels to face the witches. "Oh my *gawd*!" The middle one balks, straightening when he spots them. "The Sanderson sisters!"

Sarah's sisters peer around her shoulder at the man, and he gives a shriek of laughter. His friends are beaming, too. He extracts his arms from around their shoulders but stumbles backwards. "You ladies look fab," he says. "Can I get a selfie?"

"A—" Winifred looks at her sisters, perturbed and uncertain. "A *what*?"

"A selfie," he repeats. "I'll be quick." He hiccups, then shakes his head as if trying to knock some sense back into himself. "Okay, let's work it." He pulls out a box that resembles the one in Mary's hand. He poses in front of the confused sisters, and when the box lights up with a brilliant white burst, they shriek and jump back. The man laughs.

"You ladies are so spot-on. I love it." His curls all seem to gather at the top of his head, spilling down a little over his forehead. He combs them back with his fingers and slings his arms back around his friends.

"And *you* are sooo drunk," one friend grunts at him, giving the sisters an apologetic smile. "Night, ladies."

"We have need to enter this shop," says Winifred. She points at the dark locked door of The Oracle Stone.

"They're open tomorrow," he says, nodding at a sign with the store's hours. "But come early. It'll be packed the rest of the weekend for post-Halloween sales."

The three men wander off, the stumbling one in the middle shouting *"I put a spell on you, and now you're mine! Mine! Mine! Mine!"* as they veer off down a pedestrian alley.

Winifred watches them go.

"Hooligans," she mutters.

"Beautiful hooligans," Sarah agrees dreamily.

Winifred turns back to the shop and zaps the brass handle with a quick bolt of lightning. She thunders into the store and looks around, skirts billowing around her.

"It isn't here!" she exclaims, voice shaking. "That memory box *lied* to us!"

The shop smells musty and spicy, especially near one table where candles sit next to carefully arranged bundles of dried herbs and baskets of sticks that exude the scents of earth and tumbled leaves.

There are shelves of books on spirituality and the occult, each section propped up by bookends made from huge agates, their polished faces rippling with bands of colour. There are jewellery displays shining with polished stones and burnished metals. Sarah claps her hands, plucking up a necklace of huge black pearls surrounding an even larger purple gemstone.

"Win-Winnie," Mary ventures. "The box – I believe it summons—"

"I will not trust that blasted chattering box again," snaps Winifred. "Sarah, come. We'll find the house of that traitorous bottom-dweller of a sister, and we'll turn it inside out!"

"But Winnie," Mary says, following her sisters to the shop door. "It's been three hundred years. What if her house does not stand there any—"

Winifred whirls around and bears down upon her. "And three hundred years later, our own house stands the same, does it not, Mary?"

"Yes," Mary yelps. "Well, except that everything is broken now, thanks to—"

"Enough," Winifred says, sniffing with disgust. She turns on her heel and heads back to the front of the store.

"Enough! Enough! Enough!" chimes Sarah, stomping her boots and twirling her skirts.

"But what if Sarah could call the children through the box?" Mary blurts.

Winifred freezes, unused to being challenged by either of her sisters.

"Sarah can already call the children, you dalcop."

"Yes, if they can hear her," Mary says quickly, trying to fit all her words into one breath, "but what about the ones who are too far away to—"

In the background, an oblivious Sarah slips a ring onto her finger and holds it up to the window, examining the shine.

"Go on, Mary," says Winifred with disdain, turning and stepping towards her brunette sister. "What if I am wrong and thou art not wrong? Is this thy meaning? Hmmm?"

"Yes, I mean, no, I mean, of course not," Mary says, quailing under her sister's stormy gaze.

Winifred leaves the shop, snatching at Sarah's wrist as she passes her. "Our brooms! They're gone!" Winifred calls out.

Sarah stumbles after her, throwing Mary an apologetic look. "We shall find more brooms!" Sarah replies cheerily.

Mary turns away with a sigh. She sees a piece of fool's gold – pyrite, her mother called it – and runs one finger along its rough ribs. She still remembers the day she found a piece of this at the age of six and told Winnie she'd made them all rich. Winnie, with the superiority of several years and her own mistakes, replied that Mary was a stupid, gullible girl.

Mary picks up the worthless stone and examines it in the thin moonlight. *"I'm always just the sister on the outside,"* Mary sings softly. *"I'm always just the sister without a ride."* She pauses to swallow a sob. She sucks her lips into her mouth, steadying herself, then opens her hand to see the stone again.

After a moment, she turns towards the open front door and continues to sing: *"I can't see past that look inside your eye."* Around her, gemstones float slowly into the air, catching the light of streetlights filtering through the front windows. *"I can't tell what you're scheming of tonight."* Her voice lifts higher, stronger: *"I don't know where I've done you wrong – but I'm not slow."* Mary strides towards the door with more determination. *"Oh, this ain't love – oh, Winnie, I know."*

Mary swings onto the street, but her sisters are

nowhere in sight. A trail of gemstones follows her out, sparkling and criss-crossing as she twirls down the street by herself, her voice gaining confidence. *"Ever since your first words and your first hex – long before your powers and your projects – you always thought you're better than me. You're top dog and I'm the flea."* She freezes in front of a second-hand shop, checking her reflection in a standing mirror on display. *"But that's not true, the world's not for you,"* she insists, spinning away. *"You're not in charge – the world's always been ours! I don't know where I've done you wrong – but I'm not slow. Oh, this ain't love – oh, Winnie, I know!"*

As Mary passes Dot's Music Store, a trumpet in the window floats up and plays a soulful riff, its sound muffled by the thick glass like a 1930s jazz intro. A narrow drum sidles up to it, sticks rapping in time with Mary's sashaying footsteps. *"Oh! Winnie, I know! Winnie, I know!"* she belts out, arms spread wide to take up all the space she can. The musical instruments burst through the plate-glass shop window and trail her down the walk. *"Tonight, I'm doing everything! I'll show you who I'm meant to be! Tonight, I'll prove that I'm worth your time. I'm full of witchy energy. I don't care what you've got planned, or if it's grand! Oh, this ain't love. Oh, I ain't slow. Oh, Winnie, I know!"*

She spins around, pirouetting in the warm light

of the moon, and frolics down a row of huge houses, throwing her arms out as she dances, her toes barely touching the ground.

"You might not want it to be true, Winnie! But I'm more than what you see in me, Winnie!" The freedom is intoxicating, and the gemstones and musical instruments form her own glittering entourage. *"Tonight, before sunrise – I'll push back on your lies! And I'll be more than a bore – oh, so much more than you thought I could be – Winnie! Oh, this ain't love – oh, Winnie, I know. I'm taking a stand – tonight's the Mary show!"* She ends with a dramatic flourish, chest heaving.

Beside her, someone clears her throat impatiently. Mary pivots, stones and instruments crashing down on the pavement.

Winifred watches her with distaste, two red eyebrows arched almost as high as her hairline. "Art thou quite finished?"

Mary draws her limbs close to her body and smooths her skirts self-consciously. "Yes, Winnie, sorry, Winnie," she says, watching her feet.

"Good," says her sister crisply. "I have a plan."

The three sisters hurry through the picket fence surrounding a beautiful white house – one of the few homes on the street whose lights are still on. Inside, a handful of teenagers in costumes dance to loud music. Another group is sprawled on a selection of chairs and sofas.

There's a cauldron on a table near the door, and Sarah hurries over to it, picking up one of the items inside, which is wrapped in a crinkling brightly coloured paper. She peels open the wrapper and tastes the contents with the very tip of her tongue. "Chocolate!" she says, and then spits, throwing the thing down. She goes to grab an item with a different wrapper on a platter of iced cookies, but as she's bringing the salmon-coloured thing to her mouth, Winifred elbows her in the stomach. Sarah gasps as she drops the sweet and clutches her middle.

"Get to work," says Winifred.

With a huff, Sarah pulls the talking box from the depths of her skirts and goes to the nearest young man, who is dressed in a black cape with blood spattered down his unbuttoned white shirt. "Well met, good sir," she says, batting her eyelashes and giving him a warm smile.

"Uh—h-hi," he says around pointed plastic teeth, trying very hard not to look at her low-cut bodice.

She shows him the box, which is balanced daintily on the tips of her fingers. "Wouldst thou explain to me how this contraption works?"

Behind her, Mary chews her lip nervously as Winifred grins.

"So, you're saying we need a fragment of *bone*?" I ask Elizabeth.

My eyes flit behind her to Travis, who is talking in a low voice to Binx and Emily.

My phone buzzes to life with an incoming call, interrupting us.

I pull it out of my pocket and look at Isabella. "Uh, where's your phone?"

Isabella blinks and tilts her head. "My phone got left behind in my peacoat when they turned me into *this* magnificent creature."

"Well, you're calling me."

"*What?* I don't even have opposable thumbs!" she retorts.

I turn my phone down to show her.

"Poppy, where's that photo from?" she asks. "I like it. I didn't know you took it."

I turn my phone back to me and see the visual that pops up when she calls. It's a shot of her in a woolly jumper at the beach, gazing out over Salem Harbor with this beautiful faraway look on her face. I took it shortly after the start of the school year.

"And I thought you didn't like taking photos on phones," says Isabella teasingly.

"It's… convenient," I say, trying to shrug it off, but she can probably tell I'm embarrassed.

"It's okay," she says. "It's a nice picture. I'm glad you took it."

Blushing, I answer the call and press the phone against my ear, grateful to stop that conversation in its tracks. "Hello?" I ask.

"Poppy, that might not be—" Isabella's voice fades out of my range of hearing, like a car radio spun down to low.

The world takes on a milky hue, as if the light reflecting off leaves and blades of grass has a blurry filter on it. The thoughts in my head slow and spiral, and all I can think about is the beauty of the song looping through my brain.

> *Come, little children…*
> *I'll take thee away…*

I've never tasted words before, but these words taste like… buttercream icing.

I look at Isabella, whose black-and-white face is pressed close to mine, and I realise I've collapsed onto my back in the grass, though I don't remember when I did that. She looks concerned, and I hear a distant whimper that seems filtered through layers and layers of cotton balls.

Suddenly, the idea that Isabella could be trapped as a dog forever seems impossible. And my parents?

My parents will be fine. Maybe Hell's even a welcome break for them. Nothing to do? No pressure? It sounds… nice. Besides, the witches just wanted some time to enjoy Halloween night – and don't we all, really? Anyway, I have a blood moonstone to track down for Sarah. And where's the spell book? We have it, don't we? I look at my friends. No. My *enemies*?

Isabella whimpers again, and I want to share this song with her to help her understand the mission. I want to share this song with everyone. I could dive in and swim through its warm, slow waves of dark chocolate and cinnamon… I think I will…

The phone is ripped out of my hand and the voice disappears, leaving me with an aching sense of loss.

"Why did you do that?" I shout at Travis, who has ended the call and taken away all the comfort that came with it. "Give it back!"

He looks at me with wide eyes and shakes his head. "No phone for Poppy."

Elizabeth crouches beside me, taking both of my hands in hers. "That was the voice of my sister Sarah," she says. "I'd know it anywhere. But how did she speak to you through that thing?"

My thoughts are fuzzy and running slow, and I'm not sure how to answer.

Elizabeth seems to notice. She touches my cheek, and the chill of her fingers spills over my face and down my neck.

I shiver, and when I do, the last of the song's effects seem to vanish.

"Sarah has a gift," Elizabeth adds, "but all her life she's used it selfishly."

Travis's phone rings then, and we both turn to look at him.

"Isabella," he says, showing us the screen, where there's another incoming call from... Isabella Richards.

"They took your phone and they're working through your contacts," I say to Isabella.

"My recent calls," she agrees. "Oh, no. My mom. My dad."

"I'm sure they're okay," I say, trying my best to sound reassuring.

Isabella nods. "Can't think about that right now. How did they get it to work?"

"There's a lesson about locked screens in here," says Travis, rejecting the call with a quick swipe of his thumb.

The three ghosts are looking from each of us to the next, clearly puzzled.

"These phones allow you to talk to people far away," explains Isabella. "You can even send written notes and photos."

When Binx knits his brow, Isabella hesitates. "Photographs. Sorry. I forgot they weren't around when you—" She breaks off. "Never mind. The point is, Sarah is calling people I know and trying to cast a spell on them, but I don't understand why. Poppy, didn't you say that last time they flew over Salem to cast a spell on everyone? Doing it one by one – isn't that slower?"

"I don't know. Hearing it made me want to sing it to all of you. Maybe it's like some game of telephone, but with her spell," I say, looking to Travis. "It's a good thing you didn't let her finish." I shake my head.

"Perhaps," says Elizabeth. "But if Winifred is involved, there is some other scheme in play. You must find that moonstone, Isabella, or my sisters surely will. Find it, and destroy it."

Isabella nods. "Show us how to cast that spell you were telling us about earlier."

"Well, as I was saying," says Elizabeth, "we must first find a fragment of bone, along with the fruit of the earth, leaves deceased and a bed of soil." She studies Isabella for another long moment. "You're going to make a great witch one day, you know. You've already got the cunning and bravery." She smiles. "It's a good thing, too. You're going to need them both."

Travis and I scour the dark woods for holly berries while Isabella scratches in a clearing that's well away from any fresh graves. Emily and Binx help by picking through the freshly turned dirt, pulling out any leaves and bits of grass that might stifle the spell. Isabella reappears after a few minutes with a sharp splinter of bone in her mouth.

"Where did you find that?" asks Travis, eyeing it. "Actually, you know what? Forget I asked."

I put the berries in a heap at the centre of the dirt circle, and Elizabeth sets the bone down beside them. Travis takes a handful of dead leaves and twigs and adds them on the other side of the bone.

"You'll need to add a piece of yourself to it," Elizabeth says. "Winnie would recommend blood, but I think that's a bit too morbid, don't you?"

"I've been shedding," says Isabella, shaking her whole body like a dog trying to air-dry. "Will that work?"

"We shall see," says Elizabeth.

I stoop and pick up a short stray hair of hers from the ground, then add it to the pile of items.

"My mother taught me a spell after she gave me the moonstone, so that I might always be able to find it should I ever lose it. But she made me swear never to tell Winifred or the others. It's not in the book," says Elizabeth. She then leans down and whispers directions to Isabella, who repeats the spell in a strong, clear voice: "'Blood of family, blood of stone. Over, under, backward roam. On mountain high, in graveyard deep, show me where the moonstone sleeps'."

The leaves and twigs rearrange, sketching a map that turns piled foliage into hills and valleys and drawing lines that might be borders or roads. The berries roll, too, clustering along one winding line of bare, wet earth.

"Those are buildings," Elizabeth says, leaning down and pointing at each berry. "The chapel. The milliner's house. Mine." A lone berry tumbles far away from the others and nestles into a soft bit of earth. "That's my childhood home. And this one was the Binxes' house." She looks up at Emily. "Do you remember, poppet?"

The girl nods solemnly, then a sad smile breaks over her face.

The bone is beginning to tumble now, too, end over end, until it reaches an outcropping of leaf-land bordered on three sides by damp soil. It digs itself into the lower right side, like a particularly ghastly drawing pin.

"That is where the blood moonstone is," says Elizabeth, pointing.

I squat down to get a better look at the makeshift map. "Where is that?" I try to imagine modern-day Salem overlaid on the berries and wet dirt. "Winter Island?" I look from Travis to Isabella, and then to Elizabeth.

"Yes," she says thoughtfully. "Winter Island. There was a fort for defence of the town, but it was also a place for selling and drying fish. Dozens of ships passed through there every day."

"It's a park now," I say. "People go there to camp and vacation."

"A park with a lighthouse," Isabella says, looking thoughtful. She gazes up to meet my eyes. "If anyone knows anything about the lighthouse's history, it's Principal Taylor. We need to talk to him right away. He might know if anything was dug up when they built the lighthouse, or when they tore down the old port."

"Okay," I say slowly, trying not to commit, "but what are the chances? He's not exactly our biggest fan."

"Poppy," says Travis. He uses the tone he adopts whenever he wants to snap sense into me. "Principal

Taylor may have been a bully in high school, but he's not a monster."

I sigh. "I hope not."

"You know I'm right," says Travis. "As always. And you're going to be the one to ask him, since you can remind him what a jerk face he was to your dad."

I smile faintly, recognising the insult he's picked up from Aunt Dani. "You know, maybe we *should* go check out the Taylors' place. Besides, I saw Principal Taylor leave our party. I bet he's home with the lights off keeping trick-or-treaters away, if he's not already asleep."

"I know a shortcut," says Isabella.

We all look at her.

"Katie and I… used to be friends," she says.

Confirmed. Travis and I exchange glances, then give her a look, inviting more explanation.

"What? It was a long time ago," she says. "Like, when we were little kids."

I can tell she doesn't want to talk about it, which just makes me more curious. "All right, we'll revisit *that* bombshell after November first," I say.

"Katie Taylor? *Really?*" Travis cuts in. "Not that we're judging you," he adds quickly.

I shoot him a look, then turn to Isabella. "Ride or die, right?" Realising what I said, I spin to face the ghosts. "No offence." But I don't see them, and I'm filled with a sudden sense of loss. They were my only line of communication to my family. I look around frantically. "Elizabeth? Binx? Emily?" I call out to the chilly night air. I spin back to my friends. "Where did they go?"

"I don't know, Pops," says Travis. "Looks like we've been ghosted."

DON'T LET MY
RESTING WITCH FACE FOOL YOU

Twenty minutes later, Travis, Isabella and I sneak past the houses near the Common.

We go in single file because we're trying to be covert, so when I spot Jenny and a couple of other football girls from school walking in step in a clump, I hold out one arm to keep Travis and Isabella back. I peer around the corner of the brick building we're hiding behind.

Katie isn't with them, but the five girls don't seem to be talking to each other anyway.

"There's something wrong with them," I hiss.

Each girl hums the same eerie tune, and they make their way slowly across the square, splitting up to look under park benches and in rubbish bins. It's freezing out, but the girls are still in their football shorts and flimsy shirts from Mum's party, and they don't seem to mind the chill.

"It's the song," says Isabella. Her pointed ears perk up as she tilts her head to make sure. "I can hear it."

"Yeah, it's the angry mob spell to hunt us down!" I whisper.

Juan wanders into the square, and I jump back so he doesn't spot us.

Travis tries to push past me to get to his friend, but I grab him by the lab coat and push him against the wall.

Juan continues, his vampire cloak flapping around his ankles. He has a faraway look on his face and doesn't seem to notice us, even though he walks right in front of us. His phone is pressed to his ear, and I catch the faintest trace of a song as he slips past. My mouth fills with the taste of buttercream icing again, and the need to hunt down the moonstone, the spell book and ourselves. I swallow hard and try to block out the sound until he's safely past.

I shake my head. "The best way to help him is to get the stone," I whisper.

"She's right," adds Isabella.

Travis nods, looking resigned, but his eyes follow Juan until he disappears down an alley.

"It'll be okay," I say, and I really hope I'm right. It

doesn't seem fair to leave the football squad or Juan wandering around in the cold and the dark – but then none of this seems fair.

"Principal Taylor's place isn't far," says Isabella.

Once the coast is clear, she trots ahead of Travis and me, venturing back out onto the dark square. We follow her down a pavement along a row of houses, looking left and right.

Isabella stops short in front of a charming yet aging house. "We're here," she says.

The garden is home to several sycamore trees with thick crowns of rounded leaves. Even in the moonlight, I can tell they've turned to bright yellows and oranges with the recent cold snaps. A bed of leaves covers the lawn and drifts onto the pavement. I've walked past this house a thousand times – I've even thought of photographing the contrast of the leaves against the trees' pale, scarred trunks – but I never knew Katie Taylor lived here.

I lead us down the walk and cross to the front steps, with Travis and Isabella right beside me. I can feel their eyes on me as I ring the bell to the right of the white double doors.

The sound echoes through the house, and the following pause is long enough that I decide the place is deserted. That, or Principal Taylor is actually fast asleep.

I turn to my friends. "Great. Now what do we do?"

Travis waves his phone. "Google's got nothing."

"Think, think, think," says Isabella from where she paces on the porch.

We turn to go just as a click and a snap tell me the locks on the door are being undone.

One of the front doors grumbles and swings open, and we spin around to face it.

Principal Taylor is standing there, in slippers and striped pyjamas, looking uncertain.

"Why are you here? Is Katie with you?" His eyes swing past us to the empty street. They search up and down it, linger briefly on Isabella sitting near my feet, and return to meet mine.

"She's not. We actually came here because we need your help," I say. My voice breaks when I do, and I wince, angry at myself. I clear my throat. "My family needs your help."

"Not interested," he says. "Have a good night." He slams the door in our faces.

"So, that went well," says Travis.

Isabella plants her front paws on the door, scrabbling at it. "Principal Taylor!" she shouts. "Principal Taylor, it's the mayor's daughter, and I'm not leaving until you talk to us."

Principal Taylor swings open the door again, examining the lower third of it, then looking back at me.

"If your dog has scratched the paint, tell Isabella Richards that I'll charge City Hall," he says dryly, looking around for her and obviously not realising she's literally right under his nose.

I prickle at hearing him threaten Isabella.

Poppy, focus. Your mission.

"We *need* your help," I say firmly. "Please."

"Not interested," Principal Taylor repeats in a clipped, measured voice.

"Come on, we just have a question to ask you," adds Travis.

"Not you, too," Principal Taylor says, narrowing his eyes at him.

"Yep, me too," says Travis. "And I'm quitting Quiz Bowl if you don't help us."

"I regret to inform you, Mr Reese, that I do not give two figs about the Quiz Bowl team."

"We're national champions!" Travis says. "I know you use us for fundraising appeals."

I clear my throat. "Principal Taylor, I know you and my dad weren't exactly friends growing up. But if you help him now, it's a chance to make up for old times. Please don't leave us hanging."

"Yeah," says Travis eagerly. "We're helping you help yourself. Something terrible is going to happen to Salem if you *don't* help."

Principal Taylor turns bright red, and his thin lips twitch. "Leave you 'hanging'? Choice words, Miss Dennison," he says. "If anyone should have a guilty conscience over leaving anyone *hanging*, it's your father."

At my look of confusion, he pulls the door open a little wider. "Didn't know that about your dear old dad, did you?" he asks, raising his voice. "Well, *he's* the one who should be *making up for old times*."

"He…" I trail off, not sure what to say or where this is going. *"What are you talking about?"*

"I did try to get cigarettes and lunch money from your father, sure. I even tried stealing candy from his brat of a little sister. And then loony witches locked me and my best friend Ernie in cages. That was bad enough. But it was Max Dennison who left us for dead on Halloween night. After they summoned those three witches in the first place… Never you mind what happened!"

I falter and look from Travis down to Isabella in shock.

Principal Taylor knows the truth about the Sanderson sisters coming back?

Principal Taylor was there *twenty-five years ago? And Dad left him and Ernie for dead?*

"Well, good news is you got out in one piece," says Travis sheepishly.

I glance back at Principal Taylor. His eyes have gone

wild and slightly unfocused, as if he's landed right back in that cage from twenty-five years ago. He shakes his head at Travis's words.

"I—I had no idea," I say. "So... so you know about the Sanderson sisters."

"Oh, I know all about those three. After they locked us up, they were going to eat us! If Ernie and I hadn't taken turns screaming," he says, voice rising again, "no one would've found us. But we did scream, and they did find us, and then Max Dennison – again, your father, in case that is still not clear – spread a rumour that Ernie and I did it to ourselves, wandering into the old house and thinking it would be funny to get in the cages, then losing the key. And you know what? The whole town believed him.

"Do you know what that's like, Miss Dennison? To realise people you've known your whole life would rather believe the new kid than believe you? To know that someone would do a thing like that – like leaving you locked away in an old haunted house a quarter mile from town without food or water and then never apologise – never even *acknowledge* it – for *twenty-five years*? Why, Ernie moved all the way to Oregon to start a new life as a park ranger. Said he didn't want anyone to be lost and scared the way we were that night.

No, no. I don't owe Max Dennison *or* his family squat."
He goes to shut the door again.

This time I shove my foot between it and the doorframe.

The door bites hard into my boot and I wince.

I don't want to believe him, but I saw the cages in the house – and he knows about the Sanderson sisters. This isn't a story someone makes up, and especially not Principal Taylor. I've also never heard him say so many words together at once.

"I'm sorry," I say, because it's clear someone has to apologise on my dad's behalf.

He looks at me, sceptical, and I sense there might be a chance to get him to help us. We have to ask him if he knows anything about the blood moonstone, get to Winter Island, and locate the stone.

Right now, we don't even have a car.

"I promise I didn't know," I say. "But since you've encountered the witches before, then you'll believe me when I tell you that they're back, right here in Salem."

"They—they're back?" His face goes ghostly pale.

"Yes! My mom and dad and aunt are in Hell right now, and the witches are out there doing who knows what, and they turned Isabella into a dog."

"It's true," she says.

Principal Taylor screams and jumps a foot in the air at the sound of her voice.

"Do you know anything about a blood moonstone? Is there one at the lighthouse?" she asks him.

He stares at her and stammers incoherently, and then his eyes sweep the night air behind us.

"I don't know anything about that," he says. "But you shouldn't be outside. And neither should I. We're not safe. Go on home. Go!"

"Katie's out there somewhere, probably under their spell. Don't you want to help her?" says Travis.

"Katie… Katie is just fine," Principal Taylor says, narrowing his eyes at us. But his hand trembles as he raises it to close the door.

"But—but what about everyone else?" I ask.

"They'll be fine come morning," he says. "They were last time."

"This is *different* from last time," I insist.

He leans forward then, just over the threshold. "I wouldn't know," he says gruffly. "Last time, *I* was locked in a cage!"

I take a step back, and he slams the door in our faces. Then I hear the sound of the locks being bolted and heavy footsteps receding quickly into the house.

"Well, that didn't go as planned," says Travis.

"We're screwed," I say. "Totally and utterly screwed."

"That was some heavy stuff," he says. "Maybe your dad *was* the jerk face, Pops."

"Apparently," I say. "Isn't there an old saying about how history has two sides?"

"Now how are we going to find the blood moonstone?" Isabella chimes in. "It could be anywhere on Winter Island! We could spend *months* looking."

"Well, I guess at least that's a start," I say. "But how do we get there?"

Across the street, five little girls skip through the park holding hands. They're dressed as Tiana, Mulan, Cinderella, Belle and Merida, and none of them is older than seven.

"Go, little children," they chant in creepy angelic unison, *"hither and yon, search in the starlight and up until dawn. Find stone and book with the Sanderson claim; wrap them up and summon my name."* They unlink hands and scour the street, clambering into tree branches and running their fingers through the water of a fountain. Then they come back together, rejoin hands, and start the chorus again.

"That's got to be the least effective and creepiest way to assemble a search party in the history of man," says Travis.

"Let's maybe not be in the wide open?" suggests Isabella.

We step away from the front door and crouch behind a tree.

"What now?" I whisper.

"Even if Winnie has her little mob find the moonstone before we do, we still have this," Travis says, motioning to the spell book in his hands.

"Right. Maybe you shouldn't be waving that around? Just a thought," I say, watching as another group of kids in costumes races through the streets chanting the Sanderson spell in unison.

Travis chuckles sheepishly and tucks it under his lab coat. "Good call."

"So, we've got to find the blood moonstone before their search party does," Isabella whispers urgently. "Let's get to the lighthouse and start looking."

"One small problem. The lighthouse is miles and miles away, up the coast, and we don't have a car," I say.

"Or any clue where on the peninsula the stone could be," Travis adds quietly.

"Think, think, think," says Isabella, running in tight circles.

"Will you quit doing that? It's making me dizzy," whispers Travis.

Just then, a car pulls up the driveway and parks, and Katie Taylor steps out. She's got warm-ups on under her shorts and a STATE CHAMPS jumper on over her shirt.

Her hair is tied up in a ponytail, which glows gold in the moonlight, and her zombie makeup has been scrubbed clean.

When she sees us, she looks repulsed. "What the hell are you doing here?" she yells.

I freeze, not sure what to say.

Travis looks at me, shrugging.

Isabella's ears stand straight up at attention.

Katie approaches us with her arms crossed. "I should've known you'd be behind the zombies. Weirdos."

She's lobbing her usual insults, but her tone betrays her. Katie Taylor's definitely freaked out.

"This is the last thing I need right now." She's only inches away, and Travis and I step aside and let her pass as she beelines up to her front door.

"Katie, wait—" I start, but Katie cuts me off.

"No, Dennison. The whole town's gone full *Night of the Living Dead* and I'm getting inside before they develop an appetite for brains or something. Get out of my way."

I spin around to face Katie. "We know. We saw them, too."

"My best friend is acting like she doesn't even know me. People are lumbering around, humming and singing like they've lost their minds," says Katie, turning the key in the lock.

"Did she get a phone call?" I ask.

"What?"

"Jenny. Did she get a phone call? Did you see her pick it up?"

Katie leans against the door, huffs, and turns to face me, rolling her eyes. "Yeah. Why?"

"We know what's happened to her," I say, "and we're trying to fix it. We can save everyone, including Jenny."

"But we need a ride," Travis says.

Katie scoffs. "Why would I give you guys a ride *anywhere*? Forget it. I'm out."

"Coward," says Travis.

Katie freezes.

"Pretty pathetic for the captain of the soccer team to run and hide when the rest of the team needs her," Travis says a little louder.

"Where are you going with this?" I whisper to Travis.

"Trust me," he hisses out of the corner of his mouth.

Katie turns, eyes narrowed. "You don't know the first thing about team sports, nerd."

"I know that when your team's out on the pitch and the other guys have you on your heels, the captain isn't supposed to hand the armband off and take a seat on the bench until things get easier." Travis takes a step forward. "The captain's supposed to push through it. Get ahead. Find a way to stay in the game. The field's for those who *can*; the sideline is for those who cannot."

Katie seems to thaw a little at his words.

"Good going, coach. Where did you get all that?" I whisper.

"I play a lot of FIFA," he whispers back.

Katie's hand leaves the doorknob, and something like resolve comes over her. She moves past us, back to her car. "Get in," she sighs. "But if you're lying to me…"

She's obviously too worried about Jenny to come up with the perfect insult.

She climbs into the front seat, and Travis climbs into the back.

"Katie, thank you," I say.

Katie falters then, and I realise she's just as shocked as I am that I've thanked her. She recovers quickly, a hand on the open door. "Your resting witch face doesn't fool me, sweetie."

I let her snide comment go. "How fast can you get us to Winter Island?"

She considers this. "Depends on how many kids are blocking the streets, but not too long, I'd imagine," she says. Then she glances at Isabella. "But do we have to bring the dog? It's going to shed all over my leather seats."

"Yeah," I say protectively. "The dog's kind of key to the whole thing."

"Okay," she says. "But you're paying to get the upholstery cleaned." She slams the driver's side door shut.

I slide in behind her, and Isabella hops up onto the seat between Travis and me before I close the door.

The front door of Katie's house opens and her dad runs down the walk to the driveway. He's pulling on an old faux-leather jacket over his striped pyjamas. "Katie, you come back inside this instant!" he shouts. He stumbles in his slippers, which actually remind me a lot of my dad's.

Katie rolls down the window. "Stay inside, Dad." She raises the window and locks the car doors. As she pulls out of the driveway, she mumbles, "I can't believe I'm doing this."

COME, LITTLE CHILDREN,
ON DOWN TO THE BAY

As Katie's car pulls out onto the street, it's quiet except for the whir of the heater.

Zombie kids fill the street, and Katie tensely manoeuvres around them. "So if I drive you to Winter Island, you'll help Jenny get back to normal?" asks Katie.

"Right," says Travis.

"Why do you want to get to Winter Island, anyway? Talk about random," says Katie.

"There's something there we need to find to break the spell," I say.

"*Spell*? Okay, you need to explain more about that," she says. "Does this have anything to do with your family's bogus Sanderson sister story? Is this all some kind of *sick payback*?"

"No. And you can start by telling us what happened to Jenny," I say.

"Way to redirect the conversation. Fine. After your lame party, I went to Jenny's for a while, but she got a call from Bella Richards," says Katie over her shoulder.

Isabella lets out an indignant yip. "Hey—" she starts.

I lean in and whisper to her, "Maybe keep the talking dog stuff on the DL for now. One bombshell at a time." Then I shoot Katie an apologetic look in the rear-view mirror reflection.

Katie glances back toward Isabella, frowning. She seems to shake it off, though.

"I got a call from Bella, too. But, I mean, who talks on phones any more?" Katie continues. "Anyway, Bella must be as much of a freak as your parents, because everyone started acting weird when they talked to her on the phone."

I clench my jaw hearing her call Isabella a freak but take a deep, calming breath.

"I thought that was a prank, too," Katie continues. "Then Jenny went off the rails, mumbling about finding a stone and a spell book, and I knew she couldn't be joking." Katie gestures out the window.

A group of boys dressed as superheroes in red spandex and black boots have broken out shovels and started digging in someone's flower garden.

"So, you know how to fix this?" says Katie. "Then that means you do have something to do with this, don't you, Dennison? I want answers, or you're back on the street faster than you can say 'witch hunt'."

"What? No," I say. "This wasn't me."

Then I remember that I am technically the one who summoned the Sandersons back. So I am, at least in part, responsible for this – whatever it is.

"You're two of the only people in our class who are still normal," she says. "Well, normal for you, anyway. That's more than a little suspicious."

I'll admit that she has a point there.

"If I'm right and you're behind this, you're the only ones who can tell me what the hell is going on. And help me get Jenny back." She seems more rattled than I've ever seen her. Her tone is as flat and irritated as it always is, but she's white-knuckling the steering wheel and it's clear that she's a long way from nonchalant.

"You really care about Jenny," says Travis.

"How heartless do you think I *am*?" Katie retorts.

At the speed we're driving, we leave town behind within minutes and hit the open road of the narrow, wooded Salem Neck. Katie turns on her high beams as we streak through a grove of trees that totally obscures the moon. A power line runs along the road on the driver's side.

I watch the moon through the windscreen. Its reflection stretches over the bonnet of the car. Isabella is curled up on the seat next to me, head up and looking out the window.

I can't get what Principal Taylor said out of my mind. How could my dad have done that to him? And how could he have never told me, especially during all his talks about looking out for others and being a good person?

"Does your dad ever talk about my dad?" I ask Katie.

She purses her lips, then shrugs. "My dad doesn't really *talk*," she says.

"Oh. I thought that was just a school thing," I say quietly.

"It's cool," she says, but I can tell she's lying. She pauses, then adds, "We were close when I was a kid. He'd bring me up here and I'd swim in South Channel or Cat Cove while he worked on the lighthouse. Taught me how to fish and how to boat." She shrugs again. "But he's, like, really paranoid. Especially around Halloween," she adds.

I think about how my parents shared everything

with me, and how Katie's dad kept his run-in with the Sandersons a complete secret.

"He won't tell me why, but I'm not blind. It has something to do with your family, Poppy," she says.

I keep quiet.

"I heard your story about the Sandersons and your family earlier today at Allegra's, and it's totally ridiculous, but… when I was younger, my dad used to shut down any talk of the Sandersons. I'm starting to think that wasn't a coincidence."

"It wasn't," I say. "Your dad was there. He saw the same things. It's his story, too. He just hasn't told it."

"Great, so both our families share the same strange story." Katie pauses, like she wants to come up with a good zinger, but then she says, "Sorry I was such a jerk about that."

I lock eyes with her in the rear-view, eyebrows raised. I don't think I've ever heard those words – or anything close to them – escape Katie Taylor's mouth.

"It's all good," I say, and I mean it.

"So, *what*, the witches are back?" Katie asks sincerely.

"Yes," I say.

"And we have to stop them?" Katie asks.

"Bingo," I say.

Katie slows as the night sky breaks through the trees more easily.

"Hey," says Travis suddenly. "There's a spell in here to send evil spirits back to Hell."

I look to my left and find Winifred's spell book open in Travis's lap. He's looking at a page with intricate letters spelling out GATES OF HELL. There's a sketch of a gaping pit filled with fire and smoke. He flips to the next page: on one side is a spell to reveal and destroy a succubus, and on the other a charm for flavouring newt livers. A shaft of warm yellow light hovers above the pages as he continues to flip, revealing more spells, with names like SPELLS TO RESURRECT THE DEAD and MAGICIAN'S PACT and EXCRUCIATING PUNISHMENTS.

"Don't open that!" I shout.

Travis shuts the book with a bang.

Katie jumps, punching the brakes. "What the hell are you doing back there?" she says, looking at Travis in the rear-view mirror.

"Nothing!" Travis and I shout in unison.

Ahead of us, the road is blocked by a low metal gate secured with a chain and padlock. The gate is little more than a triangle outlined with aluminium pipes, so it'll be easy to climb over.

"We're here," says Katie. She throws the car into park, kills the engine, and gets out.

Isabella and I both turn to glare at Travis.

"Do you remember zero of my family's story?" I whisper to him.

"Or what Elizabeth told us?" adds Isabella.

"Until forty-five minutes ago, their story was *fake*, remember?" Travis whispers.

"That *thing* can call the Sandersons when it's open," I say.

"Yeah, Poppy's right. It'll betray us the first chance it gets!" says Isabella.

"So whatever you do," I tell Travis, "don't. Open. It. Again."

He rests it on his lap. "Don't open it again," he parrots. "One accidental spell and Sandy Sanderson over here thinks she's Head Witch in Charge." He looks back up at me, flashing a smile to show he's joking.

I sigh loudly, giving him a sidelong smile, and open my door to let Isabella hop out.

Katie is standing a few feet away, arms crossed over her chest as she surveys the poorly lit greenery of the park ahead of us. "Okay, now what?" she says grumpily.

There are a few sporadically placed streetlights that look like they haven't been updated since my parents were hunting witches. The lighthouse is a darker smudge right on the water, maybe a mile away, but its light isn't on. It's mostly just a historic monument now, I guess.

I can't imagine what it looked like here back when Elizabeth was alive. I try to picture her house, and all the other homes, and I wonder where her husband would hide a moonstone.

"I'm glad the Sanderson search party hasn't arrived here yet," says Travis.

"That's comforting," I say sarcastically.

"So, what are we looking for again?" Katie asks. "And you're sure whatever it is will fix whatever's going on with Jenny and the rest of the town?"

"Yes," I say, hoping it's true, and hoping against all odds that it's even still here.

"We're looking for a rock," says Travis, climbing out of his side of the car.

Katie looks over her shoulder at him. "Are you *kidding* me?"

"A magical rock," he clarifies.

"Jesus," she says, starting towards the gate. "Remind me why I agreed to help you guys."

"Because you want to get your BFF back," Travis points out.

That shuts her up.

The three of us climb over the gate, and Isabella squeezes through it.

There's a small building in front of us, the booth where the park ranger usually sits and accepts payment for parking, but it's dark and deserted at this time of night.

Travis enters it and returns with a shovel. "Score!" he says.

"How old is it?" Katie asks us.

I give her a confused look.

"The magical rock you're looking for," she says, using a tone that suggests she'll abandon me on Winter Island if I can't keep up.

"Old," says Travis. "Like, buried-three-hundred-years-ago old."

She pauses to process this new information, then starts walking again. "If it's from the seventeen hundreds, it's probably buried here, in the middle of the green. The lighthouse was built in the late eighteen hundreds, and they ripped up a lot of the old buildings on the island when they turned it into a park in the nineties." She leads us down one curve of the roundabout that encircles the booth, and then continues along a road that runs the length of the clearing before curving towards the lighthouse.

She's practically Principal Taylor 2.0 – and a fountain of lighthouse facts to boot. *Perfect.*

"Where's *your* new BFF gone off to?" Katie asks me.

As if on cue, Isabella runs beside her and heels.

"Well, about that…" I say, trying to think of what to do.

"You know, Bella used to be my friend," Katie says. "Like, when we were ten," she adds, clearly expecting us to be sceptical. "Back when she actually still wanted people to call her Bella." She sighs. "I don't blame you if you don't remember. Me or the nickname. Sometimes I don't think Isabella does, either."

I wonder why they stopped being friends.

"What happened?" Travis asks, as if reading my mind.

Katie shrugs. "She was nice. And she was busy. Future SCOTUS clerk and all that. I guess we just took two different paths. She always defended me, though. Even after we got to high school and people realised the principal was my dad. She wouldn't sit with me at lunch, but she never let anyone call me Tattletale Taylor without giving them a piece of her mind." She looks at me. "I'm surprised she's not here now. You're her new charity case, aren't you?"

The insult feels phoned in, even for Katie, but it still hurts.

I shrug and shove my hands into the pockets of my jeans. *So much for playing nice.*

Isabella heads back to me and whispers, "I guess this would be a bad time to chime in?"

I nod.

"Fine. Let me see if I can sniff out this blood moonstone." Isabella puts her nose to the ground and weaves amongst us. We all keep walking, returning to the head of the loop, where a thicket of bushes separates the road and the field. Finally, Isabella leaves the road and sniffs among the foliage, vanishing into the ferns.

"I never knew you had a dog, Poppy," says Katie. "So is he like one of those truffle-finding pigs?" she asks, jerking her chin at the bushes.

I shrug again, though it's a better explanation than I could've made up. "She's a *she*, actually," I say.

"Okay," says Katie. "So is *she* like one of those—"

A bolt of yellow lightning forks through the air, making contact with something beyond the line of bushes separating the road from the small field beyond it. My stomach lurches.

"Isabella!" I race towards the site of the lightning strike with Travis by my side.

"You named your *dog* after Isabella Richards?" Katie asks, jogging to keep up.

I shove my way through the bushes, which scratch at my legs and arms, and enter a grassy field to find a park bench, a few trees, and a clear view of the dark, vast ocean far below.

I also find Isabella, who turns to me and wags her stumpy tail. *Thank god she's okay.*

As for the patch of earth in front of Isabella, it's charred and smoking.

"Sorry!" Isabella says. "I started feeling weird – like the air had too much static – but I didn't know *that* would happen. But I think this is exactly where we should dig." She runs in a circle around the charred earth.

"What, did lightning just show us where X marks the spot?" I ask, flabbergasted.

"*I'm* not asking questions," says Travis, starting to dig.

"I wish Elizabeth were here to shed some light on what happened," says Isabella.

Katie looks around. "Uh, Bella? Where *are* you?"

"*Isa*bella," she corrects.

Katie eyes the dog. "Very funny," she says. "Ventriloquist much?"

"Not so much," says Isabella.

This time, Katie sees her mouth move.

Katie stumbles backwards, her eyes widening. "No," she breathes. "No, no, no, no, no."

I take pity and walk over to steady her before she falls over from shock.

There's the bench nearby, so I steer her over to it and help her sit down.

Isabella follows us.

"Okay, what the *hell* is going on?" Katie points at Isabella, who backs away. Katie narrows her eyes at me. "You owe me an explanation, Dennison."

I think of Principal Taylor telling me he doesn't owe my family anything, and for a fleeting moment I imagine doing the same to Katie. But then I think of how that made *me* feel, and I know that she's right.

I spill everything while Travis digs. I don't hesitate, even though Katie's expression moves from concerned to shocked to disbelieving right before my eyes. I even tell her about her father and mine, even though she admits she overheard everything I said to Isabella earlier at Allegra's – was that only just today? I continue giving my dad's side of the story and then her dad's side, and explain why we went straight for her dad's house and why he turned us down.

"That would explain his paranoia," says Katie, shaking her head.

Travis's shovel makes a solid *thunk*.

"Anything?" I call to him.

"Just rocks and roots," he replies.

Beside me, Katie puts her head in her hands and lets out a deep breath.

"Katie," I say slowly, "I know it's… a lot to take in."

She looks up at me with wide, desperate eyes. "This is unbelievable."

I shake my head. "It'll be okay," I tell her. "We will find this blood moonstone and destroy it, and I'll get my family back, and you'll get Jenny back, and Isabella won't have paws any more—"

Katie bolts up off the bench. "We're just a few hours away from daybreak!" she cries out. "We'll never make it!"

Her words hit me with more impact than I expect, and I feel sick.

"I got nothing," Travis says and dumps out another shovelful of dirt. "It was a long shot anyway. I mean, digging where lightning strikes isn't the most logical reasoning." He throws down the shovel and wipes his hands off on his lab coat. "So, who's hungry?"

"That wasn't just any ordinary lightning." Isabella pads over and walks a wide circle around Travis and the hole he's dug. She shakes as if trying to dispel water from her coat. "It's happening again!" she says. "You should probably move."

Travis climbs out of the hole and joins me and Katie near the bench.

Isabella narrows in, sniffing and wagging her tail as her circle gets smaller and smaller, until her nose is pressed against the edge of the pit. She sniffs one last time, then comes to a complete stop and stares off towards the shore, a distant look coming over her face.

Silence sweeps over us, the sound of crickets seeming

to arise out of nowhere, and a slight breeze is cold on my skin. Then comes a rumbling crash and another bolt of yellow lightning. It's so bright and powerful that we all shriek and stumble backwards, clutching one another.

"I *told* you to move," Isabella says.

"You didn't say how far," Travis grumbles in response.

"What is happening? Are you having some kind of witch allergy?" I ask. "But instead of sneezing, you're… lightning-ing?"

"Maybe!" says Isabella. "Your guess is as good as mine." She goes to the precise point where the lightning touched down, which is just an inch or two away from the hole Travis was working on. As she digs, dirt begins to fly everywhere, settling in a fine dust over her back.

After a minute or so, Isabella stops and shakes hard.

She turns to reveal a limp, disintegrating pouch, and spits it out.

"Ugh. It tastes like death," she says.

I get up, walk over to her, and pry the damp bag open. I reach in and pull out a porous red stone. I hold it up to the moon, letting the light stream around the edges.

"Yes. We found it. The blood moonstone." I cheer, holding it up high in my fist.

"The lightning actually *worked*!" says Isabella.

"Yeah! What she said!" exults Travis.

"Whatever," says Katie, approaching me. "Now what do we do with it?"

"We have to smash this thing, stat," I say.

"Totally," says Isabella. "But how?"

"It's not working!" Winifred exclaims, exasperated. She paces in front of the living room windows of the large house they'd entered, but not a single soul scurries up with a blood moonstone or her precious spell book in their hands. Behind her is a fireplace, but the fire has long since died in the hearth, leaving a smell of burnt wood that Winifred finds strangely comforting. It reminds her of winter mornings spent eating hot raven's wing porridge while Mother fussed over a bubbling cauldron.

Mother, who will be reunited with her soon, she thinks fondly – and hopefully.

Nearby, Mary is inspecting the table of food along one wall. There's a bowl with lozenges wrapped in white paper and attached to paper sticks. The wrappings all have faces drawn on them – some of them uglier than others. Mary sniffs one, then tosses it back. Instead, she picks up a long, pale thing and nibbles. "The sign says these are the fingers of *ladies*," she tells no one in particular, "but they taste like cake." She spits the stuff into one of the lozenge wrappers and returns the treat to its bowl.

Sarah sits at a table in the other room. She leans over the memory box and sings diligently into it, but Winifred knows it's only a matter of time before her sister tires of spreading her song from one person to the next – or, more likely, becomes distracted.

A shiver of energy crackles through the air and over Winifred's tongue. She glances surreptitiously at Mary, who doesn't seem to notice anything is amiss. Instead, Mary is chewing something that looks like a brightly coloured earthworm. Mary might be better at smelling children, but Winifred has always been better at sensing magic. That's why, she tells herself, she's the best suited to give directions.

"Sisters," Winifred cries, trying her best to contain her excitement. "Sisters, there is magic in the air!"

Mary sniffs delicately. "The magic smells like macaroons," she says. "Or is it *macarons*?"

"No, *that* smell is from thy *sister's singing*, dimwit."

Winifred hurries up the stairs and about the upper floor until she finds a door on the ceiling that, when drawn down, leads up into the attic. She crosses the low, dusty room to one of the small windows and crouches there, hands clasped in her lap and a grin like an overeager child's spreading on her face. She waits patiently. And then she just waits.

Then Winifred feels something else, right there in the attic, so close to her. Her eyes comb over cardboard boxes and stacks of plastic bins, and she wonders what it could be, but then, as quickly as it came, the wavelength of magic dissipates, and she slouches and sighs, redirecting her sight back out of the window to try and pick up the energy she first detected.

Winifred's confidence is beginning to lag when a second roll of distant thunder pulls her attention to the far coast in the distance. A bolt of yellow lightning springs out of the clear sky, a storm cloud forming and then dispersing as soon as its energy is spent.

"The girl," she says, pushing away from the window and hurrying back downstairs. "The feral, flea-bitten mutt has found it for us!"

Sarah looks up from the memory box on the table, blue eyes hopeful. "May I stop?" she asks sweetly.

"Yes, poppet."

A voice rises from the speaking box. "Hello? Hello, Isabella? Are you—?"

Sarah presses a bony finger against the device and silences the voice.

Winifred opens the front door of the house. Its

garden is plain, unlike the houses nearby. In fact, the only mark of decoration is a small hand-painted sign beneath the porch light, which reads THE DENNISONS. "Book!" Winifred calls, as one would call for a dog or a particularly doltish spouse. "Boooo-ook!" Nothing happens. "Book! Come to Mummy, now."

Mary comes out behind her, clinging to the doorframe. "They've still got it, Winnie, remember?" she says timidly.

"Of course *I remember*!" Winifred shouts. Then she softens, looking out into the dark, cruel world that has stolen her poor book. "Those blasted children are keeping it from me. What gives them any right?"

"Well," Mary says, with little more confidence than before, "the girl is our great-great-great-great-great-great-great—"

"Silence!" The look Winifred gives her could melt gold. "That meddling creature is no relative of mine," Winifred says. "No more than, well, Elizabeth." She wretches at saying her name.

"That is not really for thou to decide, though, is it?" asks Mary.

Winifred huffs and hustles back inside. "She makes me ashamed to be a Sanderson."

"The girl did—the girl did find the stone before thee," says Mary, cowering as she says it.

This time, Winifred turns very, very slowly on one heel to face her sister. "I do not need reminding," she hisses. "Sarah!" She turns quickly then, becoming more herself. "Sarah, dear, please do your little song again and have the children tell us where that dog and my book and my" – she pauses and corrects herself with a strained gulp and forced smile – "*our* stone has gone."

"But thou said I was finished," Sarah whines, rubbing her neck.

"And now I say thou aren't," Winifred says. "Mary, find us something on which to fly." She eyes the shining chandeliers and polished mantel, top lip curling in distaste. "There must be a broom somewhere in this hideous place."

"Yes, Winnie." Mary bows and ambles into the next room.

Sarah coughs and swallows, wishing she had a pint of scorpion juice for her dry mouth. "Cadaver, cadaver, cadaver," she sing-songs, correcting her pitch and relaxing her lips and tongue. "Bloody bones, bloody bones, bloody bones." Satisfied, she presses the button, clicks the next name on the list, and waits patiently as the speaking box casts its spell. It makes a soft chiming sound, then pauses and repeats the noise.

"Hello?" says a voice, sounding somewhat dazed.

"Hello," says Sarah brightly, and then she begins to sing: *"Come, little children, on down to the bay..."*

Winifred smiles with satisfaction and turns away from her sister. She goes over to the buffet table, picks up one of the lady's fingers Mary discarded, and takes a tentative bite.

"Cake indeed," Winifred says, spitting the wretched thing onto the floor.

#SpellOnYou

I set the pale, round blood moonstone on the grass, and we all stare at it, transfixed.

I'm sitting next to Travis on his muddied lab coat, which he's spread out on the ground. Katie sits cross-legged on the bench across from us. She's pulled out her mobile phone and is typing away, probably trying to pretend that none of this is happening. Under the circumstances, I don't blame her. I can't help feeling sympathetic towards her, with our shared family history and all. Isabella paces beside us. I still can't get over the fact that she's now a canine – or any of this night, really.

"So, let's take this shovel to it already," Travis says.

"How do we know that would do the trick?" I ask.

"I don't know! What if we… threw it in the ocean?"

Travis muses, miming tossing an invisible rock over Katie's shoulder.

"But that won't destroy it," says Isabella doubtfully, still trotting back and forth.

"We should get the police, is what we should do," mutters Katie.

Travis, Isabella and I exchange a look. *Like that'll do any good.*

"I'm not sure that'd go over so well. It never seems to work in the movies," I say.

"You're right. Besides, I already called them," Katie goes on, talking mostly to herself, "and my tax dollars apparently don't fund enough phone lines for DEFCON Witch–level emergencies."

"Okay, back to what Isabella said," says Travis.

"Would it crack if we threw it in a fire?" I ask. "Don't some rocks crack if they get thrown in fires? Is that a thing?"

"Yeah, maybe." Isabella snuffles along the side of the stone. "It's too bad the kiln is broken," she says with a grin. "I bet it would've actually worked in this case."

"What if we climb up the lighthouse and drop it onto the rocks below?" I ask.

Travis scratches his chin as he looks at the top of the lighthouse in the distance. "I don't think it would make a dent."

"I mean, we could *try* it," I say.

Travis lifts his shovel and brings it down hard on the stone.

The head of the shovel shatters with a thunderous bang.

I shield my face as metal shards fly every which way. "Holy crap!" I shout.

Travis's jaw drops and he holds up the shattered shovel handle. "Well, we can rule out cracking it with a shovel," he says in a daze, tossing the broken handle off to the side.

"I hate to break it to you guys," Katie says, holding out her phone so we can clearly read the bright screen, "but we're about to be surrounded by witch zombies."

"What?!" says Travis, leaning in towards her phone.

On the screen, under the list of trending items, are SALEM, MA ('ZOMBIE' HORDES CONVERGE ON THE SLEEPY EASTERN SEABOARD TOWN AND MOVE TOWARDS WINTER ISLAND), #SPELLONYOU (MOBILE PHONE CALLS REPORTEDLY HYPNOTISE THOUSANDS ON HALLOWEEN NIGHT) and RIHANNA (TEASES NEW ALBUM IN LATEST INSTAGRAM POST). Katie takes her phone back and taps around on the screen, then reads aloud:

"'Emergency lines are being overwhelmed as worried friends and family report their loved ones' strange behaviour. Although the damage is concentrated in

Massachusetts and surrounding states, with the hordes reportedly now heading in the direction of Winter Island, calls have been reported as far away as Seoul, South Korea. Authorities have urged the public to turn off their phones and avoid calls – even when they seem to come from recognised numbers – since those who are afflicted have used conference lines to entangle up to five recipients at a time'." She looks up at us, her face lit eerily by the light of her phone. "Talk about six degrees of separation," she says.

"I don't think that's how that works," says Isabella.

"Well, hopefully we can figure out how to destroy this stone before the zombies get here," says Travis. "What if we tried—"

"Umm, guys," Katie says, startled. Her eyes are wide. She lifts her phone in the direction of the tree line and points. "They found us," she breathes. "I knew I hated crowdsourcing."

We all turn and see specks of white light coming through the trees – I realise the lights are phones, their lock screens blinking on and off as the people carrying them stumble over rocks and tree roots. Dozens of kids and teenagers wander, zombielike, through the dark woods that connect Winter Island to the rest of Salem, drawing nearer and nearer to us. This is *so* not good.

"Where do we go?" I stand up. "We can't just stay here!"

"I'm going to tweet at the governor," Katie says, typing

madly. "Bella, isn't there anything your dad can do? He's the mayor, for crying out loud."

"Um, Katie, I think we should move," says Isabella. "Now."

Travis stands and snatches up the blood moonstone and spell book.

Over the sound of wind, I can hear the advancing crowd humming the eerie spell song. They're so close now. There's the rustling of leaves. The snapping of twigs. Katie yelps and runs over to join us and Isabella follows, hiding behind Travis. We put the park bench between us and the zombie horde.

As if a few pieces of wood and metal can help protect us.

Behind us, the cliff drops off to the ocean.

We're trapped.

But I'll be damned if I won't fight to protect my friends.

The bewitched kids close in quickly. Teens still in their Halloween costumes stagger towards us, their faces expressionless, their hands outstretched. They're all chanting under their breath: *"Find stone and book with the Sanderson claim,"* they utter in monotone unison. *"Wrap them up and summon my name. Find stone and book..."*

"The *stone*!" a teen girl in a football uniform gasps, pointing at Travis's closed fist.

"Jenny?!" cries Katie, stepping out from behind the bench and moving towards her.

I put an arm out and stop Katie in her tracks. "Katie, she's not herself!"

"The *book*!" another bewitched teen yells, charging towards us.

"So, this is an interesting turn of events," says Travis, skirting around the bench. "Since we're surrounded by water and all." He leaps out of a zombie kid's path and tosses the book to me. "Catch!"

I take it, tuck it under my arm like a running back, and race towards the cliff's edge and away from the zombies with Travis, Katie and Isabella close behind.

"We could jump, but we'd never clear the rocks," Katie says, scanning the ocean far below.

"Well, that's helpful," Travis says sarcastically. "Pops, I think it's time we open the book and look for a flying spell!"

We all spin around. My heel digs into the dirt. One more step back, and I'll fall. The zombies have formed a solid line and advance slowly, with only five feet separating us.

Now four feet.

Isabella takes a firm stance, staring them down. She's brave, even as a dog.

But as much as I deeply admire her pep, I have no clue what we should do.

"Isabella, can you make that lightning hit them?" I ask her.

"I'm not sure," she says.

"It's okay," I say, at a loss for any other ideas.

In the assemblage, I recognise a few kids from school. A zombie teen I've never seen before, dressed as a stormtrooper but missing her helmet, lunges at me, and I take a step back, lose my grip, and feel the earth fall away beneath me.

Katie catches my hand, and my body slams into the side of the cliff, dangling.

"Help!" I scream, trying not to let go of the spell book.

Far below me, the ocean rumbles, and waves spray white against the sharp, craggy rocks.

"I got you!" Katie yells over the wind.

Travis joins her, and together they pull me back up. My feet try to find footing in the crumbling soil, and finally, I'm bent over back on the cliff's edge, trying to catch my breath.

The zombies grab my friends' shoulders.

Isabella valiantly rips at the fabric of their costumes in an attempt to fend them off.

I stand up and push them away, but they keep coming, keep pressing in on us.

Over the tree line fly three figures outlined by the moon, unmistakable even in the dark night. A blanket of stars wraps heavy around their shoulders. Winifred cackles as they descend, their clothes catching the light of the moon. Mary is riding a flat mop, rocking dangerously on its swivelled base. Sarah is perched on a robot vacuum cleaner, swinging her legs as she descends, and Winifred is riding what looks an awful lot like a cordless vacuum cleaner.

Winifred's the first one to touch down, and she swings the vacuum cleaner over her shoulder as she approaches. "Three nasty children, all in a row," she croons. "All dressed up, with no place to go!"

"Three nasty children and a *dog*," adds Travis.

The zombies freeze, watching us with vacant eyes. I see Juan, whose cloak looks much rattier than it did a few hours ago. I see Cory, too, and Adena, and Patsy, and several other people from school. None of them seem to recognise us or know what's going on.

"Thank you, my pets," Winifred says, scratching the top of Jenny's head. "Now, where's my book?"

They uniformly point at me.

I hide the spell book behind my back.

Winifred turns to me and grins. Then she strides towards me, arms outstretched.

"We need to find a way back to your car," I say under my breath, glancing at Katie.

She's too busy staring, disbelieving, at the witches, but she gives one quick nod.

"Ooh, he's just *so* handsome," says Sarah, batting her eyes at Travis.

Winifred stops short of me and puts a hand to her mouth. "Smells like wet dog!" she spits, squinting her eyes at Isabella.

My blood boils at the dig.

"Looking for this?" Travis shouts at her, waving the moonstone.

It's just the distraction we needed.

"Go!" shouts Katie, shoving Winifred aside, and we all make a break for it, manoeuvring around the bench and the zombies and heading back towards the road leading to where Katie parked.

Isabella and I hang right while Travis and Katie take a left, and by splitting up we seem to confuse the sisters, who spin around, shocked and torn, as we pass them.

"Get them!" shouts Winifred.

"Which one?" asks Mary.

"The one with the stone, you miserable stockfish!"

"Oh." There's a pause. "Which one is that?"

"Get them!" Winifred shrieks again, and a few zombie kids turn towards us as if slowly puzzling out her command. Jenny reaches for me, and I twist away from her and plough into three basketball players. Two are in pyjamas, but the other is dressed as a baby with a rattle.

I quickly straighten and race ahead to catch up with my friends. We dodge into the thicket and emerge onto the road. The witches are still behind us and haven't moved from their spots. Ahead of us is the park ranger's booth, and beyond, the gate.

Lucky for us, the zombie horde found a way to smash through the gates, so we won't have to climb over again.

Unlucky for us, there are more zombies standing in our way between the open gate and where Katie's car sits somewhere on the other side. The place is packed. I can't figure out how to shove through them and make it out, and from the looks of it, neither can Katie or Travis.

"Go!" shouts Isabella, ducking under some of their legs and skirting wide to avoid the gate altogether. "I'll be fine!" she calls back.

As much as I want to follow after her, I have no choice but to take her word for it. I hope she'll be okay.

The rest of us duck our heads down and shoulder

people out of the way. Hands snatch at my hair and jumper and limbs, seeking the book tucked under my arm. I elbow and twist and wriggle until I'm close enough to the gate that I can see Katie's car just where we left it. It's a relief that the zombies haven't already slashed its tyres. And a relief that I've still got possession of the coveted book.

Beside me, I hear Katie shout. It's a breathless, frightened sound, and I turn in time to see her body flying through the air, a lasso of green lightning wrapped around her waist. The door of the park ranger's booth opens and she flies in, slamming hard into the back wall. She slumps to the floor, vanishing out of sight, just as the door slams shut after her, crackling with veins of electricity.

"*No!*" I shout.

Travis is already there at the booth, yanking on the door handle, but it won't give. A visible spark of electricity leaps from the handle into his body, and he falls backwards into the mass of zombies, cursing as he clutches his right hand. In the same movement, the blood moonstone flies out of his hand and lands somewhere in the crowd.

Zombies mumble indistinctly, and the crowd bristles around the spot where the stone landed.

Well, that *backfired*.

Travis's hand appears in the throng, giving a thumbs-up. "I'm okay!" he shouts.

I wish I could say the same for Katie and Isabella, but there's no sign of them.

If anything happened to Isabella, I don't know what I'll do.

The witches are now close by, cackling. Marching over to them, I fend off the zombies who claw at me, whacking one over the head with the book, until I'm face-to-face with Winifred and her two horrible sisters.

I'm shaking with fear and anger, full-on *shaking*, like I'm freezing cold and boiling hot at the same time. "You're *monsters*!" I scream.

"Oh," Winifred titters, batting a hand at me as if I'm just too much. "Thou art too kind." She twists her wrist again, and another shock of lightning jumps from her fingertips to Travis, this time hitting him in the stomach as he emerges from the zombie mob. "Hand me the book, or I light him up like a Christmas tree!"

"Stop it!" I yell, stomping even closer towards her. "You're horrible—"

"No, honeysop." Winifred takes a threatening step towards me, making me falter in my own forward advance. "It's the world that's horrible." She trills her Rs dramatically. "I—" She smiles coyly, regarding her sisters, who stand obediently by her side. "*We* just want to rule it."

I can hear banging, and I turn to see Katie pounding on the booth's window.

Before me, Winifred raises her hand again.

Energy crackles between her fingers like a deadly spider's web.

"Leave them alone," I say through clenched, chattering teeth.

Isabella's by my side. "I'm right here, Poppy," she says. "You got this."

"Mmm…" Winifred pretends to consider this, playing with the ball of green-tinged electricity in her palm. "No. No, I don't think I shall." She snaps her fingers. "Unless…"

I feel my heart sink into my stomach. "Unless?" I ask.

"Unless you hand over my book!" she screams. "Booook!"

I feel the book come to life in my hands, and I realise that it must have fallen open as I've been holding it. I feel it move, like it's being pulled by a giant magnet, and it takes all my strength to maintain my grip on it. I dig my heels into the soil. It's pulling me towards Winifred, but I stop it in its tracks by finally managing to close it.

"As for the stone, I'll get it one way or another, girl. Thou might as well tell me where it is now, and spare thy friends the pain of losing their – what's the word, Mary?"

"Bowels?" Mary asks hopefully.

I give her a disgusted look, then glance at where the stone landed, where the zombies stagger around, bumping their heads against one another as they scour the ground. The witches didn't see it land there, and the zombies apparently haven't found it yet. *What do I do now?*

"Yes," Winifred says, and a cruel smile comes over her face. "That's it."

Travis groans, and I turn to see him doubled over. A long bolt of electricity runs from Winifred's hooked fingers to his stomach. He clutches at his guts, trying to shield himself from her magic without much luck. His eyes are clenched shut and he screams. I can barely look.

"*Tsk tsk,*" Winifred chides, closing in on Travis. "If your friends would only hand over my book and my stone, then this could all stop!"

I consider throwing the book at Winifred to make her stop, and look down for a second opinion, but Isabella's nowhere in sight. *Please be safe.*

Suddenly, Katie, who's been slamming the small windows of the booth with both of her fists, shatters a window with a bang. She stumbles through it, causing

Winifred to freeze, turn towards Katie, and shoot a snake of electricity at her. The other witches turn towards Katie, too.

Travis twitches on the floor in front of a semicircle of statuesque zombie onlookers.

I'm about to throw myself at Winifred's turned back to tackle her when Travis catches my eye. He waves weakly at me and pantomimes holding a phone in his hand.

He's telling me to answer my phone. Why?

I feel my phone buzz in my pocket. I pull it out and see Travis's face grinning back at me. I answer because I trust that this is what Travis is motioning for me to do. He jabs a finger at his own mouth, miming a yell. *Speaker phone.*

I put my phone on speaker.

"Now where was I?" asks Winifred in her shrill voice, turning back to Travis.

Her voice is loud enough that both our mics pick her up.

Two more Winifreds echo back: *"Now where was I?"*

She looks around, startled, splayed hands at the ready, like she thinks someone is going to attack her. "Who said that?" she demands.

My phone and Travis's answer: *"Who said that?"*

"You did, Winnie," says Mary, and two Marys repeat her statement, too.

I see Katie painstakingly dig her phone out of her pocket, and a second later my phone starts to vibrate again. I merge her into the call with a covert swipe.

Winifred is too busy searching the treetops to notice.

"I summoned your past and future selves, Winifred Sanderson," announces Isabella from somewhere in the bushes. She's too far away for our microphones to pick her up, but all of us can hear her loud and clear. "And the paradox of time travel says that if you meet one of your other selves, your world collapses."

"That's not true!" says Winifred, turning again.

Now three voices echo shrilly back to her.

She covers her eyes with both hands.

"Winnie, I'm scared," says Mary, scurrying over.

I race past them to Travis and help him to his feet. "Are you okay?" I ask him, careful to keep my voice low.

"Yeah," he breathes. He regards the spell book in my hand. "Pops, where's the stone?" he whispers.

"I don't know!" I glance at the zombie mob. None of them seem to be proudly waving it.

"What?!" he whispers. "That's not good."

"Well, the witches don't know, either," I say. "Let's count our blessings."

"Go away!" shouts Winifred. Our phones are close enough now that they echo and echo in a repeated loop. "Make them go away!" The louder she yells, the louder the phones yell back. All three sisters are cowering now, covering their eyes to avoid seeing their other selves.

Isabella runs through the clearing again, cackling with laughter this time. It reverberates through our phones, sharpening with static as it loops and loops and loops.

Mary wails and buries her face in one of Winifred's sleeves.

I shove Travis in the direction of the car and sprint to Katie, the spell book still clamped firmly under my arm. With Winifred and her sisters looking away, and with the zombies now on their hands and knees crawling through the grass as they comb it for the moonstone, there's no one there to stop me as I help Katie up. She's shivering when I shove her towards the gate, too. Luckily, she seems okay.

Travis is already waiting at the car, which is barely visible once again in the sea of zombies, but Katie's the one with the keys. When she unlocks it, the beep echoes through our phones, too.

I freeze just as Winifred looks up, suspicious.

Her lips purse as her mind works out the situation.

"Step on it!" I shriek, racing with Katie for the gate.

My own command mocks me as I elbow past a few dazed students.

"They tricked us!" says Winifred, incredulous. She shoves her sisters away and hustles after me.

I'm over the gate and making my way through the assembly of zombies towards the car.

Who cares that we don't have the moonstone? We can worry about it later.

All that matters is we're all in one piece. *For now.*

Katie climbs into the driver's seat, and the car roars to life. Travis climbs in, too, and I race in after him, followed by Isabella. Katie reverses with dirt flying, then pulls forward.

"Drive!" I scream.

A bolt of green lightning hits the windscreen and the glass shatters.

"No!" I cry out.

The car swerves and hits a tree. The bonnet smokes silently.

"Ugh!" Travis groans.

"Is everyone okay?" asks Isabella.

Another bolt of electricity pries the backseat door clean off the car.

I look out at Winifred and her sisters, arm in arm and strutting towards me. With another flourish of her hand, Winifred sends her electric-green lightning right at me. It slams me between the shoulders. I feel like I'm flying for a moment, and then I feel like a puddle of pain. My body falls out of the car and lands flat on the ground, and no one part of me hurts less than any other part. The spell book is a foot away, faceup in the grass, and I crawl forward and grab it.

I hear the car door creak open behind me and Travis stumbles out.

I'm not sure where Katie and Isabella are, but I hope they're unharmed.

"Travis, run," I gasp with whatever air is left inside my lungs.

"*Hell* no," he grunts, lifting me up, but the next shock of electricity hits us both.

By the time Winifred stalks over to us, I'm a mess of limbs and pain.

I want to push her away, but my brain seems to have lost coordination with my muscles. I'm helpless as she leans over us, smiling ever so sweetly, and yanks the book from my hands.

"There, there, kitten," she says to me. "Now was that so hard?" She gazes lovingly at the book in her talons. "My darling," Winifred croons. "I knew you would find your way back to me." The green eye on its cover blinks sleepily, making Winifred titter at it even more fondly.

"Oh, I've missed you so!" she simpers. "Yes, I have!" She tickles the book like it's a cute newborn.

From the corner of my eye, I see Isabella emerge from the car. In her mouth, she's got the blood moonstone. She drops it at her feet. "Leave my friends alone. It's me you want!" she yells.

"What, mutt?" shouts Winifred. She holds up the spell book triumphantly. "Every dog has its day!" She starts to cackle and throws a bolt of lightning in the direction of her several-times-removed great-grandniece's barking.

Isabella picks the moonstone back up in her mouth and starts to take off. *Go, go, go!*

Winifred grins. "And a zip, and a zap, and a zilch!"

The lightning hits Isabella, and she collapses, dropping the stone instantly.

No.

All at once, the commotion around us fades away.

Winifred continues to cackle, but everything that isn't Isabella becomes background noise. My heart jumps into my throat. I can't tell if she's breathing. *Please be okay.*

"You *yap*, I *zap*!" Winifred cackles. "Sisters, grab the stone!" she commands.

Her sisters try to make themselves useful. They stoop to grab it at the same time, knocking heads against each other, then attempt it once more with the same result.

Winifred strolls over to them and swats them aside, then plucks up the stone and smiles. She looks up from the book and the stone and shouts, "My—*our*—time has finally come. We shall bring Mother and Master back from beyond the veil, the exchange spell shall be complete when the sun rises, and we shall live forever!" Her lips curl over her teeth. "Now, seize the brats!"

Her sisters move into action, reaching for a limp Isabella, who surprises them by righting herself and dashing off into the ferns. *She's alive. Thank god.*

Mary and Sarah don't bother entertaining the idea of chasing her down. Instead, they drag a motionless Katie from the car and an unconscious Travis from the ground into the clearing of quiet, watchful zombies, where I lie, unable to do more than wiggle my toes.

"Minions, leave us!" commands Winifred.

The mobile phone zombies disperse and head home in a daze.

We failed. The witches won. I let my family down. I hope Travis and Katie are okay. *At least Isabella got away.* A pair of rough hands seizes me, and I know this is the end for all of us.

With a disorientating lurch, we leap into the sky.

ETERNAL LIFE POTION 2.0

My wrists are tied behind my back with bits of cloth that Winifred made a bereft Sarah rip from her dress, and as we float over Salem I let my head loll back to avoid looking at the ground.

Talk about a broom *with a view.* I see Winifred's wild hair arching past a backdrop of stars and wispy clouds. *They have the spell book and the blood moonstone. We failed my family… and let so many others down.* I catch a glimpse of Travis hanging from Sarah's robot vacuum cleaner and Katie clinging to Mary's mop. They're both awake enough to hold on for dear life, though I notice Travis's hands are bound with the scarf he was wearing earlier and there's a good amount of dried blood caked on Katie's temple, most likely from the car crash.

I think of Isabella, who vanished into the woods, and feel a stab of hope. *Has she gone to find Elizabeth, Binx and Emily to ask for help?* What a scrappy rescue party they would make: three ghosts and a Boston terrier dragging a wagon full of graveyard dirt. But it could be the only chance we've got before the witches bring back 'Mother' and 'Master' and god *knows* who else, in exchange for more innocent people. And what'll become of my friends? My family? *Me?*

I just hope Isabella is okay, wherever she is.

The sky seems lighter than an hour ago, and I wonder how far off dawn is. I try not to think about Mum and Dad and Aunt Dani, but I do, of course, and then I start to feel tears again, cooling on my cheeks as we soar through the freezing night air warmed by the moon's light.

"Don't get salt on my dress," mutters Winifred, shoving me with her shoulder.

I gasp, feeling like I'm going to fall, and the fear keeps me silent the rest of the way.

The witches navigate through the dark mass of trees around the Sanderson house, land unsteadily, and walk us up the rickety steps to the open door. My knees feel weak, but I've never been so glad to be back on solid ground. Winifred prods a sharp finger into my back and I shout out, then follow Mary, Katie, Sarah and Travis into the dim, dirty hovel.

I step over my mum's red vintage coat and my aunt's Halloween wig and remember my camera, lost among the melee of the witches' first arrival. Hobbies. Photography seems like a trivial thing now that I'm in survival mode.

I snap back to attention when every candle in the room catches fire with a hungry *whoosh*, and Winifred tosses me on the ground like dirty laundry. She slams the door shut with a swipe of lightning. A feeling of cold dread tells me that the door won't be opening anytime soon.

I'm just recovering when my whole body freezes up, my veins burning. Next thing I know, I've crashed into one of the big skeleton cages that's on the floor. Winifred throws another careless bolt of green lightning in my direction, and the door to the cage slams shut and locks me inside with an electric hiss. Next to me, the other cage lies useless on its side against the wall: it was bent beyond repair in the windstorm fiasco that brought the witches here in the first place.

I feel the side of the cage and find a lock. *Too bad I never learnt how to pick one.*

Now I know what Principal Taylor and his friend

Ernie must have felt like. Trapped like poor, helpless rats.

Across the room, Sarah is tickling Travis and giggling as he thrashes and kicks at her.

Mary pushes Katie into a straight-backed chair and ties her wrists to its wooden arms. "You smell like roses," Mary says, nose wrinkling.

"It's called soap," Katie says through gritted teeth. "I can tell you've never heard of it."

"Soap?" says Mary. "I love soap! Tomato soap. Bat and barley soap. Oh, and children noodle soap."

Katie strains away from Mary's face, groaning.

Winifred clutches her spell book to her chest like a favourite child. "My book, oh, how I've missed you so, my darling." She looks up and yells, "Mary! Right that table for me!"

"Yes, Winnie, as you say, Winnie." Mary hurries over to lift the spell book's podium.

Sarah gives up on her tickle-torture of Travis when he realises it's most helpful to lie as still as a corpse. "Rest up," she says, stroking his hair. "I'll keep you as a pet until we have to eat you." Then she tightens the knots that bind his wrists behind his back and leaves him sitting on the floor near Katie, who struggles against her own ties, which shackle her to the cursed, ancient chair.

Winifred places the book reverentially on top of the

podium Mary sets before her. Then she flips it open, pulls the blood moonstone out of her pocket, and sets it on the page. She turns with a clap and a beaming smile. She summons water into the cauldron. "Mary!" she calls shrilly. "Find me dried peppermint and powdered angelica root to strengthen thy spell."

As Mary heads towards Winifred, Katie sticks her foot out to trip her. It's sneaky and savage and I kind of love it. The witch catches herself, but just barely. She gives Katie a dark look, and Sarah joins her sister's side to glare, but Katie just stares back with equal venom.

I should've known that if the Sanderson sisters had one match in Salem, they'd find it in Katie Taylor.

Travis leans against Katie's chair, his head resting on the arm. He looks at me and at first his face is so hopeless and forlorn I feel like my heart is going to break, if it hasn't already.

He raises an eyebrow at me the way he did in US History class when I told him I'd be okay at the front of the room.

I give a sob of a laugh. *How is it possible that was just this morning?* It's been the longest day of my life, and if I can't save Isabella and my parents and Aunt Dani and all of Salem – and the world? – it's going to become one permanent nightmare.

My thoughts are slowly starting to piece themselves

back together, and as they do my body finds the wherewithal to respond to my brain. The end hasn't come, not yet. There's still time to do something. *But what?* I sit up a little, leaning against the metal bars of my cage. I have my phone in my pocket. What good could that do? And the key ring with the two rusty keys. I manage to fish them out of my pocket, but Sarah pries them out of my hands and waves them.

"Winnie, she had *these*!" she exclaims.

Winifred dismisses her with a wave, and Sarah tucks the keys in the loft for safekeeping.

Even if those keys didn't fit this lock, I'm all out of fresh ideas.

I glare at Winifred. "How can you live with yourselves?" I ask.

"Just fine, thank you," she says primly. She adds a milky liquid to the cauldron, then, glancing furtively at Mary, takes a swig straight from the bottle.

"Maybe if you weren't so horrible, you wouldn't've been killed in the first place," I tell her.

"Yes," says Winifred without bothering to look at me. "That worked out so well for my dear, pure-of-heart sister Elizabeth."

"She died," Sarah says helpfully, pausing mid-pirouette.

Mary picks through the scattered rubbish, blowing

flakes of dust and glass from salvaged herbs as she collects them. She finds a few unbroken bottles and tastes the contents, occasionally wrinkling her nose.

I jump at the touch of something wet against my wrists, but then I hear a familiar voice whisper, "Shhh."

Isabella. Relief washes over me. I scoot slowly to the side to give Isabella a better angle for hiding. She nibbles delicately on my fabric restraints, careful to avoid nipping my skin.

Thankfully, the witches don't seem to notice. Winifred and Mary bustle around the cauldron, filling it up and stoking the fire to make the contents boil quicker.

"I've never been happier to see you," I whisper to Isabella.

She pauses and looks up at me with her round, dark eyes, her head tilted at a forty-five-degree angle. From a dog, it's almost comical, but I've studied her face enough to see past the dog's body she's trapped in. The look Isabella – the *real* Isabella – is giving me is a never-been-happier-to-see-you-too look. Isabella looks back at the cluster of witches and ducks further behind me. Her teeth get back to work on my binds, this time with more tugging and desperation.

"Thou hasn't got much to say now, hast thou?" Winifred asks, casting her eyes in my direction.

"What are you making, anyway?" Travis breaks in, pulling attention back to his side of the room.

"We are planning to boil a delectable and fortifying brew," explains Winifred, rolling her Rs once more.

"Ooh, should we add rabbit ears and newt livers?" asks Mary.

"It need not be *that* delectable, Mary."

Sarah has unwound a bracelet from her wrist and is nibbling one end. It looks like a piece of leather or twine, but I have an uncomfortable feeling it's something else entirely.

"Didn't we try this potion once before?" Mary asks.

"Not the Life Potion, you dimwit," Winifred chides. "A *new* spell, if your miserable memory serves you." Winifred points to the spell book with a long, gnarled finger punctuated with a long, sharp fingernail. There are ancient red letters at the top of the page reading EVERLASTING LIFE ELIXIR. "It requires the blood moonstone. We've discussed this, Sister!"

"Winnie," Sarah says, "you promised! You *promised* that after we made the immortality elixir, that we could invite some guests to join us in our celebration. Billy Butcherson, perhaps? Ooh! Or the dockworker's boy. The pretty one. What was his name?"

"Peter," says Winifred, clearly trying to end her sister's daydreaming as quickly as possible.

"Peter," repeats Sarah with a happy sigh.

"After we possess everlasting life, we're not just inviting *anyone* back, you silly girl," says Winifred. "We're bringing back Mother and Master in exchange for these brats!"

So, that's truly their grand plan, is it? And what, we're the ones who they're going to exchange? I can't say I expected less from them. On the plus side, maybe I'll see my family again. *Poppy, get a grip.* I twist my left wrist carefully and feel the fabric slacken. Slowly, carefully, I work both hands out of their weakened knots and flex my fingers to help blood flow back in.

When Winifred turns away to check the quickness of the boil, I hear a crackle of electricity and see a shiver of yellow lightning dance over the cage's lock.

It's the same yellow lightning that struck at the cliff that showed us where the blood moonstone was buried, and that struck inside the Sanderson house earlier, and that jumped between Isabella and me at school, making my hair stand on end... If Isabella is the source of the yellow lightning, that would be so badass. Especially if she can control it to get the upper hand over her distant witchy relatives.

The lock gives way with a soft click, and the door slides open by a centimetre or two. I glance back at Isabella to thank her, but she's already disappeared. I look back at the unlocked cage door, contemplating how to play out my escape without getting quickly caught. *Think.*

Isabella's white fur flashes in the space between Katie and Travis, but then he shifts to the side and she's hidden again. I'm holding my breath as I watch. *Please don't get caught.*

"You know," says Winifred then, and I see Travis's body stiffen. "Maybe you're right, dear Sarah. Maybe I dismissed you too quickly."

"Oh?" Sarah says, turning and beaming. Then her voice comes out flat and perplexed: "Right about what?"

Off to her side, Mary looks downright miffed.

"About having just any old guests to dinner." A conniving glow comes over Winifred's face, and it gives me the chills. "What good is it to rule without others who will be jealous of our triumphs? Who else dost thou think might turn positively emerald with envy, sisters?"

Sarah bounces on her heels, clapping. "Peter!"

"Well, yes, probably," says Winifred. "But no."

Sarah deflates.

"What about Gunnilda Arden or Mathilda Picardy?" Winifred asks, turning to her. "Or Isolde Fitzrou or Frances Harvey?"

"But those are all witches," says Mary.

"Yes," says Winifred, turning to her now. "Precisely."

"But Winnie," Sarah pleads, coming over and taking her elder sister by the arm. "Witches are terrible dinner guests. They try to show off and—and—steal all your turtle teeth."

"Yes, they do, don't they," says Winifred. "But our dearly descended niece has given me great inspiration. First things first: our eternal life potion is almost complete, and we shall finally live forever."

"Are you sure, Winnie?" asks Mary. "That's an awful long time…"

"Silence! We've had plenty of time to form this plan, and we're sticking to it. Now all that's left is gathering souls ripe for the exchange," says Winifred.

"How many souls can we bring back?" asks Sarah, delighted.

"There are three hundred and seventy-three witches on the other side," replies Winnie.

"How many mortals would we need?" asks Sarah, counting on her long fingers.

"Three hundred and seventy-three, you dolt!" says Winifred. "We shall drink the potion, cast the spell, free our sisters and start a new cruel and crafty coven right here in Salem. Besides, Master will enjoy the new playthings, and Mother will enjoy stepping foot back to life!"

"Master," says Sarah wistfully.

"Yes," Winifred says, as if warming to her own plan. She starts to stir the cauldron and sing softly under her breath. *"Everlasting life will be ours. No more blemishes nor scars. We'll be young and beautiful"*.

Sarah and Mary chorus *"young and beautiful."*

"No more trick nor daft delay," sings Winifred. *"I'm—* erm—we're *here to stay!"*

A snake of red smoke lances out of the brew, then dissipates. The cauldron simmers, and a blood-red mist churns across its thickly bubbling contents.

Winifred hands the ladle to Mary, who continues to stir the cauldron. Winifred pulls a knobby bone-hilted dagger from her robes, dips it into the cauldron, and licks the blade. "Tasty!" she exclaims. Winifred then consults her spell book. "Ah, the trusty everlasting life elixir – let's see." She runs her long, crooked talon of a finger down the yellowed page, and stops on instructions that she reads aloud: "'Lastly, add blood moonstone'." With a proud purse of her lips, Winifred lifts the stone and carries it to the cauldron. She pauses at my cage.

"Now, whose life force shall we sup on first?" She leans forward to give me a wide, ugly smile through the iron bars. "I say you," she teases. "You remind me of a girl I once tried to eat."

"I'm afraid I'm a little tough for your palate, witch breath," I growl.

Then I push myself up and forward in one fluid motion, grabbing on to the bars of the door without letting them stop me. The door swings open, knocking Winifred off-balance.

The blood moonstone falls from her clawed hand, skitters away, and comes to a stop in a slimy pile of wilted herbs. I quickly snatch it up and shove it into the pocket of my jeans.

There's a shout, and I turn to see Mary falling. She was coming after me with a frying pan, but Isabella's sunk her teeth deep into the witch's plump calf.

Isabella jumps onto Mary's prone body, scrabbling over her shoulders and tangled hair.

Travis is at my side.

Katie has already got the front door open. "This way!" she shouts.

Travis and I run towards her.

"The spell book!" calls Isabella.

I turn, but the podium holding the open spell book is on the other side of the room. Bolting for it would mean I'd risk getting caught again.

"Poppy, hurry," says Katie.

I gun it past her, with Travis and Isabella racing beside me, until we're down the steps, out of the front garden, and in the woods. We take cover behind a downed tree. Seconds later, the sisters emerge from the house. Winifred clutches her spell book, whose eye swivels, searching for us.

We duck back down.

"Sisters! Leave them. We mustn't abandon our everlasting life elixir," I hear Winifred instruct her sisters. "Besides, we'll get the stone back soon. With a little help."

I peer up to watch Winifred and her sisters turn and head back into the house.

Isabella stares up at me and Travis. "Please tell me one of you has the stone!"

"I do," I say, patting my pocket.

"You *rock*, Pops," says Travis.

But neither of us laughs, like we'd normally do. We're both still too frazzled.

"Good work, Poppy." Isabella paces the length of the fallen tree and back. "Now what?"

"I don't know, but it's not long before the zombies are back," says Katie.

"I don't—I don't think dogs can cry," Isabella says softly. "But I want to."

"We'll figure it out," I say.

Isabella shakes her head vehemently, then takes a deep breath. "How?" she grumbles.

"We'll find Elizabeth," I say. "She'll know what to do. Besides, we have the stone. They can't cast the immortality spell without it. And we just have to find a way to break it to undo the exchange spell, right?"

"Easier said than done," Travis says. "Besides, it sounds like they're about to cast another exchange spell using the book."

"You're right—the witches—we can't destroy the moonstone ourselves—and more people are at risk of being—and everything will become permanent," stammers Isabella.

I've never seen her so shaken. I just want to comfort her.

"Isabella," I say softly. "Trust me. We'll be okay."

She shivers, then nods. "We'll find Elizabeth," she says. "We have the stone. We'll break it. Then all their spells will be undone." It sounds like she actually believes it.

"Right. And then we'll send those thirsty witches back to Hell," Travis adds.

"And turn you back into a human," says Katie.

Isabella looks up at me, searching my face.

I'm not exactly sure what she's looking for, but I nod and give a brave smile like I know she'd do for me.

"We will," I say, surprised at how calm and confident I am, despite everything.

"Thanks, Poppy," Isabella says. "I needed that."

I feel a warmth in my heart.

Travis and Katie are both watching us.

"Any time," I tell Isabella, surprised at how tender I sound.

"Yeah," she says. She sounds a little more confident this time. "We didn't get this far without each other. We have each other's backs. We make solid plans. We get things done."

"Exactly," I say. "Now let's go find Elizabeth. We need her advice."

Isabella turns and hurries down the trunk of the tree, leaping over the roots and into a deep pile of leaves. She shakes them off, and we follow her through the woods to the road, then across it to the graveyard, dodging from shadow to shadow so that no prowling zombie teens or flying witches can spot us.

As I'm quietly closing the gate behind us, Katie leans in.

"I'm not good at this," she says, "but... I'm sorry. Again."

"What?" I ask.

"I really want you to know that I am so, *so* sorry. For being a total witch to you. You didn't deserve it. I never want to be a mean girl again. That is, if I get the chance to live long enough to redeem myself."

Isabella is far ahead already, loping up the hill towards the chapel, with Travis not far behind her.

"The truth is, I think I was just jealous that you and Bella started hanging out, and she kind of ditched me. It hurt, to be honest." She runs a hand through her hair. We follow the others to the clearing. "And then when I overheard you telling her about the Sanderson story, that was my chance to be a total mean girl. I feel like such a jerk. It's just, your family seemed perfect. And hearing something so weird about them, no offence, made me feel better about my own family. As you know, it's hard having a parent in charge of your high school, and it's harder having a single parent who barely says two words to you because he's too busy making sure the windows and doors are locked. Now I know why. He was witch-proofing the house."

I nod. I think about my parents again – how good Mum was at prepping the house for the party, and how she and Dad and even Aunt Dani had busted out Halloween costumes for the first time since I was nine or ten. For the first time since they told me about the Sandersons. I realise that maybe I haven't been protecting my family secret this whole time – I've just been protecting myself from ridicule. And that maybe the only Dennison who hates Halloween is *me*.

"I forgive you. And hey, I owe my parents and aunt an apology, too," I say.

"Yeah," she says thoughtfully. "And I owe my dad one. He was just trying to protect me."

I sigh dramatically. "Is this what growing up feels like?"

"I hope not. I feel like I've been microwaved and lived to tell the tale." Katie laughs hard at that. She stops walking to offer me an open palm. "Truce?" she asks.

I look from her hand to her face, where a few strands of blue hair are sticking to her jaw. I accept her handshake, and we both hurry up the road and towards the chapel. Luckily, the graveyard is zombie-free. Just ghosts – and friendly ones at that.

Binx is sitting on the chapel's bottom step.

Emily has created a hopscotch board from broken sticks, and she tosses a pebble and skips after it, balancing on one foot as she leans forward to scoop the stone back up.

"I never thought I'd be so happy to see ghosts in a graveyard!" Travis exclaims.

"We have good news and bad news," Isabella says.

"What's the bad news?" Binx asks, rising. He and Emily glide towards us.

Elizabeth appears in the doorway of the chapel, but only watches us, her face expressionless.

Isabella glances at me, wagging her tail. Her eyes

drop to my hand, which is still grasping Katie's, and she seems to falter. She glances at my face, then turns back to the ghosts. I give Katie's hand a gentle squeeze and let go of it, wrapping my arms around myself.

"The Sanderson sisters have the spell book and are going to cast the exchange spell to trade living souls for all the dead witches in Hell," Isabella says.

Binx gapes at us, putting a hand on Emily's shoulder. "What's the good news?"

I take the moonstone from my pocket and hold it up for everyone to see.

Elizabeth nods, then turns to Binx with a look of determination. She takes the words right out of my mouth: "That it isn't over yet."

ELECTRIC-OR-TREAT

"How couldst thou lose the stone?" Winifred demands, blaming her sisters.

"Well, Winnie," Sarah says, twisting her own fingers, "thou wert there also."

This earns her two arched eyebrows from Winifred.

Winifred may have been angrier at another point in her life, but the memory isn't coming to her in this particular moment. They've lost the blood moonstone, as well as their supper – and she isn't getting any younger. She slams her book onto the wooden planks. It emits a whimper that only she can hear. The sound makes her even angrier at herself. She whirls on her sisters.

"Never in my life have I met such blundering, club-clawed stampcrabs," she says.

Sarah and Mary cower and busy themselves at the

cauldron, taking turns stirring the incomplete potion, one more gracefully than the other.

After a pause, Winifred turns her back on Sarah and Mary, afraid that she'll wield her lightning magic in their direction if either sister opens her hopeless mouth. Slowly, Winifred lifts the cover of her book and smooths an apologetic palm over its title page, then holds her hand over the pages and takes a deep breath.

The pages flip of their own accord.

When the exchange spell that Winifred desires appears, the pages settle and still.

She leans close to the book, studying the text of the spell in the dark.

Behind her, her sisters lean forward, too.

"Bring me some mortals," Winifred says to them, eyes fixed on the window.

"Children?" asks Mary.

"It matters not to me," says Winifred, grinning. "Any mortal will do... Sarah, summon old and young alike."

Travis and Binx emerge from the groundskeeper's shed and approach us with a big steel toolbox.

"Something in here's gotta be able to crush this stone," says Travis. He takes a hammer to the stone, and then a pair of pliers, and then he tries to crush it by overtightening a clamp, but when he loosens it again, the stone bounces out into his palm – completely unscathed.

"Does a blacksmith still reside in Salem?" asks Elizabeth. "Perhaps he could fire the stone and break it with his mallet."

"No," says Katie sadly. "The blacksmith unemployment rate became untenable about a century ago."

"We're wasting our time," I say. "It'll be dawn soon."

The sky is still dark and the moon is still high.

"She's right," says Isabella. "We've been running around for hours, and we don't even know how to break the stone."

"I just really wish we had the spell book," Isabella says, swiping at her own head with a front paw. "I know we're not supposed to use it, but wouldn't it be better than *not* having it?"

"I'm not sure," says Elizabeth, looking nervous. "I've told you my sister's book can't be trusted. It sees all and knows no allegiance except to Winifred. And I know its contents all too well. The exchange spell is single-use, meaning it can only be used on the same person once. So even if you incanted it, it would not work on them."

"So destroying the moonstone really is our only

hope." I keep staring at the horizon, where the black sky fades into a charcoal-coloured sea. My heart aches. "But… morning is coming," I say quietly. A fresh wave of despair rushes over me. I turn to Binx. "Can I talk to my family again? I need to tell them I'm sorry."

"We don't have time," says Katie, pacing frantically in front of the chapel. "And besides, you can't think like that – we can't give up. Not yet."

"Poppy, she's right," says Isabella. "We have to act quickly."

"Act quickly we must." Elizabeth slowly descends the chapel steps. "It isn't time yet to lose hope. The blood moon is bloodiest before the dawn."

"Did she seriously just say that?" quips Katie.

I can't help cracking a smile.

Elizabeth kneels down in front of Isabella and touches her small round head lovingly, as if touching a human cheek. "I was not given the chance to watch my daughter, Ismay, grow up," she tells her, "but I hope that your kindness and bravery come from her. You aren't afraid to find out who you are." She tips her head to the side. "Though we are family by blood, you come from many places, Isabella.

"When I was alive, I was always afraid that if I were myself, no one would accept me. So instead, I pretended to be the person I believed everyone – or everyone I cared about – wanted me to be. I was a baker, and kept my life and my family hidden for fear of persecution."

Travis slips an arm over my shoulders and the other over Katie's. "I thought we couldn't waste any time?" he murmurs.

"Shhh," I hiss. "Let Isabella have her moment."

"In the end," says Elizabeth, "my pretence didn't matter much: the spell book betrayed me, and the rest is history. You're a brave young woman, Isabella. And you are smart, and you are curious. Those are good and dangerous things. But you are also a witch, and that is a good and dangerous thing on its own."

Isabella backs away. "I'm not," she says.

"You've seen your powers today," says Elizabeth softly.

"The—the lightning? That was an accident. That isn't me," says Isabella.

"That's what I believed, back then," says Elizabeth, laying both hands across her lap. "I didn't want to be a witch, because I didn't want to turn into my sisters – greedy and selfish and hungry for blood in more ways than one. I didn't end up like them, but I still had my life stolen from me. I was as much a witch then as you are now, but you have shown me that you can be a witch, and even a Sanderson, without being cruel."

"Is there going to be a blood pact or fire dancing or something?" Katie whispers. "'Cuz I'm here for that."

Travis chuckles, and I throw them a pinched look and shake my head in mock disappointment. "Heartless," I say. "Both of you."

Katie winks at me and Travis offers her a fist bump.

"We sent Poppy's family to Hell," Isabella chokes out, drawing our attention back to her and Elizabeth. "And I'm a dog."

I feel myself tearing up at her words.

"Oh, ducky," says Elizabeth affectionately, "none of that is any of your faults. The day Emily died, I blamed myself for not going after her. I'd seen her that morning lured to the woods by my sister's spell, but I hadn't realised just what terrible magic was at work. If I'd just gone after her, I could have saved her, and saved Thackery, too. If I had just stood up to my sisters, I could have driven them from town and no one in Salem would have been hurt. I felt a tremendous guilt, and it was easier to sit with that guilt and hide than to defend myself. Now, I can help make things right. We all can."

Isabella looks hopefully at Elizabeth. Behind them, Emily and Binx smile wanly.

"We all make mistakes, poppet," says Elizabeth. "The trick is learning how to move past them – and, when you can, to use them to your advantage." She pauses and offers both of her palms to Isabella. "Now it's my turn," she adds.

Isabella rises up on her back legs and places one paw in each of her ancestor's hands.

"While you were away," says Elizabeth, "I was chatting with Poppy's family, and they had an idea for how to turn you back into a human that doesn't involve the spell book. I don't know if it'll work, but let me try it."

I want to ask if they're okay, but there's a crackle in the air, and the wind seems to shift.

As Travis, Katie and I look on, a spark of searing-white electricity snakes around Elizabeth's hands and Isabella's paws. The light fizzles and fades, then reappears, swirling around Elizabeth's left wrist and up her arm before piercing her shoulder and disappearing.

Another snaking line of electricity – this time yellow – loops around Isabella's legs and body, sinking into the base of her spine. Soon bolts of bright electricity have twined themselves around the two witches like a single glowing rope that sparks and snaps and disappears.

Isabella's body starts to shift, growing and twisting.

Thick curls sprout from her head and her arms lengthen, fur retreating and skin shifting.

The light around her is so bright I have to look away.

There's an explosion of sparks, and the light snuffs out.

I look back, ghosts of the rope lights squiggling through my vision.

Isabella has transformed back into a human.

She's kneeling in front of Elizabeth, their hands tightly clasped. Isabella is wearing her all-white Athena costume, which by now is worse for wear. She looks down at her hands, flexing her fingers for a moment as if she can't believe her eyes. Then she turns to us, beaming.

I can't *begin* to describe how happy I am.

Isabella jumps up and throws her arms around me, squealing. "Hands, not paws!"

I want to tell her I'm glad she's back, but I realise she was never really gone.

I'm at a loss for what to say to her. All I can do is smile.

She gives me a tight squeeze, and my heart soars.

Then we part, and she runs over to hug Travis, who's grinning broadly.

"Good to have you back, Dog Breath," he says.

Aunt Dani would *reel* at that nickname.

"Thanks," Isabella replies, batting him playfully on the shoulder. She turns and pulls Katie into a long hug.

At first, a look of surprise passes over Katie's face, but then she puts her arms tightly around Isabella, too, and smiles. Neither girl says anything, but I see a thousand versions of *I'm sorry* and *I missed you* and *I forgive you* pass between them through that hug. It makes me smile.

Isabella pulls away, and Katie lifts her arm so Isabella can do a twirl as I cheer her on.

"Take a bow," Katie laughs.

Isabella stops in front of Elizabeth and pauses to catch her breath. "Thank you!" Isabella exclaims. "I mean, I wish you'd done it a bit sooner…"

"I only wish I had thought of it myself," Elizabeth says. "Magic isn't always as simple as reading a spell. It wasn't until Poppy's mother asked if you had lightning powers, too, that I realised there might be a way to transform you back without the spell book's help. Luckily, it worked." She pauses, and a little smile appears on her face.

"Thank goodness!" cries Isabella.

"Seriously," I add.

"If your lightning magic is as strong as I think it is," continues Elizabeth, "you'll need to learn how to control it. Watch." She lifts her hands over her head and white sparks crackle between her fingers, then blossom overhead in a dazzling miniature firework.

Isabella bites her lips and holds out her own hands. "What if I can't do it?" she asks.

"There's nothing to *do*." Elizabeth touches Isabella's arms and elbows, making small corrections and helping her relax. "Now," she says softly, leaning over Isabella's shoulder, "breathe deep and…"

Yellow lightning flies from Isabella's hands, making a great crack and releasing a fireball that bursts in midair. The recoil sends her backwards, shooting right through Elizabeth and crashing into me.

I react with just enough time to steady myself and keep us both from toppling over. "Well, okay," I say.

"Thanks for always having my back," says Isabella. She laughs and takes a step backwards. "Wait till Stanford hears about this," she says, watching yellow sparks jump from her fingers.

I snort, and Katie smiles.

Elizabeth just looks perplexed.

"This explains the static and all the zaps of electricity that kept happening to us today," I tell Isabella. "It all makes sense." An idea hits me. "Hey, can you zap the stone? Maybe that'll break it!"

"Always full of ideas, Poppy. I have always liked that about you. Let me give it a try," says Isabella.

Elizabeth's expression changes to one of worry.

I place the moonstone down on the grass, and Isabella stares hard at it and takes aim.

Bolts of yellow lightning crackle around her knuckles like fiery wires.

"Stop!" Elizabeth exclaims, standing between the stone and Isabella.

Isabella startles and releases her fist.

The bolt ricochets and hits a nearby tombstone with a skull and crossbones, which cracks and smokes.

"What? Why?" she asks, suddenly frazzled.

"Yeah!" says Travis. "Using Isabella's lightning magic to zap the stone is the best idea we've had all night!"

"Speak for yourself," Katie chimes in.

Elizabeth looks from the stone to each of us. "The moonstone is made up of energy. A great, powerful kind of energy. Trying to destroy its magic with your magic could be dangerous and result in a fiery blast. It could be large enough to endanger the town. You'll need to do it in a place with a lot of open space. Somewhere to take the brunt of the shock to minimize the damage. But that should do it."

"The lighthouse," Travis says.

We all turn to look at him.

"What do you mean?" asks Isabella.

"I have an idea!" he says.

"Travis, explain," I say impatiently.

When we continue to stare, he points in the direction of the coast. "If we can blast it off the lighthouse and over the water, no one gets hurt," he explains.

"Then if everyone's in favour, it's settled. Let's head back to Winter Island," I tell them.

"Wait," says Isabella, faltering in a way I'm not used to seeing from her. "What if I can't do it?"

"You can," I say with conviction.

Isabella steels her expression and nods, but she still looks unsure.

"Besides, dear," adds Elizabeth, "I'm coming with you."

A Touch Stringy When Stewed

We're standing outside Travis's house in his driveway, staring at his closed garage door.

"What's taking him so long?" asks Katie, crossing her arms.

I knew we shouldn't have split up. I knew Katie and I should have followed Travis and Isabella through the already open front door to his house. I stare at the dark windows and listen intently. Beside me, Katie holds a bucket. Inside is the soil we dug up from the cemetery since Elizabeth wanted to join us. She hovers above the bucket and looks from me to Katie.

A minute feels like decades.

"Should we go after them?" I ask.

Suddenly, there's a motorised whirr, and the garage door begins to rise.

Travis's face peeps from beneath the moving door. "Well, we were right about my family. They're not here, and none of them are night owls, which only means one thing: they're part of the zombie mob. At least my siblings are."

I step forward. "Travis, I'm so sorry."

Isabella appears beside him in the garage. "The good news is, we got four bikes."

The door shudders into place, and the motor stops.

I peer into the dim garage and see the four bikes leant up against the wall. Isabella starts to pull them out onto the driveway, one by one, and I help her. Katie walks up to one with a milk crate attached to the front and plunks the bucket into it, then saddles up. Travis hands a helmet to her, then clips on his own and offers two more to me and Isabella.

"Hey, Isabella, you sure you can't make these bikes fly?" he asks her. "We'd get to Winter Island much faster."

She shoots him a look. "I'm working my way up, okay?"

"Hey, Dennison," calls Katie, tossing her car keys to me. "My pockets suck. I'm trusting you with these."

I take the car keys and see there's also a key with a plastic lighthouse covering the top. Then I clip on my helmet. "Let's go."

Sarah and Mary stumble out of the Sanderson house and onto its depressing front lawn.

They find five humans under Sarah's spell, searching hither and yon for the moonstone.

The people crouch and look under leaves and rotten planks of wood. One of them is a sleepy-looking teen boy in a long black cape. A set of pointed plastic teeth sits on the rough wooden table in front of him. Another is a teen girl wearing a football shirt and shorts. Her ombré hair, stuck with leaves and twigs, falls around her face. The other three humans are children, who stare up at Mary with vacant expressions.

Mary glances at Sarah with a sloppy sideways smile. "Nab 'em!" she growls.

Moments later, Winifred inspects the ragtag group of human sacrifices her sisters have gathered for her review inside the house. Winifred stalks around the humans seated on the debris-strewn floor. Ruddy moonlight falling through the window soaks everything, making their clothes and faces look flushed. Mary and Sarah stand beside the smoking cauldron, waiting to be thanked. Sarah whispers something to Mary, which makes her giggle.

Winifred shoots them both an icy look. "Five? Only

five?" She sighs. "I *suppose* they'll do," she says. "For now. It's a start."

Sarah claps her hands, delighted.

"Tell me, snoring plague sore," says Winifred, leaning over to meet the teen boy's eyes, "dost thou believe in magic? Ghosts? Spirits?"

He yawns. "I s'pose not," he says.

Winifred smacks the back of his head.

"Why does she get to play with him?" Sarah pouts at Mary, who puts a comforting arm around her sister's narrow shoulders.

"Very well." Winifred turns to her spell book splayed open on its pedestal, clears her throat, and reads the exchange spell: "'Some inside and some without, one believes and one holds doubt. On—'"

"'All Hallows' Day'," Sarah interrupts eagerly.

Winifred glowers at her. "'On All Hallows' Day ere twelve is struck, trade—'"

"'Four'," prompts Mary.

Winifred purses her lips and corrects her sister, saying, "'—*Five* souls until sunup'." Winifred snaps the book shut. "Thank thee very much." She gives her sisters a devilish grin.

One by one, with individual popping sounds, the five humans vanish.

Winifred taps her fingers together expectantly.

A thin pair of pale hands appears in thin air, prying open a glowing green door.

Winifred beams then.

Sarah and Mary can't help smiling, too.

"It's been centuries since we had a true living coven," says Mary.

"Yes," says Winifred, and her simple agreement makes Mary's smile grow.

The first witch climbs awkwardly out of the tear in the emerald veil and lets it snap shut behind her. Her skirts are hitched up high, revealing striped lacy white stockings beneath a cascade of a dress that looks like a racy wedding cake. Her lavender hair is almost as pale as her skin, and her eyes are a watery green.

The prim and proper witch smiles at Winifred. "Winnie Sanderson," she purrs. "I never dreamed I'd see you again. It's a shame that Hell keeps friends so far apart. We've been in the 'plague-carrying squirrel' part of Hell."

"Gunnilda, what a *pleasure* it is to have you back," says Winifred with a tight smile. "We were relegated to the 'attending all of your exes' weddings on the same day' circle of Hell."

The green-glowing tear in the veil stretches open again, and four other witches drag themselves out.

One has a black snake curled around her ankle. As she regains her footing, the snake curls up her calf and disappears beneath her dress, reappearing from beneath her scalloped collar and encircling her neck instead. Another has a shock of white hair, wide white eyes and teeth pointed like a shark's. The fourth is a hawkish witch holding a staff with a phoenix carved on it. The last has scarlet skin and an armoured dress that looks like dragon scales, with a collar pitched into a high silver-tipped fan behind her head.

"To what do we owe the pleasure?" asks the dragon skin-clad witch.

Winifred answers with a dark smile. "To *whom*," she corrects, then adds: "To me."

There's a distant rumble, and all the witches turn towards the window.

Outside, a small lightning storm seems to have descended over the forested peninsula to the north of Salem, except that in this storm, not all the lightning arcs from the sky to the earth; instead, some of it branches backwards, stretching up for the clouds. The bolts are varied shades of yellow, punctuated by a bright, blinding white.

"Pray tell, Mathilda," Winifred says to the poshest of the newly resurrected witches, "how dost thou feel about terrier?"

"It's a touch stringy when stewed," the witch replies in a rich English accent. "But roasted, it's quite lovely."

"Yes, Sister," Winifred answers, her smile growing. "I thought you might say that."

The horizon has gone hazy, but the edge of the sun hasn't cracked it yet. The blood moon has reddened.

I'm standing on Winter Island's shore by the lighthouse and its boathouse where we stashed our bikes. In the daytime, the lighthouse is quite striking – a dizzyingly tall white column with rust-streaked sides and a black 360-degree balcony at the top, just outside the glass windows housing the light. It overlooks an outcrop of huge cracked boulders and the ocean, and there's the small empty boathouse not far from its base, where I stand now.

Elizabeth's ghostly image levitates above a bucket of cemetery dirt – sort of like the ghostly version of teleporting. Isabella stands beside her, casting bolts of lightning around the grounds, trying to gather enough energy to destroy the moonstone in one blast.

The plan is relatively straightforward, if a little cobbled together: we'll put the moonstone in the small boat on the dock and wait for it to be carried away from shore. Then, from the top of the lighthouse (and what we hope is a safe distance), Isabella and Elizabeth will strike the stone with lightning and, with any luck, destroy it without hurting anyone.

It's simple, but it also means we only have one shot at making it work. If the moonstone isn't destroyed, the chances of finding it at the bottom of the bay are pretty much zilch.

"How's it going?" I ask Isabella gently.

"Could be better," she groans. "I don't think I have enough power. I'm just not…" she trails off.

"Hey," I say, taking a step closer to her. "You got this."

She looks doubtful.

"I mean, you're Isabella Richards," I say, smiling. "That moonstone will rue the day it crossed your path."

Isabella laughs a little at that, then takes a deep breath. "Thanks, Poppy," she says. Then she casts another bolt, and I swear it's a little stronger this time.

I look out over the dark, choppy water, trying not to think about how little time we have left to fix this mess. Adrenaline pumps through my veins and goose bumps prickle my skin. Jeans and a jumper aren't nearly warm enough for such a cold night.

Er, cold *morning*, I guess.

I look to the sky and see a flock of birds.

No. Not birds.

Witches.

"Uh, guys?" I say. Isabella and Elizabeth turn to look at me, taking a moment's rest from what looked like their ultra-condensed version of Lightning Casting 101. Katie leans around the threshold of the boathouse, a bit dishevelled from what sounded like a *lot* of rummaging through metal objects, and sporting a *Spit it out, Dennison* expression.

Travis is working on the circuit breaker, trying to fix the fuse that blew when we'd tried to turn on the lights, but he stops fussing with the wires long enough to give me roughly the same look.

I point up to the sky. "Witches incoming," I say.

Katie steps out of the boathouse, wielding an oar. "Looks like it worked, then." She looks to me. "You ready, Dennison?"

I nod, hoping that my expression doesn't betray the doubt that's settling in my stomach. "Not much choice," I say.

I clench the blood moonstone tighter in my fist.

Then a menacing crackle fills the air, followed by the sound of Travis's voice.

"Ow!" he yelps, jumping back from the circuit breaker, which is now emitting a small stream of smoke.

I'm about to ask what's wrong, but the words die in my throat as the light in the tower a few dozen feet above us flickers on, casting a blinding beam into the sky.

"What the—" Katie begins, but she trails off as we watch one of the witches, caught in the beam, waver and then fall from her broom. The light stays on a moment more, then flickers out.

It isn't much, but we'll take any advantage we can get.

"Travis," I say urgently, turning to him. "Can you get that thing working a bit more… permanently?"

"I-I don't—"

He sees the look on my face that clearly says, *Do. Or do not. There is no try.*

"I think so," he says.

"Good. Isabella, you and Elizabeth get to the catwalk up top. Katie and I will be right behind you," I say. "Travis, we'll buy as much time as we can, but if you can get that thing working, we might be able to turn the tide in our favour."

"What's your plan here, Pops?" Travis asks.

"Light," I say simply. "They're no vampires, but it ain't easy trying to fly a broom with a thousand watts in your eyes. Hopefully it'll annoy the hell out of them long enough for us to come up with a plan B."

"Good enough for me," Isabella says. Without

hesitation, she picks up Elizabeth's bucket of dirt and ducks into the lighthouse, clamouring up the metal spiral steps within.

"What have we here?" says a now-familiar pernickety voice.

I look up to find Winifred Sanderson hovering above us on her cordless vacuum. "A wayward beef-witted miscreant. You called?"

I stiffen when I realise Winifred is not joined only by her sisters.

Five additional women appear in the sky behind Winifred, along with her sisters, and all of them look dangerous. One uses a lace parasol to fly, reminding me of Mary Poppins, but deadlier. Another wears what looks like armour made from snakeskin: she seems to be able to walk on air without any help at all. A third, who hovers perched on a rake, seems to have a moving tattoo around her neck, but then I realise it's a live snake, twisting as it circles her neck and shoulders, restless. *So they've begun to exchange more innocent lives for their nasty friends.*

"I have something you want," I say, narrowing my eyes at Winifred.

Winifred sniffs primly. "Where is my scruffy little niece?"

"Don't worry about her," I say.

"It seems rather like a runaround if I don't."

I hold up the blood moonstone.

My hand is sweaty, and for a brief second, I'm afraid I'll drop it and ruin the plan.

I feel all eyes on it.

Winifred advances on me herself, raising her left hand to signify for her coven to hold back. She levitates a dozen feet or so above me, tucking the spell book into her robes.

This next part is important.

Winifred's eyes are wild and frightening, gleaming in the dim glow of the blood moon, and her talons are outstretched.

When she's close enough that I can see every ghastly detail of her gravity-defying hair, I turn and sprint towards the lighthouse tower.

I open my mouth to shout at Katie, but she's two steps ahead, literally taking the spiral steps two at a time.

"Mary," I hear Winifred bellow behind me, "follow them. Don't let the miserable little snobs out of your sight."

I pick up speed, chancing a glance over my shoulder to see Winifred soaring higher, approaching the balcony of the lighthouse, where Isabella stands in Elizabeth's pale, ghostly shadow.

Mary tumbles onto the ground, lifting her mop and the hem of her heavy plaid purple skirt and taking off after me, grumbling indistinctly, but she's still thirty yards behind me as I close in on the tower. Behind Mary, Sarah glides over on her robot vacuum cleaner to where Travis is working on the breaker.

I'd be worried about him if I didn't know that he's more than capable of outsmarting the witch, who's a long way from the coven's sharpest – even by seventeenth century standards.

Ignoring the burning ache in my muscles, I enter the dark, muted quiet of the tower and bound up the steps, vowing to do more cardio if we survive this. I can hear my own heart beating in my chest. And before I even reach the deck, I hear the sound of Katie taunting Winifred and the crackle of several bolts of homespun witch lightning.

One way or another, this ends here, with Travis, Isabella and me fighting alongside *Katie Taylor* and *a ghost* to save Salem from the wicked reign of a coven of long-dead witches. I guess Mum was right – the blood moon really does have a way of wreaking havoc on the status quo.

I reach the balcony and squeeze my eyes closed for just a moment, summoning something that I hope is strength. Then I burst through the door and enter the cold, whipping winds at the top of the tower, joining Katie, Isabella and Elizabeth, the blood moonstone in hand.

Afoot! Afoot! Afoot!

can hear Mary making her way up the stairs behind me as I slam the door to the deck, then brace myself against the thick glass of the balcony.

Just beyond the railing of the tower, Winifred and the newest additions to her coven are circling in the air.

Isabella and Elizabeth attempt to hit the witches with bolts of lightning, but they're moving too quickly, spinning in tighter and tighter circles as they become emboldened.

"So much struggle before certain death," calls Winifred over the wind. "Just as well. A painful ending is always more fun." Winifred regards Elizabeth. "Good to see thee again, Sister! Though you're looking a bit pale!" She howls with laughter.

"Oh, Winifred," Elizabeth replies, "sincerity was never your strong suit."

On the other end of the deck, Katie raises her oar like a giant softball bat, swatting at the witches as they pass just barely out of reach.

"I appreciate thine heroics, dear," says Winifred, clearly patronising. "But even *thou* must realise that the game is lost before it's begun. Hand over the stone, and we may spare one or two wretched souls tonight."

"Not a chance," I say through gritted teeth, tightening my grip on the moonstone. Out of the corner of my eye, I see one of the witches pull the oar from Katie's hands, very nearly pulling her over the railing with it.

"That's it," I hear Katie growl in a tone that, just four hours ago, would've had me running for the nearest emergency exit. "Hope you're ready for a good old-fashioned *witch* slap." With that, Katie picks up a piece of sheared-off railing from the deck, wielding it like a weapon.

"Very well," Winifred says, drawing my attention once again as she feigns boredom. "Then thou shall lose everything here tonight, dear."

Then she lowers her body to the handle of her cordless vacuum and barrels towards me with impressive speed.

I lunge out of the way, narrowly escaping her clutches,

but she banks hard and comes at me again moments later.

"Give up, girl," Winifred cackles, rushing towards me again. "I'll burn thee like a plague-ridden corpse!" Her windswept hair and forest-green cloak billow around her like angry flames. Her face is twisted into something even uglier and more vengeful than before.

Isabella and Elizabeth are still casting errant bolts of lightning with limited success, both beginning to look exhausted from the strain of it. Katie delivers a swift kick to a passing witch's broom, but is very nearly caught by another.

It's looking bleak. We're outnumbered and considerably outmatched, considering we're up against eight witches with centuries' worth of experience in evildoing.

Then the light flickers faintly at our backs.

Katie, Isabella, Elizabeth and I turn to look at it in unison.

It's not much. Just a few sputtering flashes of light.

But here, with witches circling and everyone I care about staring down the barrel of eternal damnation, it looks an awful lot like hope.

"Isabella," I shout over the commotion of the witches' cackling and the wind kicking up in the wake of their aerobatics. "Can you use your powers to kick it into high gear?"

I'm no expert electrician, but I'm hoping that a shock to the lighthouse's old system might be enough to kick-start the light and, with any luck, give it some next-level juice.

Isabella nods and then she and Elizabeth turn their attention to the light, communicating silently before they lift their arms and send two bolts of lightning into the base of it.

Before I can find out if it did anything, I gasp at the sight of Winifred charging at me again.

This time though, there's nowhere for me to go.

I back up against the railing, trying to put as much distance between me and her as I can without falling.

Winifred sees that I'm cornered, though, and a wicked smile spreads across her face as she picks up speed. She doesn't bank or waver and I know well before she raises her hand and sends a wave of energy straight towards me that this isn't going to go the way I planned.

It hits me square in the chest with enough force to push all the breath from my lungs. Behind me, the centuries-old railing of the lighthouse balcony groans, its rusty metal no match for an especially windy day, let alone a burst of supernatural energy.

With an ominous crack, the railing gives way.

There's a funny thing that happens when things take a turn and suddenly the worst gets worse. Everything turns to pure instinct, to a sense of self-preservation so strong that it overrides every thought and impulse that's not immediate survival. It's instinct that has my hand reaching out, even as I fall and the only thing I can really *think* to do is panic, and stubbornly, narrowly, *triumphantly*, I grab hold of the element-battered metal of the deck, the blood moonstone still clenched in my other fist.

It's not exactly a decisive victory. I'm holding on by the tips of my fingers, and as the witches continue to dive, soar, and swirl, I know it's only a temporary stop on the way to certain death, which is a pretty permanent problem.

"Poppy!" I hear Isabella shout moments before I see her face above me. She reaches out towards me. "Give me your hand!" She puts one hand over mine on the deck, as if trying to keep it from slipping.

Behind her, the light flickers; then it surges to life, bursting forth with illumination.

I nearly laugh with relief.

"What demon is this?!" Winifred cries, carefully dodging the beam, somewhere between gleeful and annoyed as she circles above us. "Hast thou no regard for luminary discipline?!"

Please let this work, I think, willing the light to do *something*.

And it does.

It flickers… then it goes dark once more.

"Poppy!" Isabella cries again. "Hand. Now!"

Though I'm focusing nearly all of my effort on hanging on, I swing my hand overhead. "Take the moonstone!" I shout.

But as I go to pass off the stone to Isabella, I feel it slip between my fingers and fall away. I reach out to grab it in the same motion, but I miss, and the force of the movement almost tugs me from Isabella's grasp.

Isabella leans further over the side. "Take my hand," she says.

"But the moonstone!" I say, glancing down. The stone landed on a ledge of the lighthouse. If I just reach down, I could maybe grab it. I go to reach for it. My fingertips almost touch it, but I can feel my other hand slipping from Isabella's hand.

"Leave it," Isabella says. "You have to. We'll get it back, I promise." Even from this angle, I can see the tears pooling in her eyes. "*You're* the thing that we can't lose. That *I* can't lose."

It's hard to tell if my heart's hammering away at jackhammer speed because I'm dangling a few stories above jagged rocks and dark water that looks angrier than Principal Taylor on senior prank day, or because of the look Isabella's giving me right now – a signature blend of incredulity, fear and unmistakable tenderness – but somehow, it's getting harder to hear everything that's happening outside of the two of us.

"This might be it," I say, not sure if I mean for me, or for the plan if I don't get the moonstone back.

"It's not." Isabella shakes her head. "Poppy, give me your hand." She takes a deep breath and looks me right in the eyes. "Trust me."

Something about the way she says it settles the question.

Suddenly, leaving the moonstone and taking her hand is the only choice.

Keeping my eyes on hers, I reach up and take her hand.

With one swift motion (and more strength than I expected), she pulls me back up onto the solid metal of the deck.

I take a moment to catch my breath, slumped against the part of the railing still intact.

Isabella cups my cheek in her hand. "Poppy?" she says. "Are you all right? Are you hurt?"

I look at her for a long moment, trying to place something in her voice that I've never heard before. "I'm okay," I say. "I'm good."

She looks like she's going to say something else, but she's cut off by an earsplitting squeal of satisfaction that pierces the air. Winifred rises on her cordless vacuum just beyond the railing, the blood moonstone in her palm and a look of pure menacing delight on her face.

"'Twas a noble effort, dear," Winnie trills, tone patronising.

I pull myself to my feet and see that the ground below is alive with activity now.

It seems as though everyone from Salem is emerging from the trees, mobile phones at their ears as they put one foot in front of the other, entranced. Even from a distance, it's unnerving – like a slow-moving zombie horde on hold with customer service. They stand like sentries among the trees in a wide semicircle around the lighthouse, awaiting orders.

"Too bad it was all for naught," Winifred says as she pulls the spell book from inside her robes, balancing it impossibly on the cordless vacuum. "First we shall bring back *all* our sisters. And then, I shall be on my way to plunk this stone into my everlasting life elixir. And there's nothing you *twerps* can do about it!"

She clears her throat. "Surely there's at least one

nonbeliever in this pitiful horde," she says. Then she begins an incantation that's becoming all too familiar. "'Some inside and some without. One believes and one holds doubt!'" she cries.

Katie appears beside me, the long piece of railing in her hands. "Heads up, Poppy," she says.

Then, without hesitation, Katie steps up onto the lower bar of the railing and takes a swing at Winifred, connecting with her hand. The moonstone flies from Winifred's grasp, making a high arc through the air and catching the light of the blood moon as it begins to descend.

Legs still shaky from my brush with death, I move to the edge of the deck, making up in speed what I lack in grace.

Eyes wide with horror and fury, Winifred utters the final words of the spell. "'On All Hallows' Day ere twelve is struck, trade three hundred and sixty-eight souls until sunup!'"

Even as my fingers close around the moonstone once more and I haul it in, shielding it protectively, it does nothing to stop what happens next.

Below, green flickers of light appear in the trees surrounding the lighthouse. One by one, the mobile phone zombies are replaced – snuffed out – as beings from beyond the veil claw their way into our world and allow each glowing tear to close behind them. It's like dozens of green-flamed candles being lit and extinguished in quick succession, leaving a trail of witches from Hell in their wake. Without taking a moment to adjust to their new surroundings, they press forward, ready to swarm the lighthouse.

"Oh, no," I mutter. "That's a lot of evil witches."

"At least they don't have brooms," murmurs Isabella, ever the one to look on the sunny side of things.

Winifred cackles. "Perhaps I underestimated thee, foolish girl," she sneers at me. "It appears that the game is afoot."

Somewhere below, I hear the sound of Sarah's gleeful voice, chanting, "Afoot! Afoot! Afoot!"

I chance a look over the edge of the deck and see the beings below fanning out over the grounds from the forest's edge to the dock and from the narrow stony footpaths to the boathouse.

The boathouse. Travis.

He's still down there.

They'll be after him immediately.

I feel an icy dread creep over me at the thought.

Then, as if on cue, he bursts through the door and out onto the lighthouse deck.

"Big problem," he pants. "Huge problem. We've got—"

"Zombies?" Katie fills in. "Yeah, we caught that." She

rolls her shoulders and wields the piece of railing turned Witch's Worst Nightmare, looking ready to take out anyone foolish enough to get in her way.

"We need to destroy the blood moonstone," says Elizabeth. "It's the only way. There are too many of them. They'll be up here any minute."

"I'm sorry," Travis says. "The light… I tried, but…" he trails off, shaking his head. "I blockaded the door below, but I don't know how long it'll hold."

With a grunt, Katie leans over the railing and wrests the oar back from one of the witches flying around the tower. She tosses it to Travis. "Here," she says. "Let them come."

Travis, never terribly athletically inclined, catches it with more gusto than I'd imagined he had in him. "I don't know how to—"

"Pretty simple, nerd," says Katie. "If something gets within oar distance, you make sure it doesn't stay there."

He nods once, then grips it with resolve.

Travis, Katie, Isabella and Elizabeth are all looking to me, searching for something between assurance and direction.

I open my mouth to say something, but I stop short as the space around the tower lights up around us.

Brilliant jets of purple and green slice through the air as conjured ropes knot themselves around the railing, pulled taut as the fiends of Hell on the ground below begin to ascend the tower.

Katie rolls her shoulders again, preparing, and Travis tightens his grip on the oar, doing an admirable job of looking like he's ready for whatever's about to come sailing towards us over the railing. Isabella raises her hands in preparation to conjure her magic, blinking away exhaustion.

The timing isn't right. If we refocus our efforts on using Isabella's and Elizabeth's powers to blast the stone to smithereens, it will only be a matter of seconds before the eight flying witches and the crowd of witches from below will be upon us, and we can't afford that. We have to keep them at bay long enough to put together a new plan for destroying the moonstone. I put it in my pocket.

The sky around us is getting brighter, which doesn't do much to boost morale.

The witches in the air hover around us, poised like snakes ready to strike.

The ground below is teeming with witches, some of which are climbing the sides of the tower.

And then, the light in the balcony gives a faint flicker.

Isabella and Elizabeth share a look, then go about focusing their energy on it, sending controlled streams of lightning into the base of the lamp. It brightens, surging to life, becoming at once more radiant than it ever could've been on its own.

Warm light pours from it and, with a clumsy groan, it begins to rotate.

It's blinding, and on instinct, we shield our eyes in unison.

The witches in the sky disperse like a swarm of sparrows chased by a hawk.

It's all according to plan. Sort of. With a little luck, we *might* be able to keep them at bay long enough to figure out how to destroy the stone... for good.

"Keep going!" I shout over the sound of aging metal grinding through decades' worth of rust and briny wear.

Isabella and Elizabeth outstretch their arms further, palms out, lightning streaming forth.

A hand finds its way onto the metal of the deck.

Then another.

A head appears, clad in a peaked, tattered hat, below which is a face twisted with hate and disgust. It's hard to tell if it belongs to a witch or a demon or something in between, but it's pretty obvious that whoever it is isn't coming bearing tidings of comfort and joy.

Katie's there in a flash, swinging her makeshift staff expertly. She connects with an arm.

With a flurry and a shriek, followed by a *thud*, the path is clear once more.

It doesn't last, though.

More witches make their appearances – some tall, some short, some grisly and some disarmingly inhuman. As soon as they reach the level of the deck, though, they're stopped by the light. Whether blinded or burned, they hesitate, and Katie and Travis spring into action, batting them away and making sure that nothing comes near Elizabeth or Isabella.

It's working, I realise. At least for now.

We have the upper hand – and something Winifred wants.

"Don't you dare come any—" Katie's comment is cut short, though, and she vanishes.

Where she stood only milliseconds before, there's now a green glow at the edges of another invisible tear. A moment later, there are hands, then a cloak, a face and hair that rivals even Winifred's in its disregard for the laws of physics.

The witch stands in Katie's place, blinking rapidly as she takes in the scene around her.

My friends and I watch, stunned. We take in her short black hair, threaded with hints of blue, which curls in waves and hugs her pale face. Her perplexed expression features puckered red lips and twinkling, watchful hazel eyes. She wears a fur-trimmed gold brocade cloak atop what I can only imagine must've been a very fine dress by seventeenth century standards, black gloves, a feather hair fastener and more jewellery than I thought existed in 1693. The way she holds herself shows she is a dignified witch of great power and status.

"Mother!" Winifred cries triumphantly, hovering just beyond the railing on her cordless vacuum once more. "I told thee I would bring thee back, and I have delivered."

The witch, the Sanderson sisters' *mother*, raises a dramatically arched eyebrow. "It appears as though you have, Winifred." She's reserved and regal, unlike her daughters, and resembles none of them. Her face is severe and shows only the signs of aging that were stubborn enough to stick around and suffer her.

Standing straight and lifting her chin, she regards each of us with a suspicious, hawkish stare.

"Now," she says, "where is my stone?"

DRUSCILLA THE DREADFUL

O n top of the lighthouse tower, it's all a cacophony of cackles and shrieks as the assorted baddies from the great beyond make their way onto the metal deck.

Isabella and Elizabeth keep the light on and turning, but without Katie, we're being overrun, despite Travis doing his best to run interference.

"The girl has the stone, Mother," Winifred says, pointing a long, gnarled finger at me. "Just one little girl stands between us and ruling Salem – no, the *world* – for all eternity." She throws back her head and lets out a long, sinister laugh, in a way that implies she's showing off even more than she usually does and putting on a show for good old mummy dearest.

"Don't be stupid, Winifred," the elder Sanderson

barks. "There is no 'us'. There's only room for one witch on the ruling broom." A chilling grin spreads across her face. "Me."

Winifred balks, blinking and pursing her enormous blood-red lips.

"You didn't really think we'd be some sort of evil ruling family, did you dear?" Winifred's mother asks. "That's so… old-fashioned. Who needs a line of succession when you're immortal?"

I turn to Elizabeth, who's regarding the scene with shock, clearly not expecting this turn.

"But Mother," Elizabeth butts in, "you told me to protect the stone. To keep it from being used for evil."

Her mother rounds on her. "I did, dear," she says. "I meant that you should keep it from being used for evil *by anyone but me*." She grins wider. "And what have I told you about calling me 'Mother'? It makes me sound positively *ancient*. It's Druscilla. Druscilla the Dreadful, to those who know me best."

A look of betrayal, hurt and confusion crosses Elizabeth's face. "But I—I… then…" she begins, but trails off, unable to find the words.

Druscilla wheels back to face me and extends her gloved hand. "Give me the stone, dear, and I may turn you into one of the more dignified animals for the rest of your days," she says sweetly. "A horse, perhaps? Maybe a pig? They're actually quite intelligent, you know."

"Over my dead body," I growl.

With conviction that I can only hope runs bone-deep, I stand my ground, ready to fend off the big bad witch with whatever I have left. To my credit, I only falter when the sound of boots landing heavily on the metal deck is followed by hands on my shoulders and a blade to my throat.

Winifred has landed behind me and dropped her cordless vacuum, the bone hilt of a dagger in her hand. I can almost see the cruel smile spreading across her face. "*That* can be arranged." She drops the spell book onto the metal platform, near her feet, and its eye regards us warily.

I freeze, feeling Winifred's hand steady itself against my chin as she strains for control.

"Winnie," Elizabeth says, "please. Can you tell me, truly, that the balance of these forces is in your favour?"

"Get thee back, Sister," Winifred spits, pronouncing the word *sister* like she means *snake*. "Thou hast foiled me for the last time!"

"*Foiled you?*" says Elizabeth. "My dear sister, I've never foiled you at all. Winnie, you foiled yourself. And Mother foiled us both."

"You didn't exactly make it difficult, you dim-witted ditherspoons," Druscilla interjects.

Elizabeth presses on: "The village would have let you live had you not taken one of the children to make yourself young again. What is the value of youth, Winnie? You were meant for greater things than being young."

"Thou wouldst try to flatter and distract," says Winifred, shaking her head furiously.

A teen witch touches down on the balcony to our left, broom in hand. "Your Wickedness," she says, offering a mason jar to Winifred. "I believe this belongs to you."

"Thou believes correctly." Winifred snatches it with her free hand. Inside, blood-red fluid sloshes from side to side, and red steam curls against the seal. The teen witch nods and takes to the sky.

Travis catches my eye, oar still held aloft and at the ready. "It's the potion," he mouths.

"It's not enough to complete the spell," Elizabeth tells her sister.

"One drop is all it takes for the spell to be complete!" retorts Winifred. "And it's only missing one *final* ingredient."

I feel the blade barely touch my bare neck, and I wince as its sharp edge bites my skin.

"You don't have to do this, Winifred," says Elizabeth.

I realise that she really does mean this last plea to her sister, even if her family never *really* treated her like family. "You can use your powers for good, Winnie. You can use them to help yourself and others."

"This world has mocked me for the last time," says Winifred. "All my life I've been ratty-haired Winnie, wild-eyed Winnie, long-toothed Winnie. When I am done with this night, witches will rule Salem and all the world!"

"Quiet, girl," says Druscilla, bored. "Stop this ridiculous power-tripping. Get the stone for me and get on with it."

Winifred digs the knife deeper against my neck and whispers, "Drop it."

Isabella and I lock eyes. She looks torn, as if she's debating whether she should strike Winifred with her lightning. I shake my head once, just barely. It's too close.

Travis rounds the curve of the balcony, oar in hand. Winifred pauses, looking up.

"Not so fast, Warty Wonder." He steps in front of me and swings the oar in a fluid motion at Winifred.

But just before it connects with her, Druscilla sends a blue bolt of energy from the tips of her fingers, stopping the oar, then fires a bolt directly at his chest.

Travis recoils, stunned, but quickly shakes it off. He furrows his brow and redoubles his efforts, parrying her attacks and advancing on her without an ounce of trepidation.

"Winnie, Mother, please," says Elizabeth as Travis and Druscilla draw nearer to the place where her bucket of dirt sits.

"Oh, give it a rest, you prattling skelpie-limmer," Druscilla chides, then sends a bolt directly for the bucket.

For a moment, it teeters.

Time seems to slow as I watch Isabella's eyes widen, her arm outstretched, reaching forward to stabilise the bucket.

A grim grin of victory flashes on Druscilla's face, and before Travis can even think about reacting, one of Druscilla's bolts hits him in the leg and he crumples.

Several feet away, Isabella's too late, too far away to stop what's already been set into motion. Elizabeth's ghostly eyes flash with fear, and the bucket tips, the dirt within spilling onto the deck and quickly scattering on the wind. Elizabeth flickers and disappears.

"No!" Isabella shouts, dropping to her knees, trying to shovel the little bit of dirt that's left back into the bucket.

It doesn't do any good, though.

Elizabeth doesn't reappear.

Isabella deflates, shocked into inaction.

"Poor girl," Druscilla titters. "Mean something to you, did she? Who knew she'd kick the bucket – again?"

Isabella's saved from having to reply, though.

Travis groans, then lifts the oar and strikes Druscilla swiftly in the abdomen.

Druscilla looks stunned for a moment. Then she stumbles backwards, winded, and tumbles over the railing.

A faint shriek follows her down, but the deck is otherwise silent.

Travis looks back at me, expression unreadable. The air around him begins to turn that familiar shade of electric green.

My stomach drops. "No," I breathe. "No, no, no."

Travis shoots me a wink. "See you on the other side, Pops." He puts on a brave face, and with a flash of green light, he's gone.

Out of the tear emerges a tall, grizzled witch perched atop a broom. With a chilling cackle, she takes to the sky and disappears from view.

Moonstone's Last Light

"Travis!" I cry, struggling against Winifred's grasp, but it's no use. She presses the blade harder, painfully into my neck.

"Don't do anything rash, lubberwort," Winifred taunts. "He's gone now. And so is my rotten, ungrateful excuse for a mother!" She spits to the winds, smirks, and attempts to adopt her mother's regal posture without much success.

I look to Isabella, who's standing again, eyes locked on mine as she moves around the deck, inching closer.

Winifred is distracted, watching gleefully as the beings below swarm. Without Katie, Travis and Elizabeth to run interference, the witches below have a clear path and begin to ascend the tower once more.

"Sister?" comes Sarah's voice, moments before I see

her float up to the tower's railing to my left, perched atop her robot vacuum cleaner. She touches down on the deck. "Dost thou have the stone?"

Mary appears behind her, struggling to stay upright on her mop. "Are we immortal yet, Winnie?" She crashes to the deck, trying and failing to play it off as a dismount.

"Silence!" Winifred bellows. She turns her attention back towards me, keeping the blade of the dagger pointed squarely at my throat. "Now. Where were we?"

Isabella is drawing nearer. My eyes flit back to hers, and immediately I can tell she's trying to tell me something. It doesn't take much – just a few subtle gestures and a head tilt or two and I know exactly what she's trying to say.

I nod once, just barely, letting her know that I understand as I begin filling in her plan with a few flourishes of my own in my head.

"Hand over the stone, girl, and perhaps I'll spare you and your friend," says Winifred, holding out her hand. "Is it really more carnage you want tonight? More suffering?" Her vile voice is hot in my ear.

I try not to think about Travis. Or Katie. Or Mum or Dad or Aunt Dani or anyone else who's in Hell – because of me.

Closing my eyes and forcing myself to breathe normally, I stick my hand into my pocket, my fingers trembling as they close around the only thing that can get us out of this mess without being damned for all eternity. As I pull it from my pocket, I open my eyes again, looking to Isabella for assurance.

"Good girl," Mary says. "This really is what's best. We *promise*." She smiles in a way that I'm sure she thinks is nonthreatening.

I hold out my hand, fist still clenched tightly.

Winifred holds out her own, ready to snatch the blood moonstone from me.

I can't believe I'm doing this.

Telling myself that this is the right move, that this is how we get out of here alive, I open my hand and pitch the precious object over the side of the railing, down towards the sharp rocks below.

With a collective gasp, the Sanderson sisters turn, leaning over the railing, trying desperately to see where the stone landed.

I take their distraction as an opportunity to move away from Winifred and closer to Isabella, hoping that I have at least a few seconds before they figure out that it was Katie's car keys and not the stone at all, which is snug in my other pocket.

It's only a second before Winifred rounds on me, though, arm raised, dagger in hand, and eyes burning with a kind of rage that is both unnerving and surprising, even from her.

"*You*," she growls, voice low and dangerous. "You've ruined *everything*, you stupid, insolent little—" She lunges.

Isabella steps in front of me, shielding me as she casts a bolt of lightning at Winifred, which knocks Winifred backwards.

Winifred looks stunned for a moment before her features return to anger, and she lifts her hands, casting her own bolt in our direction.

Isabella doesn't hesitate, and her bolt collides with Winifred's in midair with a shower of sparks and a bone-chilling crackle. Behind Winifred, Mary and Sarah seem to be trying to hide behind one another, but they only keep bumping into each other.

Faces grim with concentration, Isabella and Winifred struggle to battle for the upper hand, neither quite getting it.

I look on, unsure how to help, when Isabella chances a glance at me.

"Now, Poppy!" Isabella shouts over the crackling of the lightning, then nods her head in the direction of the water, the shore and the rocks below. It takes me a moment as I try desperately to put together what she's trying to say. But then it clicks.

"Oh. Right." I stick my hand into my pocket, this time withdrawing the real blood moonstone. Pulling back my arm, I launch the stone into the air, tossing it high above the water in a quiet, graceful arc. I pray this works. "You yap—" I shout to Winifred.

The movement catches Winifred's eye and she wavers, her attacks on Isabella interrupted as she watches the stone soar through the air. "The stone!" Winifred shrieks.

"The stone!" Sarah echoes. "The stone, the stone, the stone!"

Mary's mouth tenses. "Uh-oh," she mumbles, eyes wide.

Winifred is stunned, face frozen in disbelief.

Isabella doesn't waste a second, though. "—*we* zap!" shouts Isabella. As soon as the stone's clear of the tower, she shoots a bolt of lightning straight for it, and the bolt and stone connect almost immediately in midair.

The result is blinding.

As the yellow bolt strikes the stone, it lets off a brilliant, searing white light that blooms in a halo around it. It lights up the water, the tower, the trees and the witches scrabbling below.

The Sanderson sisters draw their hands up, covering their eyes, howling.

The light hangs there for a long moment and the air around us goes still and silent. It's like the world's on pause as we look on, squinting against the intensity of the display. The water's parted off the shore like there's a massive crater in it that goes all the way to the rocky and sandy bed below. Then, all at once, the halo of light begins to rush back towards the stone in a radiant flash. The water rushes back with a roar, collapsing in on itself.

With a deafening *whoosh*, a shock wave barrels from the stone, rushing towards us with tremendous force. I reach out and grab the railing, hoping it's strong enough to withstand the blow.

To my left, the Sanderson sisters are scrambling, trying to stay on their feet as the shock wave makes landfall.

On my right, Isabella is doubled over, hands on her knees, exhausted from the effort. She doesn't even see it coming.

I open my mouth to shout at her, to warn her, but it's too late.

The shock wave reaches us like a tidal wave, and Isabella's hit with the full force of it.

There's no time to think about it, no time to calculate odds or make a plan. There's just this moment, this force, and Isabella being swept away from me. So I don't think.

I let go of the railing and dive forward, reaching for her, wrapping my fingers around her forearm. And then, at the last possible second, I throw my other arm out and barely catch the railing, holding on as tightly as I can.

The Sanderson sisters are swept off the tower with a blood-curdling yowl.

"Hold on!" I shout to Isabella above the noise.

She grabs on to my forearm, holding tight as the shock wave lifts us both away from the lighthouse tower, floating, anchored only by my grasp on this centuries-old railing.

After a few seconds that seem to drag on for minutes, the shock wave passes, and we begin to fall.

For a brief moment, I'm positive that we're about to fall from the tower or crash into the rusted, steely exterior or, if we're really unlucky, both.

But then Isabella lifts a hand and, with what seems like herculean effort, conjures a bolt of lightning like a rope, her brow furrowed in concentration as she directs it, wrapping it around the tallest point on top of the tower (and far away from the metal railing). I can feel the charge of electricity where our skin touches. It doesn't hurt, really, but it feels like my entire body is vibrating with energy. Sort of like that too-much-coffee feeling amplified by a thousand.

Isabella pulls us towards the balcony with a final surge of energy, and we clatter onto the deck. It's not a soft landing, but it's better than a bed of sharp rocks a long, long way below.

I lie still for a moment, trying to figure out if anything's broken.

Bruised but otherwise intact, I pull myself up.

"I-Isabella?" I stammer.

Next to me on the deck, Isabella lies motionless.

My heart stops.

"Isabella?" I try again, louder, moving towards her. "Isabella, can you hear me?" With one hand on her shoulder and the other on her cheek, I try to wake her up.

But nothing happens.

No.

Hot tears splash down my face.

I shake Isabella again, feeling her neck for a pulse. "Please, no. Please," I sob.

She remains still, and my world shatters into a million pieces.

A Bit Like Magic

My whole world is spinning again and it's like every ounce of breath has left my lungs all at once. My vision blurs with tears. This can't... *she* can't... I didn't even...

A pained groan.

Isabella opens her eyes slowly, blinking. "Magic... sucks..." she manages to get out. Then she pushes herself up, leaning against the tower wall, and cracks a small smile.

"Oh, thank god," I breathe, throwing my arms around her neck and pulling her in, holding her tightly. "I was so afraid that—" I don't finish the thought.

Isabella wraps her arms around me, too.

Behind us, the light still spins, creaking and groaning

with every rotation and bathing us in warm light that's now *just* this side of blinding.

"Yeah," Isabella says quietly, "me too."

There's a long beat of silence as we stay like this, grateful to have survived but afraid of what comes next.

Our families. Our friends. The rest of the town. Are they just…

"Look," Isabella says, pulling back but keeping an arm around my shoulder. She points towards the trees and the ground far below.

There, in the faint light of pre-dawn, hundreds of green wisps appear and extinguish. Stunned witches give way to humans. One by one, dazed citizens of Salem appear, taking in the trees, the still-churning water and the early morning light.

"Travis," I say quietly, standing and looking over the edge of the railing. I don't see him, not among the growing crowd of humans trying to piece together what's going on. He's not by the trees or the boathouse or the gate.

And then I hear him.

"Poppy!" He jogs into view from the base of the tower, waving his hand above his head, beaming.

"Travis!"

I grab Isabella's hand without thinking and pull open

the door to the balcony, flying down the now cracked and crumbled spiral steps two at a time until I'm on the ground, bursting through the door.

He's there, grinning, and I throw my arms around him, hugging him tightly.

Laughing, he does the same. "Worried, were you?"

"Just a little," I say, shrugging nonchalantly.

"Glad you're okay, Travis," Isabella says, pulling him into a hug.

"Thanks," he says, grinning. "The highway to Hell is shorter than I thought."

Isabella and I groan in unison, rolling our eyes, but I can't fight the smile creeping across my face.

"Dennison, what the hell are my keys doing in a *tree?*"

Katie rounds the corner, trying and failing to pull off her signature scowl before breaking into a grin.

No one is more surprised than I am when I step forward and hug Katie, who hugs me back, even if it's just for a second before she steps away.

"Looks like you did it, weirdo," she says, but there's no hint of malice in her voice. She smiles, somewhere between impressed and relieved.

"Couldn't have done it without you, Katie," I say truthfully. "Thanks. For sticking around."

She plays it off, but I can tell it means something

to her. "Yeah, well. You're right. You definitely couldn't have done it without me," she says. "I mean, I was *kind of* a badass."

"You were," I laugh.

Travis and Isabella hug Katie in turn, and I'm about to ask whether this means our friendship group is growing by one more when I hear something that stops me.

"Max, don't touch that," comes an irritated voice from the other side of the boathouse.

It's a voice I'd know anywhere.

"Aunt Dani?" I whisper, almost afraid to believe it. I follow the sound of the voice, slowly at first, then picking up speed until I'm jogging around the side of the lighthouse. There, near the dock and the rocky shoreline, are Mum, Dad and Aunt Dani.

Dad is crouching near the ground, picking up what looks, from afar, like a piece of broken glass. As I get closer, I see it's a shard of the blood moonstone, glowing faintly.

"Poppy," Mum sighs in relief, rushing forward to gather me into a crushing embrace. "We were so worried."

"Same," I laugh, relieved. "You have no idea."

Aunt Dani and Dad stand behind Mum, grinning.

"Looks like you pulled it off, kid," Dani says, beaming proudly. "Told you you could do it."

Dad puts a hand on my shoulder, his eyes crinkling

at the corners as he smiles. "You did good, Poppy," he says. "We're so proud of you."

"Thanks," I say, relishing the feeling. I look back over my shoulder to see Isabella talking animatedly with her parents, Travis gathering as many of his siblings up into a hug as he can, and Katie and Principal Taylor having what looks like an uncharacteristically warm conversation. "I didn't do it alone," I say, turning back to my family.

"You're still grounded, though," says Mum.

"Oh, totally," Dad nods. "Very grounded."

"What?!" My mouth drops open. "But I brought you back from the *literal* pits of Hell!"

Aunt Dani smirks. "Riiight. But you also sort of sent us there, so it was really the least you could do."

I open my mouth to issue a rebuttal, but I stop short when I feel a hand on my shoulder.

"Poppy?" says Isabella from behind me.

"Yeah?" I ask.

"Can I talk to you for a second?" she says, looking unusually shy.

I turn to follow Isabella, who leads us around the other side of the lighthouse, away from the crowd and closer to the water.

"I just want to thank you," she says, turning to face me. She talks fast, as if she's only mustered twenty seconds' worth of courage and doesn't think she can fit everything in before it runs out.

"For what?" I ask. "I didn't do anything. I mean, you destroyed the moonstone. You were incredible."

She gives an emotional snort, tears pooling in her eyes. "So were you. Poppy, you were a hero today."

"I mean, 'hero' feels like a strong word, but I'll take it," I say, smirking. "It was a team effort."

She cracks a smile, but just barely. "Sorry, I'm just… bad at this."

"Isabella Richards, bad at something? Never," I say jokingly. But it's clear that she's actually trying to tell me something. "What's going on, Isabella?" I ask.

She's staring at the ground, so I dip my head to look her in the eyes.

"Hey," I say. "What is it?"

In truth, I feel like I kind of know what's going on for the first time in weeks, but I can't tell if it's all just in my head. All this time, Isabella stood up and did the right thing. She went all-in to help me fix everything, and although there were many things I liked about her before, tonight has shown me that there are seemingly endless things to like about Isabella Richards.

Her eyes are shiny with tears as she looks at me, and I want to wipe them away, but that seems too intimate.

"Look, Poppy, I'm so sorry. For everything," says

Isabella. "I had no idea that the Sanderson house and the spirit board would lead to..." she trails off, looking down at the ground. "I can't believe you almost lost your family because of something that *I* did."

"Hey," I say again, tilting her chin up gently so that I can see her eyes, which are shiny with unshed tears. "You couldn't have known. This wasn't your fault. I'm the one who insisted we follow through."

She takes a deep breath. "It was my idea, though. And I just... I'm sorry that being my friend almost got you killed."

"Worth it," I say with a shrug, trying to play nonchalant. "Though... I'm still a little confused as to why the coolest girl in school wants to hang out with me at all."

Isabella smiles a little and looks up at me. "Come on, Poppy," she says. "Can't you tell?"

My emotions are suddenly spinning out of control. "Can I?" I feel confused, and I'm fighting like hell to keep myself from giving in to hope here.

"Yeah," she says shyly. "You're a cool girl, Poppy. And you're beautiful. And I like that you have dreams that are bigger than Salem, but you still love this place. I like that you try to see the best in everyone. I like that you'd do anything to protect the people you love — including battling a coven of evil witches on top of a lighthouse tower. I like *you*." She pauses, her eyes huge and dark. "This has been the strangest, scariest night of my life, but I got to spend it with you… and strange and horrifying as it was, I wouldn't take it back. Not a second of it."

With that, she leans forward, pressing her lips to mine.

Her breath is soft and warm, and when her lips touch mine, I feel a crackle of electricity. It moves from her hands to my hands and up through my arms into my chest, and my heart soars. She puts one hand on my cheek, and an electric current races through my veins, thrilling but not painful.

I've never been kissed before, but I know this is what a first kiss should be. A movie theatre kiss, blown up on the big screen. A kiss for the history books. A kiss that feels like…

Well, a bit like magic.

We pull apart, but her hand drops to mine.

"Me too," I say awkwardly. "I mean, I like you, too. A lot."

We grin at each other, and Isabella looks down at her feet again. I've never seen her so vulnerable, and it makes her even more beautiful. I want this moment to last forever.

Aunt Dani comes around the corner and smiles when she sees we're holding hands. "Hey, you two!" she calls out. "Let's get home and eat! I'm starving. Plus, I haven't had one single cookie of your mom's, and I was in Hell for" – she checks her watch – "way too long."

We turn and walk back down the hill towards my family, Isabella's arm brushing against mine. Halfway down, I glance over at her, and she gives me a little grin.

Dad is waiting for us at the bottom of the hill, and Principal Taylor stands by his side. As we get closer, I can hear the two men talking.

"I'm sorry I left you hanging that night, Jay," Dad says. "That wasn't right."

Principal Taylor looks a little embarrassed, but he takes a deep breath and looks Dad in the eyes. "It's all right, Hollywood," he says, smiling. "Ancient history now. I mean, that was an entire Witchpocalypse ago."

He extends his hand, and Dad takes it, shaking it heartily.

"Too right. Maybe we shouldn't leave all the hope and change to the kids," says Dad.

Aunt Dani races ahead of us towards Mum and Dad. "Hey, Allison, how much party food do you have left? Because I could really go for a junk food brunch. Plus, we haven't really wrapped up the Halloween festivities yet, so it's not too late to watch our *favourite* Halloween movie."

Mum and Dad both groan.

"Come on!" she cries pleadingly. "It's a cult classic. We've watched it every Halloween since we were kids!"

She shoves her way between them and links arms with them. "It'll be fun!"

I can hear them sigh, and I laugh to myself. It happens every Halloween, and every Halloween Aunt Dani gets her way.

I look at Travis, Isabella and Katie. "We did it," I say proudly. "And if we can save Salem from a trio of evil witches, we can do anything."

"Together," says Isabella with a smile.

"Together," I repeat happily.

"All right, saps, we get it," says Katie, rolling her eyes but cracking a smile. "Four's a coven, right?"

MATERIAL GHOST

"I can't believe you have us back here already, Dennison," says Katie, stooping to examine a headstone that's almost invisible under the cloudy night sky. "In a cemetery less than twenty-four hours after the invasion of the Real Witches of Inferno County. Bold move."

"Seconded," says Travis. "Not that I'm not *totally* supportive of witch hunt two-point-oh. It just feels… weird."

He's right. It does feel weird to be back in the cemetery, so close to where this whole thing started. Next to me, Isabella's quiet, but I sense that she's anxious.

"I'm sure she's fine," I whisper, taking Isabella's hand and giving it a gentle squeeze. "She's here somewhere."

Isabella nods, squeezing my hand in return, but says nothing. She looks nervous, and there's lingering exhaustion written on her face. I know how she feels. We're all still recovering from our flirtations with death and an eternity spent filling in for some malevolent witches in Hell.

"I can't believe that you all came here with a spirit board after Allison warned you about the blood moon," says Aunt Dani, hands in the pockets of her jeans. "It's like you heard 'increased magical activity' and thought, 'I know, I think we'll summon the dead, maybe commit a misdemeanour or eight and see where the night takes us'."

"It seemed like a good idea at the time." I shrug.

I hear Isabella laugh lightly next to me. "I think it worked out," she whispers, bumping my shoulder gently with hers.

"Me too," I say with a chuckle, happy to hear her laugh. She's spent most of the day worried about Elizabeth. Ghosts disappear with the dawn, but the last time we saw her, she was being scattered with the wind all over Winter Island.

A moment later, Isabella's smile falters and disappears.

"We should go," she says. "It's getting cold and there's no sign of her. Maybe she's just—"

"Apologies, dear," says a voice from behind us. "Taking

this form is exhausting, and after the evening we had, I'm afraid I've been resting most of the day."

Isabella turns around slowly, like she isn't quite ready to let herself believe what she's hearing.

But when I look back over my shoulder, there she is. Elizabeth is standing among the headstones near the chapel, hands clasped in front of her.

"Whoa," Aunt Dani breathes. I know what she means. Though I just saw a ghost for the first time last night, it's difficult to fully appreciate or remember just how strange they are in the... well, *not* flesh, I guess. I can't imagine what it's like to finally see a ghost again after all these years. She's described Binx plenty of times, but at a certain point, words just fall flat.

"Elizabeth," Isabella says as she strides over to stand in front of Elizabeth's translucent, shimmering form. "How did you...?"

"I can only move from here temporarily. I am, for better or for worse, tied to this place forever. Wherever I go, I am always here."

"Not confusing at all," Katie mutters. I shoot her a look.

"Are you okay?" Isabella asks.

"Aside from discovering that my mother used me as a pawn and that she makes my sisters look positively benevolent by comparison?" she asks, smiling wearily. "Fine. Like you, I suspect, just a bit tired."

Isabella nods. "Thank you," she says, "for helping us. For helping me. I never would've been able to—"

"Of course you would've, Isabella," says Elizabeth, moving closer to Isabella. "You may not know much about your powers yet, but you are an extraordinary witch and you're meant for extraordinary things."

Isabella shoots her a shy smile and, for a moment, falls speechless. "Did you get what you hoped to?" Isabella asks. "Out of helping us?"

"All of that and more," says Elizabeth, reaching forward to touch Isabella's cheek. "I am so very proud of you. Of all of you. You showed great courage. Without you, this would've been a dark day followed by many more to come."

"That's something of an understatement, I think," says a new voice.

Binx materialises next to Elizabeth, followed by Emily, who stands beside him.

"Binx!" Aunt Dani rushes forward, stopping just in front of him and grinning.

"It's good to see you this side of the veil," Binx laughs. "Is everything all right now?"

"Well, we're not in Hell any more, so can't complain.

Also, you were capable of appearing this whole time and you didn't *once* think of dropping by to say hi?" She crosses her arms petulantly. "So much for 'I shall always be with you', jerk face."

"Well, you didn't exactly pop by the cemetery for a quick chat," Binx shoots back. "And ghosts making house calls is typically frowned upon. Terrible for real estate prices."

She frowns for a moment longer, then breaks into laughter. "Touché."

Emily looks towards me, then, steps forward, pulling her hand from behind her back to reveal my camera.

"No way," I say, taking it gently and inspecting it. Save for a few scuff marks, it's intact. "You found it."

"I figured you might want it back," she says with a shrug. "I'm still not sure what it does, but it seemed ever so important."

"Thank you," I say, popping the cover off the lens. "Do you all mind if I try something?" I ask the three ghosts.

They shake their heads, but are clearly confused.

I put my eye to the viewfinder, make a few adjustments, then snap a photo.

"For posterity," I say.

"You live in a very strange world, Poppy Dennison," Binx muses. "But I hope that one way or another, you always find what it is you're looking for." He puts a hand on Emily's shoulder and smiles, then they both fade gradually, leaving only Elizabeth.

"Pardon me for speaking quickly, dear," Elizabeth says, turning back to Isabella. "My energy is waning. There's so much I'd like to tell you now, but it will have to wait for another day. Until then, it is essential that you understand one terribly important thing."

"This doesn't sound good," Travis says under his breath.

"You can never really kill a witch," Elizabeth continues. "My sisters are gone, but so long as there is wickedness in this world, there will always be a place where evil finds a home."

"What are you saying?" asks Isabella, her tone quiet but nervous.

"I'm saying that Salem needs to be protected," says Elizabeth, "and that you've proven yourselves more than capable." She looks at each of us. "Remain vigilant. Weed out hate and ignorance and persecution whenever and wherever you can. And hold tight to one another." She smiles sadly. "If I'd had the support of friends like yours, I imagine that things may have ended differently for me."

Elizabeth begins to fade.

"Wait," Isabella says, "there's more I want to… I need to… I have so many questions."

"You'll always be able to find me here, Isabella," Elizabeth says. "But I think you'll discover you already have the answers."

And, with a knowing smile, she disappears.

Silence falls over our small group, all of us stunned into remaining quiet. At least for a moment.

"Wow," Travis says, running a hand over his hair. "That's... a lot."

"Yeah," Isabella says quietly. "It is."

"So it isn't over? Is that what I'm getting here?" asks Katie. "Because I have to be honest, I'm really looking forward to sleeping for about twenty-four hours and taking a nice long break from thinking about witches and ghosts and Hell."

"Sounds like we might not have that luxury," I say.

"Fighting evil is going to have to wait, though," says Aunt Dani, putting a hand on my shoulder. "We promised your parents we'd have you home in an hour."

Isabella nods, walking back towards me as we all turn and make our way out of the cemetery. She links an arm through mine.

"Thanks for coming back with me," she says. "I'm just so glad she's okay."

"Of course," I say. We walk in silence for a moment. "So, how are you doing?" I ask. "Ghostly ancestors and a new set of magical powers is a lot for one night."

She considers that for a moment. "Honestly? I feel a little relieved," she says. "I always felt like there was this part of me that was... missing. And finding Elizabeth, finding out about all of this and who I really am... it's a relief. It feels right. Even if it's terrifying." Isabella bumps her shoulder with mine once more. "I'm feeling like I'm ready to take on whatever comes next," she says, smiling gently.

"Well, *I'm* feeling like I'm ready for pizza," says Travis. "And bed. And a twelve-hour nap."

We all laugh in agreement and head towards the car.

Isabella's right — it is a relief to know that there's more to Salem than made-up stories and a disturbing preoccupation with a particularly dark period of history. But I can't shake the feeling that there's something we're missing. Something we forgot.

And then, all at once, the realisation hits me like a freight train.

Winifred's spell book is missing. Again.

Eye for an Eye

ONE YEAR LATER...
SALEM, 2019

osters of a missing teenage girl plaster telephone poles, postboxes and the Salem post office.

They were put up over a year ago, but someone keeps pinning up fresh printouts over the old, weathered ones. On a bustling residential street filled with trick-or-treaters, there's a lamppost with one of the posters attached to it. Illuminated by the moonlight, it shows the pretty girl, beaming as if she just won the lottery. Under her photo, the sign reads:

MISSING

SHAY WOMACK

Last seen in Salem Common, Salem, MA

Date Missing: October 31, 2018

Age: 17

Height: 5′ 3″

Hair: Long, Brown

Last seen wearing white T-shirt and jeans.

Please call the Salem County Sheriff's Office.

A teenage boy regards it. "Thanks again for switching places with me," he smirks. "Not that you had much of a choice in the matter." He tears down the missing poster, laughing, and slinks across the pavement.

"Nice costume, mister!" shouts a little trick-or-treater dressed as a princess.

The teenage boy dips his chin, obscuring his face with the wide brim of his pointed black hat, and keeps walking, his long emerald-green cloak swirling fiercely in his wake.

He turns up a red-brick walk – moving half like a shadow and half like a snake – and stops in front of a colonial-style two-storey house with white clapboard siding and dark shutters. Party music and bright light flood from its open windows.

He crumples the poster in his fist and tosses it over his shoulder, then regards the house for a moment longer. He takes a step closer to it.

When the front door opens, a warm glow from within spilling onto the walk, he sidesteps into the shadows, avoiding the light.

Under the cover of darkness, he turns and leaves the property, dashing across the suburban streets amidst a flurry of eager trick-or-treaters. He passes happy homes and streets full of laughter, barely staying out of sight, but deftly blending into the crowd and the night. It's only when he reaches the edge of the town's quiet cemetery that he slows to a stroll.

As he makes his way past ornate tombstones, simple grave markers, enormous stone crosses and grand mausoleums, his eyes scan the grounds, looking for something in particular. When at last he finds it, he stoops, squinting as he inspects it. The headstone's once-detailed surface is blurred by the forces of time and nature. Still, he can make out the simple skull and crossbones atop the inscription.

He stands and pulls Winifred's spell book from the folds of his cloak, smirking at the confused swivel of the book's single cloudy green eye.

He gazes back down at it, his remaining eye glowing a matching shade of green. "There, there," he says gently, stroking the puckered lid and the delicate silver filigree that surround the eye. His other hand rises subconsciously to his face, touching the empty socket. He still misses it. The eye in the book blinks once or twice, each blink slower than the last, until it seems to fall asleep.

The boy licks his thumb and pages through the book, almost lazily. "Yes," he says, as one might say to quiet a sleeping child. Then he parrots the ghost who had stood in this exact spot one year ago: "You can never really kill a witch. Especially," he chuckles, "if you don't know he's there." He finds the page in the spell book he's been seeking and reads aloud: "'Unfaithful brother long since dead, deep asleep in thy wormy bed. Wiggle thy toes, open thine eyes, twist thy fingers towards the sky. Life is sweet, be not shy. On thy feet, so sayeth I'."

Before the last syllable even leaves his lips, the ground begins to violently shake and quake. Nearby, the other tombstones lay still, but the one in front of him sinks into the ground.

An old wooden coffin slowly rises from the dirt as the boy looks on triumphantly.

The ground goes as still and as quiet as the night.

The top of the coffin creaks open, shudders, and slides off as a figure slowly sits up.

The teen witch grins. "Welcome back, Billy. Great things await us."

ACKNOWLEDGEMENTS

This book exists because the Sanderson sisters and the actresses who portrayed them gave the world unforgettable magic, mayhem and joy.

It also exists thanks to several unsung heroes. I'm grateful to my fabulous editor, Eric Geron, for his help in spinning the tale; to incredible artist Matt Griffin for illuminating it; to Amy and Logan for always lighting candles when I find myself in the dark; and to so many more who infused these pages with heart, sweat and other witch-worthy ingredients.

I'm also grateful to you, reader, for keeping the *Hocus Pocus* spirit alive and well. May your cauldron overflow with something sweet, and may your broomstick never be purloined.